Roya

In the lap of luxury what a difference a prince
Can fairytales really come true?…

3 glamorous romantic fantasies

In March 2006, By Request
brings back two collections each
containing three favourite romances by
our bestselling Mills & Boon authors:

ROYAL PROPOSALS

The Prince's Pleasure by Robyn Donald
A Royal Proposition by Marion Lennox
The Sheikh's Proposal
by Barbara McMahon

SWEET REVENGE

Rome's Revenge by Sara Craven
The Sweetest Revenge by Emma Darcy
A Seductive Revenge by Kim Lawrence

Royal Proposals

THE PRINCE'S PLEASURE
by
Robyn Donald

A ROYAL PROPOSITION
by
Marion Lennox

THE SHEIKH'S PROPOSAL
by
Barbara McMahon

MILLS & BOON®
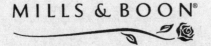

*All the characters in this book have no existence outside the
imagination of the author, and have no relation whatsoever to anyone
bearing the same name or names. They are not even distantly inspired
by any individual known or unknown to the author, and all the
incidents are pure invention.*

ROYAL PROPOSALS © by Harlequin Enterprises II B.V., 2006

The Prince's Pleasure, A Royal Proposition and *The Sheikh's
Proposal* were first published in Great Britain by Harlequin Mills
& Boon Limited in separate, single volumes.

The Prince's Pleasure © Robyn Donald 2002
A Royal Proposition © Marion Lennox 2002
The Sheikh's Proposal © Barbara McMahon 2002

ISBN 0 263 84667 9

158-0306

*Printed and bound in Spain
by Litografia Rosés S.A., Barcelona*

THE PRINCE'S PLEASURE

by

Robyn Donald

Robyn Donald has always lived in Northland in New Zealand, initially on her father's stud dairy farm at Warkworth, then in the Bay of Islands, an area of great natural beauty, where she lives today with her husband and an ebullient and mostly Labrador dog. She resigned her teaching post when she found she enjoyed writing romances more, and now spends any time not writing in reading, gardening, travelling and writing letters to keep up with her two adult children and her friends.

CHAPTER ONE

THE hotel events organiser burst into the drab staff cloakroom with all the drama of a star going nova, her frown easing dramatically when she saw the woman there.

'Alexa! Thank heavens!' she cried. 'I was afraid you weren't going to be able to make it. This wretched flu has struck down just about every waiter with security clearance.'

'Hi, Carole,' Alexa Mytton said cheerfully, smoothing sheer black pantyhose up her long legs. 'I didn't know I had security clearance.'

Carole looked a little self-conscious. 'With all the high-powered bankers in Auckland for this conference— not to mention the Prince of Dacia's security man, who is driving us crazy—head office insisted we run checks on everyone,' she said. 'You're as clean as a whistle, of course.'

Something in her voice alerted Alexa. 'Did you mention that I'm a photographer?'

A grimace distorted Carole's perfectly made-up face. 'No, because paranoia reigns! I could see I didn't have a hope of convincing the Prince's man that you're an up-and-coming studio photographer, not one of the dreaded paparazzi!'

Five years previously, when Carole had owned the top restaurant in the city, she'd hired Alexa as part-time help. A first-year university student, with no family and no money, Alexa had been grateful for the job, and still enjoyed helping her former boss in emergencies.

'Security men are paid to be paranoid,' she said cheerfully, straightening up to pull a long black skirt over her head. She patted the material over her slender hips and shrugged into a classical white shirt.

'He's not too bad, I suppose.' Carole surveyed Alexa with a professional eye. 'I thought you might have stopped taking casual work.'

'No, I'm still saving for that trip to Italy to research my grandfather.'

'Tell me when you're planning to go so I can take you off the roster.'

Alexa's long fingers flew as she buttoned up the shirt. Laughing, she said, 'It'll be another couple of months. But even if I had the tickets I'd have jumped at the chance to see the Grand Duke Luka of Dacia close up.' Opening her wide ice-grey eyes to their fullest extent, she batted long black lashes and simpered. 'He's not a regular visitor to unfashionable countries like New Zealand, so this might be my only chance to admire the gorgeous face that's sold so many millions of magazines and newspapers.'

Carole leaned forward, her voice dropping into a confidential purr. 'Mock all you like, but he's a seriously, seriously beautiful man.'

'Let's hope I can control my awe and fascination enough not to tip the crayfish patties over him.'

Oh, to be twenty-three again, Carole thought, before remembering what it had been like to ride that rollercoaster of emotions. But it would be great to *look* twenty-three again! Not that she'd ever come up to Alexa's standard. With her warm Mediterranean colouring of cream skin and copper hair the younger woman glowed like an exotic flower in the cramped, utilitarian confines of the room.

'*Not* patties,' Carole corrected briskly. 'They went out with the fifties. Did the Italian university have any information about your grandfather?'

Alexa shrugged. 'A big fat nothing so far.' Skillfully and swiftly she began to plait her thick hair into a neat roll at the back of her head. 'Either they won't give out information, or my Italian is so bad they didn't understand my letter!'

'That's a shame,' Carole said with brisk sympathy, glancing down at the clipboard she carried. She looked up to add, 'By the way, dishy though he certainly is, Luka of Dacia is no longer Grand Duke. Since his father died a year or so ago he's the hereditary Prince of Dacia, sole scion of the ancient and royal house of Bagaton.'

Alexa searched in her bag for a tube of lipgloss. 'What do I call him if he says something to me?'

'Your Royal Highness the first time, and then sir.' Carole sighed. 'It doesn't seem fair, does it? For a man to have it all—power, money and looks. Oh, and intelligence.'

Alexa laughed. 'Intelligence? Come off it, the man's a playboy.'

'He didn't get to be head of one of the top banks in the world without brains.'

'The fact that his royal daddy set the bank up might just have had something to do with that,' Alexa suggested drily, producing the tube from its hiding place in the bottom of her bag. 'If the gossip columns and royal-watchers of the world are right, the Prince simply hasn't got enough time to be a high-flying banker. He's too busy wining, dining and bedding fabulous women all over the globe.'

Carole grinned. 'Just wait till you see him. He's—
well, he's overwhelming.'

'I haven't been able to open a magazine or newspaper
for the past ten years without being overwhelmed by
photographs of him. I agree—he's sinfully good-looking
if you like them tall, dark and frivolous.'

'Frivolous he is not, and photographs don't do him
justice. Whatever the definition of charisma, he's over-
flowing with it. And trouble.' Abruptly sobering, Carole
went on, 'Overseas photographers have already approached several of the staff with outrageous offers.'

'I knew I should have brought a camera—I could have
hidden it down my front, James Bond style,' Alexa said,
skimming her generous mouth with colour. 'One photograph of him carousing with bankers would probably
finance my trip to Europe.'

'You're not big enough to hide anything much there.
Neat, but not overblown, that's you. Have you got a
camera with you?'

Alexa shook her head. 'Didn't seem tactful.'

'You're so right,' the older woman said, adding
thoughtfully, 'The Prince of Dacia is not a man I'd like
to cross.'

The hand wielding the lipstick suddenly still, Alexa
met Carole's shrewd eyes in the mirror. 'A puffed-up
playboy princeling, is he? Full of his own importance?'

'Far from it, according to those who've dealt with
him. The staff say he's lovely.'

'But?' Alexa finished applying the gloss and snapped
the case shut, scanning her reflection. She looked up and
said quickly, 'Don't answer that—I'm sorry I asked. I
know you have to be discreet.'

Carole said thoughtfully, 'He's the sort of man you
notice, and it's not just the overwhelming combination

of a handsome face, a great body and a height of about six foot four! It comes from inside him.'

Intrigued by the older woman's unusual gravity, Alexa turned her head. 'What does?'

'Charisma, I suppose. I saw him talking to the manager, being welcomed to the hotel—the sort of thing he's probably done thousands of times before. But there was no sign of boredom.'

Alexa's brows rose. 'They train royalty from childhood in that sort of PR. They probably have lessons in charm, and how to control the facial muscles!'

'I know, yet I'll bet my paua pearls he's no aristocratic figurehead. I got the impression that simmering beneath that very worldly surface there was a kind of fierce energy. He looks powerful.'

'So did King Kong. Now you've made him sound interesting.'

Carole shrugged. 'Unfortunately, not just to you. If someone starts asking questions about him, or for information about his movements, tell Security.'

Pulling a disgusted face, Alexa dropped the lipgloss into her bag. 'I will.'

'And thanks again for stepping into the breach.' Carole glanced at her watch. 'Help—I'd better go! If you get into trouble, smile—it's a killer, your smile.'

'It won't work if I ruin someone's designer outfit,' Alexa said pragmatically. 'I've been practising a demure, respectful expression all afternoon. Thank heavens a cocktail party's nowhere near as arduous as a silver service dinner.'

Carole shuddered. 'As of five minutes ago we've got a full muster of waiters for the banquet. Pray that it stays like that! Come on, I'll take you down. You might get a chance to use your Italian.' She opened the door to the corridor. 'Apparently Dacian has close similarities.'

Alexa had learned Italian at school and later, after her parents' death, at university, preparing for the day she'd go to Italy and find her grandfather's grave—perhaps even discover family there.

Of course an illegitimate granddaughter might not be welcome, but it would ease some inner loneliness just to know that she wasn't entirely on her own in the world.

During the turmoil of last-minute preparations, Alexa gave her respectful, self-effacing smile another couple of work-outs before she picked up a silver salver exquisitely decorated with tiny, tasty oyster savouries. Holding it steady, she set off into the room where the most powerful and influential people in the financial world, and their wives or mistresses—with a sprinkling of important politicians and local dignitaries—were meeting for drinks before dinner.

There she circulated slowly, careful not to let her interest in the women's clothes get in the way of her job.

She was covertly eyeing one trophy wife, clad in what appeared to be almost transparent scarlet clingwrap, when an autocratic female voice commanded from behind, 'Waitress, this way, please.'

Alexa's helpful, obliging smile slipped a fraction. There was always one snag.

Lovely, and superbly dressed, the snag was definitely not a trophy wife. She had a conscious air of power, Alexa decided as she eased her way through the crowd.

'Are those made with oysters?' the woman asked.

Alexa smiled, demure, self-effacing, and answered, 'Yes, they are,' as she proffered the salver.

Smiling up at the man beside her, the woman said in

an entirely different tone, 'Do try these, sir—they're a New Zealand speciality. We consider our Bluff oysters to be the finest in the world!'

'A big claim,' a deep, cool male voice responded with courteous confidence.

Alexa stole a glance through her lashes at an exquisitely tailored dinner suit that revealed wide shoulders, lean hips and long, strongly muscled legs.

Aha, she thought flippantly, the charismatic, much-photographed Prince Luka Bagaton of Dacia. And every bit as handsome as his photographs! The superbly chiselled features made an instant impact, as did a mouth that managed to combine beauty, strength and formidable self-discipline.

And then her eyes met his. Tawny-gold, the colour of frozen fire, they surveyed her with unsparing assessment.

Alexa stiffened as though she'd been measured, judged, and found wanting, and the salver in her hands quivered. Carole had chosen the right word for that formidable, potent aura of compelling maleness and authority. Prince Luka of Dacia was overwhelming—a devastating prince of darkness.

Heart juddering against her breastbone, Alexa concentrated on holding the salver steady while he took a savoury in a long, elegant hand.

'Thank you,' he said in that controlled voice with its fascinating slight accent.

Although Alexa had intended to step away without looking at him, her gaze flicked up to be captured by eyes gleaming with mockery. Yet a flare lightened their golden depths as the Prince of Dacia's bold warrior's face hardened into ruthlessness.

'Thank you, that's all we need.' The woman's voice, crisply territorial, slashed across Alexa's startled silence.

With a brief, meaningless smile she turned away, took two steps and offered the salver to the next group.

Nobody had told her that charisma burned, she thought once she drew breath again. Ridiculously, she felt as though the Prince's brutally emphatic energy had reached out and claimed her, branding her with a mark of possession that scarred her all the way to her soul.

Striving desperately to recall her sense of humour, she ordered herself not to be so idiotic. He'd looked at her; she'd looked at him. And, being a strongly visual person, she'd overreacted to the most gorgeous man she'd ever seen!

Shaken, still tautly aware of the Prince in the middle of the room, she avoided his area and kept her gaze well away until everyone obeyed some unspoken signal and trooped into the banqueting hall.

Much later, when her shift was over and she was heading for the staff cloakroom, Carole appeared, looking slightly less harried. 'The banquet went off really well—so far, so good,' she said on a quick, relieved note. 'What did you think of the Prince?'

'Grand Duke suited him better—he's entirely too grand,' Alexa said, aiming for her usual blithe tone and just missing. 'Who's his minder?'

'The stunning blonde? Sandra Beauchamp, the under-secretary for something or other. Apparently she's an old flame.'

Repressing a stark stab of primitive emotion she would not dignify with the name of envy, Alexa drawled, 'Old? She wouldn't like to hear that.'

Carole gave her a sharp woman-to-woman grin. 'Warned you off, did she? I don't blame her—she'd be mad not to try for another chance with him. So, what did you think of him?'

Alexa hoped an ironic smile hid her erratic emotions. 'He's a fabulous man, like something out of a fairy story—one of the dark and dangerous ones.'

'He gave a fantastic after-dinner speech—funny, moving, intelligent and short!'

'I hope he paid the writer lots.'

'Methinks I detect a note of cynicism,' Carole said as they turned towards the service lift. 'Don't you approve of the monarchy?'

How could she say that Prince Luka had made such an impact on her she couldn't think straight? It sounded foolishly impetuous, like falling in love at first sight.

Alexa shrugged. 'As an institution I think it's probably on its way out, but our lot have done pretty well by us, so who am I to tell the Dacians how to run their country? If they like their Prince, that's fine. And I gather he's doing great things for them with his bank.'

Pressing the button to call the lift, Carole said in an awed voice, 'The bank uses the Dacian crown jewels as security.'

Suddenly tired, Alexa covered a yawn. 'Crown jewels?' she said vaguely. 'Oh, yes, I remember—don't they have fabulous emeralds?'

'And the rest! Literally worth a prince's ransom.' The lift slid to a halt in front of them, doors opening. 'Have you got your car?' Carole asked, jabbing the button to keep the doors apart.

Alexa shook her head. 'It's in dry dock. Something to do with the radiator, I think. Whatever, it made funny noises.'

'Then take a taxi—and keep the receipt because you'll be reimbursed.'

'I'll drop it off or post it to you. Goodnight.'

After the lift had whirred Carole upwards Alexa took

the next one down to the ground floor, but one glance at the foyer changed her mind about trying to get a taxi there.

People were pouring out, taxis leaving as soon as they'd arrived, doormen moving fast to clear the crowd. Not to worry—the nearest taxi rank was only a couple of hundred yards away, just around the corner of a well-lit street. And as the hotel car park opened onto the same street there'd be enough passing traffic to make it perfectly safe.

Slinging her bag over her shoulder, Alexa set off, shivering slightly because it had rained while she'd been offering delicious food to the rich and powerful.

Down in the basement car park, in the restricted area, Luka of Dacia stood beside the anonymous car his agent had hired and listened courteously to his head of security.

'At least let me follow you in another car,' Dion said urgently. 'I don't like anything about this—why do they want you to go alone to meet them?'

Luka said calmly, 'These men have been fighting a desperate war for the past twenty years—a war that's turned brother against brother, father against son. I don't imagine they trust anyone any more.' He understood their behaviour. His life had been built on a lack of trust.

'That's no reason to put yourself in their power,' Dion expostulated angrily. 'Luka, I beg of you, think again! Your father would never have permitted you to take such a risk.'

'My father judged risks differently from you.'

Dion said in exasperation, 'Your father would have risked everything for Dacia. This is not for Dacia—these people are nothing to you—their Pacific island is as far from Dacia as any place can be. Let them fight their futile war until they're all dead!'

Luka's brows rose but his voice was crisp and abrupt as he said, 'Somehow I don't think it's quite as simple as that. Apart from my obvious neutrality, they must have a reason to choose me as an intermediary between them and their opponents.'

'What possible reason can they have?'

'That's what I plan to find out. These people aren't rebels—they are the elected government of Sant'Rosa. So they're not going to kill or kidnap me. And apart from the humanitarian aspects I have also to consider that although their country may be in ruins now it has the largest copper mine in the Asian Pacific region, not to mention other extremely valuable minerals, and the possibility of a flourishing tourist industry. Good pickings for the bank.'

Dion, who knew perfectly well that it was the humanitarian aspects that had persuaded his Prince, said angrily, 'Why ask for this secret meeting late at night and alone?'

'Possibly because they don't want to lose face. If tonight leads to further discussions between the two factions on Sant'Rosa, and if I can persuade them to accept some sort of protocol for peace, the Bank of Dacia can help them rebuild their economy. By ensuring their prosperity, I can help promote ours.' He paused, then added coolly, 'My father would have thought any—every— sacrifice worth that.'

Dion's frown deepened at the complete determination in his Prince's voice. 'Let me come with you,' he said, knowing it was hopeless. 'No one will know I'm there.'

'I will know,' Luka said inflexibly. 'I gave them my word I'd go alone, and I intend to keep it.' He looked down at the man he called friend and demanded, 'Give me your word you won't do anything to jeopardise this meeting.'

Dion met the Prince's hard eyes with something like anguish. 'You have it,' he said stiffly, and stood back, holding the door open to let his ruler into the car.

Luka slid behind the wheel, his face sombre as he turned the key and heard the engine purr into life. Although he was early for the meeting, he was also a stranger to Auckland, so in spite of memorising the route he'd probably make enough wrong turnings to use up the extra hour.

Putting the car into gear, he eased it out of the parking bay and through the car park, slid his card into the slot and waited for the grille to roll back.

A security man posted there gave him a keen look and a respectful nod—another instance of the meticulous attention to detail by the conference planners.

The wet street appeared deserted, but his eyes narrowed when he saw a woman striding towards the corner; adrenalin pumped through him as he noticed the two men coming up behind her, leashed violence smoking around them like an aura. They were taking care not to make a noise—hunters with prey in their sights.

Luka's hand thudded onto the horn and he stamped on the accelerator. The stalked woman jumped and whirled, mouth opening in a scream he could hear even over the squealing tyres and revving engine. By the time he'd driven across the footpath between her and the men she'd backed into the wall, hands in front of her in a classic posture of self-defence.

Trained? No, but ready to defend herself, Luka guessed with approval, himself expert in a lethal martial art. He leapt out of the car, but the two men were already sprinting across the street.

Luka ignored them. 'Are you all right?' he demanded harshly.

The street lamp revealed a face he recognised, a face that had lodged like a burr in his mind since she'd offered him a savoury before dinner. A highly appropriate offering, he'd thought then—oysters for sexual stamina. He'd looked into eyes, like a blast of winter set between black lashes and brows, and wanted her with a violence that startled and irritated him.

'I'm fine, thanks to you,' she said, the words coming clumsily.

Although she was pale her wide, soft mouth was held under tight discipline. Unwillingly Luka admired her self-control even while some part of him wondered what she'd look like when she lost it.

Wild; those fantastic ice-grey eyes half hidden by heavy eyelids, her hair tossed and tumbled like skeins of copper silk... The flush of passion would turn her skin to peaches and cream, and her mouth would soften into a sensuous welcome.

To take his mind off that purely male speculation—and the stir it created in his body—he suggested quietly, 'You can drop your hands now. You're quite safe.'

They fell to her sides. She managed a rapid, set smile and said, 'Thank you.'

'For what?'

Her teeth bit into her bottom lip for a moment before she answered, 'For getting involved.'

'Why wouldn't I?'

'Some people don't,' she said, dragging a sharp breath into her lungs.

Luka wrenched his gaze from the extremely interesting lift and fall of her breasts. In a voice he realised was too harsh, he demanded, 'Who are you, and just what are you doing in a back street at this time of night?'

'I'm Alexa Mytton,' she answered, stiffening as her chin came up, 'and I'm going to the taxi rank around the corner.'

'Why not ask one of the doormen to get you a cab?'

So he'd recognised her. Something warm and satisfied, a kind of purr of femininity, smoothed over Alexa. Afraid she'd fall apart if she relaxed, she straightened her shoulders and said quickly, 'I'm not a guest at the hotel. Thanks very much for being so quick to respond. I'll—I'll go now and get a taxi.'

'I'll walk there with you,' he said with a crisp purpose that warned her he wasn't going to leave her there alone.

Clamping down on a shiver, the aftermath of the terror that had surged through her, she said feebly, 'You can't leave your car blocking the way.'

'Then can I offer you a lift to the rank? You are really in no fit state to walk there by yourself.' A hint of impatience threaded his decisive voice.

Alexa knew she should say no and head briskly off. She glanced up into a face carved in granite, and then looked away, her stomach knotting; although definitely a dangerous man, there was no criminal menace about him. The peril radiating from him was the simple, sensual danger a potent male represented to a woman's composure.

'Thank you,' she said tightly, repressing another shiver.

With courteous speed the Prince put her into the front seat beside him and drove around the corner.

And of course the taxi rank was empty—as was the

street, apart from one man lurching from lamppost to lamppost. Alexa stifled a little hiss of dismay.

'If you'll trust me with your address I'll take you home,' the man beside her said with an aloofness that should have reassured her as he pulled into the empty space in the taxi rank, clearly not at all concerned by the prospect of any cruising cab-driver's outrage.

'Thank you, but you don't need to do that,' she told him swiftly. 'Perhaps you could take me to the nearest police station—if it's not too much trouble,' she added swiftly when he hesitated.

'Of course,' he said remotely, and put the car into gear again. When she'd given him instructions he said evenly, 'Promise me that you won't again walk by yourself at night in the inner city.'

'I don't make a habit of it. I was just in the wrong place at the wrong time,' she defended herself. 'I suppose they thought it would be easy enough to grab my bag and get away before anyone arrived.'

'Perhaps. And perhaps they didn't want money.'

'What else would they have wanted?' she asked, then flushed at his derisive glance. A slow cold shudder tightened her skin. She'd only had one glimpse of their faces before they'd turned and sprinted across the street, but they were imprinted on her mind. 'They can't possibly have thought they could get away with…assaulting me on a public street when traffic and pedestrians could arrive—'

'You forget the car,' he broke in. 'And surely your mother told you that beautiful women are always prey.'

'What car?' His words chilled her, yet she tingled because he'd called her beautiful.

The swift blade of the Prince's glance skimmed her

profile. 'They'd parked down that little alley over the street. Didn't you hear them drive off?'

'No.' Because her whole attention had been focused on him. Fear cramped her stomach as she realised how close she'd been to disaster. Alexa muttered through teeth she had to clench, 'It was just bad luck—'

'And foolishness,' he said with a bite in his tone, startling her by pulling into the kerb and shouldering free of his jacket.

Before she had time to say more than, 'What on—?' he tossed the garment at her. It landed on her lap, warm and as superbly cut as the dinner jacket he'd been wearing in the hotel.

'Wrap that around you,' he commanded, when she stared mutely at him. 'You're shocked and cold.'

Startled and dismayed, she pushed at the garment. 'I'm all right—'

'You're shivering,' he pointed out. When she didn't move—couldn't move—he commanded, 'Lean forward.'

Alexa reacted to the crack of authority in his words with automatic obedience. He dropped the garment around her shoulders, pulling it down to cover her arms.

As the cloth enfolded her sensation splintered in the pit of her stomach. Still warm from his body, the jacket sparked a violent, primal tug of awareness deep inside her, an awareness made keener, more intense by the faint, clean scent that had to be his—scent only a lover would recognise.

'All right?' he asked, frowning. He dropped his hands over hers, clasping them as he said more gently, 'You've had a very nasty experience, but it's over now. You're safe.'

'Thanks to you,' she muttered. Safe? When every cell in her body was drumming with a wild, strange need?

He said something in a language that sounded like Italian before freeing her and turning away to set the car in motion. As it pulled away from the taxi rank he asked in English, 'I have forgotten where we turn next.'

Still shaking inside, she gave him directions. Had he really said something like 'dangerously beautiful' in what must be his mother tongue?

Of course not. She tried to straighten her trembling mouth. In spite of a superficial resemblance, the Dacian language was not Italian.

But he found her attractive.

So what? Being rescued from what might have been an exceedingly nasty situation was no excuse for behaving like a halfwit. Prince Luka Bagaton of Dacia might possess courage and some kindness, he might even think she was beautiful, but he was way out of her reach— and she wasn't reaching! A quick fling with a visiting prince was not her style.

Alexa stiffened her spine and her shoulders. When the car stopped outside the police station she groped for the door handle and said in her most formal voice, 'Thank you very much for your help. I hope you enjoy the rest of your stay in New Zealand.'

After a quick glance at his watch, he said, 'I'll come in with you.'

Alexa objected. 'You don't need to become tangled up in this. You were on your way somewhere...'

To Sandra Beauchamp's bed, perhaps?

Without looking at her he said, 'I saw them too. I may be able to help identify them.'

'I…' She hesitated, then blurted, 'You don't want to get involved.'

'You're right,' he said, courteously inflexible, 'but it is my duty.'

CHAPTER TWO

HALF an hour later, after separate interviews, the sergeant complimented them both. 'I wish all our witnesses were as observant as you two! With such good descriptions we should nail them before they do any damage.' She looked at Alexa and said, 'We'll contact you if we need to.'

Alexa nodded. In the small room where she'd made her statement and drawn a sketch of both assailants she'd been given tea and some bracing, professional sympathy. It had helped, but her insides still felt as though someone had taken to them with a drill, and weak, irritating tears kept stinging her eyes.

Luka's firm hand on her elbow ushered her out to his car. 'You'll have to direct me to your address,' he said after a searching glance.

In a monotone Alexa guided him to her small flat in one of the inner city suburbs. He drove skilfully and well, although a couple of times she had to fill him in on New Zealand road rules.

Once they'd drawn up outside what had used to be a Victorian merchant's house, now converted to flats, she said sincerely, 'Thank you very much for everything you've done.'

The words stumbled to silence when he looked at her with cool, dispassionate irony, his angular features clamped into an expression of aloof withdrawal. Tension sparked through her, lifting the hair on her skin. Delayed shock, she thought protectively.

Swallowing, she continued with prickly determination, 'I don't like to think of what might have happened if you hadn't come along.'

'Don't think of it. Your scream would have brought someone running. I did nothing,' he said negligently and got out, swinging around the front of the car to open the door for her. 'But promise me one thing.'

Clinging to the door, she braced herself. He was too close, but even as the thought formed he stepped back and she pulled herself upright on quivering legs.

'What?' she asked, her throat tightening around the words so that they emerged spiky with caution.

His smile was a flash of white in the darkness—sexy, knowledgeable and implacable. 'That from now on you will call the doorman when you leave the hotel.'

'From tomorrow I'll be driving my own car, but I promise I won't go walking alone at night,' she responded quickly, groping in her bag for her keys. In her turn she smiled at him. Keep it impersonal, she warned herself, angry because she was so acutely conscious of him, tall and lethally masculine, his dark energy feeding some kind of hunger in her. 'And I don't work at the hotel,' she added.

His eyes narrowed. 'I saw you—'

'Handing out snacks,' she agreed. 'I'm on the emergency roster and I was called in tonight because flu is laying the staff low.' It seemed days ago now, as though the telephone call had summoned a different woman.

For someone who wanted to keep things on an impersonal level, she was failing miserably. Get out of here, she told herself silently. Now!

Walking carefully past him, she went up the steps to the front door, unlocked it and turned, to flinch back with dilating eyes at the tall, dominant silhouette that blocked out most of the light.

'I'm sorry,' he said harshly, hands closing around her upper arms. Warm, strong, unthreatening, they gave her support and steadiness. Frowning, he said, 'You're too pale. You've had a shock, and you should have someone to make sure you're all right.' His arms closed around her, pulling her into the hard warmth of his body.

In spite of the warnings hammering her brain, Alexa let herself lean on him, accepting the male comfort he offered with a purely female gratitude.

'You were brave,' he said on an unexpected note of gentleness. 'I saw you gauge your options and decide that screaming and fighting back offered the best chance. Quick thinking, and a refusal to accept being a victim. Do you know how to defend yourself?'

'No. I've always thought I should do s-something about it, but I've never s-seemed to have the time.' She stopped her stammered explanation to drag in a quick, shallow breath. It was dangerously sweet to be cosseted. Forcing a brisk note into her voice, she pulled away, both relieved and disappointed when he released her instantly. 'I'm sorry I interrupted your evening.'

He frowned, the dim light emphasising his brutally handsome features. 'It was nothing. Can I ring someone for you?'

'It's really not necessary—I'm a bit shaky, but a good night's sleep will fix that.' Alexa suddenly remembered his coat, still keeping her warm. 'Oh, your jacket!' She set her bag down on the balustrade and struggled to get out of it, hauling at the material so recklessly that her shirt lifted free of her waistband.

The Prince's hands skimmed the silken skin on either side of her waist, then jerked back as though the touch burned him. Alexa's breath froze in her throat. She stared up into eyes that glittered in the light of the street lamps, into a face as hard and tough as a bronze mask.

For the space of several heartbeats neither moved until Alexa regained her wits enough to leap back and hand over the jacket. Both were careful not to let their fingers touch.

'There,' she said in a strained, hoarse voice. 'And *don't* say it was nothing.'

His mouth compressed. In a voice that could have splintered stone, he said, 'I don't lie. Go inside.'

Taut with a forbidden excitement, Alexa opened the door and escaped into the hall. 'Goodbye.'

His dark head inclined. 'Goodbye, Alexa Mytton.'

Incredulous, she thought she heard an echo of aloneness that mirrored her own. She looked up sharply, but his hard face revealed nothing except self-contained assurance. Heart hammering, Alexa pushed the door closed with an abrupt thud.

She listened until the sound of the car engine was lost in the noise of other vehicles, and then walked along to her flat, thinking that of all the idiotic things to suspect in Prince Luka loneliness was probably the most unlikely.

Yet he was far from the playboy prince she'd imagined, a handsome surface-skimmer, all machismo and conceit. He'd changed from a warrior, quick-thinking, formidable and exceedingly dangerous, to a man who offered aloof kindness and an inherent protectiveness that still surprised her.

Luka Bagaton was a complex, deeply interesting man. 'S-sexy, too,' she said aloud.

In the chilly security of her own flat she glanced at her reflection in the mirror, wincing at the feverish gleam in her pale eyes and the hectic flush along her cheek-bones.

She had every right to feel jumpy and restless, but she wasn't going to be able to sleep like this. Still trembling inside, she made herself a cup of milky chocolate, took it across to her computer and sat down to log on, searching for Luka Bagaton on the internet.

An hour later she switched off the computer and got up, stretching muscles that had locked as she'd read about Prince Luka of Dacia.

'No wonder he's so self-contained,' she said, picking up the empty mug of chocolate.

At eighteen his father had succeeded to a princedom on the verge of being invaded by a country across the narrow strait separating the island of Dacia from Europe. Then, amazingly—and probably desperately—he'd married the only child of the dictator who'd threatened his country. His ploy had worked—Dacia had kept a limited independence. A year later the only child of the union had been born.

'I hope they fell in love,' Alexa said, yawning. 'Otherwise it would have been hell for them both.'

Ten minutes before she had to leave for work the next morning, Alexa's bell pealed. Her brows drew together as she pushed proof sheets into an envelope and went out to answer the chiming summons.

She opened the door to a man carrying a huge bunch of Peruvian lilies, delicately formed and fragile in shades of copper.

'Miss Alexa Mytton?' the messenger asked. At her nod he held them out.

Alexa automatically took the lovely things, looking down at the envelope with her name written across it in

bold, very definite letters. Her heart jolted as she said,
'Thank you.'

Back in her flat she arranged them in a glass vase in
front of the window, admiring the way the autumn sunlight glowed through the silky, almost translucent petals.
Had he chosen them to match her hair?

Only then, overcoming a kind of superstitious reluctance, she opened the envelope. *I hope you are feeling
much better this morning,* he'd written, signing it with
an arrogant 'L'.

A swift shimmer of excitement took her by surprise.
They were lovely, she thought, touching one of the lilies
with a gentle forefinger.

Oh, all right, he'd probably said to someone, Send
some flowers to this address, please, and forgotten about
it immediately, but it was thoughtful of him. She swung
around and caught up her camera. If only she could catch
that silken transparency...

Glancing at her watch, she regretfully put the camera
down. It would have to wait.

Alexa stamped into the flat late that afternoon, still tense
after a hideous session with an actress who'd insisted on
being photographed with her pair of psychopathic
Dobermanns, laughing brightly every time they made a
determined attempt to eat Alexa's equipment.

The Peruvian lilies gleamed like copper tulle when
she turned on the light, and her strained irritation mu-
tated into a sweet, futile anticipation.

Carole had rung to say she had a full roster, so Alexa
knew she wouldn't see Prince Luka again, but she'd always remember his kindness and his flowers. She'd written a note to thank him for them, and would drop it off
at the hotel in a few minutes.

The front doorbell jangled through the room. 'Oh, great!' she said, slinging her bag onto a chair. Perhaps it was a friend who'd called in for coffee.

But the man who waited there was no friend, although he looked vaguely familiar.

Before she had time to place him he spoke in an accent that told her what that familiarity was. 'Miss Mytton?'

Her heart picked up speed. 'I'm Alexa Mytton.'

'The Prince wishes to see you,' he told her impassively, although the dark eyes that lingered on her face were shrewd and perceptive. 'I'm sorry it's such short notice, but if you could come with me...'

When she hesitated he frowned and said, 'I am sorry.' He drew out a card and presented it with some ceremony.

He was Dion, followed by a long Dacian name. Alexa turned the card over, her eyes scanning the writing on the back—Prince Luka's writing.

Please accompany Dion, it said, the brief note followed by that same 'L'.

She was probably being paranoid after last night, but she wasn't getting into a car with a total stranger. 'I'm going past the hotel in ten minutes,' Alexa said. 'I'll call in on my way.'

He looked taken aback, but said politely, 'Yes, of course. I will meet you at the elevators on the third floor.'

Secretly, shamefully glad she was wearing a sleek trousersuit in her favourite bronze, with a silk mesh tank top under the blazer-cut jacket, Alexa closed the door on him and scurried back into the flat to renew her lipstick, before scooping up her car keys.

Why did Prince Luka want to see her? Expectant, yet

strangely apprehensive, she parked in the visitors' car park and took the lift into the hotel.

Sure enough, Dion with the mile-long name was waiting. Although he greeted her cordially enough she sensed his reservation as he opened another elevator with a key and ushered her inside. Kites jostling in her stomach, she stared at the wall until the lift stopped at the penthouse, where a security guard opened the door and ushered them both into a foyer.

'In here, madam,' her guide said, opening another door for her.

He stood back as Alexa walked through. Stopping when the door closed behind her, she ignored the huge, opulently furnished room to fix her eyes on the man who turned from contemplation of a crimson sunset to look at her with dangerous metallic eyes.

From somewhere Alexa remembered that when confronted by royalty you waited until you were spoken to. So, although she had to bite back the words that trembled on her tongue as he surveyed her with comprehensive and intimidating thoroughness, she stood silently.

But her eyes sparkled at his unsparing scrutiny, and her mouth tightened as she jutted her chin at him.

'Have you seen today's newspaper?' he asked in a deep, cold voice.

Frowning, she abandoned any attempt at formality and protocol. 'No. Why?'

He gestured at one spread out on a coffee table. 'Perhaps you should read it now. In the last section, page three.'

After a baffled glance she walked across to the table and picked up the paper. The conference had made the front page, but the part he referred to was a lifestyle pullout. And there, in the gossip column, someone had ringed an item with a slashing black pen—the same pen that had written the letter 'L' on the paper accompanying her flowers.

Incredulously Alexa read the item.

The Prince of Dacia, heaven's gift to romantic royalists now that the Prince of Illyria is married, is clearly a connoisseur of more in New Zealand than our scenery and wine. Last night, a small but dedicated bird told me, he was seen driving one of Auckland's busiest young photographers home after the opening banquet of the banking conference. And she was wearing his jacket. What, we wonder, can this mean?

With scornful precision he asked, 'Did you leak this?'

Alexa's head jerked upwards. Bitterly—foolishly—hurt, she transfixed him with a furious glare. 'Of course I didn't!'

'Then how did it get into the newspaper?'

She didn't know what intimidated her more—his anger, frozen and harsh as a blizzard at the South Pole, or his flinty control.

'I don't know,' she told him, clinging to her composure. 'Someone saw us at the police station, I'd imagine. Fortunately she hasn't linked you with any specific person.'

'Perhaps your name will be in the next sly little morsel,' he said with a cutting edge to his voice.

Her head jerked around and she met the full shock of his gaze. Dry-mouthed, she asked, 'Why should there be a next one?'

'Because whoever fed this to the columnist will make sure of it.'

'Look,' she said, trying to be reasonable, 'it's irritating and naff, but it isn't the end of the world. People will forget it.'

'I won't forget it,' he said, watching with hooded eyes the way the light smouldered across her hair, loose now around her face. With silky precision he said, 'I don't like being used, Ms Mytton.'

In the face of his scornful arrogance she felt hot and foolish and furious. Covering a stab of pain with seething denial, she asked indignantly, 'Why would I want to *use* you?'

'Usually it's for money,' he returned caustically, killing Alexa's jab of sympathy by adding, 'But often for notoriety—and I imagine that a link to me, however tenuous, would help you advance in your profession. I hope you took no photographs of me last night.'

Pale eyes glittering, Alexa almost ground her teeth. Her quip to Carole about hiding a camera came back to taunt her, bringing colour to her skin—which he noticed. 'Not a single one,' she retorted crisply. 'And I don't leak titbits to the press. This rubbish—' she gestured contemptuously at the newspaper '—is your area, not mine. And it's totally without any foundation.'

'Do you really believe that?' He crossed the room in two strides, stopping her instinctive retreat by grasping her shoulders.

The previous night Alexa had noticed the strength and support of his hands; now, knocked off-balance by hurt and anger, she felt nothing but the promise of their power.

'I wish I could believe that there is no foundation for the sly innuendo in that rubbish,' he said, mockery gleaming in the frozen fire of his eyes, 'but I am a realist above all else.'

And he bent his head and kissed her.

Afterwards Alexa tried hard to convince herself that it was the sheer unexpectedness that kept her locked unprotesting in his embrace.

But she lied. The second she'd seen Luka she'd been acutely, forcefully aware of him—and in spite of his steely control, she'd recognised a like response. Each time their eyes had met they'd exchanged hidden messages that bypassed logic to kick-start a flagrant hunger.

Fed by clamouring instincts, that secret communication—primitive and involuntary—had grown in quantum leaps, burning away common sense and caution.

Without realising it, she'd been waiting for this moment, all that was female in her knowing it would come. In mute surrender, she relaxed against his taut body.

At the first touch of his mouth something buried inside Alexa split and broke, as though she'd emerged from a chrysalis.

And then, after a kiss as short, brutal and impersonal as a slap, Luka lifted his head to survey her with chilling detachment, the hunger that prowled his eyes disappearing behind their opaque, enamelled surface.

It took every ounce of self-command she could summon to ask sweetly, 'Had enough?' letting contempt sharpen each word.

With a bleak, twisted smile he said harshly, 'Unfortunately, no.'

This time the kiss was neither brief nor brutal. He kissed her with fire and purposefulness, as though he'd longed for her down the years, as though they were lovers who had only this kiss to exchange before bitter fate tore them apart for ever.

Alexa struggled to remain passive, but a terrifyingly raw, untamed force sprang up to meet his open hunger, and—to the shocked astonishment of the last rational part of her mind—match it. Flames rocketed through her, eating away everything but the sheer physical magic of the Prince's flavour and subtle scent, and the heat and power of his warrior's body against hers.

It was the increasing hardness of that body rather than the sharp knock on the door that broke into her sensual enslavement. In some dim recess of her brain she remembered that this man might have spent the night with another woman.

When she pushed against his chest he lifted his head and released her, stepping back. Alexa forced her lashes up and looked into eyes as polished and impersonal as the gold they resembled. Oh, he wanted her—he couldn't hide that—but with nothing more complex than simple lust.

It shouldn't have hurt.

Yet it was pain as much as fury that drove her to ask, 'And what did that prove, except that you're stronger than I am?'

Caustic amusement gleamed in his gaze, curved the mouth that now knew hers intimately. 'It proved that you want me as much as I do you,' he returned on a note of courtesy that lacerated her composure.

'That means nothing,' she retorted, trying to convince herself. Beneath the surface control, she realised, he was blackly furious.

'An admirably liberated view,' he said, not hiding the flick of contempt in his tone.

The skin over her high cheekbones heated and she forgot tact and discretion and plain common sense to flare, 'Perhaps, but *I'm* not so liberated that I sleep with every good-looking man who wants a bit of publicity.'

'No,' he said lethally, 'you merely pander to the avid eagerness of people who want to read that sort of trash.'

Hot with chagrin at her humiliating rudeness, she said between her teeth, 'I shouldn't have said that. I'm sorry. But, for the last time, I did *not* notify the newspaper.'

He surveyed her with aggression bordering on menace. 'If news of those kisses makes it into the media I'll know how much your word is worth.'

'As much as yours,' she said tersely. 'I'd hate to be as mistrustful as you are.'

'I imbibed it with my mother's milk,' he said, adding with cold distaste, 'Literally.'

Shocked by the stark authenticity in his words, she muttered, 'There's someone at the door.'

'They'll wait.'

Possibly his staff were accustomed to waiting for him to finish with the woman of the moment!

Alexa turned away, paradoxically feeling safer now they were back in adversarial mode. 'They won't have to. I'm going.'

'Perhaps you should comb your hair,' he suggested in a voice that was a maddening mix of amusement and mockery. 'You look—tumbled.'

Glaring at him, Alexa shook her hair back from her face, but the heavy copper tresses clung to her hot cheeks and temples. She pushed it back with her fingers, but when his dark gaze lingered on her shaking hands she gave up. With a crisp 'Goodbye' she walked abruptly towards the door.

Halfway there, she stopped. 'Thank you for the flowers.'

'Don't throw them into the garbage just because I sent them.' He sounded more than a little bored.

'It isn't their fault they came from you.' She couldn't

resist adding, 'Although I'll bet you ordered a minion to send them!'

'Alas, the days of minions are long past,' he said, deadpan, adding, 'Have you got your car back yet?'

'Yes, thank you.' Torn by a debilitating mixture of anger and resentment and desolation, she swept out past the man who waited on the other side of the door.

Luka's eyes met Dion's and he jerked his head. Obeying the unspoken order, Dion closed the door. He'd accompany her down to her car.

Alone once more, Luka turned away and walked across to the window, to stare at the elaborate terraced garden and pool outside.

Shortly after his seventh birthday he'd screwed his courage to the sticking point and dived through a waterfall to the pool behind it. He'd felt the way he did now—as though the gleaming darkness was a gateway into some other dimension, a place of perilous beauty where he risked the slow dissolution of his innermost self.

Every muscle clenched while he fought to leash an unwanted onslaught of desire. He understood the primitive strength of his own needs and instincts, and over the years he'd caged them in a prison of will-power and discretion.

Yet Alexa Mytton's smile and the glittering promise in those pale, crystalline eyes had pushed him over the knife-edge of control.

He shouldn't have kissed her, and once he'd done it he certainly shouldn't have surrendered to that overmastering need to find out whether she tasted as good the second time as she did the first.

He tried to resurrect his anger, but primal impulses

still raced recklessly through his cells. He had work to do.

He was leafing rapidly through papers when another knock at the door signalled Dion's return. When the other man was inside Luka asked, 'Did you see her to her car?'

Dion said abruptly, 'Yes. Luka, the last sighting of Guy was a week ago, when he boarded a ship loaded with medical supplies for Sant'Rosa. I've checked, but no one seems to know where it went or what happened to it.'

Luka swore—low, virulent oaths that startled his companion.

When he stopped Dion drew in a sharp breath and said, 'You'd better tell me what this is all about.'

'Guy is a hostage,' Luka said, only a thread of steel in the deep voice betraying his emotions.

Last night's meeting had begun in an atmosphere that had reeked with suspicion, but he had thought he'd managed to convince the men from Sant'Rosa that he was an entirely neutral emissary. They had discussed the sort of peace they envisaged.

And then they'd produced their trump card in the form of his cousin.

'In Sant'Rosa? We can spring him,' Dion said instantly.

'Without alerting the government?' Luka shook his head. 'He's safe enough for the present. They really want an end to this war, and they're convinced the rebels want it too. However, they don't trust anyone—not even anyone from the other side of the world.' His voice hardened into iron. 'When Guy appeared they recognised him from the gossip columns and realised they had the

perfect way to stop me from double-crossing them.
According to the Prime Minister, he is quite safe.'

'And you believe him?'

'That far, I believe him,' Luka said deliberately. 'And
I believe that if any word of this peace initiative gets out
to the media Guy could be in serious trouble. Before
anyone knows of any possible treaty, they want the deal
to be signed and sealed, with a peace-keeping force already on the island.'

Dion frowned. 'Why?'

'Because,' Luka said evenly, 'the neighbouring state
is poised to march across the border and take over.
They'll stay on the sidelines as long as they think the
two sides are bleeding to death, but any hint of peace
will see them invade. Guy is being kept three miles from
the border on the main route to the capital city.'

Dion swore this time.

'Exactly,' his Prince said harshly. 'He's safe as long
as no one knows anything about the possibility of a
treaty between the Sant'Rosa rebels and the government.'

'So what do we do?' Dion asked, crisp and professional.

Luka said deliberately, 'From what I heard last night,
the rebels won't be too hard to persuade—especially if
they're promised a place in the new order of things. The
government has guaranteed this. I've put out feelers
amongst the local refugees from Sant'Rosa—apparently
there are several with direct links to the rebels.' He
looked at Dion, recognising the other man's frustration
and need for action. 'Make sure the jet's ready to fly—
we may need to airlift them into Auckland and take them
up to the beach house. Apart from that, you'll do nothing—yet.' He smiled ironically. 'And before I start work

on a peace plan that will satisfy both sides, I plan to swim.'

Dion said, 'Guy is tough, Luka. He'll probably get himself out of there.'

Luka gave a crooked smile. 'I know.' He paused and said abruptly, 'There is something else you can do. Make sure Alexa Mytton is not permitted into the hotel until after the conference is over.'

Although he turned up the jets in the private pool to full power, swimming didn't clear his mind. Instead of working out a way to free his cousin, or bring both bitterly divided sides to a neutral meeting place, all he wanted was to feel Alexa's hair around him like some silken tent, each coiling tress caressing his skin into feverish ecstasy. He wanted her to look at him with her ice-clear dangerous eyes smouldering with desire, in the full knowledge of what she was doing. He wanted to feel that passionate mouth on his skin...

He hauled himself out of the pool and strode towards the shower, sweat gathering on his forehead as his body responded to the goad of his thoughts.

More than anything in the world he craved to take her, bury himself deeply in her strong slenderness, mark her by his possession so that any other man's touch on her would be unthinkable—an insult, an unbearable horror.

Because he was fastidious—and circumspect—there hadn't been many women in his bed, but without conceit he knew he was a good lover. Partly it was his true appreciation of women's needs, his pleasure in their softness and their curves, his understanding that making love was an infinitely greater risk for a woman than for a man. But it was the self-mastery taught to him by the courtesan his father had summoned as a sixteenth birthday present that brought his lovers to sobbing fulfilment before he yielded to his own climax.

And it was that control that enabled him to keep himself emotionally distant from each one. He'd been trained in a hard school to think of his country before anything else.

Yet now he'd been ambushed by a hunger that clamoured to take a woman hot-bloodedly and without finesse, loosen control and let mindless white-hot passion ride him to satiety.

A photographer, for God's sake! And sniffing around now, at the very worst of times. One hint of publicity and the desperate men he'd met last night would disappear out of New Zealand and back into their tropical jungle, and more people would die, more children would grow up uneducated, knowing only war and famine and disease.

And Guy, his younger cousin, could well lose his life.

With a quick, savage flick of his fingers he turned the shower onto full, and when that didn't tame his rampant body he punched the palm of one hand with a clenched fist and fought the dangerous frustration with hard common sense.

Where had he seen those astonishing eyes before, so pale they were almost transparent, their colour a violent contrast to her warm Mediterranean colouring of creamy skin and copper hair?

A knock on the door brought his head up. 'What is it?' he asked with harsh precision.

'A message, sir,' his private secretary said urgently. 'The one you've been waiting for.'

That night, as she cooked dinner and ate it without tasting a mouthful, Alexa replayed over and over again that scene with Prince Luka.

It didn't take a psychologist to explain the electricity that had scorched through her at his touch. She'd been caught off guard by potent physical attraction, the kind of sensual intuition that splintered the bars of caution and common sense to whisper alluringly of feverish, compelling sex, to counsel surrender to a passion she'd never expected to feel.

Basic, earthy, almost entirely amoral, it should repel her. Emotionally and intellectually it did.

Unfortunately some rash, previously unsuspected part of her found Prince Luka wildly exciting. He'd kissed her like a conqueror, and she'd let him—worse than that, she'd gloried in it, because she'd known she'd breached some barrier in him.

Even more intriguing was that hint of vulnerability, of hidden secrets. Perhaps she could do some research on him—

'No!' she said, outraged.

And she should stop beating herself up! It wasn't as though she was the first woman to have found him attractive. Every magazine and newspaper in the western world was a witness to the number of women who'd fallen for his particular brand of Mediterranean glamour. And as well as being dynamically sexy, he'd been surprisingly kind when she'd started falling to pieces.

The telephone rang. 'Alexa,' Carole said in a flat voice, 'something's happened that's rather—upsetting.'

CHAPTER THREE

'I'VE just been speaking to Mike, my boss,' Carole said, with no sign of her usual dramatic delivery. 'He's suggested that you be—that you're not…' She hesitated before continuing bluntly, 'Alexa, he doesn't want to see you in the hotel for the duration of the conference.'

Stunned, Alexa asked, 'What? Why? He can't do that!' But he would, she realised with a clutch of nausea, if someone with enough power asked him to.

'I'm afraid he can, and I'm also afraid I must ask you not to lose your temper and try to force your way in,' Carole said, dropping her tone by several notes.

'Of course I won't embarrass you like that.' Alexa steadied her words. 'I'm just—gobsmacked. Did your boss give you a reason?'

'He was told officially that you're a photographer,' Carole said, 'and at the moment photographers are very much *personae non gratae*. Of course I vouched for your integrity, and pointed out that you'd worked here before and that you had security clearance. Mike knows that, but he's in a cleft stick; he said it's temporary, and no reflection on you.'

Fighting a raw sense of betrayal, Alexa unclenched her jaw with difficulty and ignored the faint questioning note in the older woman's voice to say, 'Carole, it's all right. As it happens I've got a full programme for the next week, so I probably wouldn't have been able to do anything for you anyway.'

Carole sighed, a sure sign of her panache returning.

'Thanks for being so understanding. A model tried to sweet-talk her way into the Prince of Dacia's suite yesterday—and almost got there. Apparently she sold a story to an English paper. Management is stressing out collectively and individually over security, so when someone said you were a photographer it was the final straw.'

And Alexa knew who that had to be! The Prince of Dacia was no slouch when it came to quick, ruthless decisions. She said brightly, 'Don't worry, I'll keep well away from the hotel. Are there likely to be any repercussions for you?'

'Me? Oh, no. Alexa, Mike *knows* you're trustworthy,' Carole assured her earnestly. 'He's under pressure from someone, and you can't blame that someone. It's just a pity you're the one to suffer. I have to go, Alexa. Thanks.'

After carefully putting the telephone down, Alexa strode furiously across to her window and threw it open. Salty air from the harbour, almost overwhelmed by petrol fumes, floated in, bringing with it all the noises of the city.

Talk about brutal misuse of power! she thought vengefully. How she'd like to tell Prince Luka of Dacia what she thought of people who used their status to intimidate.

A glance at her watch revealed that she had half an hour to go the gym and work off both her temper and the stupid, baseless sense of bereavement that kept breaking through.

She was a modern woman and Luka Bagaton was fresh out of the Middle Ages—protective of the weak, impersonally kind, hard, ruthless and chauvinist to the core. They had nothing in common, so this unsuitable, reckless attraction would die as soon as it had sprung up.

A week later she folded the newspaper so she couldn't see the Prince, lethally aristocratic and authoritative amongst the other bankers in a final posed photograph on the museum steps. Buttering toast with a vicious sweep of the knife, she said to the empty kitchen, 'I wonder just how much being superbly photogenic has helped his career as a banker. Lots, I'll bet.'

A swift glance through the window revealed a mellow autumn day, perfect for travelling. She planned to touch up her tan for ten glorious days at the beach house owned by the parents of a schoolfriend on an island forty miles north of Auckland. She had it all organised: days of glorious solitude stalking the perfect shot that was going to win her a competition.

Still chewing toast and honey, she cast a cold glance at the newspaper. The morning after that icy interview with the Prince the gossip columnist had struck again wondering archly:

What is going on between gorgeous Prince Luka and the lovely photographer? The same little bird that saw them together on the first night of the conference noticed the photographer emerging from the Prince's private elevator with tumbled hair and distinctly bee-stung lips. Watch this space!

So by now he'd be convinced she was feeding the wretched woman information.

Not that Alexa cared. 'Not even the tiniest bit,' she said, smiling brilliantly—and lying.

The island, she decided three hours later, manoeuvring

her friends' elderly four-wheel drive vehicle over the narrow winding track from Deep Harbour, was the ideal place to blob out—and to chisel a dangerously magnetic man out of her brain.

The Thorntons had sited their bach on the ocean side of the island, more exposed to the waves and the winds than the gentler leeward side. That fitted Alexa's mood perfectly, as did the comfortable middle-aged house crouched above a sweeping beach with sand the colour of fine champagne.

And the forecasters were predicting that the weather would stay in Indian summer mode until after she returned to Auckland.

Determined to enjoy herself, Alexa opened glass doors to let in the air, turned on the power and the water, and began to unload the vehicle. That done, she rang Sally Thornton in Auckland to tell her she'd arrived safely.

Then she ran down the beach for a quick dip to wash off the road grime. At last, clad in denim shorts and a sleeveless blue-green T-shirt that gave some colour to her eyes, she strolled out onto the deck and stared out to sea.

'Not another house in sight,' she said with satisfaction. The ruinous farmhouse along the beach, crouched defensively behind thick old trees, didn't count.

Smiling, she dragged a lounger out onto the deck and squinted along the bay, mentally framing at least three superb shots. Tomorrow she'd go out and see what else she could find. She wanted to play with black and white shots.

Out of nowhere sprang the image of Luka's face when he'd accused her of leaking gossip to the press—a face with the kind of hard, forceful bone structure that photographed magnificently.

'Oh, for heaven's sake,' she muttered in frustration.

Absurdly sensitive to beauty she might be, but it was ridiculous to obsess about a man she'd only seen three times. OK, so he kissed like a dark angel, but punishing kisses had gone out with her mother's generation. No, her grandmother's!

Alexa grinned suddenly, recalling her grandmother— bright, modern, and tough enough to be a solo parent when it would have been a lot easier to put her son up for adoption. Gran would have had no truck with punishing kisses either. Her smile faded swiftly as loneliness rolled over her in a dark tide.

Her happy, charmed life, so safe and secure, had come to a bitter end. Her mother had died after a long illness when Alexa was just fourteen; two days previously, on the way home from the hospital, Alexa had been the only survivor of a motorway accident that had killed her father and grandmother. Stunned with grief, and left without relatives, Alexa had spent the rest of her school years in a foster home.

Yet, unlike some of the others there, she'd had happy memories. Just what sort of memories haunted Luka of Dacia, who'd admitted to imbibing distrust with his mother's milk?

'Get out of my head!' Alexa commanded the man who'd had her dismissed like a dishonest servant.

Late that night, woken from a deep sleep by something she'd barely heard, she pulled on a woollen jersey against the chilly air and made her way out onto the deck. The timeless silhouette of the hills brooding against the night sky and the subtle obsidian sheen of the sea beneath the stars usually satisfied something deep in her soul, but not tonight. The warm glow from the small lamp in the sitting room beckoned much more strongly.

She'd swung around to go inside again when a point of light stopped her. Adrenalin powered up her pulse-rate by several beats a minute. No one had lived in the old house along the beach since the owner had been forced to spend his final years on the mainland.

'Well, someone's there now,' she said aloud, then froze as a noise from the sea boosted her heart into over-drive. With night-attuned eyes she made out the shape of a large launch in the bay; the sound she'd heard was the creak of oars as someone rowed ashore.

Nothing unusual in that, but she stayed motionless until the autumn chill drove her inside.

Unable to pin down the source of her uneasiness, she retired back to bed, this time locking the door onto the deck. Probably the neighbouring property had changed hands, but there was a possibility—so remote it was barely worth considering—that someone had broken into the house and was lying low.

The next morning the peacock waters of the bay spread out a gleaming, serene emptiness beneath the sun. Brows knitting, Alexa rang Sally in Auckland.

'Oh, I forgot to tell you!' her friend said cheerfully. 'After Mr Patrick died it was sold to some millionaire who demolished the old house and built a very upmarket bach there. Well, not a bach—more a mansion! He's got riparian rights to half the cove, but I don't think he's ever stayed there. I suppose he bought it as an invest-ment.'

Amused at the mindset of anyone buying land in such a glorious place for that prosaic reason, Alexa said cheerfully, 'He seems to be in residence at the moment because I saw a light there last night.'

'That'll be from the caretaker's house a bit further along. A nice middle-aged couple—you'll like them if you meet them.'

So much for night-time uneasiness—the launch in the bay the previous night had probably ferried the caretaker back from a fishing trip! Five minutes later, a small pack over her shoulders, Alexa pushed a hat onto her head, donned her sunglasses and picked up her father's old camera. Time to go exploring.

Halfway along the pale curve of the beach a soft scrabble in the scrub froze her into stillness. Wallabies, brought across the Tasman Sea more than a century ago by one of the original settlers, could sometimes be seen hopping along the sand, lending the beach a bizarre Australian air. A gap in the teatree scrub might indicate a track.

Narrowing her eyes, she checked the light. Perfect, and with the splendid iconic pohutukawa tree in the background it would make a surreal image.

Slowly and silently she eased herself behind a large wave-smoothed rock and readied the camera.

After ten minutes of motionless waiting with the sun radiating off the rock, Alexa itched in several places and longed for a drink. Experience warned her that any hiding wallaby would decide to hop down onto the beach at the exact moment she reached for her water, only to be spooked into cover by her movement.

The back of her neck prickled. Concentrating ferociously, she stopped herself from glancing behind.

No small grey animal emerged onto the beach. Sunlight sizzled across sand tinted pinky-gold by the fragments of millions of shells, and shimmered in fascinating patterns over lazy, glassy waves. A gull shrieked from behind her—probably defending some choice titbit. Camera at the ready, Alexa fought an eerie feeling of being watched.

Finally she could stand it no longer. Patiently, carefully, she turned her head.

And looked straight up into eyes of frozen fire—contemptuous eyes in a handsome, autocratic face. Her heart crashed against her breastbone; instinctively she jumped sideways, and the camera dropped from her numb fingers onto the rock as she fought to keep her balance.

An iron grip stopped her from falling ignominiously onto her face and set her on her feet in the yielding sand. 'Are you hurt?' Prince Luka of Dacia demanded.

'I'm all right.' Fighting for control, she twisted away from hands that opened instantly and let her go. She dropped to one knee to pick up the camera case, catching back a small cry of dismay as it flexed ominously.

'What the hell are you doing?' Luka asked with harsh distinctness. 'This is private property.'

'But not *your* private property. I have every right to be here.' Astonished by the flood of sheer physical excitement that threatened to overwhelm her, Alexa stood up, clutching the shattered camera and lifting her head to stare aggressively at his wide, straight, alarmingly sensual mouth. 'You're the trespasser, not me.'

His hard handsome face froze.

Recklessly Alexa pushed her luck. 'So, what are *you* doing here?'

For a second he looked dangerously close to losing his cool. Perversely, Alexa hoped he would. It seemed only fair. He'd scared the life out of her, startled her into smashing her father's camera—one of the few mementoes she had of him—then had the nerve to look at her as though she were a slug in his lettuce.

'I am on holiday,' he said in a tone that could have sliced granite.

Alexa struggled with the impulse to tell him to go to hell. 'So am I,' she stated, her hand clenching over the camera case. When something jabbed her finger she fought back sudden bleak tears as she jerked it away.

'What's the matter?'

'Nothing,' she snapped.

But he'd seen the blood. Saying something short and untranslatable in the musical language that was presumably Dacian, he stooped and caught her hand, lifting it to examine the cut. 'Is the glass still in there?'

'The lens isn't broken,' she muttered, the small pain vanquished by the sudden uproar of her senses. How could one man's touch cause such mayhem? 'It's just a cut from the shards of the case.'

Luka hauled a handkerchief from his pocket and mopped the bead of blood away. Black brows drawn together in a formidable frown, he checked the cut carefully before wrapping the cloth around her finger. Then he looked up.

And caught her watching him.

He returned her gaze with flinty eyes reflecting the shimmer of the sun on the sea. 'Where is your boat?'

'Boat?' Bemused by the jumble of sensations rioting through her, Alexa said, 'What boat?'

Although his fingers didn't tighten around her wrist, she knew she didn't have a chance of pulling free.

Ice-cold, he said, 'The one you arrived on.'

'The only boat around here is the one that came into the bay last night—the big launch I presume you arrived on. I came by car—a four-wheel drive, actually.'

Silence—taut, stark and thrumming with unspoken words—stretched between them. The sun swathed gold over his skin, highlighting stark cheekbones and gleaming golden eyes half hidden by heavy lids and long lashes. He appeared to be thinking hard and fast. With silky indolence he pointed out, 'This is an island, Alexa.'

'I know it's an island.'

Insultingly, relentlessly polite, he asked, 'So how did you manage to reach this beach by car?'

She retorted with frosty hauteur, 'You have no right to cross-question me.'

'Answer me.' *Or we'll stay here all day.* His tone and the implacable cast of his features said the words for him.

Chills skimmed the length of her spine. For the first time Alexa realised how vulnerable she was, alone on a lonely beach with a man who paid the salaries of the nearest people. Not far beneath Luka's sophisticated surface lurked a warrior, with a warrior's outlook, formidable and ruthlessly practical.

But this was New Zealand! He was the interloper here, not her.

She said crisply, 'I drove to the Spit, left my car in the car park, caught the ferry to Deep Harbour and picked up the four-wheel drive my friends keep garaged there. Then I drove over the island to my friends' bach.' She jerked her head backwards. 'Along the beach. And you, I conclude, are the millionaire next door?'

Hooded eyes narrowed further into smouldering chips. 'I'm certainly next door.'

With Sandra Beauchamp?

Angry with him for interrogating her—but furious at the incandescent, unwilling response of her body to his touch—Alexa twisted her wrist away.

Luka's fingers relaxed instantly, although he didn't

step back. Instead he watched with narrowed eyes as she unwound his handkerchief and examined her finger.

'It's stopped bleeding,' she said practically. Her voice sounded as prosaic as the words, which was a relief, because her tense body was humming with adrenalin, ready to run. Or surrender...

Ignoring that degrading thought, Alexa stooped to pick up the other small shards of plastic from the destroyed camera case. When she'd recovered every one she could see, she dropped them into his immaculate handkerchief. Well, immaculate except for the scarlet stain of her blood. Carefully she flicked the last dark splinter into the white linen and tied the handkerchief into a loose knot.

Luka said conversationally, 'I'm surprised you use such an old camera.' His voice altered. 'What have I said?'

With an inelegant sniff that didn't hide the dampness in her eyes, Alexa said truculently, 'It was my father's. He—he was interested in photography—he bought me my first camera and when he died I—I managed to salvage this one.' She bit her lip to stem any further confidences.

'Salvage it from what?' Luka asked in a deeper, gentler voice.

Unwillingly she told him, 'When my parents died I was sent to a foster home. The government organisation that cared for me sold everything we owned except for my things and a couple of mementoes.'

'How old were you?' he asked.

'Fourteen.' She looked down at the little parcel of plastic.

He said quietly, 'I was fourteen when my mother died.'

Alexa looked up sharply and surprised a fleeting expression on his handsome face that twisted her heart. 'Not a good year for losing parents,' she said wryly, adding, 'At least you had your father.'

'I don't suppose any year is a good year to lose a parent.' Luka looked past her to the Thorntons' bach. 'How long are you staying?'

His patent eagerness to get rid of her was like a slap in the face. For a moment there she'd thought they'd achieved a tenuous understanding. Shrugging, she said, 'Ten days. It doesn't matter, you know—I'll stay out of your way. You can always avoid me by swimming in the pool up at the house instead of off the beach—the rip can be dangerous.'

'Been snooping, Alexa?' he asked silkily, heavy lashes hooding his eyes.

'No need to,' she returned, chilled yet defiant. 'Millionaires always have pools. It's part of the mindset— like paranoia.' And arrogance.

Schooling her face into an expression of calm dismissal, she held out the handkerchief with its bloodstain and its little cargo of plastic.

Angular features tough and forbidding, he stood motionless. Sharp fierce tension throbbed between them while the waves crisped against the sand and the sun beat down, hot and heavy as summer, summoning blue from the black depths of Luka's hair and lovingly outlining the compelling angles and planes of his face. Alexa fought an impulse to run.

Even when at last he took the handkerchief from her she couldn't relax.

He said levelly, 'I want privacy, Alexa. I'd be happy to organise a holiday for you somewhere else—Hawaii, northern Australia, the Islands. England in the spring is very beautiful.'

Good resolutions forgotten, she returned with a steely fury she'd later think ridiculous, 'I don't want to go any-where else. I'm perfectly happy here.' Flicking her hair back from her suddenly hot face, she said with a taunting smile, 'Perhaps you could get a stick and draw a line down the beach on the boundary. I promise I won't cross it.'

The silence that followed those unwise words was as brittle as the case of her father's camera, until Luka said, 'But how much can I trust your promise?'

Alexa knew she'd regret letting her normally even temper get the better of her, but at this moment it ex-hilarated her. Coolly defiant, she said, 'Enjoy the rest of your stay in New Zealand.' With a brisk little air she held out her hand.

After a moment Luka's long fingers closed around hers, lifting them so that he could kiss the little cut. Thick black lashes half hid his metallic eyes, and as his mouth branded her skin Alexa crossed a hidden bound-ary into wild, unknown territory.

But it wasn't until he turned her hand over and bit it delicately on the fleshy mound beneath her thumb that her body went crazy.

She yanked her hand back and stared at him. White-faced, grabbing for composure, she said shakily, 'Is that how you say goodbye in Dacia?'

'That's how we say *I want you very much* in Dacia,' he drawled. 'Why look so shocked? You already knew that.' Unforgivably he finished, 'And you want me too. I hope you find it as irritating as I do.'

Alexa could have kicked herself for giving him such an opening. She swallowed. 'I'm going. Goodbye.'

His laugh was low and unamused, totally cynical. 'I think we'll see each other again.'

'Not if I see you first,' she shot back, and set off for the bach.

Marching steadily along the beach, she could feel his gaze bore into her shoulders. What had been an enjoyable five-minute walk half an hour ago now seemed to take hours, and by the time she reached the house she was parched and slightly dizzy.

'So drink your water next time,' she said staunchly, shrugging out of her pack and opening the bottle in it. She drained the slightly warm liquid and set the bottle down with a small defiant crash.

Luka of Dacia might want her but he certainly didn't like her. Well, that was entirely mutual.

Of all the wretched coincidences! And why hadn't she been able to keep a guard on her tongue?

Every time she saw him the devastating impact of his sexuality burned away her confidence. Like some dark enchanter he paralysed her common sense and her willpower and sent her hormones crazy.

'It's quite simple. You're a strongly visual person,' she rationalised, 'and heaven knows he's got enough good looks to stock a model agency. Of course he affects you—you'd be a lousy photographer if he didn't.'

So why not leave the island?

Because that would be ceding some sort of victory to him in this intense, irrational war they were fighting. If she tamely gave up and ran away she'd be surrendering.

Dion watched his Prince stride across the room and come to a halt in the window. 'So what do you plan to do?' he asked in a neutral voice.

'I have no choice,' Luka said harshly. 'Alexa Mytton

will want to keep our whereabouts as quiet as she can so that she can earn the utmost from her photographs and copy, but if she does let slip that we're here the bay will be crawling with paparazzi within hours. Last night the Sant'Rosans revealed that they've been having discussions with the New Zealand government, who are prepared to send a peace-keeping force as soon as an accord is signed, but until then they want secrecy. Guy will be in real danger if news of those meetings gets out.'

'Only if we don't get to him first,' Dion said urgently.

'If we make an attempt to rescue him we can give up any chance of peace there,' Luka said, an austere note hardening his voice into grimness. 'I understand what it is not to trust anyone.'

Which was why he couldn't let this ridiculous hunger for a flame-haired beauty stand in his way.

Forcing himself to ignore the persistent clamour of his senses, he went on, 'If Alexa Mytton is not paparazzi she has links with them, and I won't risk my cousin's life for a pair of brilliant eyes.' And a body that still tormented his dreams. He gave a hard, unamused smile. 'As my father used to say, ''Never trust anyone. And especially never trust a woman.'''

'It's a cynical creed to live by,' Dion observed, watching him closely.

'One that works.' To save his island realm from invasion his father had married the only child of the dictator poised to crush Dacian freedom. He'd sired her child, and in the fifteen years of their marriage he'd never trusted her.

Repressing memories of the quiet, weary woman who had loved him, Luka said, 'I might give Ms Mytton the benefit of the doubt if it weren't for the other items of gossip in that damned column. As it is, I dare not. I can't permit her to tell anyone I am here.'

'I agree,' Dion said, nodding. 'So, to get back to the point, what are you going to do?'

Luka shrugged. 'Whatever I have to,' he said in a flat, lethal voice.

'Trust the Sant'Rosans?'

'Oh, no,' Luka said coolly. 'You will organise a group to snatch Guy; get them as close to Sant'Rosa as you can, without alerting the islanders, and tell them to wait until you contact them before doing anything.'

Dion nodded. 'And what about Ms Mytton?'

'Run another, more complete check on her. I want to know everything—friends, family, professional standing, lovers. Bank account.'

A knock at the door turned both men's heads. 'Come in,' Luka said.

A stolid, middle-aged man entered and bowed. 'Your Highness,' he said after Luka had greeted him. 'The woman is taking pictures.'

Luka's stomach contracted, as though warding off a blow. Angry at this sign of weakness, he asked, 'Of what?' surprised that his voice stayed so level.

'Of the sand, and some birds, but mostly along the beach.'

Luka exchanged glances with his head of security before saying, 'Thank you. Go back and continue watching.'

The man hesitated and Dion asked, 'What is it?'

'I think perhaps I was careless and let the sun catch the lens of my binoculars,' he said apologetically.

Dion said sternly, 'Make sure it doesn't happen again.'

The man saluted and sketched another bow before disappearing.

'I'll pay another visit to Ms Mytton,' Luka said with a flat, deadly intensity. He sensed he'd startled the other man, but he was gripped by a disappointment that consumed him until he could barely breathe. Somehow the spirited, fiery Alexa Mytton had got to him so hard he couldn't think clearly for wanting her.

Never, since that first treacherous affair, had he wanted to trust a woman so much. Well, that was a lesson he'd learned very well.

CHAPTER FOUR

ALEXA removed the film from the camera, telling herself sternly that by obsessing about the man she was giving him power over her.

She didn't care about Prince Luka. 'Not at all,' she said aloud. He was someone from another world, a glamorous, exotic world where duty meant everything and love nothing. She knew exactly what she wanted in life—a satisfying career, a man she could love, and children. A family to replace the one torn so brutally from her, and an ordinary life with all the ordinary pleasures and some, certainly, of the ordinary pain.

Luka was far from ordinary.

But when a thickening of the atmosphere pulled her head around and she saw his big, lean body silhouetted in the door a shameful flare of anticipation shortened her breath and pulled every tiny hair on her skin upright. She'd rather cross swords with this man than kiss another.

Clutching the container of film, she said bluntly, 'I didn't hear you knock.'

'I didn't, and I'm not waiting for an invitation to come inside either.' He walked in and glanced around with the searching concentration she'd seen on the news from those anonymous men whose job it was to take bullets for their masters. As well as the room, that hard, swift survey took in her camera on the table, the film in her hand, and the special bag she kept her other films in.

'You're quite safe,' she said evenly, suppressing a

shaft of sympathy. No one should have to live like that, wondering who was aiming what at them. 'No hidden photographers waiting to pounce.'

'How about hidden cameras?'

'No,' she said shortly. 'Why should there be? To what do I owe the pleasure…' her voice lingered with delicate scorn on the word '…of this visit?'

His eyes narrowed. 'I came to this island for a private holiday. I know that you have links to whoever writes that gossip column, and are a friend of the hotel events manager. Naturally I find your presence here suspicious.'

Did he suspect Carole? Chin jutting, Alexa said, 'Besides being excellent at her job, Carole Molloy is a consummate professional—she wouldn't tip off a gossip columnist.'

'I didn't say she had.'

'You insinuated it! Carole doesn't deserve to be blamed for—'

He interrupted her with a hint of cynicism. 'You're very loyal.'

'She was good to me when I needed help,' Alexa said fiercely, 'and she has nothing to do with any of this.'

'That doesn't matter now,' he said, dismissing Carole with a careless arrogance that set Alexa's teeth on edge. 'She is no longer a player. You, however, are.'

'All I want is to spend a peaceful holiday taking photographs for a competition!' Alexa told him stonily. 'I am not—repeat not, not, *not*—interested in you or whoever you have visiting you!'

Again that dangerous hooded glance, keen and lethal as the blade of a golden dagger, contrasting with the calm pleasantness of his tone when he said, 'I don't trust you, Alexa Mytton. I don't believe in coincidences, especially when they concern journalists. One item in a gossip column could be bad luck. Two are extremely suspicious, and three—'

'Three?' Alexa echoed, startled.

'Three times. Yesterday she mentioned that you and I were spending time together on a romantic island tryst.'

Alexa's mouth fell open. 'I don't believe it.' Her mind raced over people who might possibly have known where she was going—only her friends, and they certainly wouldn't be talking to any gossip columnist.

'I can show you the newspaper if you want to check it,' he said with exquisite contemptuous politeness.

Biting her lip, Alexa said, 'No, if you say it's there, I believe you. But that lets Carole off the hook. She didn't know I was coming here.'

'I've already told you I am no longer interested in Carole Molloy.' He waited, but when Alexa remained silent, he went on, 'I want any films you've exposed. And I won't pay you for them. I despise blackmailers.'

'And I despise bullies. I don't know how on earth that wretched columnist knows where I am,' Alexa sputtered, still stunned, 'but I am not in the business of selling spy shots—not even of you, not even if you stripped naked in front of me!'

His eyes gleamed. 'No matter how much you were offered for it?'

'No,' she retorted.

'Do professional photographers habitually try to kiss their way out of trouble?' he asked, watching her with an intent, unsettling gaze.

The blatant unfairness of this set fire to her temper. '*You* kissed *me*.'

'It was an experiment. You had only to resist and I'd have let you go. You didn't resist,' he said coolly, watching her with hard, analytical eyes. 'Why?'

An *experiment*! The colour faded from Alexa's face, leaving her clammy and furious. He was right, damn him. She was the one who'd lost it, totally and embarrassingly, responding to him with all the fervour of a schoolgirl kissed by her first love.

Thanks to a temper she hadn't known she possessed until she met this dictatorial man, things were way out of control. Time to try calm reason. Summoning a cool smile, she said, 'Whatever, that's got nothing to do with photography, which is my job and my passion.'

'What were you doing down on the beach?'

'Trying to catch the difference between summer and autumn.' His raised brows persuaded her to continue, 'I'm intrigued by the subtle variations in seasons. An autumn day can be almost as hot as a summer's one, but there is a difference in—in texture, and one of these days I'll catch that difference on film.'

A mocking lift of his brows revealed that he didn't believe a word. 'We can do this easily or with difficulty.'

She stared mutinously at him. 'Easily for whom?' she demanded crisply.

His smile was worldly and ironic. 'Give me any cameras you have, plus films, with a promise not to take any more. They'll be returned to you when you leave.'

'And the easy way?' she asked, winged black brows shooting up above pale, seething eyes.

He laughed abruptly. 'That *is* the easy way. If you refuse I'll have you kept under guard.'

Furiously, she scanned the speculative amusement in Luka's face as he watched her search for words.

When she'd recovered enough to speak, she said calmly and coldly, 'This is New Zealand, not your own private fiefdom. If you so much as lay a finger on me I'll see you in court on a charge of assault, and not even

being a prince will be enough to save you from that here.
New Zealand is a democracy.'

'So is Dacia,' he said, bored. 'As for touching you…'
His gaze swept her mouth.

Heat fountained through her, fire to match his smouldering gaze. Her breasts tightened and became heavy,
the nipples thrusting urgently at the thin cotton over
them.

'Who would believe you?' he asked softly, surveying
her with a flick of contempt. 'You respond so vividly to
me that I'd have no problem convincing any enquirers
that you came away with me and then tried to blackmail
me into paying you off. You'd get your day of notoriety—possibly even some money from the gutter press—
but if you *are* a serious photographer you'd lose all cred-
ibility.'

Alexa made a small panicky movement, then lifted
her head proudly. 'You wouldn't dare.'

He shrugged. 'I would,' he said softly, and she believed him. His voice changed, deepened, and his smile,
free of anything but warm, ironic humour, hit her like a
blow to her heart.

'Alexa, privacy is important to me. Can you not simply enjoy your time here without taking photographs?'

She recognised calculated charm when she saw it, but
even then it washed over her like a sensual tide and she
wanted to surrender, give him what he wanted.
Contracting every muscle in her body, she said, 'I do
understand—I think—how angry and frustrated media
attention must make you, and I can see why you're suspicious—'

'So you do accept that I have reason to be?'

Where had that wretched columnist got her information from? 'I've just said I do. But I have as much right

to be here as you. You have my word that I won't take
any photographs of you.' Drawing a long bow, she
added grandly, 'Or your guests. Please go now.' She
turned away.

He reached her in two strides, stopping her with a firm
grip around her upper arm. Before she could react, he
seized the hand clutching the canister and forced her
fingers apart. The little container toppled, was caught
with another of those swift movements, and she was
free. Outraged, Alexa launched herself at him, only to
be held away with one strong, merciless hand.

'You are an intransigent woman,' he said harshly as
he flicked off the top and shook out the reel.

'No,' Alexa cried, abandoning her retaliation when
she realised that he intended to expose it to the light.

Grim-faced, he paused. 'Creative anguish?' he
drawled, eyes as cold and hard as crystals, searching her
horrified face. 'Or the prospect of losing a lot of
money?'

Alexa opened her mouth, but before she could speak
he went on with brusque irritation, 'All right, I'll get
them developed first.'

'You are so kind,' Alexa raged, knowing it was futile,
knowing she didn't have a hope of getting her film back.
How she wished she'd taken self-defence lessons!
Nothing would give her greater pleasure than to severely
hurt him.

Cold logic told her that, attack training or not, she
wouldn't have had a hope. Luka had moved with the
lethal speed and skill of a professional warrior, using
just enough strength to keep her away from the film, and
even now he was watching her, ready to counter any
attempt on her part to get it back.

Alexa knew when she was beaten. In a low, tense

voice she said, 'One day you're going to pay for that, I promise you. Now you've got what you came for, get out.'

'Not before I collect any other cameras,' he said.

'By the time I've finished with you, you'll be in prison for years!'

'I doubt it,' he said tersely. 'But unless you let me take your photographic equipment I'll send one of those minions you're so scathing about down to search the house.'

'I'd prefer that,' she retorted. 'At least he'd be just doing his job.'

'Is that what you want?'

She hesitated, then said reluctantly, 'No.'

'So show me your cameras.'

Furiously she said, 'This is the only other one I have here, and if you break it too I'll—'

He said forcibly, 'I won't break it. And I want any unexposed films you might have.'

Alexa bared her teeth. 'Get them yourself.'

Lips clamped together, she watched him pick up the bag and glance into it.

'I will of course return them,' he said courteously. 'And now I need your mobile telephone.'

Of course. If she had been a journalist, the mobile phone would be a logical way of dictating copy or sending text messages. It was sitting in full view on the bookcase, but she was damned if she was going to meekly hand it to him.

'Get it yourself.' Recklessly Alexa pushed her luck. 'I'm not your servant, so don't expect me to curtsy and run around after you.'

'You're not my subject,' he said, in a tone that could

have sliced granite, 'so nothing more formal than a hand-shake is expected.'

She waited until he'd slid the phone into the breast pocket of his well-cut shirt before saying with brittle precision, 'I ring my friend every morning.'

'Then every morning I will come down with the telephone so that you can speak to her,' he said courteously. 'Unfortunately I will need to listen in to the conversation.'

Alexa sent him a glittering glance. 'It will be a pleasant constitutional for you.'

He smiled, but went on, 'Do you have a computer?'

'Yes.' He paused, and she said truculently, 'There are no telephone lines into the bach, so I can't send anything out.'

'Why did you bring it?'

She flushed. 'It's none of your business.'

'But you will tell me just the same,' he said with silky menace.'

Alexa shrugged. 'All right, I'm using software I've just bought to fill in details of my family tree.'

His frown dissipating, he said, 'That's an unusual hobby for one so young.'

Bestowing a smile edged with mockery on him, she said sweetly, 'For those whose family history is well-documented, perhaps it is, but mine is not. And because I'm the only one left on my particular branch of the family tree, I'm very interested in finding out if there are any others.'

'You are completely alone in the world?'

She lifted her chin. 'I've got friends.' *Which,* she allowed her tone to imply, *is more than you have.*

His brows drew together. 'You're bleeding!'

As she followed his gaze to her hand he dumped her

gear onto the table and strode across the room to where she stood. Their tussle for the film had opened the small cut in her finger, releasing a thin line of blood.

Colour heated Luka's arrogantly defined cheekbones. 'I'm sorry,' he said in a rough voice, 'I didn't mean to hurt you.' And as though compelled he lifted her hand to his mouth and sucked the tiny bead.

Alexa gave a choked gasp, her entire world narrowing to the intense pleasure his mouth called into life inside her.

Returning to sanity, she jerked her hand free, but it was too late; he caught her close and looked into her eyes with a fierce stare that claimed something from her.

Rash excitement burned away the last fragment of common sense in Alexa. The word he crushed against her lips was his name, and she melted into him, adrift and lost in uncharted seas.

If the first kisses had been dynamite, this one was a volcano, she thought dizzily. But she'd think about that later...

When he lifted his head she was so far gone that her mouth unconsciously followed his, seeking a return of the heady magic.

He laughed softly and his arms tightened about her, bringing her even closer to his tense, fully roused body.

'What is it you want?' he asked, heavy-lidded eyes promising unimaginable sensual pleasure, while the lazy note in his voice told her that he knew exactly what she wanted—and what she was inviting if she didn't stop this right now.

Alexa brought all her will-power to bear, ruthlessly quashing the images her treacherous brain supplied only too eagerly. He had a nerve.

'I am not a toy to amuse you,' she snarled, twisting away from him.

He proved just how little the kiss meant to him by releasing her instantly.

Her body throbbing, she threw at him, 'If you think you can come in here, steal my belongings, threaten me and then kiss me into stupidity, think again. I'm not an idiot.'

Stiff with hauteur, he said, 'I do not force women. You wanted that kiss as much as I did.'

It wasn't *fair*! Alexa wanted to yell her fury at whatever malevolent fate had brought Prince Luka of Dacia into her peaceful life. Her hair felt as though she'd been caught in a lightning chamber, and every muscle ached with the tension of frustrated lust and a terrifying loss of control. She wanted to stamp and pound and break things, because in spite of everything her body still ached for him.

Instead she said in a tight, strained voice, 'You've got what you came to get. Now get out of here before I start throwing things.'

'I can't leave you like this.' His voice was deliberate, steady.

'I'm all *right*.'

He pushed up her chin and scanned her face with hard, unsparing eyes. Ignoring her protests, and the closed fist she punched into his solar plexus, he picked her up and put her into a chair, his big frame taut and determined.

'It serves you right,' he said savagely as she cradled her painful knuckles. It had been like attacking a rock. 'Of course I tightened the muscles there. Do you have bandages for that finger—some cream?'

Alexa unclenched her teeth enough to spit, 'No.'

'Then I'll bring some down.'

'No! I don't need anything from you.' She closed her fingers into another fist. 'It's just a cut—it'll heal.'

Another swathe of swarthy colour licked along his magnificent cheekbones. 'I'm sorry,' he said, as though she'd wrung the words from him. 'I don't normally behave like a clumsy savage.' He swung on his heel and strode into the kitchen.

Alexa watched his black head above the bar that cut off the kitchen from the living room, and realised that he was pouring her a glass of water. He was, she thought dazedly as she began to come down from the adrenalin high, a complex mixture—both protective and antagonistic. She watched him warily as he came across the room.

Half-closed eyes, grimly gold, surveyed her through a thick layer of black lashes. 'Here,' he said, handing over the glass. 'Drink it all down.'

The water slid cold and refreshing down her throat, easing it enough so that she could say, 'Thank you,' politely and hold out the glass.

He gave her another of those searching glances before, apparently satisfied, taking it back into the kitchen.

Alexa got to her feet and wooed calmness. Memories forced their way into her brain—the unconstrained strength of the arms that had held her, the heavy, driving beat of Luka's heart, and that tantalising, elusive scent. And his warmth, the feeling she'd had of being protected as well as bewitched.

From behind, Luka said, 'You look better—do you feel it?'

'Certainly,' she said with composure, turning to face him. 'You overreacted to my natural irritation with myself for consorting with the enemy.'

His laughter startled her. 'One thing I'll say for you,'

he said, collecting the camera and the bag of films with an easy movement, 'you're not dull.'

Alexa gave him another fulminating look, refusing to back down. 'Don't patronise me. Unfortunately,' she said between her teeth, 'you are entirely predictable.'

'Enjoy your holiday,' he baited her with a sarcastic courtesy that set her teeth even further on edge.

Childishly—a state he seemed able to inflict on her at will, she decided savagely—she cleaned her teeth, scrubbing the taste of him out of her mouth. As she stripped off her clothes to shower she thought he should find a way to bottle his natural scent and sell it as a stimulant.

It was humiliating to be so helpless against his sexual power; whenever he came into the room her will-power fell to pieces as messily and comprehensively as a pavlova tossed onto the floor. Attacking her treacherous body vigorously with soap, she wondered why she hadn't bitten him when he'd kissed her. Her hands slowed.

'Because it never occurred to you,' she said irritably. 'You went under without a murmur.' But she'd like to bite that olive skin—and then lick the small mark—

'Oh, stop it,' she wailed, horrified. 'What am I going to do about this man?'

Perhaps running back to Auckland would be sensible. Her mouth compressed. No, that would be surrender. It was time Luka of Dacia realised that the world hadn't been constructed to suit him alone.

'So I'll stay here, but keep well away from him,' she answered grimly, and got out her computer and the sheets of information she wanted to transfer onto it.

Halfway through an afternoon of sheer stubbornness and many mistakes, she realised that Luka had accepted her word that she had no other cameras.

CHAPTER FIVE

ALEXA woke with panic kicking her in the stomach and the sound of a dull roar echoing through her mind. Wind howled around the eaves, and the first onset of a squall exploded like small bullets on the roof. She relaxed and snuggled under the duvet, drifting off to sleep again to the drama of the storm blowing in from the sea.

The following morning, however, after waking to a still, placid day gilded by sunshine and perfumed with freshly wet grass, she discovered that the bach had no electricity. Which meant no shower, no toast, no coffee…

Fortunately there was the sea, and the barbecue. Half an hour later, after a brisk dip, she ate a piece of bread and honey while watching a battered pan steam gently over the gas jets. She'd have to call the power board, and to do that she needed her telephone, but the first priority was caffeine.

She cast a glance over her shoulder, almost dropping the bread when she saw Luka, the dark prince himself, striding along the beach. In spite of her sternest commands, her heart began to race as he approached, formidably tall and dominating.

His brows rose when he took in the sight of the barbecue and the pan and her salty, slightly sticky wet hair. 'Breakfast al fresco?' he asked coolly.

'No power,' she told him, cloaked in the tatters of her composure.

His brows drew together. 'What happened?'

'I don't know.' She shrugged against the hard topaz gaze. 'I assume the wind last night brought the line down.'

He flicked out her mobile phone—*her* phone!—and punched a number into it. After speaking briefly and incomprehensibly in Dacian, he frowned at the answer, then turned it off and said levelly, 'Someone's going to check the line. In the meantime, you'd better come back with me.'

That macho protectiveness thing again! 'I'm fine,' she said immediately. She gestured at the simmering saucepan. 'I have all I need—coffee and bread and honey.'

'Very rustic.' He surveyed her with a glimmer of amusement that brought her chin up.

Their eyes clashed, hot fire versus pale ice, until the sound of gas hissing and spitting made her jump. Sure enough, the water in the saucepan had begun to boil over the sides and hiss onto the gas.

When Alexa had switched off the gas and poured the water onto the coffee grounds in another saucepan, she looked up to see Luka scanning the barely visible tops of two huge water tanks buried in the bank behind the bach. Of course he noted the piece of rope she'd used in a futile attempt to haul off the hatch.

Frowning, he said, 'I assume you've no water?'

'Not now I've used up what was in the electric jug, but I'll dip it out once I get the hatch off.'

'Leave it—it's far too heavy,' he said.

She kept her eyes firmly averted from his broad shoulders and tightly muscled arms. 'Perhaps you could haul it off.'

'I could,' he drawled, 'but why bother when I can offer you a hot shower and coffee made properly? Come over and have breakfast at my house.'

She gave him an insouciant smile. 'That's very kind of you, but, as you can see, I'm fine,' she said sweetly. 'And barbecue coffee has a taste all on its own.'

Luka lifted his brows, meeting her smile with one of his own—deadly in impact. 'In that case, why don't you offer me some while we find out what's caused the power cut?'

'I'd better ring my friend in Auckland first,' she said, not giving an inch. 'It's her bach—well, her parents'— so they'll need to be told what's happened.'

'It would be better to wait until we know what's happened to your power supply,' he said calmly. 'I still have electricity, so it must be something between here and the junction.'

Irritated by the good sense in this suggestion, Alexa nodded and turned away, giving the coffee grounds in the pot an unnecessary stir.

'Did you get your data transferred to the genealogy software?' he asked idly.

She gave an ironic smile. 'After I'd worked out how to do it, yes.'

'How did you end up being so singularly bereft of family?'

She hesitated before saying defensively, 'My mother was an orphan, and on my father's side my grandfather died young and my grandmother never remarried.' She was not going to tell him that her grandparents on her father's side had never married, her young Italian grandfather dying before he knew his lover was having his child. 'And my mother was ill for a couple of years. Dad took Gran and me to see her in hospital, and on the way back we got hit in a tanker pile-up on the motorway. They were killed instantly. It was just bad luck.'

'It sounds more like tragedy,' he said, his voice very deep.

Because she didn't want to like him at all, she said pertly, 'I suppose you come from a very large family.' And then, pink with embarrassment, recalled that although he was related to most of the royal houses of Europe he was as bereft of immediate family as her.

He shrugged. 'Several hundred distant cousins of varying degrees, but close to me only two.'

His voice had—not hardened, exactly, but become remote, a vocal *No Trespassing* sign. Rebuffed, Alexa turned away.

'What was life like in that foster home?' Luka probed.

Alexa stirred the coffee grounds again. 'The first one was not good, but—'

He said something under his breath, then asked quietly, 'How bad?'

Stupid tears stung her eyes as she shook her head. 'I just didn't get on with their kids. I fitted much better into the second one. They were kind, and most of the other kids were all right. They kept coming and going, but I—well, I was lucky. I knew my mother and father had loved me. It gave me something to cling to when things were bad. Most of the other kids didn't have that.'

'Yes,' he said simply. In a tone she didn't recognise he said, 'It's very important, that knowledge.'

Had his mother loved him? Or his wily, hard father?

He added, 'Your parents must have been delighted that they had a child as sunny and vital as you.'

Startled, she looked up. He was watching her with a hooded glance, not sombre or calculating or grim, but as though she was something new and unusual. Well, ordinary people probably *were* an unknown quantity to him!

Carefully keeping the grounds in the bottom of the saucepan, Alexa poured a mug of coffee. 'We were happy together,' she said. 'I didn't realise how happy until it was over. I need another mug—I'll go and get one.'

'I'll go. Tell me where they are.'

'In the right-hand cupboard above the sink.' She watched as he casually scooped up the telephone and left her.

They drank their coffee on the deck, looking out over a sea so brilliantly blue that only the surf still lashing the rocks recalled the storm in the night. Luka asked questions about her genealogy software, and she made him smile when she told of her struggles with it and her triumph when eventually she worked out the logic that drove it.

Halfway through her mug of coffee Alexa discovered that she was enjoying herself; although a potent, sexually charged tension still seethed beneath the fragile surface somehow Luka had sidestepped it, and they were talking like—well, like friends.

Don't get excited, she warned herself. Making small talk would be another thing royalty was taught from the cradle.

When the telephone rang, Luka excused himself and answered. Alexa's gaze lingered on the powerful male beauty of his face. Purely as a photographer she admired the strong, angular framework and magnificent colouring of olive and gold and black. Although his handsome face echoed his Mediterranean heritage, the dash of Slav in the cheekbones gave his face a tang of dynamic virility.

She blinked her eyes and dragged her fascinated stare away just in time. After a word that clearly meant the equivalent of goodbye, he said in English, 'The line is down—a lightning strike, by the looks of it. You had better let your friend know.' He handed over the telephone.

Alexa keyed in Sally's number and told her what had happened. 'Bummer for you,' Sally said, clearly in a rush. 'Don't worry about it, Alexa. I'm off to Queenstown in half an hour, but I'll get in touch with Mum and Dad and they can organise it from this end. Thanks a million for letting us know—bye!'

'Bye—have fun skiing!'

Luka held out his hand for the phone.

With a shrug Alexa gave it back, and he said easily, 'You had better come to stay with me until the line is fixed. Apparently it won't take too long.'

That was when she realised that of course he wouldn't let her go back to Auckland; he still didn't trust her not to spill the beans.

Yesterday she'd have scorned his invitation, but yesterday she hadn't sat out on the deck with him, drinking thick, smoky coffee and talking about the complicated tricks software could play. If he'd used that conscious charm on her she'd have told him to go to hell; the Luka who had made her laugh with his lazy wit and humour was very easy to like.

And although he was smiling at her it was with wry understanding, as though he knew how torn she was between indignantly refusing the command hidden in his invitation, and an overweening curiosity.

Because that was all it was. She wanted a peek at his house, and if the price of that was a few hours spent in his company while the power company fixed the line, then she was prepared to pay it. A salty tangle of hair sliding across her cheek decided it for her.

'All right,' she said, adding with a half-smile, 'If I can shower there. A swim is no substitute.'

'Certainly you can.'

Suddenly nervous, she scrambled up. 'I'll get something to change into.'

She had enough self-control not to choose her most flattering outfit, but it was a close-run thing. Alexa packed a few clothes into a small pack and came out to see Luka standing on the deck. Deep inside her some unknown, unsuspected emotion lurched into life, and then slotted into place.

Don't be stupid, she warned herself. You know what he's like—autocratic and high-handed and formidable. And a prince.

As though he'd sensed her approach he turned to meet her, and held out his hand for her bag. 'So,' he said, suddenly very foreign, 'let's go.'

He asked questions about the wildlife while they walked along the beach, describing with humour his surprise the first time he'd seen a family of wallabies eating grass on one of the hillsides.

His gardens extended right down to a wide area of grass beneath the huge pohutukawa trees leaning out across the sand, their roughly barked branches making sweeping statements against the bay. On the way up to the house Alexa noted subtle barriers between the sand and the plantings. As they went through a gate she glimpsed a security camera mounted high to survey the foreshore.

Chilled, she thought angrily that no one should have to live like that. It hadn't even been Luka's choice; he'd been born into the life, with no way out.

She recalled some of the photographs she'd seen of him, many taken with long-range lenses at a time when he'd thought himself free of surveillance. And years before she'd read an article by one of his lovers, describing their most intimate moments in salacious detail. A sliver of resentment dissipated, washed away by compassion.

When, after this holiday, nothing appeared in any newspaper, perhaps he'd realise that some people could be trusted.

She smiled up at him, almost staggering at the ferocious response that roared through her when he smiled back.

He felt it too—fire kindled in the depths of his eyes—but his expression didn't alter. 'Welcome to my house,' he said, his voice a little thickened.

Shaken, Alexa forced herself to gaze about with interest as they walked along a wide paved path.

'It's like a series of pavilions,' she said warily, wondering what such a building said about Luka. From a man of his background she'd expected something luxurious and solidly conventional, harking back to Europe, but this—this was exotic and fascinating, as beautiful as the setting.

'It is exactly that,' Luka told her. 'A young Auckland architect designed it, and did an excellent job.'

'It's stunning.'

Luka escorted her across a wide, partly roofed terrace overlooking the lush gardens and the sea. Alexa noted luxurious cane furniture arranged in conversation groups with a view across the garden.

He took her into the house, tiled with the same tiles as the terrace, and along a wide hall with glass on both sides.

Luka opened a door at the far end and said, 'There is a bedroom you can use.' He gave her another of those slow, glinting smiles. 'It has a bathroom *en suite*.'

Once inside, bag in hand, the door closed firmly behind her, Alexa let out a soft exhalation of air. Furnished with a simplicity eminently suited to a holiday house, the room was luxurious yet soothing. And it had curtains to cover the windows, so she wasn't exposed to any stray security man, seagull or prince who happened to wander by.

'So relax,' she muttered between clenched teeth as she pushed open a door into a surprisingly large bathroom. Spare and practical, it had been put together with the same unobtrusive opulence and the same attention to detail.

A horrified glance in the mirror revealed a face topped by a bird's nest of copper hair. As she stripped Alexa admitted that, in spite of being an autocratic, infuriating throwback to medieval times, Luka of Dacia had a strictly modern sensibility when it came to interior decoration.

Of course he'd probably just snapped those lean, strong fingers and someone else had done all the work, but was all this understated discretion, this almost aggressive coolness of colour and line, a reaction to growing up in a country with a dark, often bloody, always dramatic history?

He might be an ogre, but he was an interesting man.

And a very clever one. Every woman who saw him sensed a sexy, exciting challenge, because such tightly leashed self-control hinted at passion beyond the usual. And every woman wondered if she'd be the lucky one to unleash it.

Alexa turned away and set the shower going.

'I'll bet no woman ever has. I don't think there's a chance of smashing through his defences,' she murmured. 'I can't even make him lose his temper!'

She suspected that Luka carried his country in his heart's core, a man trained—probably from birth, poor little boy!—to repress everything else to his duty as a ruler.

Although according to the woman who'd sold her story, he'd been a perfect lover: tender, passionate, controlled and—well, generally magnificent.

'So he's great in bed,' Alexa said cynically, walking into the shower with a sigh of relief. Sternly ignoring her half-scared, half-feverish shiver at the thought of him as a lover, she told herself, 'You know that's not everything.'

Damian had been a good lover, and she'd really believed she'd loved him, yet in the end she had left him because she'd loved his large, cheerful, noisy family as much as she'd loved him. More, if she was honest.

And she wanted more than that; she wanted what her parents had had, and her grandmother—a once in a lifetime love.

She wasn't naïve enough to let her fascination with Luka blind her. Sexual attraction was notoriously brittle as a sensible base for any sort of relationship—

'Whoa!' she said out loud, shocked by the thought.

The hand soaping her hair stopped. *Relationship?*

Oh, no. No, no, no! Although no man had affected her as Luka did, she wasn't going to fall into that trap and assume she must be in love with him.

Her unwilling response was solely physical. She felt nothing more for him than anger at his arrogance, respect for his intelligence—and a humiliating surge of hormones.

Without emotion and understanding sex offered no more than a momentary pleasure and a sour aftermath.

Ignoring a stab of pain somewhere in the region of

her heart, she finished washing, dried herself down on an enormous bath sheet and dressed rapidly in the well-cut jeans and a honey-coloured shirt.

She was not going to let herself become obsessed by a man she didn't know and didn't trust. Apart from the huge gulf between a New Zealand woman and a European prince, when this interlude was over he'd go back to Dacia and she'd never see him again. Which, she reminded herself sternly as she gathered up the clothes she'd discarded, would be a good thing; she was far too susceptible to the spectacular charm, which was as much a weapon as his intellect—and used just as ruthlessly.

Someone was in her bedroom when she went back—a thin, middle-aged woman who looked up from straightening cushions on the chair when Alexa stopped in the doorway.

With a hint of reservation, the older woman said, 'Hello, I'm Jill Martin, the housekeeper. If there's anything you want, let me know.'

'Thank you,' Alexa said, smiling.

It wasn't returned. Jill Martin said, 'The Prince asked me to tell you that morning tea will be served by the swimming pool in half an hour.'

CHAPTER SIX

A FEW minutes later, eyes masked with sunglasses, Alexa walked out of the bedroom.

She hadn't taken two steps before the housekeeper reappeared, greeting her with that reserved smile. 'The Prince asked me to show you the way.'

'Thank you.' Alexa walked sedately beside her along the seaward terrace and down some wide steps towards a pale apricot stucco wall, wondering why the woman was so reticent.

Accustomed to making people feel relaxed enough to photograph, she went on, 'This must be a fabulous place to work—a far cry from noisy, busy Auckland.'

'We love it here,' Jill Martin said politely, standing back to let her go through a door in the wall.

Alexa persevered. 'I know it's very new, but the garden looks so established.'

'The landscaper brought in a lot of mature trees, and of course some, like that coral tree, were already here.' The older woman gestured towards a large tree that sheltered a long, low cabana, its claw-like scarlet flowers already bursting free of their buds.

Beyond it a pool glittered under the benign sky. Lounging furniture had been arranged on two sides of the walled enclosure, some in full sun, some in the shade of a pergola, under which Luka was reading. Sprawled along a lounger, he should have looked relaxed and lazy, in spite of the papers he was flicking through, but his big, powerful body radiated leashed purpose beneath the scarlet bouganvillaea cascading above him.

Alexa's gaze flew to his face, strong and angular and harshly compelling. Her breath rasped shallow through her lungs and something splintered in the region of her heart. Every sense was so acutely honed that the cool breeze slashed at her skin and the mellow autumn sunlight flailed it. Even the ironic mew of a gull scraped across her eardrums.

Briefly she closed her eyes, willing herself back into her usual composed self.

Luka glanced up, then got to his feet. Helplessly Alexa noticed the way his T-shirt and trousers tightened across his shoulders and lean hips, calling attention to the length and muscled power of his legs, the balance and co-ordination that combined to forge his masculine grace.

'Thank you, Jill,' he said.

The caretaker's wife smiled at him with real affection before disappearing back to the house.

Luka's voice deepened. 'You look—charming.'

'I—thank you.'

In contrast to the cool courtesy of his words, the sculpted mask of his face remained urbane, almost bland, yet Alexa sensed something relentless and detached behind it. He didn't want her here.

Well, she thought, trying to hide a surprisingly acute twist of pain with brisk common sense, she didn't want to be here either. Yet she didn't entirely blame him for being so suspicious; that third item in the gossip column was pretty damning. If she'd thought he was a member of the pack of photographers who bayed after celebrities like greedy hounds, she wouldn't have wanted *him* anywhere near her.

'Come and have some tea,' he invited.

Alexa poured a cup for herself, and some inky black coffee for him.

Sitting back down in the lounger, he said pleasantly, as one would say to a guest, 'What made you decide to become a photographer?'

'I fell in love with a camera when I was eight.'

'Eight?' His brows rose.

'My father loved photography, and he showed me what to do. The minute I realised I could imprison time with exciting images I was hooked.'

'Imprison time?' he repeated, eyes suddenly keen. 'That's an interesting way to see it—especially as the camera can lie.'

She said, 'A good photographer reveals the truth.'

'Whose—the subject's or the photographer's?'

Alexa hesitated. 'The truth of that moment.'

Although his brows drew together he wasn't exactly frowning. 'I'm sorry you dropped your father's camera.'

'It was just a sentimental thing.' She shrugged. 'Don't worry about it.'

'I will replace it, of course,' he said without expression.

'That won't be necessary. I was the one who dropped it, not you.'

He ignored that to ask, 'Exactly what sort of photography do you do? Portraits? Weddings?'

She'd already told him, but perhaps he was trying to trip her up. Smiling in a way that hinted of teeth, she said, 'Portraits. And some magazine work, even a bit of fashion work—it's all good discipline. Wedding photographers need far more courage and stamina and sheer dedication than I'll ever have. It's like swimming with tiger sharks—dangerous. Mothers of the bride are notorious!'

Entranced by the difference laughter made to his expression, she watched him through her lashes. Nothing would ever soften his face, but genuine amusement lifted it beyond gorgeous into blazingly charismatic.

Sobering, he commented drily, 'Not to mention pageboys and flower girls,' and added, 'Have you noticed that there is always one child everyone watches with a mixture of dread and anticipation?'

'Usually the cutest one,' she said, surprised in her turn by his observation. But then, he was a man who noticed things.

'Tell me about Dacia,' she suggested, to move the subject off herself—although she'd developed a curiosity about the place that had produced a man like Luka. 'I know it's an island, and very beautiful, and I know it's had an interesting history, but I'm afraid that's about all I know.'

Luka wondered why she was bothering, but to keep his mind—and his body—off the way the sunlight poured through the flowers onto her vivid, sensuous face, he said, 'What would you like to know?'

'How is it still a monarchy when every other country around is a republic?'

'Not every one. Illyria has a prince who married a New Zealander.'

Alexa nodded. 'We heard about that in spades—the newspapers called it the romance of the century. Were you there?'

'Yes. We know each other quite well, Alex Considine and I.' Another smile hit Alexa with sledgehammer charm. 'Illyrians consider us a Johnny-come-lately state because Dacia has been independent only four hundred or so years, whereas they claim descent from the original Illyria in Roman times. And of course there's Monaco, on the French side of Italy, and a couple of others. We're all accidents of history, and we owe our existence to clever, cunning rulers who were willing to sacrifice almost everything on the altar of their little realms.'

'As your father did,' she said quietly, dark winged brows pleating above her pale, exotic eyes.

He saw the moment she remembered that his mother had been the daughter of the man who'd threatened Dacia with invasion. Colour ran up beneath her silken skin in a manner he found oddly endearing as she looked at him with stricken regret, and his ingrained, carefully constructed suspicion began to crumble.

But only for a second. Her clear, candid gaze invited trust, but Luka remembered a woman who'd looked at him with erotic fervour one night, and the next morning sold every detail of their lovemaking, bargaining with the ruthless skill of a huckster to extract the utmost money from the press.

He'd never spoken of his parents' marriage to anyone, not even his friends. The impulse to tell Alexa how it had been was just another indication of how she'd got to him, like wine laced with poison, he thought fancifully.

Aloud he said neutrally, 'Dacia wasn't big enough to win a war, and when it became obvious that we were on our own my father was forced to temper his actions to the inevitable.' He gave a hard smile. 'He yielded on those things he had to, but within the limits imposed by my grandfather he stood between the people of Dacia and the sort of hell the Illyrians suffered.'

He drained his glass, then set it down. Coolly, without emotion, he said, 'My mother's father was an old-style warlord, but although he kept my father on a tight rein my mother was able to soften a lot of his harsher decrees. She was his only child.'

Alexa felt as though she were walking across fish-hooks. 'So the marriage worked out?'

He gave her a brief, oblique smile, but ignored her comment. 'He knew the time for warlords was passing, and I suspect it satisfied something in him to know that one day his grandchild would rule Dacia.'

'Did you like him?' she asked curiously.

His expression didn't change, but she knew she'd intruded across some invisible barrier. 'I didn't know him well,' he said evenly.

Had his father and mother loved each other?

With that unnerving ability to read her mind, Luka drawled, 'Dynastic marriages can be quite satisfactory if both parties understand the rules.'

'And what *are* the rules?' Alexa enquired dulcetly.

'That the couple provide support for each other, and that after producing the required heir—or two—love and excitement may be sought outside the marriage, but always discreetly.' He directed a sardonic smile at her rigid face. 'I can see you don't approve.'

'It sounds remarkably cold-blooded,' Alexa said quietly, gazing out over the glinting water of the pool and feeling profoundly sorry for both his bartered mother and his wily, duty-bound father. And for him, growing up in what must have been a hell of tension.

'So you would demand passion and romance in marriage?' he asked with silky, goading precision.

'Don't most people? As well as respect and liking and companionship, of course.'

'You *are* a romantic,' he said, his voice deep and

taunting. 'Where do you expect to find this paragon of male perfection?'

'I'm not actively looking right now,' she retorted, trying to conceal her bristling hackles.

'And do children enter the equation?' Politely he offered her a plate of delicious little muffins.

Helping herself to one, Alexa said, 'If that's at all possible, yes.'

Although his expression didn't alter his searching scrutiny tightened her skin, and she suspected he understood the source of her deep-seated longing for a family.

Hastily she said, 'For a dynastic marriage to be a success you'd have to be brought up where marriages of convenience are the norm.'

'So you can't see yourself entering into one?'

'Never,' she said crisply. 'But I do think that any relationship should have ground rules, and if both parties agree with them and stick to them the relationship should work.' She added snidely, 'Especially if the expectations are limited. I assume that's the sort of marriage you plan to make?'

He leaned back in his chair and surveyed her with half-closed eyes. 'Probably,' he said indolently, 'unless I find another woman like Ianthe of Illyria, who wears her love for her husband in her face.'

'And does he love her?' Alexa asked, a little more tartly than she'd intended. OK, so she'd given him the opening, but his cold-blooded decision to marry for practical reasons hurt her in some fundamental way.

Luka smiled, all prowling, sexual charm beneath unreadable eyes. 'It's hard to tell. He doesn't give much away.'

'It certainly wasn't a *practical* marriage,' Alexa said before she could stop herself. Ianthe of Illyria, born plain

Ianthe Brown of New Zealand, was a scientist who walked with a limp, a beautiful Cinderella who'd won the heart of her prince.

'Not practical at all,' Luka agreed without inflection.

Something in that level, unemotional voice made Alexa wonder if he even believed in love.

He went on, 'Of course Considine was brought up in Australia after he and his mother fled Illyria. No doubt he absorbed different attitudes and values there.'

Alexa said carefully, 'I hope he and his Ianthe are very happy together.'

Luka's smile had an edge to it. 'Have you ever been in love?'

'Four or five times,' she told him, her cheerful voice ringing hollow even to her own ears. 'How about you?'

His brows rose, but he said evenly, 'A couple of times in my youth, when anything seemed possible.' He glanced across the swimming pool. 'Would you like to swim?'

Another abrupt change of subject. But what did he mean by 'when anything seemed possible'?

Possibly that a man who'd been trained to distrust everyone would never learn to love.

The thought sent icy little needles of pain through her. Such a waste!

'A swim sounds wonderful,' she said sedately, getting to her feet and beginning to stack the dishes on the tray. A swim would also douse the slow, simmering heat permeating her body. 'I'll take this inside and change.'

He accompanied her back to the house, silent beside her while she wondered why on earth she'd agreed to swim. Because he'd challenged her to do it, and she'd responded with a flare of bravado.

If she kept this up she'd be heading into trouble, she

thought on an odd little pang—serious trouble. Although she'd packed her most demure bathing suit, the thought of Luka watching her in it sent sneaky little thrills up her spine.

'The kitchen's through here,' he said, opening the door.

A large room, magnificently set out with every conceivable gadget a cook might lust after, it was empty. Alexa set the tray down on the bench, surprised when Luka began to put the dishes away.

With a swift smile he closed the refrigerator door. 'You see, I'm not entirely without domestic skills.'

She laughed. 'Oh, great skills—putting milk and sugar away and stacking the dishwasher! Can you sort clothes to go into the washing machine?'

'I have tried,' he told her with a vastly different smile, one that set her heart thudding uncomfortably against her breastbone, 'and I've decided that such knowledge is genetically coded into the female of the species.'

'How chauvinist and convenient for you!'

'I'm afraid that goes with the territory.'

The note of warning in his voice chilled Alexa. When he wanted to Luka could be amusing and entertaining, and she enjoyed matching wits with him—enough, in fact, for it to become addictive—but there was always that invisible barrier.

It shouldn't matter, but somehow it did.

If he'd been the seriously sexy, lightweight playboy prince from the headlines, instead of a man with formidable intelligence and uncompromising authority, she wouldn't be feeling this complicated mixture of emotions. The raw sexual attraction, although intensely potent, was probably the easiest to deal with—at least, she thought with a sudden catch of her breath, as long as he didn't touch her.

What frightened her was her growing fascination with the complex and intriguing man beneath that darkly handsome mask.

She looked up sharply when a man walked into the kitchen—the man Luka had sent to bring her to the hotel that day he'd accused her of sending information to the wretched gossip columnist.

Luka frowned, but said pleasantly enough, 'Alexa, you have already met my head of security.'

'I have. Hello,' she said with a smile.

He gave a formal half-bow and said, 'Ms Mytton.'

Luka's voice was cool. 'Dion, what have you discovered about the power to Ms Mytton's house?'

Straightening up, Dion said, 'Not good news, I'm afraid. The line was not brought down by a branch or a tree; it seems that the transformer was struck by lightning.'

'Which means?' Alexa asked.

Luka cut in with smooth reassurance, 'Merely that it will take a little longer to fix. Don't worry about it now—Dion will find out when it will be done. In the meantime, I think we should enjoy that swim.'

Five minutes later, Alexa was wriggling into her periwinkle-blue bathing suit, originally chosen because it lent her eyes some colour. It covered everything, but it was skintight. Normally she'd have worn it quite happily, but—well, this was not a normal occasion.

Trying to ignore the insistent, secret excitement thrumming through her, she pulled her shirt over the suit, then went to the bathroom in search of sunscreen.

She found an unopened bottle—along with other beautifully packaged, untouched cosmetics—in the top

drawer. Uncapping the bottle of lotion, Alexa pushed the
drawer back in with a quick twist of her hip. A sharp
rattle revealed that she must have dislodged something;
she pulled the drawer right out to see a tube of lipstick.

Feeling oddly empty, she twisted the lid free. It had
been used. Alexa stared at the neatly rounded top as
though it were a snake, Sandra Beauchamp's beautiful
face flashing into her mind.

'So why the shock?' she said robustly. 'According to
the magazines he's not in the habit of holidaying alone!'

She was jumping to conclusions—if Luka had had a
woman here, surely she'd shared *his* bed and *his* room?

Perhaps he valued his privacy too much to share a
room with a woman.

Recapping the gold case, Alexa set it on the marble
counter and with deft, angry movements applied sunscreen to her lips and skin.

Ten minutes later she re-emerged, sunglasses worn as
a visor, her face an aloof mask, hoping that Luka
wouldn't recognise how absurdly sensitive she felt about
the long bare legs emerging beneath the hem of her shirt.

Or see the foolish jealousy seething beneath the glossy
surface she'd manufactured.

The housekeeper was walking along the terrace when
she emerged into the sunlight. Keeping an eye on her?
Before she had time to wonder whether it was sensible,
Alexa said, 'Ms Martin, I found a lipstick in a drawer
in the bathroom. It's been used, so someone must have
left it behind.'

The older woman nodded and said pleasantly, 'I'll
deal with it.'

'Thank you.'

Still slightly shaky with a horrible mixture of anger

and jealousy, and a possessiveness she'd never experienced before, Alexa continued on to the pool.

Whoever had designed it had chosen tiles the exact colour of the sea on a sunny day, and organised the water to fall gently over an unseen lip so that the pool and the ocean mingled without an obvious boundary. An infinity edge, and swimming in it would be like floating into space—exhilarating, dangerous, something she'd never done before…

It seemed like a slap in the face when she saw Luka already in the water, striking out fast and purposefully, sunlight gleaming richly on his olive skin.

Watching the sinuous movement of the coiled, powerful muscles in his wide shoulders and long legs, Alexa suffered a spasm of forbidden desire so intense it felt like agony.

Only a few minutes ago she'd been complacently telling herself that she could cope with this elemental response! Instead, she burned in feverish need, every cell in her body aching with a hunger she couldn't control, a hunger that honed the emotions already churning inside her, feeding off their intensity and adding to them.

Like every other woman he met, she'd fallen under Luka's spell. Why else had she just spent half an hour talking to him instead of berating him for treating her like some piece of plunder?

Actually, she decided more reasonably, he'd treated her like an obstacle to neutralise. And now he was swimming as though he'd forgotten her.

Not that she *wanted* him to be interested in her.

Taut with tension, and thoroughly disgusted with herself, Alexa shrugged off her shirt and threw it onto a hammock, tossing her sunglasses onto a low table. After shucking off her sandals, she executed a neat racing dive into the pool well away from Luka.

Cool water sleeked deliciously along her body, but did nothing to douse that treacherous fire inside. Alexa set herself to emulate Luka's determined pursuit of fitness, striking out with her own classic crawl stroke. Well-taught herself, she recognised the signs of an excellent coach, and thought sourly that no doubt he'd had the very best of tuition for anything he desired.

Making love, too. All those impossibly beautiful women who'd shared his bed and his body…

She missed a turn and breathed at the wrong moment. Choking, gasping, she sank to the bottom, pushed off again and shot to the top.

Strong arms snatched her up, lifting her out of the pool. As she lay coughing on the tiles she felt Luka turn her onto her side in the recovery position, holding her there until she stopped spluttering water.

Finally, when she was able to breathe again, she sat up and looked at him with streaming eyes, muttering, 'Th-thanks.'

He was kneeling, his dark face grim with concern. 'Are you all right?' he demanded, tilting her chin so that he could see her face.

'Apart from my wounded pride,' she said with a determined smile. 'I've known since I was three that breathing underwater doesn't work…'

He got to his feet and bent down, his arms closing around her in a tight, warm embrace as he pulled her to her feet. She had to stop herself from curving into him, abandoning herself to his support.

'I thought you were drowning,' he said roughly, picking her up.

He carried her across to the hammock, setting her on

the edge and holding her and the hammock still so that he could see her properly. 'Can I get you something— a little brandy, perhaps?'

'No,' she said, trying to stifle another bout of coughing. 'I'm all right. Sorry to interrupt your swim. As soon as I get my breath back and dredge up some self-esteem, I'll join you again.'

Arms tightening around her, he started to laugh.

'Truly, I'm fine. You can't drown a water rat,' she muttered, confused and scared, yet aching with a tense need that threatened to overturn the warnings thundering through her mind.

He scanned her face thoroughly. Strident heat stormed up through her skin, but she met his darkening eyes fearlessly.

'Actually, you *can* drown a water rat,' he said with a strange half-smile, partly cynical, partly aggressive. 'Don't do that again. It scared me.' Almost absently he lifted his hand to trace the soft outline of her mouth.

Dimly, through the wild hammering of her pulses, Alexa knew that he might have decided to use the incandescent attraction between them to keep her docile. At that moment it didn't matter, not when Luka was looking at her from intent, molten eyes and his fingers were moving with tantalising lightness against her lips.

Dazzled, bemused, enchanted, she caught one of those maddening fingers between her teeth and nipped—not hard, just enough to stop it. He tasted of sun and salt and water, and a potent male flavour all his own.

As though her bite had been a signal, he tipped her into the hammock in a tangle of arms and legs, twisting halfway to land on his back beneath her.

'You've got tiger's eyes,' he said, kissing the hollow of her throat, where her heart thudded in delicious panic, 'cool and challenging, with an edge of danger, and you've been giving me some very tigerish smiles and glares.'

'What did you expect? You've been behaving like a marauder,' she said, trying to sound as confident as he did.

'Mmm.' He tasted the skin above that fluttering skipping pulse, sending violent jolts of sensation right down to her toes. Laughter gleamed in his tawny eyes. 'I'm not a marauder—just a man with a problem.'

CHAPTER SEVEN

'I CAN feel it,' Alexa muttered, scarlet-faced.

Luka's problem—an urgent, not to say *pressing* problem—was obvious. He was very aroused, and so was she, the hidden places of her body softening and moistening in preparation for his possession.

He gave another heart-shaking smile. 'That,' he said, a touch of lazy ruefulness in his tone, 'is a response, not a problem.'

Alexa opened her mouth, but before she could formulate a tart answer he wound his hands in the tumbled copper hair around her shoulders and kissed the words from her lips.

It was an oddly tender kiss, as was the one that followed, and the one after that—sweet and hungry, yet leashed by his will. Unsatisfied, Alexa lifted her head and opened her eyes, almost flinching away when she saw that hint of laughter still lurking in the gleaming golden depths of his eyes.

For him this was an idle pleasure to fill in a sunny morning—as light and meaningless as the sex he'd presumably had with the woman who owned the lipstick. Whereas what Alexa felt was wild and desperately consuming, raw and real.

She said tightly, 'It might not be a problem for you, but it's one for me.'

Cynicism replaced the amusement in his eyes. He enquired with a mocking smile she disliked, 'Proving a point, Alexa?'

'I don't know—am I?' she asked, scrambling off him. The swaying hammock made it difficult, and as soon as she'd got off it he showed her how it should be done, rising in one swift, lithe movement to tower over her.

'I think so.' This time his smile held an edge of aggression. 'But perhaps I should prove one too...'

Mesmerised, she closed her eyes when the back of his fingers came to rest on the pounding pulse in her throat.

'You remind me of a horse I once had,' he drawled.

Her eyes flew open, snapping with outrage. 'Well, thanks a million!'

'She was a very beautiful mare,' he said, that disturbing mockery edging each word. 'Tall and elegant and fast, with hair the same colour as yours. She refused to allow me to ride her.'

'So what happened to her?' Alexa ground out, pretending to ignore the blatant double meaning. 'Did you have her put down for treason?'

His eyes half closed. 'For a citizen of a modern democratic monarchy, you have a strange idea of how one works,' he said smoothly. 'It's no longer politically correct to chop off people's heads just because they disagree with you. No, I broke her to my will. It didn't take me long to have her eating out of my hand and allowing me to ride her whenever I chose.'

Pagan heat raced through Alexa's body. Defying it, she lifted her brows and said with a cheesy smile, 'How very masterful of you.'

He smiled, increasing his grip on her shoulders and drawing her towards him. The knowledge that she wanted him to kiss her rather more than she wanted to take her next breath should have terrified Alexa, but she didn't resist.

'Of course I had to gentle her first,' he said, and released one shoulder to lift her chin. 'It wasn't easy because she was flighty and suspicious and hot-tempered—a challenge I couldn't resist.'

His touch seared through Alexa's crumbling defences like a sword slashing silk. Her skipping, pounding heart echoed through her brain, drowning her thoughts in a ferocious physical response.

'Did I say she was beautiful enough to ravish a man's heart from his breast?' he asked in an abrasively sensual voice. 'Sleek and strong and glorious, like wind over the ocean, like the sun in its glory, like a tigress defending her young…'

And he kissed her, moulding her against him. For long moments they stayed locked together, until he made an odd harsh sound in his throat and deepened the kiss, and she responded with an excitement that flared into a conflagration.

Lost in the incandescent world of the senses, Alexa slid her arms up and around his neck, offering herself to his mouth, to his hands. Luka accepted that mute invitation, making himself master of her mouth as his fingers cupped the swelling mound of her breast, touching it with sure knowledge of how to please her.

Mindless, intense and perilous, wildfire blasted through her, sizzling from her mouth and her breast to the source of all pleasure in the pit of her stomach.

And then he lifted his head to smile into her dazed face with its heavy-lidded eyes and pleading mouth.

His golden eyes darkened. With a muttered oath he released her and stepped back.

Almost gulping air into her panicking lungs Alexa stared around, slowly realising where she was as memory came crashing back, accusing her of stupidity and shaming surrender.

She stumbled back, humiliated to the soles of her feet. 'How the hell do you *do* that?' she whispered, inwardly raging and bereft.

All emotion vanished from his eyes, leaving them flat and metallic. 'There's no magic spell,' he said in a voice that sliced what little composure she had left into shreds. 'You are a beautiful woman and I am a healthy man with the usual appetites.'

'I'm not talking about my effect on you,' she snarled, her twisting hands belying her tone. 'Most men are easily—' She bit back the scathing words.

His wide shoulders lifted in a shrug. 'Women are not so different from men,' he said carelessly. 'And don't try to convince me that this hasn't happened to you before—you knew what you were doing.'

At least she'd kept something of herself hidden from him. This overwhelming physical attraction was completely new and alien.

'Never without emotion,' she returned, swivelling away with his kisses still burning her lips and his touch setting every secret place in her body alight with a forbidden anticipation. 'I'm going.'

'The night we met,' he said, his thoughtful voice stopping her, 'you looked at me with a kind of shocked, defiant resistance. I recognised it because that's how I was feeling too—as though I'd been ambushed by a challenge both intoxicating and dangerous.'

His hand moved with sure delicacy to the sensitive place where her neck met her shoulder, leaving a trail of fire. Alexa shivered, and he laughed again. The next moment she was in his arms, shuddering with pleasure as he kissed the pulsating hollow in her throat.

The thin wet material of her bathing suit might just as well not have existed. When he closed his lips around the incredibly sensitive point of her breast a spasm of intolerable excitement twisted through her, banishing all thought; unable to control her response, she arched into him.

'*That* is the problem,' he said in a thick, impeded voice, straightening abruptly and picking her up. 'Breathe in.'

Aching with frustration, she dragged air into her lungs. Luka took the three steps across to the pool as though she weighed nothing, stepping off the edge with her still locked in his arms.

Cool and bracing, the water closed around them. He kissed her again, hard and heated, and then released her, pushing her upwards in a swirl of water.

Opening her eyes when she broke the surface, Alexa saw the muscles across his back bunch as he hauled himself out of the pool. She sank back beneath the water and turned to swim for the other side, pulses jumping like a jackhammer.

He was waiting, hand outstretched. Reluctantly, still in an anguish of frustration, she accepted his help and was drawn free of the pool.

'Come for a walk with me,' he said, enough command in his tone to ensure she knew it was deliberate.

'Do I have a choice?'

His eyes mocked her. 'Of course you have a choice.'

'As long as I do what you want!'

'If that were so,' he said, challenging eyes boring into her as he pushed back a lock of hair clinging to her cheek, 'you'd be lying under me in the hammock right now.'

Flushing, she jerked her hand away and almost ran to collect her shirt, her skin burning more deeply as she saw the creases pressed into it by the combined weight of their bodies. She shrugged into it, using it as a shield against his hard, perceptive gaze.

'Is that how constitutional monarchs normally behave? I thought you were brought up to duty and service and self-sacrifice?' she scoffed, casting a derisive glance at the pool and the luxurious furniture.

'Oh, I enjoy the trappings,' he said deliberately, his eyes hardening, 'but that's all they are—trappings.'

'Like sex?' Angry because she passionately wanted to be more to him than a playmate for an afternoon, she added curtly, 'Sorry, but I'm not a trapping.'

With a narrow, knife-edged smile Luka gestured towards the garden. 'Neither is sex.'

End of discussion, she thought grimly. She certainly wasn't going to continue on that subject!

The grounds had been skilfully and superbly landscaped, but Alexa noted that the walls were high enough to deter any but the most determined intruder, and discreet surveillance cameras were dotted here and there.

'I hope there isn't a camera in the pool area,' she said, her skin heating again.

He ignored her question to say blandly, 'The cameras are turned off when I'm in the garden.'

'I don't want to star in a pornographic movie,' she snapped, sure now that he spent long hours seducing women by the pool. She glared up at him. 'In fact, I want to see the films from these cameras.'

He gave a crack of wry laughter. '*Touché*. Relax—you'd find them incredibly boring.'

'Just as you'll find my negatives,' she said grimly.

Brows slightly raised, he looked at her for a long moment before smiling faintly. 'Perhaps,' he conceded.

Alexa swallowed, swiftly looking away in search of something to comment on. 'Oh,' she said gratefully, her voice suddenly soft, 'a cotton rose! My grandmother used to have one in her garden.'

Luka said, 'A cotton rose? I thought it was a double hibiscus.'

'It does look like a hibiscus, doesn't it? But the flowers last longer—at least three days.'

He nodded. 'And change colour each day.'

'They fascinated me when I was a kid—opening white, then turning that pretty rose colour and ending up this lovely dark pink.' She touched one with a caressing finger. 'Why do you need all this security?'

'You should know.' His voice was brusque. 'The night we met you were almost attacked.'

With a final glance at the cotton roses, Alexa moved on. 'That was in the city. No one knows you're here, and even if they did they wouldn't intrude. You might get a few wallaby hunters trespassing, although you could just send a minion out to warn them off.'

He laced her fingers through his. 'I can cope with those hunting four-legged prey.'

Fighting back a scorching pleasure, it took her a moment to comprehend what he meant. Appalled, she glanced up, to meet eyes as smooth and opaque as the metal they resembled. 'But this is New Zealand—we don't go in for assassinations or kidnapping!'

'It can happen anywhere,' he said, his tone suddenly harsh.

Alexa glanced up, but with a face and voice that revealed nothing, he went on, 'This is to keep the press out. And, yes, possibly I'm paranoid, but your profession is extremely determined and cunning when it comes to stalking prey.'

'I am not a press photographer,' she said between her teeth. 'I can imagine how frustrating it must be to be dogged by paparazzi, but have you ever thought that the publicity has been good for you and Dacia?'

His eyes gleamed beneath his thick lashes. Derisively he asked, 'In what way, apart from giving me an edge when it comes to business negotiations?' He answered her enquiring look with a narrow, humourless smile. 'No one expects a pin-up, playboy prince to be any good at anything more serious than skiing,' he explained.

'So they underestimated you.' She nodded wryly, knowing how the anonymous 'they' felt, because she too had taken him at surface value. 'Oh,' she said in an entirely different tone, 'who is this?'

An elderly Labrador came sniffing around the palm tree. Obviously sure of its welcome, it advanced, tail wagging in ingratiating enthusiasm. Alexa stooped and stroked its blonde head, smiling as it sighed and leaned against her knee.

'Good girl,' Alexa said, fondling the dog's soft ears, then looked up to ask with a hint of disapproval, 'Is she yours?

'No, she belongs to the caretaker and his wife.' He surveyed her with a glimmering, tawny gaze. 'Don't you think I should have a dog?'

'Dogs are social animals. They need companionship, not jet-setting owners.'

'So we agree on something,' he said ironically.

Straightening up, Alexa said, 'If you're so worried about paparazzi storming your compound, I'd have thought you'd have several Dobermanns or German Shepherds at the ready, not one darling old Lab.'

He said evenly, 'There are others around,' and bent to stroke the Lab.

Something compressed into yearning deep inside Alexa as she noted the way sunlight gleamed blue-black on his head when he bent to stroke the pleading dog. Hardly breathing, she traced the bold caress of the sun on the dense lashes that hid his brilliant eyes, on the chiselled perfection of his mouth as he murmured to the dog.

She tore her gaze away and fixed it on a tree she'd never recognise again. From behind she heard him say, 'I envy you—and old Bonny here—your serene conviction that the world is a benign place.'

'No, you don't. You think we're totally naïve,' she said quietly, setting off between banks of shrubs and flowers with the dog snuffling along behind. Compelled to discover more about him, she asked, 'Surely you trust—or trusted—someone. Your family? Your chief bodyguard?'

His broad shoulders lifted and fell in a negligent shrug. 'If you can't trust your family, who can you trust? And Dion is not a bodyguard—he's a security expert.'

The one who organised all these lights and cameras, no doubt.

Alexa recognised the evasion, but the words she'd been about to say dried on her tongue. Luka was smiling down at her, using his magnetic charm to veil a keen scrutiny.

This jaunt through the garden was a warning. He wanted her to know she didn't have a chance of sneaking into his house without being caught and humiliatingly exposed.

She was angry and hurt, yet the reluctant, uncontrollable excitement surging through her summoned an answering smile, one she strove to control.

Luka noticed the telltale steady stare, the limpid, practised movement of her full, lush mouth, and wondered cynically why he was disappointed. With himself, perhaps, because he had to fight down a stupid desire to trust her.

After hearing from Dion—who'd searched the bach and discovered no more cameras—that she'd told him the truth, Luka had even found himself concocting scenarios that might explain those three tell-tale items in the gossip column, when he knew the most logical reason was almost certainly the right one. She had sold them to the columnist.

There had been no more since he'd silenced her by removing her camera and mobile phone.

For a second he toyed with the idea of how things could have been between them, but discarded the fantasy before it had time to lodge in his brain. He'd been brought up to believe that duty was paramount, and he couldn't change now.

He had to keep his hands off her, even though the temptation to take what she offered with such reluctant ardour ate into him like a sweetly corrosive acid, filling his dreams with passion and his brain with sensual smoke.

Guy's welfare was far more important than slaking this urgent desire to strip her naked and take her, sink into the lithe lushness of her body and watch her convulse with shattering pleasure in his arms.

Once an accord between the rebels and the government had been signed, and peace-keeping forces had moved into Sant'Rosa, Guy's value as a hostage would disappear and it wouldn't matter how many columnists Alexa contacted or what she reported about him or his whereabouts. In the meantime, he needed to keep a low profile from the press; nothing must leak about a possible peace process or his involvement. He'd have to keep Alexa an unwitting prisoner, making sure she didn't leave the island or communicate with anyone else.

And the easiest way was to keep her here, where he could supervise her.

He said thoughtfully, 'I am not happy at the thought of you staying down there with no electricity.'

Those astonishing eyes splintered into ice crystals. 'I can manage,' she told him.

No doubt about that, he thought; she was surprisingly practical. 'No water, no cooking—'

'There's the barbecue,' she pointed out, square chin angling up as it always did when she crossed swords with him, 'and if someone could get the hatch off the tank I could dip water out.'

'Why not spend the night here? The power should be back on tomorrow.'

Looking down at the dog, she turned her face half away. Luka was accustomed to the untamed charge of sexual desire at the sight of a beautiful woman, but something about the straight line of Alexa's nose and the proud, sensuous curve of her mouth, the angle of her chin as it jutted slightly, punched him in the heart. It was a weakness he couldn't afford.

He said coolly, 'I won't touch you again.'

Colour smoked across her cheekbones and her mouth bloomed. Relief? He didn't think so. But although she was tempted, she wasn't going to give in. He said with a smile, 'Admit that you'll be more comfortable here.'

Alexa knew she should go back to the bach. She was dicing with danger staying here, talking to him, watching him, wondering about him. 'I'm surprised. Does this mean that you trust me not to go bleating to the nearest newspaper as soon as I get back to Auckland about my

"Secret Tryst with the Prince of Dacia''?' she said tartly.

He laughed. 'It won't matter if you do. I'll have had my peaceful holiday, and I'm accustomed to opportunist lies. Besides, I don't think that's your style.'

'But selling titbits of information to a gossip columnist is?' she flashed, hiding her chagrin and hurt with a slicing anger.

'The jury's out on that one,' he said softly, eyes lancing across her face. He smiled. 'If you stay I can promise you a much better dinner than anything you could concoct on that wreck of a barbecue. And a decent shower.'

The suggestion of trust cut her resistance into shreds. 'Appealing to my stomach is a low blow,' she said, anticipation fizzing through her. 'Thank you, I'd like to stay the night here. But I'll need some things from the bach.'

'We can walk along—or I'll send Jill down to pack up your clothes,' he said.

'I'll get them,' Alexa said immediately.

'I'll come with you.'

She started to protest, but stopped. Beneath that pleasant, lightly amused façade she sensed cold determination. 'All right,' she said with a shrug.

Before she went to bed Alexa stared at her reflection with acute foreboding. She'd spent the evening trying very hard to keep her head while Luka dazzled her with sophisticated charm and intelligent, interesting conversation. Her eyes were heavy-lidded and slumbrous, her mouth somehow softer and more curved—asking for kisses, she thought hollowly.

'You should have said no. Tomorrow, power or not, you're going back to the bach,' she told that betraying reflection. 'You only managed to hang onto your wits by a thread tonight.'

The next morning found her edgy and thoroughly unsettled, her defences crumbling more every time Luka smiled at her.

Which he did frequently. She could have resisted the smiles, but the conversation that accompanied them was fascinating and intensely stimulating.

Like the man himself—and not just physically, she told herself crossly, turning again at the end of the pool and forcing her weary arms and legs to propel her through the water. It wasn't fair that a man with such blazing physical charisma should also give her brain such a workout. And he treated her opinions with respect, which was very seductive.

Luka strolled across to the edge of the pool and observed, 'Time to come out.'

Tempted to ignore him, she floated to a stop. 'Why?' she asked belligerently, squinting up at the tall outline haloed by the sun.

'Because you're tiring.' His voice warmed on a hidden note of amusement. 'Do you want me to come in and help you?'

Sensation zinged through her. 'You don't have to,' she said loftily, and swam over to the steps.

His smile widened a little, leaving her with the uncomfortable suspicion that he understood too much of what was going on in her head.

And her body.

He tossed her a towel. 'Thanks,' she said, and dried herself down before walking across to the shaded area. Her legs felt heavy and she had to stop herself from collapsing into the cushioned lounger. She'd been an idiot to swim so long, but she'd needed to work off the restlessness prowling through her body.

'Sunscreen,' Luka said, offering her a bottle.

'Thank you,' she said again, more formally this time, and sat down to apply it to her arms and legs and shoulders, recklessly aware of his smouldering gaze as she deliberately smoothed her hands across her skin.

In a cool voice he said, 'I hope you don't make a habit of wearing yourself out in the water. It's dangerous.'

'I'm very careful when I swim alone,' she returned briskly.

His dark brows met in a frown as he settled back into his lounger. Good; at least she wasn't the only one affected by this rash impulse to flirt with disaster. Lying in the sun usually drained her of energy; she applied herself to caging the feverish desire twisting inside her.

It didn't work. In spite of liberal doses of common sense and self-derision, that disturbing, perilous hunger, compelling and merciless, simmered like a hidden volcano through every cell in her body. Rolling over, she murmured, 'It's too hot here! I'll go up and change. And then I'd better go back to the bach.'

'I'll see if the electricity is on again,' Luka decided, getting to his feet.

A woman who enjoyed solitude, she'd normally have found his constant presence irritating. It was a measure of her infatuation that she liked it, she thought despairingly as they went back to the house.

A long, cold shower did nothing to ease the fever in her blood. She put on a fine cotton shirt and a pair of slender cinnamon pants, combed her hair back from her face, and folded her clothes and toiletries into her pack before settling down in one of the chairs out on the covered deck. From inside she could hear Luka's voice.

Wired and restless, she tried to concentrate on the lush fertility of the garden below, backed by the ocean spread in peacock-blue glory to the misty line where it met the sky.

Almost immediately Luka joined her, darkly dominating the vista before her with his forceful presence. 'They haven't changed the transformer yet,' he told her, 'so there's still no power.'

She frowned. 'Nevertheless, I'll have to go.'

He sat down, putting a folder of papers on the table beside his chair. 'Stay for lunch,' he said easily.

Alexa opened her mouth to refuse, but he smiled at her and the words dried on her tongue. What harm could it do? some traitor in her brain asked. He'd go soon, and she'd never see him again; he'd stop being Luka, infuriating, fascinating, utterly absorbing, and become the Prince of Dacia, a handsome mask in the media.

'Thank you,' she said recklessly.

After lunch he defused her turbulent craving by suggesting a ride; she agreed.

Mounted on a pleasant, easy-riding mare befitting her status as a horsewoman, she tried to forget his suggestive story about the other mare while admiring his effortless control of a much larger gelding. Since his promise yesterday not to touch her again, he'd been charming but impersonal, and it was ridiculous and masochistic to miss the elemental undercurrent of awareness.

By the time they got back to the house it was late afternoon and Alexa said firmly, 'Whether the power is on or not, I'll go back to the bach now.'

'I'll check,' Luka said. He rang on the house telephone, and frowned at the reply he got to his question.

'Not yet,' he said, putting the receiver down. 'Jill rang half an hour ago to see what was happening, and they said they'll be replacing the transformer tomorrow.' He said coolly, 'You might as well stay another night, Alexa.'

Alexa bit her lip. If he'd tried to pressure her she'd have left, but it did seem silly to go back to the bach with its inconveniences when she could stay here.

And she really wasn't in any danger. It wasn't as though she was falling in love with the man! OK, she was fascinated, both physically and mentally, but that would soon wear off once he went back to his world.

One last night, and then she'd leave—and just to make sure she didn't cross that invisible line between infatuation and something more dangerous she'd go straight back to Auckland. Oh, she wouldn't tell Luka; if he still believed she was in contact with that wretched gossip columnist he'd probably try to stop her going.

Perhaps when nothing appeared in the newspapers he'd realise that he could trust one woman at least. 'Thank you,' she said. She looked down at her clothes and sniffed delicately. '*Eau de* horse and seawater,' she said. 'I'll go and change.'

Because it would be her last night she chose a soft paisley shirt in shades of gold and copper and ice blue overlong trousers, and drew her hair back from her face in a sleek knot.

'I thought we'd eat by the pool,' Luka said lazily after a swift, appreciative appraisal. He'd changed clothes too, a slim-fitting black shirt and trousers transforming him into some dangerous paladin from a more barbaric past age. 'It's going to be a magnificent sunset.'

It was, staining the sky in a gaudy rage of scarlet and crimson and gold that faded into softer pastels as day

was overtaken by night. Someone had lit the large torch
flares; in the rapid darkness their light flickered on
Luka's tanned, angular face, intensifying the burnished
gold of his eyes, the slashing cheekbones and the disciplined, strongly marked mouth.

Little rills of lightning ran through Alexa, sparking
fire wherever they touched. Luka was far from the in-
dolent playboy she'd assumed him to be, coasting
through life on his charm and his rank. His dry sense of
humour entertained her, and she knew now that he liked
blue vein cheese, and the sort of classical music she felt
needed a good tune, that he found opera entertaining but
the emotions too obvious and stereotyped, that he liked
Botticelli and Picasso....

Oh, she knew far too much about him! In fact, over
dinner, she began to suspect she could spend the rest of
her life discovering things about him.

But of course she wasn't in love with him!

'Some liqueur with your coffee?' he asked when the
meal was finished.

'No, thank you.' Although she'd drunk very sparingly
of the excellent wine, her head was fogged by emotions
she had no right to indulge.

'You're shivering,' he said, frowning.

'I'm just a little chilly,' she lied. 'I should go in, I
think.' She tried to smile, but her stiff mouth moved
awkwardly. 'In fact, I should go home.'

For the space of a heartbeat he stayed immobile, the
tough, uncompromising bone structure that gave his face
its strength and authority standing out in stark relief. A
stray breeze tossed light from the flares high into the air
so that it fell across him.

Alexa's heart stopped. He looked like a buccaneer,
dangerous and grim and ruthless.

Then, as though compelled by something even more powerful than his steely string of will, he pulled her into his arms and held her against the thudding of his heart, in the perilous heat of his embrace.

If his reluctance hadn't been so clear she might have resisted him, but the realisation that he couldn't resist her was headier than any wine, more alluring than lazy, sweet-tongued temptation itself. As though she had found the home she'd been searching for, she relaxed against him.

An ancient instinct hissed a warning.

Suddenly afraid of her own weakness, she lifted her face to meet his hooded eyes, and said in a hoarse, abrupt voice, 'This is a bad idea.'

'For once, I don't care. You've been driving me insane ever since we met, and I know it's been the same for you. Kissing you is like capturing a piece of heaven.' His glittering survey dragged her soul from her body, until he bent his head and kissed her with concentrated hunger.

Alexa's expectant body sprang into eager life. Within a charged, primal moment she was giving him back kiss for kiss, knowing where this would end and not caring that it would lead nowhere.

'Alexa?' he said against her mouth, giving her the choice.

She sighed into his mouth. 'Yes.'

He lifted her and carried her across to the hammock. Lit only by stars and the dying torches, drugged by desire, she forgot yesterday, forgot everything, and pulled him down with her as she went up in flames.

He wooed her with potent kisses, gentling her with caresses that smoothly banished the last of her fears, so that she slid her hand into the opening of his shirt, seeking a way to the sleek, muscular body beneath. He laughed under his breath and lay back beside her, wordlessly giving her access to him.

Alexa lifted herself, adjusting herself to the sway of the hammock. Carefully, watching the play of her fingers against the dark fabric of his shirt, she began to undo the buttons.

His chest rose and fell abruptly. Alexa's hand froze as she realised that he was holding back, deliberately controlling his hunger; she wanted him to be lost to the same frightening passion that gripped her.

She stared at him with a narrowed, intent look, pale eyes smouldering between their black lashes. The amusement fled from his expression and a much more primitive reaction took its place.

'Do you know what you're doing?' he asked, his voice a low growl that sent anticipatory shivers along her nerves.

'Yes.' *Yes*, she thought, smitten by a savage pleasure. He was still resisting her, but now she understood her own power; she could breach the barriers of his iron determination.

CHAPTER EIGHT

SLOWLY Alexa lowered her head. As though some other, much more experienced woman possessed her, she flicked her tongue along Luka's beautiful mouth. He lay very still, big body taut, eyes fiercely turbulent.

Then she kissed him, nuzzling his mouth open and losing herself in the deep carnality of it.

Luka's arms contracted around her, hauling her down against his lean length while the hammock rocked beneath them. Their bodies flowed together, and Alexa wanted him so much the need ate at her like a hot tide—merciless, overwhelming, and perilously exciting.

Sighing, she surrendered to the dark enchantment, going willingly when he eased her over onto her back and bent his head to her throat and her shoulders.

He had to know that her breasts were heavy and taut and eager, that his least touch through her shirt sent agonised anticipation sizzling through her. By the time he reached that acutely sensitive skin with kisses she didn't protest when he stripped off her shirt and bra.

The cool evening air breathed against her, tightening her nipples. Shivering, she lifted dazzled eyes and searched his face, each angle and plane more harshly etched than usual.

Some faint recollection of where she was penetrated far enough for her to mutter, 'Someone might come.'

Indolently, skilfully, he shaped her soft curves. Electricity sparked from his fingers, from the erotic heat of his mouth on her breast, from the sensuous contrast

116

of dark skin against pale, male strength against feminine softness.

'One of the few advantages of being who I am,' he said raggedly, 'is that no one will come unless I call them.'

The words were kisses against her breasts, the silken rasp of his cheeks an exquisite friction that dispatched more white-hot sensation through her, swift and sure as wine into every cell of her body. Lifting heavy lashes, Alexa drowned in his gaze.

Struggling to think, she asked, 'Do you have any protection?'

Surprise clamped his mouth into a straight line, but almost immediately it relaxed. 'Yes.'

Alexa closed her eyes.

Just this once she'd forget everything but this, she thought, tempted beyond bearing by the incandescent pleasure that sang in her heart, melting her last inhibition. She'd thought she knew something about sex, but Luka was teaching her how innocent she was in all the ways that mattered.

Running her tongue along her dry lips, she forced up her weighted eyelids, making herself scan his hard, intent face.

He wasn't going to persuade her. She'd never be able to believe he'd swept her off her feet—she was cooperating in her own seduction. What would it be like for him to lose that iron armour of self-possession? She suspected that no woman knew, and wondered if…

No. That way would lie disillusion. Emotions weren't trustworthy; they messed things up.

Let it be honest—a straightforward slaking of the powerful, untamed need that had sprung into sinful life the first time their eyes had met.

Responding mindlessly to the skilled tenderness of his hand on her skin, her body made the final decision for her, suddenly racked with a tension that could only be eased by arching up into him and pressing herself against his lean hardness.

Instantly, before she could pull away, his arms clamped around her and he held her stretched beneath him.

The elemental heat and pressure of his body against hers, the faint mingled scent of salty air, flowers and aroused male, set the tinder to her desire. Shuddering, she made an odd noise, half-groan, half-purr, then turned her head into his throat and used the edge of her teeth in a series of punishing little kisses along it.

His body flexed against hers, but his control held. 'Slowly,' he said in a thick, abrasive tone. 'This is not a time for haste.'

He bent his head and kissed the circle of rosy flesh at the centre of her breast, lightly, teasingly, as the nipple puckered and stood proud. An intolerable need for something more made her twist restlessly, but apart from the quickening heat of his body he ignored her silent plea and eased her trousers downwards, exposing her navel to his gaze.

His understanding of just what she craved, what gave her the most pleasure, proclaimed a vast experience of women. Alexa drove that thought to the back of her mind.

Her skin tightened as his mouth explored each breast, worshipping it with kisses, tormenting her with tiny tastes until she groaned and held his head there, fingers sinking into his black hair while she wordlessly demanded that he give her what her body had been longing for.

The tantalising pressure of his mouth increased, became ravenous, and she cried out as exquisite urgency flooded through her, replaced too soon by a dark and demanding hunger.

Her hands came up to grasp his lean hips and bring him over her. He moved, but although the pressure and rhythmic thrusting of his loins against her most sensitive part dazzled her almost to delirium, it wasn't enough. It hurt not to open herself to him, take him and enfold him and hold him in her—make him hers for a few precious minutes.

'Will this be enough for you?' he demanded.

'No,' she said harshly. 'I want you.'

He stripped her trousers away, then lay back; arms folded behind his head, eyes gleaming beneath their thick fringe of lashes, he invited, 'Take me, Alexa.'

Flushed, her body afire, she eased his clothes over his hips, fascinated by the fullness of his penis as she tried to free it from the prison of cloth.

He wasn't in the least shy; why on earth was she so fumble-fingered?

Abruptly he caught her hands and pulled them away. Shocked and humiliated, she looked up into a drawn, stark face.

Luka said harshly, 'I'm not going to last if you keep doing that,' and divested himself of his remaining clothes.

She'd expected a swift possession, but he lay looking at her as she came down beside him, his mouth compressed and his eyes narrowed. Skin puckering in a cool breeze, she met his gaze steadily.

'Sure?' he asked quietly.

'Very sure.'

He smiled and leaned over and began to explore her navel with his tongue.

Shocked, she lay rigid, until the erotic little caress stirred her senses into full clamour, storming through her with the force of an explosion.

Against the soft curve of her stomach he murmured, 'You are so beautiful—sleek and strong as silk...'

'You're beautiful too,' she said wistfully.

'But you don't like touching me?'

Startled, she protested, 'I do.'

'Then why aren't you?'

Shyly she lifted her hand and flexed her fingers against his chest, following with her hand the pattern of hair before sliding her arms around him. Drowning in touch, she learned with her palms and fingertips the taut, coiled contours of the muscles beneath his sleek, hot skin.

She kissed his shoulders, nipped along the powerful breadth with tiny bites, moving with languorous deliberation.

Until eventually he rasped, 'That's enough,' and pulled her hips into his. 'Look at me,' he commanded.

Alexa's lashes fluttered up, meeting eyes that seared into her soul.

'Say my name,' he said, easing slowly into her.

She summoned enough air to breathe. 'Luka.'

'Alexa,' he said, claiming her, and thrust home, powerful shoulders bunching as he took possession.

It hurt a little, but no small pain could prevent the pleasure that assailed Alexa. Gasping, she met the full force of his body with her own strength, gripping him tightly inside her as he pulled back, only to repeat the same voluptuous process until an unknown anticipation drove her to silently demand more than this calculated seduction.

Yet still he remained in full control, using his body as an instrument to summon pleasure, building that pleasure so slowly she could have screamed with the ravishing torture. The world narrowed down to this knife-edge of rapture, keen and savagely consuming. As Luka played her like a master musician a primal force gathered deep in the pit of her stomach, taking over her body until she soared past the limit it could bear.

Hurled into a climax so intense it almost tore her apart, she gasped his name and surrendered to ecstasy. When she could think again above the sound of her heart juddering in her chest and her breathing, she lay in his arms and wondered why of all men it should be Luka...

Always before she'd wondered whether that was all there was to it. This time she thought dazedly that any more and she'd have died. The human body wasn't built to take so much ecstasy.

But she'd been alone on that pinnacle of sensual abandon; Luka hadn't reached his peak.

She opened heavy eyelids and saw him smile. 'All right?' he asked quietly.

He knew, of course, that this had never happened to her before. For a second she almost hated him—until he bent his head and kissed a certain spot beneath her ear. Astoundingly her body responded with renewed desire as with devilish talent he coaxed the afterglow until it leapt from satiation to a sharp hunger and she called out his name in appeal.

'Soon,' he said, growling the word. 'Soon now.'

And this time it was even better, lasted longer, causing an agony of rapture as he drove towards his peak. Out of control now, Luka thrust deep and hard, and beneath him and around him Alexa convulsed and cried out, wrenched from the foundations of her world, reborn into a new one. Everything she knew about herself vanished, leaving her like an amnesiac, alone and frightened in a hostile, unknown world.

'Hush, *cara*, it's all right,' Luka said eventually in a deep quiet voice, turning onto his back. He pulled her into the comforting prison of his arms and swept back her tangled, damp hair to kiss her forehead with the sort of tenderness he'd probably give a child. 'Do you always cry, or have I hurt you?'

Alexa couldn't tell him. It was painfully clear that he felt nothing like her enormous desire to give and give and give until she had nothing left to give. Although he'd enjoyed making love to her, for him it was simply sex.

Whereas for the rest of her life she'd remember the man who'd transported her into this transcendental ecstasy. Even worse, she'd measure every other man by him.

Listening to the joined thunder of their hearts, Alexa smiled, a bittersweet smile as old as time, the smile of a woman who lies in the arms of the lover she knows won't stay.

'Alexa?'

'You didn't hurt me,' she mumbled.

'Sure?'

'Positive.'

Luka picked up a tress of hair and curled it around her shoulder like a veil of copper silk. 'Where did such warm Mediterranean colouring come from?' he asked idly.

'My father was half-Italian.'

He ran a gentle finger along the inside of her arm,

sending explicit shivers along her waiting nerves. 'And your mother was Scandinavian?'

'Scandinavian? No, she was English—well, her ancestors came from Cornwall, actually. What made you think she was Scandinavian?' Alexa asked drowsily, grasping a meagre contentment in lying like this against him and talking.

'Pale eyes like yours come normally from the northernmost parts of Europe.'

Alexa said dreamily, 'I got those from my father too. Just about the only thing I inherited from my mother was her red hair.'

He kissed a spot on her shoulder, letting his lips linger there. Alexa ran her fingers through his hair, revelling in the simple pleasure it gave her to touch him like this—tenderly, with the ravenous sexuality temporarily sated. And underlying that physical satisfaction was a deeper, more emotional contentment, because making love must mean he'd learned to trust her. A little, anyway, she amended—enough to believe that she wouldn't sell salacious details of his prowess as a lover to the media.

'So your Italian father had those amazing eyes?' he asked, each word another kiss against her skin.

'Yes,' she said bemusedly. 'And according to my grandmother he inherited them from his father.'

'Did your grandfather die young?'

Alexa paused. Once she'd told him she'd be saying goodbye for ever to any wispy, romantic hope of a happy ending. Even if Luka no longer suspected her to be a member of the paparazzi, princes made only the most basic of commitments to the children of bastards. Mistress or lover, yes, but forget anything else, anything permanent.

Well, so be it. This was a relationship destined to go nowhere. He was a prince and she was a nobody; he planned a convenient marriage with a woman who'd accept the constraints of such a union—status and sex in return for children. Alexa wouldn't settle for anything less than love.

She wasn't ashamed of her family, and that barely-formed hope was a stupid delusion!

'He died before my father was born,' she said evenly. 'My grandmother went to Italy to study the language at university and met him there—he was a student too. They fell in love, but when he died she came back to New Zealand and raised his son here. All we have of him is a photograph someone took of them both.' She said defensively, 'You can tell they loved each other very much, and my grandmother never looked at another man.'

'When were they together?'

A little surprised—and pleased—at his interest, she told him.

'What was his full name?'

Alexa shrugged. 'My grandmother never told anyone.'

Casually he asked, 'How do you feel about that?'

She hesitated before admitting, 'It's like having a hole in your life. I'm not obsessive, but it would be—well, it would be nice to know that I'm not entirely alone in the world, that there's someone else who has eyes like mine, someone who might remember what my grandfather was like.' She shrugged a little uncomfortably. 'I've tried contacting the university, but got nowhere. Mind you, I suppose a handsome grey-eyed Italian didn't give them much to go on! And any Italian family would probably disown me, as the one thing I do know is that they weren't married.'

'Italians have moved with the times,' Luka told her drily, although he seemed to be thinking of something else. 'What do you know about your grandfather?'

'I know that my father was called Nicholas Alex, after him, and he called me Alexa Nicole as a sort of link.'

He released her and rolled over, lying with an arm across his eyes. 'Your grandmother must have had courage and determination. I don't imagine it would have been easy to bring up a child without a husband in those days.'

Stupid to feel rejected! Her skin cooling fast, Alexa said proudly, 'Not easy, but she managed.'

But she couldn't concentrate on her grandmother's sad romance. She longed to run an exploratory finger over Luka's shoulder, just for the sinful pleasure of feeling the powerful muscle contract beneath her touch, but now she felt awkward about it.

Although his tone of voice hadn't changed, she thought she'd heard the sound of doors clanging shut against her.

But those doors would never have been open for her. Even if they were, she thought with a constricted heart, she wouldn't walk through them; marrying Luka without love would be walking into hell.

Slamming the doors of her own mind on that realisation, she turned on her side and pressed her face against his arm, breathing in his scent and thrilling to the taut power that seethed through him. He dropped a kiss on the top of her head, but she could sense his absent-mindedness. That hard, forceful mind was on something else entirely.

Swallowing to ease a suspicious dry patch in her throat, she sat up. 'I'll go back to the house,' she said and clambered awkwardly out of the hammock before crouching to pick up her clothes.

Luka followed her, and from the small sounds and glimpses of his movements she deduced that he too was dressing. Chilled and clumsy, she yanked on her shirt and trousers and stuffed the rest into a pocket.

'Goodnight,' she said, hurrying away from him. He didn't try to stop her.

On the terrace outside the big living room she met the housekeeper conferring in a low voice with the security man—Danilo? No, Dion—and immediately felt that the activity of the last hour was detailed in scarlet letters on her face.

It should have been a relief when Dion barely looked at her, frowning as he asked, 'Is the Prince still down by the pool?'

'Yes, he is.' Irritated at her own prissiness, Alexa headed for the door to her bedroom. Once safely in the shower, she asked herself angrily why she should be so embarrassed.

Nowadays women made love with the men they wanted without considering themselves fallen, or even slightly tilted.

And Luka might not realise it yet, but that was the second time he'd trusted her. The first had been down at the bach, when he'd accepted her statement that she had no more cameras. Surely that meant he was beginning to—

No, she thought painfully; she couldn't let it mean anything—beyond the best sex she'd ever had.

Hoping she wasn't like her grandmother, who'd only ever loved once, she shampooed her hair, scolding herself for her choice of word.

This *couldn't* be love. She wouldn't let it be love. She

didn't know him well enough to love him. He was an arrogant, autocratic prince with an arrogant, autocratic habit of jumping to conclusions and a life that she couldn't even imagine.

But she indulged in dreamy, dazed memories until her sensuous reverie was interrupted by the discovery that she'd either left her bra behind at the pool, or dropped it on the way up to the house.

Whatever—she had to get it. She wasn't going to suffer the humiliation of having the housekeeper pick it up and present it to her. After slipping into jeans and a dark T-shirt, she made her way out of her room. Once across the terrace she sneaked into the garden and searched her way down to the darkened enclosure, feeling absurdly like a thief.

At least she didn't have to worry about the security cameras—if Luka hadn't been lying when he'd said they were turned off.

No bra gleamed on the ground, so it must still be wherever it had landed when he'd tossed it from the hammock.

Her heart settling down a little, she was just about to open the door into the pool enclosure when she heard Luka speaking in a cold, uncompromising voice that froze her breath even before he said her name.

He was speaking Dacian; frowning, she concentrated, catching words that made no sense, words that sounded like the Italian for 'I can't risk that...' and 'too much to lose...' and, shockingly, 'imprisonment.'

Flabbergasted astonishment robbed her of everything but instinct. Whatever he was talking about, it concerned her, and it wasn't good. Heart juddering, she slipped behind the lush, green bulk of some glossy-leaved shrub.

Dion answered, agreeing heartily. Cold with bewil-

derment, Alexa heard him say her name—Ms Mytton—
and ask when.

Luka hesitated a moment before answering abruptly.
Straining, Alexa translated the equivalent of, 'Let her
sleep tonight. They come tomorrow at ten, so it will have
to be before then.' He paused and added levelly, 'I'll
see to it.'

Dion started to protest, falling silent when Luka
barked one word. By then Alexa had heard enough.
Sweating and scared, her heart bumping in her throat,
she slid away from the wall and fled noiselessly back
through the darkened garden, sinister now with shadows
and menace. All the way up to the house she tried to
convince herself that she hadn't heard right, that although Dacian was very close to Italian, the words she
thought she'd heard could not possibly mean what they
seemed to.

But he'd said her name and Dion had repeated it. Even
if she'd misheard or misunderstood what they'd said,
they'd been talking about her.

Who on earth was arriving tomorrow morning?

It didn't really matter. She needed to get out of there,
and fast. She'd slip out and head for Deep Cove once
everyone was asleep. Darkness would make it much
more difficult for anyone to find her, unless they were
armed with heat-seeking equipment. And once she got
to Deep Cove she'd catch the first ferry to the mainland.
If Luka sent someone to intercept her she'd scream the
place down and demand help from the islanders.

Hardly breathing, she tiptoed into the house and slunk
into her bedroom.

Only just in time. The knock on her door arrived about
two minutes after she'd got back; she jumped, but com-

posed her face and went across. Surely he didn't expect her to—

No. One glance at Luka's gorgeous, treacherous, *lying* face told her that he hadn't come to make love. He looked formal and completely self-sufficient, a dominant man in full control of his life—a prince, not a lover, and certainly not a man ever enslaved by his senses.

When he smiled at her and said, 'Sitting in the dark, *cara*?' she felt the full impact of the barriers, the remoteness he hadn't shown to her after that first night in Auckland.

She hoped she masked her pain sufficiently to fool him. Holding her voice under such extreme discipline that each word rasped huskily, she said, 'Just—thinking.'

His eyes narrowed slightly, but he reached out and touched her mouth, made tender by his kisses, and for a moment she thought she saw a shadow of regret in the tawny eyes. 'Don't think,' he said. 'Come for a walk.'

'I'm tired,' she said with a half-smile that wobbled before she could control it. 'Tomorrow night, perhaps?'

'It's a beautiful night, and I won't keep you for long.'

An outright refusal might make him suspicious, and she had the whole night to make her escape. The first ferry left at seven in the morning. Dry-mouthed, her head buzzing, she said, 'All right, then,' and came out, closing the door behind her.

Silently they walked out into starshine and the dark mystery of the garden. Undercurrents, deep and turbulent and disturbing, swirled around them in the tangy, humid atmosphere as lights set beside the path sprang into glowing life.

Without looking at the man beside her, Alexa gazed about, orienting herself. Luka took her down a white shell path they hadn't explored previously, between

high, stifling hedges to a courtyard filled with herbs and
vegetables. The hedges surrounded them, rising dark
enough to block out everything else but the indigo vault
of the sky with its scattering of stars. In the centre of
the courtyard a rose arbour still covered in blooms sheltered a fountain, softly sussurating in the humid air.

'A secret garden,' Alexa said huskily, listening to the
sound of their footsteps crunching over the shell.

Alexa bent over and inhaled the scent of a rose,
straightening only when her head began to spin with the
dizzying perfume. A shell slid beneath her foot and she
took an unexpected step sideways; Luka's hand closed
around her arm as she straightened up, then dropped
away.

'Careful,' he said evenly, a disturbing note of formality clipping his words. 'Come and look at the rest of
the garden.'

Warily Alexa accompanied him through a narrow gate
in the hedge, stepping into another charming starlit fantasy. 'How lovely,' she breathed, looking around with
delight at the closely planted flowerbeds, gleaming with
flowers and potent with scent.

'I thought you would like this.'

Alexa noticed a small building, embowered in shrubs.
'Is that the original homestead?' she asked, scanning the
simple, practical lines of the miniature house as they
walked up onto the narrow Victorian verandah, their
footsteps louder and sharper on the narrow wooden
boards.

Did he realise she'd overheard that frightening conversation with Dion?

No, how could he? Unless the cameras had been on—
and even then he didn't know she spoke Italian well
enough to understand.

'Yes. I use it as a guest-house sometimes.' He opened the door, switching on a light. 'The decorator had a wonderful time discovering original pieces for it.'

She walked in, seeing yet not seeing the tiny room, with its classical lines and furniture. Her pulses raced and adrenalin fired her with the need to get the hell out of there. Although every nerve and cell in her body was alert and on edge, she swung around and produced a fake yawn. 'It's lovely, but I'm rather tired. I'd like to go back now, Luka.'

'I'm afraid you can't.'

She froze, staring into a face carved from stone, cold and guarded as a beautiful mask.

Neatly trapped, she realised sickly. She didn't have a hope of getting to the door past him, and she had no doubt the windows were securely locked.

'I'm sorry,' he said with uncompromising determination, 'but you'll have to stay here for possibly twenty-four hours. After that you'll be free to go.'

Stunned by her own stupidity, Alexa watched him step back. But when he turned she commanded in a voice molten with fury, 'Let me out this minute or I'll scream the place down.'

'Screaming will exhaust you and achieve nothing, because the only people who'll hear you will be the men on security duty.' He paused before saying, 'I'm sorry, Alexa. At the moment I have to consider you a security risk. Please don't try to escape.'

Alexa overcame a grasping pain to demand, 'Why are you doing this? Because you still think I might leak information about you to the press?'

'Yes,' he said bluntly, and while she was still absorbing the cold, flat rejection he walked out and closed the door behind him.

Through its solid wooden depth Alexa heard the snick of a key in the lock, and a soft hiss that was almost certainly a bolt as it slid home.

So much for trust.

Still unable to believe that Luka had actually locked her in, that she was truly a prisoner, she stood motionless with bitter outrage until she was certain she was alone.

Only then, with the intense focus of a hunted animal, did she search her temporary prison. The little sitting room had one bedroom off it, with an *en suite* bathroom. Each had a window, locked and covered by wrought-iron shutters—locked also.

Alexa eyed the deadlocks with gathering frustration.

The double bed—a romantic four-poster—had been made up with linen that smelt of lavender, and on a small blanket chest at its foot stood her suitcase. She opened it, saw everything she'd brought up from Auckland neatly folded inside, along with her sponge bag. Someone had gone to the bach and collected all her clothes.

And her books. She glanced around the little room, a clever decorator's homage to a past age, and saw her computer on a side table, looking weirdly out of place.

Quickly she checked through the tiny cottage, but there was no telephone line, so she couldn't use the internet to call for help.

Face set, Alexa explored the rest of the cottage. In the tiny kitchen she dragged the door of the refrigerator open to see staples—bread, butter, cheese and milk. On the table a bowl of fruit glowed in reds and oranges and green. There were no utensils, nothing but a plastic knife, fork and spoon in the drawer. Everything was plastic, even the bowl containing the fruit and tomatoes.

Luka had anticipated exactly how she'd think. No

utensils to fashion into tools, no china to break and use, nothing metal.

A violent mixture of anguish and fear and rage churned her brain to uselessness. Luka couldn't have organised all this since she'd overheard him speak to Dion, so he'd made love to her knowing he was going to lock her in here.

Tamping her emotions down, because she had to think, to plan a way to get out of here, she continued her survey.

Each double-hung window was open at the top to let in the soft, scented air, but the deadlocks held firm, and each opening was covered by shutters. Breaking the glass wouldn't get her out.

Clearly Luka had made love to her in a cold, deliberate ploy to keep her occupied while this makeshift prison was set up.

In spite of her own complicity in the scene down by the pool, that thought hurt so much she slid hastily to another. What the *hell* was going on? Who were the mysterious 'they' he thought she might betray to the press, and what would 'they' be doing here?

She couldn't begin to think. An acute sense of bereavement, of heartshaking agony, seemed to have numbed her brain and reduced her to abject, shivering uselessness. Which was possibly exactly what Luka wanted to happen.

Galvanised into action by that humiliating suspicion, she tried the door handle again, twisting it with fruitless anger before giving up and stepping back. Even if she could pick locks there was the bolt on the outside, and for all its charming olde-worlde air the door was impregnable, held there by inset hinges and another modern deadlock.

That sly groundswell of fear chilled her skin.

So what was she going to do?

Well, she wasn't going to scream unless she knew it would get results. Luka, who'd made love to her with a fire and passion that still hummed through her body, would sedate her without a second thought.

She needed to think. Collapsing onto a delightful love seat, she fought back grief to marshal her brain into some heavy-duty scheming.

That was when she heard a helicopter coming in from the sea, low and fast, the pitch of the engine rising and steadying as it reached the house.

Who was it carrying? The 'they' who were supposed to arrive at ten tomorrow morning? Had she been imprisoned early because 'they' had changed their plans?

In spite of the best promptings of her common sense, Alexa lifted a shaking hand to her mouth as ridiculous scenarios played out in her mind.

She tried to laugh at her vivid imagination, but the emptiness beneath her breastbone and a dry mouth warned her of panic. 'Tea,' she said defiantly. 'I need a cup of tea.'

Making it gave her something to do. She was pouring it when the helicopter engine died into silence. After carrying her cup across the room, she stared out of the window and tried to think as she sipped. Luka, she decided vengefully, was going to suffer for this, if it took her all her life to come up with a suitable, satisfying revenge!

Another noise, a distant hum that rapidly turned into another helicopter, penetrated the silence. With a shaking hand she set the cup down and leaned forward, engine noise reverberating through her head. This time she saw it, lights flashing as it roared overhead and across the garden to the other side of the main house. Alexa rubbed her hand across her eyes.

Within a few minutes the harsh throbbing of the motors died into silence. Why was it so necessary for Luka to lock her away?

Bleakly she said aloud, 'I don't think it's because the Prince is coy about having a woman in his house. If I'm a security risk, these people must be here on highly secret business.'

Who were they? Slowly she finished the tea while she worried away at the puzzle.

Could it be a meeting of tycoons and captains of industry?

It didn't seem likely. By locking her up, Luka had to know he'd set himself up for charges of abduction and imprisonment, so whoever had arrived in those helicopters had to be hugely important—and possibly here on a matter of life and death.

Somehow business tycoons gathering to plot bigger and better takeovers didn't fit.

Diplomats? But why would the ruler of an Adriatic island nation be negotiating weighty international affairs in New Zealand?

Which left her with a much more sinister suspicion.

Was he involved in something illegal?

No. Not Luka. Irrational though it was in the light of his recent behaviour, she knew without even thinking about it that he wouldn't step across that line.

So what on earth was so hush-hush it had forced him to stoop to kidnapping? The only thing she could think of was the welfare of his people. If that was at risk, then, yes, she could see Luka doing whatever had to be done.

Gazing around the neat, ordinary room, she couldn't hold back a half-sob. Here she was, talking herself into the dangerous syndrome of finding excuses for Luka's behaviour because the alternative explanation—that he'd coolly, cynically betrayed her—hurt too much.

'Well, if you thought you might be falling in love with him,' she muttered, wincing at the brittle note in her voice, 'you've learned a lesson.'

Her gaze fell on a pile of magazines neatly stacked on a polished wooden table.

A suspicious warmth flooded through her, which she banished by saying aloud, 'The amenable Ms Martin probably thought of it. Amazing what some people will do to earn their living!'

She wouldn't be able to concentrate on a magazine, or any of the books from a tall bookshelf against one wall, so she washed the cup and saucer, surprised when a yawn caught her unexpectedly. A grey flood of exhaustion poured through her, weighting her bones and dulling her mind, but she set her jaw and went over the house with painstaking care, searching for some weakness she could exploit. She was not going to meekly remain a prisoner without at least trying to escape.

Much later, she had to admit defeat. She'd failed to pick the locks with her nail file, and there was nothing in the place she could use as a means of prying open the shutters or smashing the locks.

Smothering her torment with anger, she discarded any thought of changing into nightclothes and stretched out on the bed, staring into the darkness while futile, anguished suppositions raced through her mind. She listened for sounds that never came, until eventually she slept.

Alexa opened heavy eyelids to light, and bewilderment. For long moments her sluggish mind tried to work out where on earth she was. She swallowed several times to ease a throat like sandpaper, before finally deciding she needed a drink.

It was strangely difficult to force herself up from the bed, and when she stood at last she had to grab the back of the chair to stop herself from falling. Her head spun and her legs didn't want to know her.

She had, she realised, been crying in her sleep.

And of course it hadn't been a dream—Luka really had made love to her and betrayed her...

Biting her lip, she stumbled into the bathroom and washed her face. A glance at her watch revealed that it was six-thirty in the morning. She poured a glass of water and drank it down greedily, relishing its coolness, then went back into the bedroom and crawled under the sheets again.

Lying with one hand behind her head, she stared across at the window. The more she thought about her situation, the more she began to believe that Luka had intentionally used sex to control her.

Bitter chagrin roiled through her in an icy, humiliating wave. She'd been so blind, so easily tricked.

Alexa knew she'd inherited her father's good bones and her mother's superb skin, knew that her large eyes, pale as crystals beneath their sleepy, cat-like lids, fascinated some men. Yet even those assets, and the long legs and small, high breasts that helped her look good in her clothes, couldn't compare with the beautiful, sophisticated women Luka had been linked to.

She'd known that, but she'd wilfully throttled every forewarning, every instinct that had warned her to be careful. Overwhelmed by her first taste of heroic passion, she'd surrendered without a bleat, eagerly letting herself be duped by Luka's charisma and the dark sexuality that pulsed beneath his sophisticated charm.

She couldn't have made it easier for him if she'd tried.

Disgusted with herself, she muttered, 'Face it, you dumped your common sense and self-control. For a man who makes love like a god.'

A gentle curve of colour on the bedside table caught her eye. Frowning, she levered herself up on one elbow and saw a flower. Cool and soft as tissue paper, it had been tucked between two scented green feijoas—fruit she loved and had eaten with pleasure at the breakfast she'd shared with Luka.

Holding her breath, she reached out and picked up the flower, shivering when she felt the dampness of the dew still on its soft white petals.

A cotton rose.

Her throat closed up. Was it a mute apology?

No, she thought, struggling against a weak need to be reassured. Luka had made love to her in a deliberate attempt to throw her off balance. This would be the same—a lying promise of something he had no intention of delivering.

Or a taunt.

How dared he come into her room, watch her sleeping, and drop flowers and fruit beside her?

Mortified, she wondered whether he'd witnessed the tears that had been choking her when she finally woke.

She stormed out into the kitchen, pushing back the curtains as she went to let sunlight into the rooms. The lush cottage garden rioted in a profuse display of colour and form between the hedges that blocked out everything else, even the sea.

She pulled down a packet of cereal and stood with it

in her hand while her eyes stung with foolish tears. The cereal was her favourite.

'So?' she demanded, and poured some into a bowl. She didn't feel hungry but she'd eat, because she needed to keep her strength up.

When the plastic plate was empty, she forced herself to drink coffee, and after that to work on the genealogy program on her computer, filling in a day that dragged slowly by, silent and peaceful except for an occasional bark from the caretaker's dog and the ever-present feeling of being under surveillance.

Some time during the following night she was woken by the *thud-thud-thud* of the helicopters. Definitely two, she realised as she lay rigid on the bed, listening with every sense on full alert.

CHAPTER NINE

AFTER a paralysed moment Alexa scrambled off the bed. What was going to happen now?

She'd already worked out what she was going to do; moving as silently as she could, she raced out to stand behind the door so that Luka couldn't see her when he opened it. Yesterday after he'd left she'd carried a chair there. It had seemed light enough then, and how many times had she seen people on the screen lift a chair without even breathing heavily?

Probably thousands, but now the chair was heavy and uncooperative, and although she'd practised doing it several times she felt an utter fool with it hoisted above her head.

Pulses skipping and shallow, she listened as the choppers lifted and flew out to sea. A huge relief took her by surprise.

She didn't hear him come, didn't hear the bolt being drawn or the lock click, but a subtle alteration in the atmosphere warned her strained senses that he was there.

The door eased back, stopping just short of where she stood. To her intense chagrin he stayed on the doorstep.

Could he hear her breathing? No, because she wasn't. So what had warned him—the sound of her heart bounding unevenly in her throat?

She nearly screamed when Luka laughed. 'I should have guessed,' he said drily, and switched on the light. 'A chair?' he said, amusement still showing in his tone and his eyes.

'It seemed a good idea at the time,' Alexa snarled, white with rage.

She put down the chair and stepped out from behind the door. Head held high, she stared at him, her anger and aggression transmuting into concern the moment she realised that his olive skin stretched tautly over the strong framework of his face and there were dark shadows beneath his golden eyes. He looked as though he hadn't slept at all since she'd seen him last.

'It was a good idea, but you don't need to protect yourself.' All amusement scoured from his voice, he said flatly, 'It's over, Alexa. You're free. And one day I hope you'll forgive me for locking you up like this.'

He was leaving the country—leaving her. She could tell it although his tone revealed nothing. *I do not care,* she thought defiantly, while her heart twisted in denial.

'What time is it?' she demanded.

'An hour before dawn. Do you want to go back to the bach, or to Auckland?'

'To Auckland,' she said quickly, adding, 'But first I want to know what the hell is going on.'

He paused. 'I can't tell you.'

'You mean you don't trust me.' She gave a cynical little laugh. 'But what's new about that?' Good enough to make love to, just not good enough to trust.

His silence confirmed it. She drew in a sharp breath, but before she could speak he said abruptly, 'I would like to trust you, but I cannot. It is not—' He stopped, then finished with icy composure, 'It is not just you. I learned early in my life that a prince can trust no one— not his mother, not his father, not his best friend. I ask you to believe that I would never have behaved like an arrogant despot if people's lives had not been at risk.'

Lives? She must have said it aloud, because he said,

'Yes. And although it will infuriate you, I must ask you to trust me.'

She threw him a seething glare. 'Why should I?'

Luka shrugged as he admitted, 'There is no reason why you should, but this—problem is not over yet. Will you remain quiet about it, at least for a week?'

She flashed, 'So that the police will ask me why I didn't complain immediately?'

'Think that if you like,' he said indifferently, watching her from narrowed eyes. 'A week, Alexa. That's all I ask. You say I don't trust you, but there is no trust in you, either.'

She hesitated. 'And if I say no?'

'Then you'll have to stay here,' he said calmly. 'Not locked up, but as my guest in the house.'

'But if I say I won't tell anyone you'll trust me enough to let me go?'

He paused. She could sense the reluctance radiating from him when he eventually said, 'Yes.'

And even though Alexa knew she was being recklessly stupid, she muttered, 'All right.'

'Thank you.'

Setting her teeth, she said flatly, 'Well, goodbye.'

He didn't move. 'Goodbye, Alexa. Is there anything I can do—?'

'No!'

His hand closed over hers; he pulled her into him and kissed her. It started off in sweet and seducing tenderness, to be transformed into a passion so violent her knees buckled. Aware only that this was goodbye, Alexa pressed herself against him until, sick with shame, she jerked away.

'I'm sorry,' he said, letting her go. His voice was level and aloof; clearly he hadn't felt anything like the bitter yearning that clawed her. 'For everything. I hope you have a very happy life, Alexa. Try not to think of me with hatred.'

He turned, and some minutes later, still standing rigidly in the dark, she heard the sound of another helicopter start up.

So he'd put off releasing her until the very last moment. Tears ached behind her eyes, clogged her throat, but if she started to cry now she might never stop. After pushing the door wide open, she went to get her suitcase.

Scrabbling for her key, Alexa said patiently, 'No, Sean, I don't want to make you a cup of coffee.'

Her companion for the evening laughed and grabbed her wrist, using his superior strength to turn her around. 'Come on, Alexa, don't be so stuffy.'

Irritated into discarding her usual tact, she snapped, 'I don't want to kiss you either. And I certainly don't want to go to bed with you.' With a sharp twist she wrenched free. 'Goodnight. Don't keep the taxi waiting.'

Her escort had drunk just enough to make him stubborn. 'Why?' he persisted. 'I like you and you like me—what's your problem?'

Another figure loomed behind him at the top of the steps. Although Alexa's eyes dilated, she immediately discounted her response; a couple of achingly lonely months hadn't been long enough for her to overcome the tendency to see Luka in every tall, dark man.

But when the newcomer said in familiar, deadly tones, '*You* are the problem,' Alexa's heart skidded to a stop.

Frozen, she saw Sean swing around, jaw jutting as he confronted Luka. 'Who the hell are you?' he demanded.

'Nobody you'd be interested in,' Luka returned curtly. He looked past Sean to Alexa. 'Do you want him gone?'

Straining to keep a wild, incredulous hope from her voice, she unglued her tongue enough to croak, 'He's going.'

But Sean said belligerently, 'Like hell I am. I was here first.'

In the voice that probably sent shivers down the spines of his underlings, Luka responded, 'You heard her.'

The naked, brutal authority in his tone and stance got through to Sean. Shrugging, he walked past and stamped down the steps. A safe distance away, he flung over his shoulder, 'You should have told me there was a man in your life, Alexa. I don't poach.'

Unfortunately he spoilt the bravado of his exit by tripping. Tense and unbearably expectant, Alexa kept her eyes on him as he moved faster than strictly necessary to the waiting cab.

Silence stretched between the two outside the door until she broke it by saying, 'Thank you,' in a flat, strained voice.

'Who is he?' Luka asked indifferently.

'A friend,' she returned, cutting it short because the words stumbled off her tongue. Embarrassment warring with an exultant hope, she kept her eyes on the key as she thrust it into the lock and turned it.

'Do all your friends make passes at you?'

If it hadn't been for the cold distaste in his tone she might have suspected jealousy, but this was no returning lover come to sweep her off her feet into a sensual idyll.

'That,' she told him, her heart plummeting, 'is none of your business. But as it happens, no, they don't. And Sean won't try it again.'

A car door slammed and both turned to watch the taxi drive away with its resentful burden.

'I need to see you,' Luka said, looming tall and dark and ominous against the diffused lights from the street.

'Now?' Another squeaky word—he'd think she was mad. She coughed and resumed, 'It's after midnight.'

'It's important.'

Shivering, she pushed the door open and muttered, 'You'd better come in.'

What state was the flat in? She couldn't remember, and as they walked without speaking along the hall she hoped it was tidy.

Not too bad, she realised, casting a swift glance around as Luka closed the door behind him. At least there were flowers—a huge bunch of southern tulips holding up brilliant scarlet chalices. She'd bought them that afternoon because everything else in her life seemed grey.

And now the cause of her nagging, ever-present misery was in her home, watching her with icy detachment.

Skin prickling, she asked stiffly, 'How long have you been in Auckland?'

'I flew in this evening,' he told her, all cool authority, watching her with hooded eyes and a poker face. 'On a private visit.'

She sent him a glittering glance. 'I won't tell anyone,' she said curtly, because she wanted more than anything to ask if he'd come alone, or with the latest royal princess to take his fancy. According to the gossipmongers, this one was serious; Luka had stayed with her family in their château in France.

His eyes narrowed. 'I know.'

Overcoming a foolish desire to hold her breath, she asked, 'Did I finally manage to convince you that I wasn't a member of the paparazzi?'

His smile was assured and lethal. 'Yes.'

Deliberately she opened her eyes wide. 'How?'

'You didn't sell photographs or a story. And you kept your promise not to talk.'

It would have been wiser to remain silent, yet she couldn't prevent herself from saying, 'I don't renege on promises.' And because that sounded self-righteous, she hurried on, 'Thank you for replacing my father's camera. It must have taken some searching to find an identical one.'

He shrugged. 'It was nothing.'

Which probably meant he'd told some minion to find it and post it off to her, although he had signed the note that came with it. 'It meant a lot to me.'

'And you have already thanked me in a formal little note,' he said.

Which he hadn't answered. Because that still stung, she asked quietly, 'Did you organise the chance for me to work with Trudi Jerkin?'

That had come out of the blue: a week spent escorting one of the world's best photographers around New Zealand. She had learnt so much.

Watching Luka closely, Alexa saw the betraying quiver of his lashes and said briskly, 'I'm very grateful, but you don't owe me anything, you know. The day I read about the peace treaty in Sant'Rosa I understood why you'd been so antagonistic at having me wave cameras around right next door.'

When the news had broken, with the information that the treaty had been hammered out at Luka's beach house, Alexa had devoured everything she could find about it. One article she'd even cut out and hidden in her drawer.

Prince Luka, the journalist had written, was a man whose combination of old-world diplomatic skill, ruthless intelligence, charm and a brilliant financial mind were far more important than his rank—although in status-conscious Pacific societies that was no disadvantage.

By arranging this treaty the Bank of Dacia had gained considerable influence in the Pacific-Asian region. It had also set in motion the re-opening of the huge and lucrative mines closed by the fighting—and that too would be good for the Bank.

And for Dacia.

'I was on my way to meet representatives from the Sant'Rosan government when you were almost attacked,' Luka said, his tone as aloof as his expression. 'The government insisted on secrecy because the neighbouring state was ready to invade.'

Alexa nodded. Of course he would sympathise with a small state threatened by foreign troops.

He gave her a keen glance. 'The Sant'Rosans wanted a peace-keeping force in position before news of any treaty leaked out.'

Alexa loosened fingers laced so tightly together that they were almost white. 'I do understand why you felt the need for secrecy on the island—I even understand why you thought I might have links to that wretched gossip columnist—who turned out, incidentally, to have a mole in Carole's office who listened to phone calls— but I still think that locking me up was a huge overreaction.'

Luka said crisply, 'It seemed appropriate action at the time. I know that a prison is a prison, however comfortable it is, but I would do it again if I had to. I hoped that you would realise how little I enjoyed being forced to do it.'

Skin burned along her cheekbones as she remembered

the cotton rose. 'It doesn't matter,' she said in a cool voice. 'The peace treaty seems to be holding, so it was worthwhile.'

He hesitated, then said quietly, 'Sit down, Alexa. I have something to tell you.'

Alexa surveyed him with a mutinous glint, but obeyed, deliberately folding her hands in her lap. Just like that, the subject was finished with!

She glanced at his serious, stern face through her lashes, and with a sudden appalled leap of foreboding wondered if he'd come all this way to inform her that he was going to marry his exiled princess.

Why would he bother? They'd shared nothing but sex and sparring. 'Fire away,' she said tightly.

In a dispassionate, almost neutral voice he said, 'When we first met, your eyes fascinated me.'

Whatever she'd expected to hear, it wasn't this. Incredulously she repeated, 'My *eyes*?'

His mouth tightened. 'Amongst other things,' he drawled, leaving her in no doubt what those other things were. Ignoring the hot colour staining her skin, he went on, 'I have a friend with eyes exactly the same colour. I had other things to think of, so I put the coincidence from my mind. However, when you told me your father was half-Italian, and that you didn't know who your grandfather was, I became intrigued.'

'Why?' The word sounded clumsy and she realised she was holding her breath.

'My friend comes from that part of the world.'

The colour drained from Alexa's skin. Unable to speak, she stared at him, greedily noting the way the warm lamplight coaxed shades of amber and gold from the skin stretched taut over his slashing cheekbones.

Impassively Luka continued, 'Even though you bear

his names in Anglicised form, that is not so unusual—
Alexa and Nicole have been fashionable for some time
now. But when you told me they were your father's
names, and that his father had been your grandmother's
lover at an Italian university, I was intrigued. Back in
Dacia I set a researcher to find out what he could about
your grandmother's sojourn in Italy.'

'You had no right to do that,' she said stonily. 'You
don't have to pay me back somehow for locking me up.
You should have told me what you suspected, and I
could have decided what to do.'

His brows snapped together. 'There are other considerations,' he told her.

'What considerations?'

'The identity of the man who was your grandfather.'

Alexa's breath blocked her throat. Swallowing, she
said huskily, 'You found him?'

He slipped a lean, elegant hand into his pocket and
pulled out a photograph, laying it down on the coffee
table in front of her. 'Do you recognise these people?'

She gazed at it, hands clenching in her lap. 'Yes,' she
said huskily, staring at the couple who smiled at each
other in the faded snapshot. 'I've got one very like it.'

'May I see it?'

Dizzy with a mixture of anticipation and anguish, she
raced into her bedroom and brought out two framed photographs from her dressing table. 'My grandparents,' she
said, showing him the older one, 'and my parents. You
can see a family resemblance between my—my grandfather and my father.'

Luka's hard, handsome face didn't change expression
as he scrutinised them. He put them down and said,
'Yes. It all fits together very well.'

'So who was he? My grandfather?'

Incredibly, Luka said, 'It seems that at the time he met your grandmother he was the Crown Prince of Illyria. DNA testing would prove it, but all the information points to that.'

Alexa's jaw dropped. When she could speak again she said faintly, 'The one who married a New Zealand woman? No, he's too young!'

'Not Prince Alex but his father, then Crown Prince Nicolo.' Luka watched her intently. 'He met your grandmother at university in Italy and they became lovers. When her year of study was over she returned to New Zealand, pregnant with your father. Prince Nicolo can't have known because by all accounts he had an overdeveloped sense of responsibility, and I think he'd have supported her and his child at the very least.'

'It sounds like a fairy story,' Alexa said thinly, trying to sort her whirling thoughts. She bunched her hands into fists to stop them shaking. 'Too far-fetched.'

'There had to be a reason for your grandmother, who sounds a sensible and loving woman, to keep all knowledge of her son's father from him.' Luka touched Alexa's photograph. 'That man with your grandmother is definitely the present Prince of Illyria's father at the age of twenty. If your grandmother understood that in the climate of the times there was no chance of them marrying, her decision makes sense.'

'And she wouldn't have wanted to burden him with the knowledge of an illegitimate child,' Alexa said numbly. 'What happened to him when Illyria was overrun?'

'After that year in Italy he went on to university in Switzerland and Great Britain. He married just before the communist upheaval and worked secretly as a peasant in his country until he, his wife and his son Alex, now Prince of Illyria and your half-uncle, were betrayed. He died giving his wife and son time to escape.'

Alexa blinked back sudden, painful tears for a man she had never known.

'Yes, he was a hero,' Luka said quietly. 'You have every right to be proud of him.'

Alexa swallowed. 'I—don't know what to say.'

He laughed quietly. 'For perhaps the first time in our acquaintanceship.'

She bit her lip fiercely to stop it trembling. 'Why did you go to all this trouble?'

'It seemed the least I could do to make up for the indignities I subjected you to. You said that you had a hole in your life. And although you laughed when you talked of a big Italian family, you sounded wistful.'

He sounded almost bored. Another man with a strongly developed sense of responsibility, she decided painfully, because it would have meant so much if he'd done this to please her, instead of making amends.

'I—thank you,' she said, hiding the uncertainty in her words with an attempt at briskness.

'You don't need to thank me,' he returned negligently. His face hardening into a cold, bronze mask, he went on, 'Unfortunately, while researching this, my employee was careless enough to alert someone else to the possibility of a child sired by Nicolo. That information was handed on.'

Feeling extremely sorry for the careless employee, Alexa asked, 'To whom?'

'The royal family of Illyria.'

Alexa's head came up. Her eyes met his, fire duelling with ice. Lashes falling, she looked away. 'I see.' She waited, and when he said nothing she murmured, 'I don't imagine it matters. It doesn't seem likely that they'll be terribly interested in an unknown relative on the other side of the world.' It was one thing to fantasise occasionally about a large, happy Italian family; it was quite another to be presented with the reality of a royal half-uncle.

'You do Alex a disservice,' Luka said austerely. 'He is extremely interested. He contacted me, and when he realised that I had met you he asked if I could arrange a meeting.'

'A meeting?' Alexa echoed, limp with shock. So this was why he'd come.

She swallowed a lump in her throat to croak, 'Why?'

'He wants to meet you,' Luka said coolly. 'He suggested Dacia as a neutral place for that meeting. His wife is pregnant, and travelling is uncomfortable for her, but she can cope with a flight from Illyria to Dacia.'

'Dacia?' Hope, ever-present, undying, burst into life again. To quell it, she asked, 'Why Dacia?'

'It would cause too much interest in Illyria if an unknown woman with the Considine eyes and bone structure arrived there,' he told her curtly. 'Press photographers and gutter journalists would gather from around the world, sniffing out a story.'

'Is there no freedom of the press in Dacia?' she asked with a spark of malice.

He gave a narrow, cynical smile. 'My people are more accustomed to me than the Illyrians are to Alex—they allow me a private life. Outsiders I can ban, if necessary.'

Mind churning, Alexa unfroze enough to pace across to the window. Pulling back the curtain to stare into the small courtyard garden outside, she said indistinctly, 'I hadn't—it's so clichéd to think there might be royalty in your ancestry, and I certainly didn't expect to find it in mine! I don't know that I want to meet this so-called uncle of mine.'

'That's a decision only you can make,' Luka said coolly.

Chilled by his remote courtesy, she was goaded into indiscretion. Turning her head, she ignored the constriction of her heart to raise mocking brows. 'No more kidnapping, Luka?'

Tension suddenly sparked into the air. Don't be a fool, Alexa told herself. She should have learned by now that pricking at his self-control was futile.

Without moving he said abruptly, 'I hated locking you up, but I couldn't run the risk of letting you go free. Too much was at stake. I have a young cousin who is an adventurer—still reckless and eager. Somehow he managed to wangle a trip to Sant'Rosa on a ship full of medical supplies. He was recognised, and kept there as a hostage.'

'Why?' Dropping the curtain, she turned back into the room, her hands suddenly shaky. 'I seem to be saying that every second word. What happened—is he all right?'

He shrugged. 'Yes. When I told you that lives depended on your silence, his was one. The Sant'Rosans were desperate men, and they used him to force me to work for them and do it in secrecy.' He gave a hard smile. 'When I arrived to talk to the guerrilla forces—'

Horrified, she breathed, 'You went to Sant'Rosa after you left the beach? You walked into the middle of a civil war?'

'It was necessary,' he said, watching her with cool amber eyes.

'You could have been killed!'

'They needed reassurance.' As though the words were

torn from him he said, 'I understand men who don't trust anyone, not even their leaders.'

'I know.' She was holding her breath.

'My parents' marriage was—difficult. I grew up knowing that my mother was not a Dacian, that her interests lay elsewhere. It taught me not to rely on anyone but myself.'

That feeling of balancing on the edge of a precipice increased. 'I'm so sorry,' she said, thinking of a small boy with no one to turn to.

'Neither of them wished for the marriage. My mother had been forced onto my father, and he onto her, and she was both spy and hostage. Yet they loved me.'

And he had been the child in the middle, unable to bridge the gap. Tentatively Alexa said, 'It must have been hell for both of them.'

'It got worse when my father decided that I should be initiated into my duties as ruler. He warned me clearly that I could not speak to my mother about anything that I learned.' His voice was cold, as cold as the frozen fire veiled by his lashes. 'And then of course the media circus began when I reached eighteen. I grew to despise and distrust all journalists and photographers. Alexa, I dared not tell you what was going on—premature disclosure of the peace talks could have derailed the whole process and led to the death of my cousin.'

For the first time he was revealing something of himself to her. Alexa treasured every difficult word, even as she ached with sympathy.

She managed to smile and said cheerfully, 'At first I had every intention of getting even with you when I finally got out of that cell. But when I read about the treaty—well, a few hours spent locked up didn't mean much compared to the misery the Sant'Rosans have endured for so long. It was a comfortable cell.'

'My mother spent her life in a very comfortable cell,' he said with sombre intensity. 'In the end her lack of freedom killed her.'

Alexa said again, 'I'm so sorry.'

Hard eyes searched her face. 'Yes, I think you are,' he said with a twisted smile. 'It all happened a long time ago. When you come to Dacia I'll make a villa available where you and your half-uncle will have privacy. You need not see me at all.'

He couldn't have made his lack of interest in her more obvious.

Pierced to the quick, she said woodenly, 'I can't just up and go—I have a job.'

'Can't you spare a week? I will make all the arrangements—it won't cost you anything,' he said, a muscle tightening in his jaw. 'Perhaps this letter from Alex will persuade you.' He produced an envelope from his pocket and handed it to her.

Accepting it from him, Alexa bit her lip. Luka certainly wasn't trying to persuade her! His barriers were slammed firmly into place.

'Read it,' he commanded, a hint of impatience roughening the deep voice.

Alexa opened the envelope and unfolded the single sheet of paper to see what the Prince of Illyna had written.

Dear Alexa Mytton,
My wife and I would very much like to meet you, and as I know this is at very short notice I've asked my good friend Luka to deliver this. If you can come to see us, give him the dates so I can organise your

tickets. For obvious reasons I must ask you not to let anyone else but those you trust know about this.

He was hers, Alex Considine.

Alexa looked up into remote eyes. 'Why you? It's a long way from Dacia to New Zealand.'

'Not so long from Asia, where I've been for the past week. As for coming—it was my fault that your private story was made public in however minor a degree. And after discussing it we decided that you would prefer to hear this news from someone you know.'

Had he told the Prince of Illyria that he'd made love to her? Alexa cast a fleeting glance at his beautiful, disciplined face and shivered inwardly, repressing the erotic images that flashed across her mind. Why should he? It had meant nothing more than momentary physical pleasure.

And the sooner she realised that and gave up her pathetic dreams, the better it would be for her.

Before she could think of a reply he said, 'I'll leave you now to make up your mind. I'm flying to Sant'Rosa in an hour, but I'll ring you at eight tomorrow morning.' He smiled at her, amused, ironic, without humour. 'Even if you decide not to go to Dacia this will not be the end; Alex is a very determined man, and he wants to meet you.'

After she'd closed the door behind him Alexa felt light-headed, almost drunk with pleasure at seeing Luka again—yet the ice that had been building inside her since she'd left the island had advanced some more. He'd made it so plain he didn't want any contact between them.

He had looked tired, she thought anxiously, his strong features more angular and the dark energy that drummed through him a little less forceful than before. Had he been working too hard?

Stupid to care...

Alexa spent the rest of that night lying awake in the dark, listening to traffic noises. She didn't have to make up her mind—she knew what her answer was going to be. She'd spent two months trying to get Luka out of her mind, and will-power hadn't worked. Now was her chance to see if harsh reality might do the trick. According to the headlines, his exiled princess had been shopping in Paris for a trousseau.

Perhaps the tiredness she'd read in his face was simply sexual exhaustion.

To her he'd never been a prince, with all that that status implied—he'd simply been a man. Surely seeing him in his natural habitat would force her wilful heart to recognise the stupidity of hope.

And perhaps meeting her new family might ease this constant nagging grief, this longing for something she could never have, for a man who'd never love her.

CHAPTER TEN

A MONTH later Alexa was sitting inside a jet on the runway at the only international airfield on Dacia. When she'd gone to pay for her flight she'd discovered that it was already paid for, and when she'd embarked she'd realised that either Luka or her unknown uncle had booked her first class all the way.

She'd repay whoever it was, even if it broke her.

Buoyed by a stomach-churning mixture of tiredness and pulsing, heady excitement, she peered through the window. From the air Dacia had spread a green and white patchwork in a brilliant sea. Groves of trees lay like silvery fur over the central spine of hills, and beaches looped in silver crescents between high white headlands. Some of those headlands, she'd noted with a surge of excitement, were crowned with what looked to be castles.

Swallowing hard, Alexa picked up her hand luggage and followed the rest of the travellers out into the terminal.

'Ms Mytton?' a voice enquired.

Alexa looked at the smiling young woman who accosted her, and nodded. 'I'm Alexa Mytton,' she confirmed.

'I am Lucia Bagaton, and I have been sent to meet you. Please come this way.'

Alexa followed her through a door to a small, private lounge where she was reunited with her luggage before being whisked out of another door and into a car so rapidly she gained only an impression of hot sunlight, and the scent of the sea mingling with the pungent odour of aircraft fuel.

Immediately the door had closed behind them the car sped away, its tinted windows hiding the passengers from any curious gaze.

Alexa sank back as they drove away from the airport, listening to her escort's running commentary on the vineyards and olive groves. Clearly Lucia Bagaton, who had to be some relative of Luka's, didn't expect an answer.

But when Alexa gave a sharp exclamation, and twisted in her seat to stare at a honey-coloured building across a vine-patterned field, her companion said, 'That is a pre-Romanesque church built over a thousand years ago. Lovely, isn't it?'

'I've never seen such an old building,' Alexa said, gazing at it until olive trees cut off her sight. The car avoided a woman on a donkey, who waved and called out a smiling greeting.

'You are interested in antiquities?' At Alexa's nod, Lucia Bagaton said, 'We have Greek and Roman ruins here also. Perhaps you will get to see some.'

Carefully Alexa said, 'Forgive me, but are you related to L—the Prince of Dacia?'

Lucia Bagaton gave her an equally careful smile. 'A distant cousin,' she said. 'I work for him as an occasional social secretary.'

The car turned onto a much narrower road that threaded between stone walls and a pine forest until it stopped in front of elaborately wrought iron gates. The driver sounded the horn, and as Alexa watched the gates swung back, opening the way between high walls faded to a dusty, delightful apricot.

'This is the villa Luka thought you might like to stay in,' her escort said as the car eased through. She flashed a cool, professional smile at Alexa. 'You will be completely private here.'

After supervising the man who carried Alexa's bags up to a cool bedroom, shuttered against the fierce sun and the glare from the sea, she turned to Alexa and said, 'Enjoy your stay, Ms Mytton. I'd suggest a short rest, then perhaps a swim. Dinner will be served in two hours. If you need anything, ask Carlotta, the housekeeper, who will contact me. And if you wish to do any sightseeing I will be more than happy to arrange it for you and accompany you. Goodbye.'

Not exactly dismissive—very gracious, in fact—but there was a barrier there. It could be a family characteristic, or might his distant cousin perhaps be in love with Luka?

'Thank you,' Alexa said with a smile that faded into bleakness as the door closed behind her escort.

Luka had made it obvious that he didn't want to resume any sort of relationship, so it was stupid to feel abandoned. She straightened her shoulders and looked around, remembering another bedroom beside another sea. Both tiled and sparsely furnished, they couldn't have been more different. Equally beautiful and suited to the climate, this room bore the imprint of an ancient culture in the thick walls and heavy carved furniture.

Fighting a ridiculous forlornness, Alexa showered in the small marble bathroom off the bedroom, staying under the cool spray until her skin began to wrinkle. When she came back to the bedroom she found her case unpacked and her clothes hidden in a huge armoire that smelt of lavender and rosemary.

The homely scents reassured her. Surrendering to

tiredness, she lay down on the daybed and wooed her brain into quietude as the sunlight smouldering through the shutters dwindled into a copper glow.

Her brain obstinately refused to drift, embarking again on a familiar treadmill of queries and yearning hopes.

'Oh, grow up!' she exclaimed furiously, moving restlessly on the pile of pillows.

Luka was making it more than clear that whatever they'd shared was dead for him. So it had better die for her too. Obsessing about him was a waste of time and emotional energy.

Impatient with her foolishness, she finally got up and chose a long, floaty skirt in the finest cotton, pairing it with a sleeveless shell top in the same pale blue. She combed her hair back from her face and applied lipstick before walking down the stairs, feeling like a trespasser in the big, silent house.

Without looking at any of the rooms, she found her way onto a terrace at the back of the house, shaded by pink bougainvillaea. A pang of homesickness brought tears aching to her eyes.

Forcing herself to appear calm, she walked across to a keyhole window in the wall through which she glimpsed an alluring cascade of more bougainvillaea—scarlet this time. Enchanted, every sense vibrant and alert, she peered into a courtyard with palms in pots and a lily-dotted pool. Someone had set a table there—for two, she noticed, and suddenly her heart thundered in her breast and she felt alive again.

'Good evening.'

Alexa swung around. Luka stood at the door of the house, tall and dark, in trousers tailored to fit his lean hips and long legs and a white shirt with sleeves rolled up.

Absurdly glad she'd decided to wear her prettiest casual clothes, she said unevenly, 'Hello.' Oh, you've got it bad, she thought disgustedly, but her tremulous smile refused to go away.

Golden gaze fixed to her face, he came out onto the terrace. 'I hope everything is to your satisfaction,' he said formally.

Now it was. With enormous reluctance Alexa admitted that whatever she felt for him was more than desire, more than fascination—much, much more.

Resisting the implications, she said, 'I'd be very hard to please if it wasn't. This is lovely, thank you.' After a moment's hesitation she asked, 'When will—the Prince of Illyria come?'

'The day after tomorrow,' Luka told her, his deep voice laconic. 'We thought it best to give you a complete day to recover from the flight.' His eyes narrowing, he scrutinised her face. 'That doesn't please you?'

Alexa said, 'No, no, it's fine. This is the first time I've flown for more than six hours, but I don't think I'm jet-lagged. Do long flights affect you?'

'No,' he said calmly. 'I've trained myself to sleep and I drink vast amounts of water.'

'Which reminds me,' she said, 'I owe you for the flight.'

He grinned. 'Shall we quarrel about that tomorrow? This is your first night here, and I'd like you to enjoy it.'

Taken aback, Alexa said, 'I hadn't planned to quarrel!'

'So forget about it.' At her hesitation, he said lazily, 'Until tomorrow.'

'Until tomorrow,' she agreed recklessly, aware that

when he looked at her like that she'd forget anything he asked her to.

'Sit down and tell me how the flight went,' he said, going across to the table that held, she was surprised to see, a bottle of champagne and two flutes, glittering in the candlelight.

What was he up to? she wondered, trying very hard to be cynical, and failing. Excitement hollowed out her stomach, zinging along her nerve-ends like an electric current that played by its own rules.

As the sky filled with strange stars and the wind whispered across the pines, Luka poured out champagne and handed her a flute before suggesting a toast to reunions.

'Reunions,' Alexa said ironically, and sipped the golden liquid. 'Although it's not exactly a reunion—I haven't met Prince Alex before.'

'He looks enough like your father to make it one,' Luka said, his smile wry.

'He certainly does. Now that I know, I'm astonished I didn't notice before,' she said lightly.

'Because you weren't expecting to see it.'

'That must be it.' Casting about for something else to say, Alexa asked about Sant'Rosa.

Luka began to talk of the situation there. Telling herself firmly that she was glad he avoided any personal topics, she listened, her tension easing a little. She could, she thought despairingly, spend the night discussing the affairs of the world with him.

Dinner arrived, delivered on a trolley by the beaming housekeeper, who then disappeared. Over a superb meal they continued to talk, a stimulated Alexa hungrily drinking in the sound of Luka's deep voice, the way he smiled, the mellow gleam of candlelight on his strong features, his lithe male grace.

Afterwards, in the big bed in her room, Alexa replayed the conversation over in her mind, awed by his responsibilities, impressed by his acute grasp of world affairs, and fascinated by his absolute discretion, because he'd told her nothing she hadn't already read or heard in the media.

In spite of his statement in Auckland, he still didn't trust her. It didn't seem likely that he'd ever overcome that childhood conditioning.

Hopeless and unhappy, she thumped her pillow and buried her hot face in it.

But he still wanted her. Able to control almost everything else, he couldn't hide the small physical signs of awareness and desire—the flick of a muscle in his jaw and the dilating pupils that turned his eyes to smouldering topaz gems when he looked at her.

She pressed her hand against her racing heart and told it sternly to stop.

However susceptible to Luka's raw male charm, she couldn't be in love with him. Although memories of their lovemaking still had the power to send ripples of thwarted passion through her, and any relationship with him would be explosive and wild and heart-stoppingly passionate, he'd never lose control—and she'd always know that for her it was second-best.

And she certainly wasn't suitable mistress material.

'Anyway, it's academic,' she told the silent room. He hadn't made one move towards her during the evening—had carefully avoided touching her, had skilfully and ruthlessly kept the conversation on impersonal matters.

He'd probably hoot with laughter at the thought of making her his mistress. Especially now he had the perfect princess tucked away in the background.

'So stop aiming for the stars and get some rest,' she commanded, and eventually sleep hit her like a mallet.

She woke with a dry mouth and a slight headache, and muscles so stiff she realised she hadn't moved all night. Groaning, she staggered out of bed and pushed the shutters open, smiling at the fresh scent of pines and the sun leaping above the sea. A small fishing boat, its bow painted with a colourful eye, puttered around the headland and across the bay.

Hastily she scrabbled into clothes and snatched her camera, running down onto the beach to catch the exquisite light. She'd never come back here, and she wanted to imprint every moment onto her heart.

An hour later, sandy and satisfied, she returned to the villa. She'd photographed sand and sea, the gorgeous little Grecian temple above the beach, the pine forest surrounding the villa, and the view from the headland.

Now, before she showered, she asked Carlotta, the housekeeper, if she could contact Lucia Bagaton.

Although the older woman appeared to speak reasonably good, if heavily accented English, Alexa must have made a mistake, for an hour later it wasn't the distant cousin of Luka who arrived at the villa, but the man himself.

'Oh! I didn't—' Alexa stopped, bushwhacked by his smile. Leashing the response fizzing through her blood, she said brightly, 'I'm sorry—I must have got it wrong. I wanted to go sightseeing, so I asked Carlotta if she could contact Lucia to arrange it. I didn't mean to drag you away from your duties.'

'I have no duties until much later in the day,' he said, smiling at the startled look on her face.

Anticipation danced through her. 'Are you bunking off?' she asked in a conspiratorial tone.

He grinned, and she noticed that he wore clothes as casual and suitable for sightseeing as hers. 'I don't spend every hour of every day ruling,' he said. 'Where would you like to go?'

It was like being given a gift from the gods. 'Your cousin Lucia mentioned something about Greek and Roman ruins,' Alexa suggested on a hopeful note, adding demurely, 'I think she felt that lovely pre-Romanesque church was a bit *nouveau* to deserve all the admiration I was giving it.' She laughed. 'And New Zealand is such a very young country that I'd like to see the oldest things you've got!'

Later, when the day was over, she thought dreamily that it had been almost perfect. Luka had shown her a Roman archway before driving up into the hills where they'd picnicked by a small jewel of a Greek temple. They'd talked as though they had known each other all their lives, almost ignoring the wildly disturbing current of attraction that ran beneath every word and glance.

Alexa had exclaimed over herbs and cyclamens growing wild, and Luka had taken her even further into the olive-silver hills to a cave where the original inhabitants of the island had sheltered. A wall, probably almost as old as the cave, enclosed the entrance.

'How long ago?' she asked, eyeing the huge blocks of stone.

He shrugged. 'Perhaps thirty thousand years.'

Awed, she said, 'That is old.'

'The oldest man-made thing on the island.' He looked at his watch. 'I'd better get you home,' he said. 'I have a meeting in half an hour.'

Until then they hadn't seen anything larger than a village, but on the way back to the villa he took her through a bustling, thriving city still full of tourists.

She leaned forward as they drove past a large building on the edge of the harbour. 'That looks ancient too,' she commented.

'A Renaissance castle built on Roman foundations,' he told her briefly.

Chilled by its size and pomp, Alexa said, 'Judging by the sentries, it must be where you live.'

'It's the official residence,' he told her coolly. 'I spend most of my time in a much smaller, more comfortable house a few miles out of town.'

She fell silent. All day she'd managed to almost forget that he ruled the country, but that big palace dominating the city reminded her of the distance between them.

He took her to the front door of the villa and said, 'I'll see you this evening.'

She gave him a pale smile. 'Thank you for a perfect day,' she said quietly.

She went slowly up the stairs and showered, and then she waited for Luka. Oh, she didn't admit that that was what she'd done during the sleepy, hot afternoon, but now, as he came out onto the terrace this evening, something slotted into place deep inside her, and she knew.

No matter what happened, she would spend the rest of her life waiting for Luka, because she loved him. Like her grandmother, she had fallen in love with a man she could never have. At least her grandmother had been loved in return, even if only fleetingly. But she wasn't going to think of that now.

Making no attempt to hide her smile, she got up and went towards him, her long skirt floating mistily around her legs.

'Hello,' she said. 'How was your meeting?' And she held out her hand.

He paused, looking into her eyes. She knew what he saw there—surrender. His lashes drooped too late to hide the swift glitter of gold as he took her fingers and lifted them to his mouth. 'Too long,' he said against her skin.

She shivered. 'Yes,' she whispered unevenly.

But after that light kiss he let her hand go and stepped back. A subtle rejection, she thought wearily, but a rejection nevertheless.

Accepting it, she forced another smile and moved away, looking over her shoulder to say, 'I'm glad you could take today off. It was glorious.'

Luka watched with half-closed eyes the sinfully distracting curve of her throat and cheek, the smooth swell of her high breasts above the narrow, lithe waist. Copper hair swung around her lovely face, and her walk was a silent, sensuous invitation that targeted his libido with unerring aim.

'I don't spend all my life on official occasions,' he said, following her.

He wasn't going to accept that invitation, even though his body throbbed with hunger for everything he knew she could give him. This time he would show her that he could be relied on to control himself.

Alexa glanced at him as she walked across to the balustrade of the terrace. His face was closed against her, the stark, uncompromising angles and lines set in a mask of forceful self-sufficiency.

It was no use telling herself that no human being could be as controlled and assured as Luka—in spite of his physical awareness of her, he'd never shown a hint of vulnerability.

Whereas she was raw with it, her love naked and exposed. Loving him was as natural to her as breathing, as necessary as her blood.

Holding desperately to her smile, she said, 'So my half-uncle and his wife arrive tomorrow. Are they staying here?'

'If that's all right with you.'

'Of course it is,' she said automatically.

'He's suggested they stay for three days.'

'Just long enough,' she said flippantly. 'If we hate each other on sight we can politely pretend otherwise for three days.' After that she'd be heading home. Her open airline ticket could be activated any time.

'You won't hate each other,' Luka said with cool confidence.

Hoping he was right, she asked impulsively, 'What's he like? I mean, I know he's a techie billionaire, and of course I know the romantic story of his escape to Australia, but what's he like as a human being?'

'Formidable,' Luka said instantly, 'but a good man.'

The word *formidable* so exactly described the man who'd just used it that she half laughed. 'Takes one to know one.'

'You'll like him,' Luka told her drily.

'I hope so.' Alexa stared down through a feathery screen of foliage to the white sand below, prisoner of the driving, irresistible awareness that had pulsed just beneath the surface during the whole wonderful day.

She said abruptly, 'This is a very beautiful place.'

'As beautiful as New Zealand?'

Suspecting him of sarcasm, she said, 'Every bit as beautiful in a different way. It looked lovely coming in from the air. I'd thought it would be dry and harsh, so I was surprised at the forests.'

'My father was passionate about forestry,' Luka said evenly.

Alexa looked around. 'And this is an enchanting spot.'

'It was my mother's refuge,' he told her. 'Her favourite cell, she used to call it.' And in an abrupt and unsubtle change of subject he said, 'I thought we'd eat down on the beach.'

'Yes, of course.'

Side by side, yet never touching, they walked through the gardens towards the little temple, shimmering in the last rays of the sun.

Carlotta had set the table in front of the columns but instead of the silver and crystal formality of the previous night she'd used rustic china and glasses. Two tall wrought-iron candelabra held candles, and food steamed in bright earthenware casseroles on a serving wagon. The earthy sophistication of the bowls and dishes somehow suited the setting perfectly.

'I know this is going to sound incredibly ignorant,' Alexa said cheerfully, 'but compared to that lovely little temple in the hills, this one looks to be in too good repair to be original.'

Luka smiled down at her. 'You've got a good eye. It's an exact replica, but it lacks soul. A hundred and fifty years ago a romantic forebear decided that it would be appropriate to build a shrine to Eros.'

The youthful god of love, Venus's mischievous son. 'It's a charming little folly,' Alexa said, skin prickling at the dismissive note in his voice.

She accepted a glass of white wine and asked him about the history of Dacia. He gave a précis of a bleak and often bloody story, but, although she found it fascinating, she preferred the edgy intimacy of their previous exchanges.

This Luka was the monarch, compelling, decisive—
formidable!—master of his life. And, although she respected and admired this Luka, she had come to love
the man she'd crossed swords with in exhilarating bouts,
the man who'd made love with heart-stopping skill, setting a benchmark she knew no other lover would reach.

Accept it, she told herself silently, watching him
through lowered lashes. Somehow, impossibly, you've
fallen in love with him, and nothing is ever going to be
the same again.

Alexa knew then what she was going to do before the
night was through.

CHAPTER ELEVEN

ALERT as a fencer about to fight the duel of her life, she lifted her glass to hide her expression, then set it down without drinking. Delicious though the wine was, she didn't want a clouded head. Tonight she was going to experience everything, remember everything.

And so would Luka—but would he remember her as a sexual trophy, or as someone he could have loved if only his parents, forced into an unbearable situation, hadn't shattered his trust for ever?

'Are those speakers I can see?' she asked casually, nodding at the interior of the temple.

'Would you like some music?' he said, equally casual.

'I think I would,' she said slowly, adding on an unforced, husky note, 'Something good to dance to.' It was a direct challenge.

His long, measuring survey sent sensation shivering the length of her spine. Her breath hissed through her parted lips as he strode between the pillars into the dim interior. Insistent, reckless, desire drummed through Alexa.

Something about his movements reminded her of a hunter, powerful and predatory, the ruthless master of all he could see.

A moment later smooth, seductive jazz filtered through the warm air. Music to dance to? Music to make love by…

Skin prickling, she crossed to the edge of the terrace and looked out over the darkening sea.

'Alexa.'

Silently, eyes lowered, she turned. But he wasn't letting her get away with passive acceptance. A lean finger tipped her chin and he scanned her face.

Neither spoke. Alexa met his hard eyes gravely until, with a mocking smile, Luka took her in his arms. Without speaking, barely touching, they began to dance. He moved to the music with a lithe authority that overwhelmed everything but a feverish response to his lethal grace.

Bonelessly yielding to her body's urgent clamour and the violent intensity of her emotions, she melted against him. His arm tightened around her and his cheek came down on the top of her head.

'Do you like this music?' he asked into the fragrant air, a raw note rasping through the words.

'Love it,' she murmured.

Love dancing with you, her heart whispered, love everything about tonight, love you...

The heavy perfume of some unknown flower, the slight grittines of the stone terrace beneath her feet, the moody, sexy wail of the saxophone—all were integrated into the primal delight of dancing with Luka.

'So we have something in common,' he said in a cryptic voice.

Stay cool, she told herself. Striving for an easy sophistication, she said, 'We might have lots in common. We've just never bothered to find out.'

His chest lifted on a low laugh that was almost a purr. 'Too busy fighting.'

'Mmm. Instant enemies.'

'Do you know why?'

A relaxed, sophisticated woman would be lightly amused. Alexa tried for it. 'Well, there was the incident with the camera, and then the minor matter of a couple of days in a cell—'

'Before that,' he said, his beautiful mouth curving. 'Right at the start it was fireworks—skyrockets, Catherine wheels—the whole foolish, potent, mesmerising bag of tricks.'

His arm tightened a little more, pulling her closer, but when he spoke his voice was cool and reflective. 'What happened about the men who planned to attack you?'

'They were caught later that night—they attacked a woman a few streets away, but a security camera got their car number. I didn't have to give evidence,' Alexa told him, every nerve singing as he turned them both to avoid one of the white pillars, and in doing so held her for an unhurried moment against the lean strength of his body. His arms around her, the heat of his body and his subtle scent—entirely Luka and all male—overwhelmed her.

He looked at her, his autocratic face hardening in a smile of masterly irony. 'You were so inconvenient.'

'So were you! And arrogant—'

'I did overreact,' he admitted drily, pivoting again and carrying her with him. 'But I couldn't risk letting you stay free.'

Alexa nodded. 'I know.'

'I shouldn't have kissed you, or made love to you.'

A salty breeze from the sea caressed Alex's bare arms, chilling her. 'So why did you?' she asked tautly. 'I wondered if it was the old chauvinist power trip.'

His smile was unsettling with irony. 'Far from it. I simply couldn't stop myself, even though a cynical part of my brain wondered if you were prepared to barter sex for information. You slashed me with those incredible eyes, cutting as diamonds, and I wanted you more than I'd ever wanted anything else.'

Heat began to surge through Alexa in a heavy subliminal tide, drowning logic, drowning common sense.

Luka said, 'And although you were furious, you responded to me.'

Alexa stiffened and lifted her chin.

'My father discovered that the first woman I fell in love with was negotiating with one of the newspapers,' he said coolly. 'She was older than I, and had no taste for royal life; to her, it was only sensible to make what profit she could of the experience. When I broke off the affair she sold her story for a huge amount of money. I was young and foolish, but it reinforced my father's teaching that no woman can be trusted.'

'Your father was wrong,' Alexa stated.

'Intellectually I knew that. Emotionally, I still believed him.'

Quickly, to hide just how miserable that made her feel, she said, 'When I read about the peace pact I forgave you for everything. Almost—'

Laughing, he caught her fist an inch away from his ribs. 'Tigress.' With her hand wrapped in his big warm one, he bent his head and kissed her.

Yet although it began with a swift flare of passion, Alexa felt the moment his will-power slammed the gates closed in her face. Her lashes flew up as he lifted his head. Mouth clamped into a straight line, he was watching her with blazing eyes.

Driven by a fierce mixture of anger and desire and pain, she thought, Tonight he's going to lose that regal self-control.

She swayed against him, stormy hunger heating her body from the inside out. His involuntary response, a lash of darkly potent energy, swept away her last scruple.

'Luka,' she said, reaching up to run her finger across his top lip. He had shaved very recently but she felt a slight abrasion against her sensitive fingertip, a sensation that sizzled the length of her arm to explode like fire and ice in every cell of her body.

'Alexa,' he said harshly, and pulled her hand up to his mouth, biting her finger with deliberate care. And then he released her. 'I promised myself I wouldn't do this again! We need to talk.'

But she saw the hunger prowling his eyes.

'Not now,' she said, and kissed his mouth again.

He stayed rigid, asking harshly against her seeking lips, 'What do you want?'

Narrowing her eyes at him, she said, 'Can't you guess?'

He looked at her with glittering, angry intensity. 'No.' The single syllable was guttural, almost inhuman in quality.

'No, you can't guess? Or no, it's not going to happen?' She swayed into his arms again, exulting as they folded around her and clamped her against his aroused body.

Eyes dilating, Alexa saw that desperate need consume him as well, and realised the dangerous game she was playing—trying to force him into something he didn't want. A spasm of shame shattered her petty need to make him lose control.

'Neither of those. No, why fight it?' he said harshly, each word raw from his throat, and kissed her again. This time there was no holding back.

Too late she tried to let him go, but his arms tightened around her as he demanded the surrender she longed to give him. Alexa yielded, each kiss fuelling the excitement that swirled through her like rising smoke until it reached her brain and shut it down.

He tasted of love, of longing and hunger and anticipation. Ferocious pleasure cascaded through her, tearing her adrift from the world she'd always known.

When he stopped his passionate exploration she nuzzled his throat as he slid the strap of her top down her arm and followed his hand with slow, demanding kisses that liquefied her bones.

Her breath left her lungs in a moaning exclamation when he bit the smooth skin where her neck met her shoulder, gently catching her skin in strong white teeth.

Alexa knew she'd precipitated this, knew she wanted it, yet something tried to tell her that it was dangerous, terribly dangerous, and that she should pull away now while she was able to.

Except that she would die if he stopped.

Smiling blindly, helplessly, she lifted her arms and clung to him, offering herself, claiming him in the most primal and basic way of all.

She didn't resist when he picked her up. Silently she watched his face in the light of the candles while he carried her between the pillars and into the shadowed interior of the temple. Angular, stern, the handsome features revealed a self-discipline at odds with the curved fullness of his lower lip and the molten intensity of his gaze.

A sensuous rush of heat poured through her, tightening her breasts so that they thrust her nipples against the material of her top. Shuddering with delight, she accepted that if she went ahead with this she was putting her heart—her life—in the hands of a man who didn't love her.

It didn't matter. Luka wanted her and that was enough. She'd take whatever he could give, and seal this night in her heart for the rest of her life. Even if he never realised it, she'd give him the gift of her love.

As her grandmother had to her lover...

He stooped, lowering her until fine cotton cooled her hot skin, and she gazed around in astonishment. In the flickering, bobbing light of the candles through the columns she could barely discern the edges of a huge bed.

And then all coherent thought fled as Luka came down beside her. Eagerly she reached up, kissing and then licking the hollow at the base of the column of his neck where a pulse thudded rapidly.

A purring growl burst from deep in his throat. Eyes glinting like burning crystals, he thrust his hands into her hair and used the soft silk to push her head back onto the huge pillows.

Luka scanned the beautiful face raised to his, the creamy skin and the pale eyes, at once clear and blazing, as her slender fragrant body lifted against his in an involuntary invitation as old as Eve.

He could no longer resist her. Worse, he didn't want to. For the first time in his life passion fogged his brain, so that all he could think of was the hunger that devoured him, the need to bury himself deep into her and make her his own, to take everything he could from her and give in return the relentless pleasure that was already building towards a climax.

In the sensuous dimness Alexa could see nothing past the outline of his broad shoulders. Shyly she touched his face, her fingers tracing the wide cheekbones and the angular jut of his jaw, finding the contours of his mouth.

His chest expanded abruptly as he dragged in a harsh, impeded breath, and she sighed her relief into his mouth as his lips claimed hers again. When he lifted his head she was naked to the waist.

She held her breath as his mouth found her breast, and almost winced at the pleasure, keen and sharp as knives, that raced from his touch to the source of all her yearning.

'What is it?' he said against her skin, and she realised she was calling his name in a sobbing gasp. 'Alexa, tell me what you want. This…?' He moved to her other breast and the erotic torment began again.

'Or this?' he asked, the heel of one hand finding the tense, expectant place between her legs, pressing, then easing upwards in a tantalising torment.

She was ready for him, but instead of stripping her he contented himself with that tormenting imitation of the ultimate embrace until she arched into his skilful, knowledgeable, maddening hand.

'Take off my shirt,' he said.

Eyes by now accustomed to the darkness, it was a matter of moments to slide out the buttons and free him. Racked by intolerable hunger, she smoothed her hands over his shoulders and chest, delighted with the hard tensile strength of the muscles that flexed beneath her fingers.

'Yes,' he groaned.

He broke off when she slid her hand down between his trousers and his skin, her fingers delighted with the hard, hot force she found there.

Again that half-guttural, half-purring sound broke from his throat. 'Wait,' he said, and got up.

Before she had time to grieve for his absence he was back, his body as tanned and beautiful as the god for whom the temple had been built. With swift, deft movements he stripped her skirt from her and stood a moment looking down at her like a conqueror.

'I think I knew that first night,' he said, his voice harsh and dangerous, 'that this was where we'd end up.'

Words blocked her throat, refusing to be spoken. She held out her arms to him and he bent and kissed her with slow, purposeful skill until she was gasping and twisting beneath the caress of his mouth.

'Yes,' he said, that faint hint of an accent emphasised, 'now you know what it is to want as I want you...'

He positioned himself above her tense body, his long strong legs holding hers in place. She expected his previous control, but this time he thrust into her with a ferocity that almost stunned her.

It was like calling down the whirlwind. Taken over by a force beyond herself, Alexa choked out his name and moved with him, welcoming him inside her, clinging when he pulled away, winding her arms around the taut, bunched muscles of his back to hold him close to her, so that she would always remember how it felt to be his lover.

Faster and faster they moved in unison, until at last the fire swirling around Alexa tossed her into another place where sensation broke over her in merciless waves. She cried out and Luka followed her there, spilling into her as the currents of ecstasy drowned her in a sea of turbulent, erotic sensory overload.

She had no idea how long they lay there, still linked, their mutual rapture joining two people so far apart they should never have met, never have kissed, never have fallen in love.

Except, she thought, that she was the only one who loved.

But Luka had finally surrendered his formidable self-control. At the end he had wanted her as much, as recklessly, as she wanted him.

Weakly Alexa lay against him, storing up every second, every moment, every rise and fall of his chest, the sexy smell of their mingled sweat and lovemaking, the gentle swish of waves on the sand and the way the candlelight bobbed between the columns.

Eventually he turned onto his side and pulled her against him. 'When I originally came out to New Zealand,' he said quietly, 'I was planning to marry someone.'

A sneaking shame tarnished her indolence. No, she thought, no, oh, no…

But it had to be faced. She would, she promised herself in one painful flash of clarity, be mature about it. Huskily she asked, 'Are you still planning to marry her?'

'No.' He smoothed her hair back from her face, and looked into her eyes, his own hidden beneath his lashes. 'Even after we made love on the island I thought I could be like my father, using people for the good of Dacia.'

He pulled her into him so that she could feel his body coming to life again. With suppressed anger he said, 'I distrusted this violent physical attraction. At first I believed you were a modern woman, with a modern attitude to lovemaking, but when I had you investigated—'

'What?' She sat bolt upright.

'I had to find out what sort of woman I was dealing with.' A hint of arrogance brushed his voice as he pulled her down again. 'I was delighted to find that you were not in the habit of making love with every man you went out with—'

'Chauvinist,' she snapped.

'—because I hoped it meant that I affected you as strongly as you affected me.'

'How on earth did you make that out?'

He laughed and kissed the top of her head, and the throbbing little traitor in her throat. 'You made love with me the fourth time we were together,' he said outrageously.

Alexa thoughtfully sank her teeth into his shoulder. He laughed and tipped her head back, holding her in a grip that prevented movement and kept her clamped against his long, powerful body.

'My beautiful wildcat,' he said, his voice low and rough. 'I was certain that this overpowering sexual need would die when I left New Zealand, but you lodged in my mind, in my memory, like a delicious, tantalising burr beneath a saddle. After weeks of aching for you, missing you so badly that my life lost all colour and flavour, I became totally convinced that I am not like my father, able to cut my life into compartments. Fortunately I had made no overtures to my prospective bride.'

'Is she unhappy?' Alexa asked worriedly.

'No. We are very good friends, but it would have been one of those marriages of convenience you were so scornful about.'

It seemed impossible that any woman could not fall in love with Luka. Putting the princess aside for the moment, she asked, 'Why didn't you come back to New Zealand sooner?'

He paused, then said deliberately, 'I didn't know what to do. I've never felt like this before.'

'And you resented it,' she guessed.

'Resented it?' He sounded surprised.

She nodded vigorously into his chest. 'I resented it too. I was really enjoying my life and then you smashed into it, and after a while I knew nothing was ever going to be the same again. And I hate being unhappy!'

'We're a prickly pair,' he said with an odd note of laughter in his voice. 'Yes, I was angry that you could turn my life to ashes. When Alex wanted to meet you I offered my services, hoping that I would be able to look at you dispassionately as just another beautiful woman.'

'Oh, did you?' she said ominously, trying to wrench herself free of his grip.

He laughed softly and tightened his arms around her, kissing her angry, mutinous mouth with such seducing sweetness that she almost surrendered.

Luka said, 'And of course I was utterly wrong. When I saw you again I knew that you were the woman I would love until the end of my days.'

'Why didn't you say something?' she demanded, radiant with joy.

'I was sure I had made you despise me beyond recovery—and if you didn't, I thought it might be just this violence of passion, and die as swiftly as it had sprung into life, like a grass fire in summer.'

Alexa gasped as he ran an exploratory hand down her body, but before she could answer he said harshly, 'And this generous passion you give me is wonderful, but not enough. So I told you lies about Ianthe of Illyria not being able to travel so that I could persuade you to come here. And I told myself that I wouldn't make love to you.'

'I know,' she said into his shoulder. 'You posted "Keep Off" signs all around you.'

He laughed quietly. 'Being you, of course, you took no notice of them.'

Alexa's anger was fading swiftly and she couldn't help asking, 'Are you sorry?'

He kissed her. 'How can I be sorry when you can take me to heaven with one sideways glance?' He ran a hand over her back. 'When you agreed to come to Dacia I told myself that I must give you back the freedom I took from you in New Zealand. So I tried to hold aloof.' He laughed a little ironically. 'That lasted for exactly fifty-two hours.'

His grin at her sudden snort of laughter faded quickly. In a steady, almost unemotional tone he went on, 'So will you marry me, Alexa, my sweet one, my heart's delight? I love you very much, and I'm going slowly mad without you.'

She hesitated, but it had to be said. 'Even though it seems I might be related to the Illyrian Prince, I'm just an ordinary New Zealand woman—'

'I am not,' he said dangerously, 'asking you to marry me because you have some connection with Alex Considine. I would want to marry you no matter who you were. Trust is a two-way thing. Can you not trust me sufficiently to understand that you are the centre of my world, the woman I hold at my heart's core? Before I met you I was lonely, so alone and so accustomed to it that I didn't even realise it. You filled my empty heart with your vitality and your spirit and your laughter. If you won't marry me I shall never marry.'

Alexa's eyes filled with tears. 'I do trust you, and I want to marry you very much.'

'Does that mean you love me?'

'Of *course* I love you,' she spluttered. 'I think I must have fallen in love with you when Sandra Beauchamp was doing her impersonation of a piranha before that banquet!'

'I knew you wanted me,' he said in a shaken voice, holding her close. 'I hoped you'd learn to love me enough to put up with the disadvantages of living in a goldfish bowl. It seems unfair to ask you to marry me when you have no idea what you'd be getting into.'

'I don't care,' she said in a stark, stripped tone. 'I'll be with you. That's all that matters.'

But it wasn't. And those perceptive eyes saw her realisation of this. 'What is it, my darling?' he asked against her forehead. 'Whatever it is we can deal with it, I swear. If you hate the idea of living in the full glare of the media we can rapidly turn into a boring old married couple.'

Heart exulting, she said, 'It's not that.'

'Then tell me what it is.'

'Do you really trust me?' she asked quietly. 'Enough not to doubt me? I couldn't live with suspicion all the time, Luka. I love you too much. I want everything of you.'

She held her breath, but he didn't hesitate. 'I have to trust the breath in my body,' he said simply. 'I must have trusted you from the beginning. Not that I recognised it.' He paused. 'But I was certain you wouldn't go to the police with a story of abduction, and when I told you who your father was I didn't even ask myself if you would try to make money from such a story. It never occurred to me. So the trust was there, my heart, right from the start, and perhaps I should ask your pardon for ever doubting it.'

Alexa shuddered with relief. 'I'm glad,' she said inadequately.

He said soberly, 'I can't promise I'll be easy to live with, but I know in my heart and my soul that my love is safe with you, and I promise that I will take the greatest care of yours. It may take me a while to become confident enough to stop being jealous whenever you smile at another man. I can't even offer you a tranquil life. All I can promise is to love you with everything I am, everything I have, for ever.'

His stark, stripped words convinced her. She'd make him so happy he'd forget about his childhood, she vowed. Lifting her head, she looked him in the eyes.

'And I love you with everything I am,' she said unevenly, pronouncing each word like a vow. 'For ever and always, with every part of me.'

He kissed her and she melted against him.

A long time later he yawned and said lazily, 'We'll have to eat something or Carlotta will know that love has stolen all our appetites but one.'

'She knows,' Alexa said into his chest. 'Why else did she set the scene for seduction? I'll bet she thought you were being very odd last night not to stay. Mmm, you smell so good...'

'Not as good as you.' He swung off the bed and stooped to pick her up.

Alexa looked up into his beloved face. 'If you plan to jump into the water again with me,' she threatened sweetly, 'I'll do unmentionable things to you.'

A white flash in the darkness revealed his smile. 'You are a miracle,' he said quietly. 'I treated you so badly, yet you love me in spite of it. Now, if you'll put at least a layer of clothes on we can eat, and then I'll endeavour to work out how I can tactfully tell Alex Considine that he has a bride to give away.'

Three months later her half-uncle escorted her to the altar in the splendid church she'd seen from the road her first day in Dacia.

Alex Considine, Prince of Illyria, stepped back with a

smile, glancing for a moment at his now obviously pregnant wife, who smiled lovingly at him.

Clad in a silk dress the same colour as her skin, swathed in the veil that Ianthe of Illyria had worn at her wedding, Alexa looked up at the face of the man she loved.

Half an hour previously she'd panicked, but now, warmed by the special smile that was hers alone, she was totally confident. With the exquisite emerald engagement ring Luka had had made for her safely on her right hand, she held out her left and put it into his, and together they turned towards the altar and made their vows to their future.

A ROYAL
PROPOSITION

by

Marion Lennox

Marion Lennox was born on an Australian dairy farm. She moved on – mostly because the cows weren't interested in her stories! Marion writes for Medical Romance™ as well as Tender Romance™. Initially, she used a different name for each category, so if you're looking for past books, search also for author Trisha David.

In her non-writing life Marion cares (haphazardly) for her husband, teenagers, dogs, cats, chickens and anyone else who lines up at her dinner table. She fights her rampant garden (she's losing), and her house dust (she's lost). She also travels, which she finds seriously addictive.

As a teenager Marion was told she'd never get anywhere reading romance. Now romance is the basis of her stories: her stories allow her to travel, and if ever there was an advertisement for following your dream, she'd be it!

Also out this month is Marion Lennox's fabulous new novel
Princess of Convenience
from Mills & Boon Tender Romance™

CHAPTER ONE

'ALASTAIR, I know you and Belle are planning to marry, but you *must* marry Penny-Rose first.'

Silence. Marguerite de Castaliae looked as unruffled as if she'd just talked of the weather, but Alastair and Belle were staring at her as if she'd dropped a bomb.

'What are you saying?' It was Alastair who first found his voice. His Serene Highness, Alastair, Prince de Castaliae dug his hands deep into the pockets of his faded jeans. His dark eyes closed. What now? He didn't need his mother making crazy propositions. Not when he had so much else to think of...

If this inheritance didn't go through, the village faced ruin. After months of effort, he'd found no way to save it. His own fortune couldn't save this place. Nothing could.

Today he'd reached a final, joyless decision. He'd been up since dawn inspecting the cattle with stock agents, working out how much they'd make at market. He'd come in to make a final bleak phone call to his accountants. They'd given him their verdict and it was all looking futile.

The banks would never finance such a venture. The estate would have to be sold.

So Alastair was exhausted, and he didn't need this.

'Marry someone else? That's ridiculous.'

'It's not ridiculous.' His mother was wearing her I'm-about-to-solve-all-your-problems smile. 'My dear, you do *want* to be a prince?' She was probing, fishing for a reaction.

She found it. 'No!' Alastair turned to stare out the window, over the castle's lush gardens to the river beyond. 'No,' he said again. His voice was surer still, and there was

5

revulsion in his tone. 'It was Louis who was supposed to inherit all this. Not me.'

'But Louis is dead, dear,' Marguerite reminded him. 'And I won't even pretend I'm sorry, because he would have made a very bad prince. If he'd inherited…'

'It was his right to inherit.'

'He drank that right away,' his mother retorted. 'He was a wastrel and a fool, and now he's dead. So now the title is yours. And the responsibilities.'

'I never wanted it.'

'But it's yours for the taking.' Marguerite's gaze shifted from her son to her future daughter-in-law, and her probing eyes were thoughtful. 'If you want it badly enough,' she said gently. 'And if Belle wants it.' Her voice became questioning again. 'I'd imagine Belle would rather like to own this castle and be your princess?'

'Belle doesn't care about titles,' Alastair said shortly. 'Just as I don't.'

Marguerite wasn't as sure of that as her son was, but she kept her face deliberately expressionless. This tiny Castaliae principality, tucked between France and the rest of Europe, might be a very small player on the world stage, but it was a lovely place to live—and maybe a wonderful place to rule?

Wealth and position might very well appeal to Belle, she thought, but she'd have to use other ways to persuade her son.

'Alastair, the people here need you,' she told him. 'The country is depending on you.'

'We've been over this.'

'Yes, dear, but you're not listening. If you don't inherit, there's no one else to take it on.' These were hard facts to be faced, and the sooner her son faced them the better.

'If you don't accept it, the estate will be carved up and the title will disappear,' she told him. 'Most of the people who've lived here all their lives will face losing their own homes. Then the village houses will be bought by holidaymakers who'll only live here for three or four weekends a year.'

'No!' said Alastair, outraged.

'Of course not. None of us want that.' She was getting through. All she could see of her son was his strongly muscled back, but it was expressive enough. Alastair had been brought up to accept responsibility. Marguerite had every hope that he'd accept it now.

Despite Belle.

Or even with Belle's assistance...

Alastair was a good son, she thought fondly. A son to be proud of. Until his recent involvement with Belle, Alastair de Castaliae had been considered to be one of Europe's most eligible bachelors.

Well, why not? Of royal blood and with an inherited fortune, he'd been attractive even as a child. Time had added to his good looks until, at thirty-two, his mother— and a fair percentage of the principality's female population—considered him perfectly splendid.

The tragedy in his background did nothing to lessen his appeal. In fact, the distance he'd placed between himself and the rest of the world since Lissa's death had seemed only to make him more desirable.

And he *was* desirable, his mother decided, trying to look at him without bias. Alastair was six feet two in his socks— and his muscled, taut and tanned frame made him seem even taller. He was smoulderingly dark. His jet black hair, his crinkling, brown eyes and his wide, white smile had made many a girl's heart melt.

Just as his father's smile had melted her own heart all those years ago...

Sternly Marguerite blinked back unexpected tears and returned to the job at hand. Emotion wasn't any use here. It wouldn't convince Alastair—he'd held himself emotionally distant after Lissa died—and she was almost convinced that Belle didn't have any emotion to play with.

'It's only for a year.'

'What's only for a year?' Alastair turned back to face his mother, his brow drawn heavily over his deep-set eyes. 'You sound as if you have this whole thing arranged.'

'Well, I do,' she said apologetically. 'Someone has to think of the future. You've been so involved getting the estate back into working order—making sure all the workers are paid, organising the rebuilding of the stonework, doing all the work caused by two such sudden deaths—that you haven't had time to look at the whole picture. So if you'll only listen...'

'I'm listening.'

It was the best she could hope for, but he was still glowering. And all she could do was explain.

'Our problems are all caused by Louis's father changing the inheritance,' she told him. 'Louis's dissolute ways were giving him nightmares, so he put in the clause—'

'I know this.' Of course he knew. After all, Louis had bleated to him of it often enough, and the clause was the nub of his problems now. Alastair's brow descended even further. 'It decreed that Louis marry a woman of unimpeachable virtue or he couldn't inherit.'

'Yes.' Marguerite tried very hard not to look at Belle. What she was about to say now wouldn't be easy. Alastair already understood about the clause—but did Belle? 'Your uncle couldn't predict that Louis would end up in the grave three months after his own death. And now it's left us in a mess, because the clause applies to anyone inheriting the title—which includes you.'

Silence. Then...

'Contrary to what the lawyers are saying,' Alastair said softly, in a voice that sounded almost dangerous, 'Belle *is* a woman of unimpeachable virtue.'

'No, dear, she's not.' Marguerite refused to be silenced. There was no easy way to say this but both Belle and Alastair had to face it. She'd been saving it for when Alastair saw how bleak his position was, and that time was now.

'You know it, or you wouldn't be spending all this time with the accountants,' she went on. 'The lawyers are all of the same opinion. Your cousins are prepared to take legal action to see that the estate's sold and divided, and if you marry Belle that's exactly what will happen.'

'Just because Belle's been married before—'

.'And also because she's had affairs, ever since she was a teenager.' Marguerite did look at Belle now, and her tone softened. 'I'm sorry, my dear,' she told her, 'but it's time for plain speaking.'

'Go right ahead,' Belle told her. Alastair's companion sat with her hands loosely clasped on her elegantly crossed knees. She was wearing a chic, black dress, her silk-stockinged legs looked as if they went on for ever and her expression, rather than seeming offended, seemed coolly calculating. She tilted her head, causing her sleek bob of auburn hair to glint in the sunlight. It made a striking impression, and she knew it. 'So I'm not a woman of unimpeachable virtue. Fine. Don't mind me.'

'I do mind you, dear,' Marguerite said apologetically. 'But the cousins have been digging up dirt. I gather you had an affair with a married man when his wife was pregnant…'

Belle's beautiful face shuttered down at that. 'That was ten years ago. It's hardly relevant.'

'The lawyers say it is. And it means that if Alastair marries you, he can't inherit.'

'Which is damnable,' Alastair snapped, and his mother nodded in agreement. But her face didn't look hopeless.

'Yes, dear, it is damnable, but it's also avoidable.'

'I'm marrying Belle!'

'But if you waited for a little—'

'No.'

'Just a moment.' Belle rose, stretched, cat-like, and crossed to where Alastair was standing. And as she did, his mother had to acknowledge why her son had been attracted to her.

Falling in love had never been an issue for Alastair. Not after Lissa. However, he'd rarely been without a beautiful companion, and Belle was certainly beautiful. She was magnificently groomed and chic and incredibly feminine. She spoke three languages, which, in this tiny border principality, was a huge advantage, and her social skills were polished to perfection. Even in Alastair's present occupation as a Paris architect, she'd be a hostess to be proud of.

Belle was sleek and feline and clever, and she'd spent a lot of effort persuading Alastair that marriage could suit them both. For maybe the hundredth time, Marguerite wondered how she could get on with such a daughter-in-law.

But Belle wasn't thinking of marriage now—at least, not her own. Not yet. She laid one beautifully manicured finger on Alastair's arm and turned to face Marguerite, her intelligence focussed. 'Tell us your plan,' she said softly, and with a stab of triumph Marguerite realised just how hungry for the title this woman was.

She'd thought that she would be. Married to Alastair while he worked as a Paris architect, Belle would have had wealth and position, but here was the chance of more. With the death of Louis—with the chance of inheriting this magnificent estate—came the title of Prince and Princess and money to keep them in unimaginable luxury for the rest of their lives. It was a windfall Belle would reach out and grasp with both hands.

If she could.

But the old man's will stood between them. *'A woman of unimpeachable virtue…'*

'Tell us your plan,' Belle said again, and it was as much as Marguerite could do not to sigh with relief. She sat back and closed her eyes for one millisecond—to give her enough space to gather her thoughts. Then she started.

'Penny-Rose,' she said.

'Who's Penny-Rose?' Alastair demanded.

'The woman you need to marry. For a year.'

* * *

Penny-Rose O'Shea settled the final stone into the dirt with a satisfied slap. Great. Finished! It had taken her all morning to choose the slabs that would be the foundation of her wall. It was immensely satisfying work, and Penny-Rose was satisfied.

She was also extremely hot.

Midday had arrived without her realising. She put up a hand to wipe sweat from her face, and felt ingrained dirt smudge thickly across her cheek. Urk! A beauty queen she wasn't!

Never mind. It was good, honest dirt, she thought happily. She was doing what she wanted to do, and by evening she'd be even dirtier. Also, she'd have the next layer of stones complete. Building walls designed to last a thousand years might not be everyone's cup of tea, but it was hers and she loved it.

'Penny-Rose!' She looked up to find her boss waving to her from the other end of the wall.

Was he reminding her of lunch? That was strange. Bert didn't usually remind his workers it was time to knock off, but she rose gratefully to her feet.

But he wasn't reminding her of lunch.

'You're wanted,' he told her, thumbing toward the castle. 'By them indoors.'

'What?'

'You heard what I said.' Bert's weather-worn face creased even further with a puzzlement that matched hers. 'Someone came out just now and said could we send you inside. Pronto. There's no mistake.'

'They want me to go inside?' Penny-Rose stared at her boss in disbelief, and then stared down at herself. She was wearing begrimed overalls, her shoulder-length chestnut curls were twisted into a knot under her filthy cap and every inch of her was covered with dust. She grimaced. 'Why?'

'They sent a message saying they want to see you, and that's all I know,' her boss said patiently.

'You're kidding.' She glanced up at the forbidding ancestral home, where those who'd issued the summons were hidden.

'They can see me by looking out their windows,' she told her boss, and she grinned. 'That way I won't besmirch their ancestral floors.'

'Don't be clever, lass.' Bert, normally the kindest of bosses, was perturbed and it showed. 'I don't know what they want, and I can't say I like it. Do you want me to come in with you?'

'Yeah, take him with you, Penny-Rose,' one of the lads called. The whole stone-walling team was fascinated at this unexpected twist of events, and the cheekiest of the men came to his own conclusion. 'Maybe the new prince has decided to increase his harem.'

'Or maybe that other one—what's her name, Belle? Maybe she thinks our Penny-Rose is prettier and she's decided to tear her eyes out,' another added, and his comment was greeted by hoots of laughter.

The entire team was in on the conversation now. They were all male, mostly a lot older than Penny-Rose, and concern for their protégée was behind their good-natured banter.

'How would they know our Penny-Rose is prettier? *We* only see her for five minutes every morning before the dust settles back,' one demanded.

'She is pretty, though,' the first lad said stubbornly. 'Real pretty. If the prince saw her without her dirt…'

'Well, he hasn't.'

'His mother has.'

'Not without her dirt, and, anyway, what's that got to do with the price of eggs?'

'No, lass…' Bert cut across the banter and his eyes were still troubled. 'Seriously, they've asked to see you. You spoke to the old lady, didn't you? You didn't say anything to upset her?'

'No.' Penny-Rose wiped filthy hands on her overalls, thinking fast. 'At least, I don't think so.'

Penny-Rose had arrived at the castle with the team of Yorkshire stone-wallers six weeks ago, and she'd had her hands full ever since. There was so much to be done! After years of neglect, the west farmyard walls had almost entirely collapsed, and if they weren't mended soon, the north and south walls would do the same.

So she hadn't had time for socialising. The only contact she'd had with the titled landholders had been a conversation with the castle's elderly mistress.

Marguerite had been out walking, and had come across a stooped figure sorting stones. 'Good heavens, it's a girl,' the woman had said, startled, and Penny-Rose had chuckled. She'd deferentially hauled off her cap, letting her curls tumble to her shoulders.

'Yes, ma'am.'

'You're part of the stone-walling team?' the woman had demanded, her amazement deepening, and Rose had smiled and once more agreed.

'That's right.'

'But the team's from Yorkshire.'

'And I'm not from Yorkshire.'

'Now, how did I guess that? Where are you from?'

'Australia.'

'Australia!' The woman's eyes had still been creased in astonishment. 'Why on earth are you here?'

'I'm working with the best stone-wallers in the world,' Penny-Rose had told her, not without pride. 'I'm gaining my master-waller's certificate, and when I'm finished training, I can go home and demand my price.'

Then Penny-Rose had looked up at the castle where the soft gold sandstone turrets and battlements shone in all their glory, as they'd shone for almost a thousand years. Her green eyes had twinkled in appreciation of the beauty around her.

'It's great work,' she'd said softly. 'It almost makes up for having to work in the shadow of rickety old shanties like this.'

The woman laughed, seeming genuinely amused. She stayed for some time, seemingly intrigued by Penny-Rose's work. Her questions were gently probing, but maybe it was her right to probe the background of workers on her son's estate. Penny-Rose thought no more of it, and when the woman left, she felt as if she'd made a new friend.

But now...

Had she taken her joking seriously? Was she about to send a message through Penny-Rose that the team was no longer required?

Help...

'Do you want me to come in with you?' Bert asked again, her worry mirrored in his eyes. This was an important job, and both of them knew there was a lot at stake. 'Not that I think you have any need to worry, but I can't think of any reason they'd want you.'

'They're hardly likely to toss me into the oubliette for insubordination.'

'Have you been insubordinate?'

'Only a little bit,' she confessed with a rueful smile. 'Not very much.'

He groaned. 'Well, don't be now. Get in there and grovel, and only say nice things about your boss. That's me. Remember?' Penny-Rose had never been reluctant to give a bit of cheek, and Bert shook his head at her. 'Know your place, girl, and, short of letting the prince have his wicked way with you, agree to anything. I can always back out later.'

He meant he could always dismiss her, she thought, her laughter fading. If it was a choice of Penny-Rose or the team, it had to be the team.

Maybe she had been too cheeky. Was the aristocracy so sensitive? Heavens, why didn't she learn to keep her mouth shut? Still, if damage had been done, it was she who'd have to undo it.

'If I'm not back in a week, demand entry to the dungeons,' she said, more lightly than she felt. She looked down at her grimy self and thought of what she was facing. 'You really mean go right now?'

'I mean go right now,' Bert said heavily. 'That's what the aristocracy wants, so that's what the aristocracy gets.'

They were waiting.

Penny-Rose walked up through the terraced gardens toward the main castle entrance and found the head gardener waiting. They walked into the courtyard where a butler was waiting in turn. He gave her a wintry smile, turned and led her into the house.

And what a house!

The castle had been built in the twelfth century and maintained by fastidious owners ever since. Castaliae was one of the few countries in the world where the royal family had never deviated from direct succession. It had led to a certain simplicity—the family were the de Castaliaes, the estate was Castaliae and so was the country.

It was confusing maybe, but it certainly must make ordering letterheads easier, Penny-Rose had decided when she'd first learned about the place. And now, looking around the ancestral home of the country's rulers, she saw other advantages of continuous succession. The halls were filled with exquisite furniture, gathered over a thousand years, the walls were hung with fabulous tapestries and the whole place was filled with light and colour from a building designed far in advance of its time.

Every south face had been used to effect—no one here had worried about window taxes—and sunlight streamed in everywhere.

The Castaliae family had been known to sit on the fence for all the castle's history, Penny-Rose knew. The independence of this tiny principality was a tribute to the political savvy of its royal family.

Penny-Rose glanced about her with awe as she was led from room to room. For a twenty-six-year-old Australian, this was new and wonderful indeed. She almost forgot to be nervous.

Almost. She remembered again the moment she entered the great hall.

They were waiting for her.

She knew them by sight. Marguerite, of course. The new prince's elderly mother. She was the woman who'd spoken to her in the garden, and her smile was warm and welcoming.

Then there was Belle. Although it wasn't official, rumour had it that she was engaged to be married to the prince. She was a cold fish, the boys had decided, but it didn't stop them admiring her good points. She might be a cold fish, but she was a very beautiful cold fish. Belle didn't move from her seat now, and she certainly didn't smile.

And, of course, there was Alastair. Alastair de Castaliae… His Serene Highness, they said, if he could figure out the inheritance hiccups.

And why shouldn't he be the prince? she thought. He certainly had the look of it. He might be dressed for farm-work now, in an ancient pair of moleskins and a shirt that was grubby and frayed at the cuffs, but he was still drop-dead gorgeous, with a smile to die for.

Mmm! He was smiling now—sort of—as he rose to greet her. It was a smile that stilled her nerves and caught her attention as nothing else could. What a smile. And what a…

Well, what a man!

Penny-Rose had never had time to play round with the opposite sex but a lack of time had never stopped her appreciating what was in front of her. And this one was worth appreciating! He was tall, lean and hard-muscled, with long, long legs, and…

And she wasn't a schoolgirl, she reminded herself sharply. She was twenty-six years old, and she had too many responsibilities to be distracted by any man, much less royalty!

So, with an effort, she pulled her attention away from thoughts which were totally out of place. What on earth did they want?

The prince, gorgeous as he was, was looking at her like he wasn't seeing her. Belle was watching her with a calculating expression Penny-Rose didn't like. It was only Marguerite who was smiling as if she meant it.

'Penny-Rose. How lovely. Will you sit down?'

Sit? Good grief! She looked at the plush cream settee and fought a desire to giggle.

'Um…I'm afraid I'd leave a signature,' she said, and received a swift appraising look from Alastair for her pains. 'If it's all right with you, ma'am, I'm just as happy standing. If you'd just tell me what you want, I'll be off before I spread dirt everywhere.'

'But we need to get to know you,' Alastair said, in a voice that sounded as if he didn't believe what he was saying.

Penny-Rose shook her head. She'd hauled off her cap before she'd come inside so her curls bounced around her shoulders and dust floated free. 'You don't need to get to know me, and I'm not dressed for socialising.' OK, she was being blunt but she was at a disadvantage and she didn't like it. Belle was looking at her like she was some sort of interesting insect, and kowtowing to those higher up the aristocratic ladder had never come naturally to Penny-Rose.

'Just for a minute.' Alastair's voice was strained to breaking point, and she cast him an unsure glance. What was wrong with the man?

'My boss can tell you about me,' she said discouragingly. 'Or are you intending to get to know the whole team better?' That made an interesting plan, but it didn't make her smile. She felt more and more like an insect brought in as part of a collection, and she didn't like the feeling one bit.

'No, but—' Marguerite started.

'Let's just tell her what we want,' Alastair said heavily.

'Don't confuse her any further.' His eyes hadn't left Penny-Rose's face, and they didn't leave it now.

He seemed nice, Penny-Rose thought inconsequentially. He also seemed exhausted, strained to the limit, but still very, very nice. His voice was deep and grave and soft, and he sounded as if he was concerned for her.

His English was excellent—well, it would be, as his mother was English. It was only his words that were troubled.

'I'll come to the point,' he told her, speaking slowly as if measuring each word.

'What my mother wishes to know—what we all wish to know—is whether or not you can be persuaded to marry me.'

For a long, long moment nothing stirred. She stared at them in turn, taking in each of their faces. All of them looked...for heaven's sake, they looked as if they were serious!

'You have to be joking,' she said at last, and it was as much as she could do to find her voice. Her words came out a sort of high-pitched squeak. She coughed and tried again. 'I mean...you are joking, right?'

'I'm not joking.' The look of strain on his face intensified. 'Would I joke about something so serious?'

'Yeah, right.' Her eyes narrowed. 'Did you say marry?'

'I said marry.'

'Then you're either having a laugh at my expense or you're all about in the head,' she said bluntly. 'Either way, I don't think I should stay.' She gave them a last wild look. 'I...I'll see myself out, shall I?'

She didn't wait for an answer. She took herself out of the door and out of the castle, without a backward glance.

CHAPTER TWO

THE prince found Penny-Rose an hour later, when she'd been persuaded, against her better judgement, to go back to work. She was sorting stones and Alastair came up behind her so suddenly that she missed a couple of heartbeats.

As before, his voice was deep and soft and calm—as if nothing lay between them at all.

'Why do they call you Penny-Rose? Why not just Penelope or Penny? Or even Rose?'

As a question it was harmless enough, but the situation was ludicrous. She caught her breath, regretted her missed heartbeats—while this man was around she needed all the heartbeats she could get—sat back on her heels and glared.

The fact that his shirt was open at the throat and the sun was shining on the wispy curls on his chest didn't help at all…

Good grief! Cut it out, she told herself. Put your hormones on the back burner!

'Bert says I'm not to fraternise with the upper classes any more,' she said frankly. 'You've had your joke. If you want something else, ask Bert. Go away.' Already she could see her boss rising from where he'd been working. He'd been disbelieving when she'd told him what had happened, and then he'd been furious.

'It's their idea of a sick joke,' he'd said. 'It's too bad we're not back in England where I can have a word with the union.'

But they weren't back in England. They were in this tiny principality where normal rules didn't apply, and if Bert wanted to keep his team employed he had to bite his tongue and tell her to get on with stone-walling as if nothing had happened.

'They're paying excellent rates, lass,' he'd told her. 'The best. And we've gone to a lot of expense to get over here. We put up with it if we can, for the good of the team, but you're not to go near them again. Just keep working and forget it.'

So she'd agreed. It had been a big thing for Bert to take on a female apprentice, and she wanted to make it as trouble-free for him as possible. But now this creep wouldn't leave her alone.

'Go away,' she said again, and turned back to her stones. She concentrated fiercely on fitting a neat wedge between two blocks and refused to look at him.

Thankfully she heard Bert's heavy footsteps, and then her boss's Yorkshire accent. 'I'd be grateful if you could speak through me if you have anything to say to the workers, sir.' Bert's words were deferential enough, but his tone was pure bulldog.

She risked a glance up, and to her surprise she saw Alastair raking his fingers through his ruffled black hair. It was a gesture that made him seem almost as bewildered as she was.

And it was gesture that suddenly made him seem much less of a prince—and much more human.

And much more…hormone-confusing?

Get back to work, she told herself fiercely, turning back to her ill-fitting stone. Forget your stupid hormones. And don't look again!

'I need to speak to Penny—'

'Penny-Rose isn't speaking to you. She's heard what you have to say and it doesn't make sense. So leave the lass be.'

'I'm not offering her any indecent proposals.'

'If you were, I'd take my team and walk off your land right now,' Bert told him. 'Money or no money. Penny-

Rose is a good lass and a damned fine worker, and I won't have her badgered.'

Wow! Under her cap, she felt her ears go pink with pleasure. Praise from Bert was hard to earn, and valued for what it was. She'd worked hard to get this far.

And for Bert to offer to withdraw his team on her behalf... Goodness!

But Alastair was still trying to speak. 'I don't—'

'Look, what is it you want?' Bert said, exasperated. 'You've upset the lass, you've upset me. If you have anything reasonable to say, then say it. Now. In front of Penny-Rose. Clear the air, like. And then we can say no and get on with our work.'

'I hope you won't say no.'

Bert was getting angrier by the minute.

'Well, what is it?'

'As I said, I want to marry Penny-Rose,' Alastair told him, putting his hands up as if to deflect the storm of protest he knew Bert was capable of. 'I want to marry her for a year. As a business proposition. Nothing more.'

The silence went on for several moments. Penny-Rose stayed crouched by her stones. She wouldn't look up but her fingers had ceased even trying to fit her rocks together.

This was crazy.

She left the answering to Bert, because she couldn't think of a thing to say. Even the normally voluble Bert was having trouble.

'Where I'm from,' Bert said at last, in a voice that sounded as if he'd been winded, 'people don't take brides as business propositions. They take brides for life.' His belligerent jaw jutted forward. 'And just the one of them at that. The locals say you're engaged to some woman up in the house. Well, then. You hang onto her and leave our Penny-Rose alone. Bigamy is something I don't hold with and never shall, and if you so much as come near our lass—'

'This isn't bigamy.'

'Look, I don't know what your rules are—'

'I imagine my rules are exactly the same as yours,' Alastair said wearily, and once again his fingers raked his hair. He looked like he was finding this impossible. 'I'm not intending to marry twice. Or…not at once.'

This was getting crazier and crazier.

'What we want here,' Bert said conversationally, and speaking to the world in general, 'is a strait-jacket. Anyone got one?'

Amazingly, it was Penny-Rose who came to the prince's defence. That last gesture of his had got to her. For some reason this didn't seem like someone making indecent propositions. This seemed like a man at the end of his tether.

'Give him a break, Bert.' She rose and shrugged off some dirt. Then she stood back so there was distance—and Bert—between them, but her eyes met Alastair's and held.

And her chin tilted. This was the look she used when she was meeting trouble head on, and she had a feeling she was meeting it now.

This man's trouble.

'Let him say what he wants,' she told her boss. 'He isn't making sense, but we might as well listen.'

The silence stretched out under the afternoon sun, and in the stillness Penny-Rose was aware that Alastair's gaze never left hers. Their eyes were locked, and it was as if there were questions being asked—and answered—without words being spoken.

And whatever the questions were, her answers must have satisfied him because he gave a slight nod, as if he'd come to a final decision. Some of the confusion left his face.

'It could work.'

'What could work?' Bert asked belligerently, and Penny-Rose laid a hand on her boss's arm.

'Let him say.'

And he did. 'I'm serious,' he said at last, his eyes still fixed on hers. 'I don't have a choice. If I don't marry a lady of unimpeachable virtue, this entire estate will be split.'

'I don't understand,' Bert told him.

'It's the terms of the old prince's will,' Alastair said wearily. 'If I don't make such a marriage then the estate will be sold and, no matter how I look at it, there's no way I can buy it. God knows, I've tried every way over the past couple of months, but the thing's impossible. I'd assume the castle itself will go to the government and be opened to the public as a tourist venue, but the acreage around here will be split up.'

Bert frowned, but he wasn't too surprised. He'd heard the rumours. 'And the village?'

'That's the hard part,' Alastair told him. 'It's the reason I'm considering such a marriage. There are over a hundred families living around the estate. All of those homes will have to be sold, and the cousins who stand to inherit stipulate that they'll be sold on the open market.' He paused and gazed around him, over the river banks to the village beyond. 'I guess you've realised by now how desirable this place is?'

It was. The Castaliae estate contained a fairy-tale village built on the cliffs of one of the most picturesque rivers in the world.

But it still wasn't making sense. Bert was still confused.

'So?' Bert demanded.

'So they'll be sold for a fortune,' Alastair said simply. 'We know that. It's already happened to villages like ours that haven't been protected by one landlord. The locals are well enough off, but they're not so wealthy that they can match the prices of city dwellers and overseas interests.'

He sighed, his gaze returning from the far-off village to the girl before him. Now he was talking directly to her. 'If I can't save it, the village will be deserted in winter and filled with wealthy tourists and designer shops in the summer. The locals will have to move away. They can't bear it, and I can't bear it. So I'm asking you, Penny-Rose, to marry me. If you'll have me.'

More silence.

Penny-Rose's gaze didn't waver. She took him in. Not just his amazing good looks, but the grubbiness of his clothes—he wasn't nearly as dirty as she was, but he obviously hadn't had time to change since he'd been out working with his farm manager this morning—the tension of his stance and the dark shadows under his eyes. He looked like a man close to breaking point.

Then, finally, she allowed herself to look around, at the land he was talking of.

This estate went on for ever. The castle itself was built into the cliff overlooking the river, and at the base of the cliff was a tiny village. Penny-Rose was boarding with a family there, and they thought of this man as their landlord.

But this was indeed a fairy-tale village, with its soft sandstone buildings set into the cliffs on the gently flowing river. Alastair was right. Tourists would outbid any villagers for their homes. And if he couldn't bear to have the villagers evicted, she could understand why not.

'It's a stupid clause,' she said at last, and Alastair nodded.

'It is. My uncle put it in place because my cousin was…wild. What it did was to stop Louis marrying at all, and then Louis died just three months after his father.'

'So why don't you just do what Louis did? Not marry?' It seemed a reasonable solution. Surely the gorgeous Belle could be talked into being a mistress only—with so much money at stake!

'I can't inherit unless I marry.'

'But Louis inherited.'

Alastair shook his head, and the impression of weariness intensified. 'Louis never formally inherited, and the cousins started legal action to recover the property. His death forestalled that, and legal opinion is that the estate and the title is now mine—as long as I *do* marry. As long as I do what Louis didn't.'

'And…your Belle's not a lady of virtue?' Bert butted in. He had things in his stride here—almost. His fierce intelligence was working overtime. 'No?'

'Belle's a wonderful woman,' Alastair said quickly. 'But there are…shadows…in her past.'

'I'd imagine there might be.' Bert's team had little time for a woman they'd decided from the first was prone to giving herself airs. On the first few days of working here there'd been a wall collapse on one of the men. Belle had been seen at the window, watching, but hadn't enquired as to the state of Steve's health or even sent down to ask whether she should contact an ambulance.

With Bert carrying a cellphone, her disinterest had been a minor enough offence and hadn't mattered, but it had rankled.

'What…?' Bert said slowly, his eyes moving from Penny-Rose to Alastair and back again. 'What makes you think our lass here is any different? Virtue-wise, that is?'

'Hey!' Penny-Rose said, shocked into comment. 'Can we leave my virtue out of it?'

'Well, that's it. We can't,' Alastair said heavily. 'My mother—'

'I might have known she'd come into it somewhere.' Bert seemed to be almost enjoying himself now. He had the solid workman's view of the aristocracy, and he didn't mind this man's discomfort. 'Now, there's a lady of virtue.'

Marguerite, when she'd heard of the same accident a day later, had been horrified and had sent every possible comfort to Steve. Settled into the local hospital with a broken foot, Steve had appreciated the attention very much indeed, and so had his mates on his behalf.

'My mother's a lady who thinks ahead,' Alastair told them. 'While I've been seeing to the everyday running of the estate and trying to figure out financial ways of saving it, she's been figuring out the only logical way. Which is marrying Penny-Rose. For a year.'

'But—'

'Like I said, it's a business proposition.' Alastair spread his hands. 'I know this sounds intrusive, but my mother had Penny-Rose's background checked. She's employed investigators, and there's now little she doesn't know. In every respect, this is the sort of woman I need.'

He paused, and then said in a softer tone, avoiding Penny-Rose's eye, 'My mother also says she badly needs money.'

It had stopped being even remotely amusing. Penny-Rose's colour mounted to a fiery crimson and she took a step back. *Investigators*... 'My circumstances are none of your business,' she snapped. 'How dare you?'

But Bert was looking back and forth at the pair of them. 'It seems to me the conversation's getting private,' he said.

'It seems to me the conversation is over,' she flung back, and Bert nodded.

'Yeah, OK. But the man's right. You're strapped for cash, girl, and you know it.' It was Bert who organised a huge percentage of her wages to be sent back to Australia. She kept so little for herself that he'd been horrified. 'Maybe it's like the man says—you need to listen to his proposition.' Bert's sunburned face creased in resigned amusement. 'Now, what I suggest—'

'Is what you suggested first and send for a strait-jacket,' she said through gritted teeth, but Bert shook his head.

'No. The man's got a problem, and it's a real one. I'm seeing it now. I don't say his solution will work but you could do worse than to listen to what he's proposing.' He glanced at his watch. 'So... It's two o'clock. We knock off at four. When we do, you go down to the village, Penny-Rose, get yourself washed and into something decent, and you...' He turned and poked a finger into Alastair's chest. 'You take her out to dinner. Properly. Pick her up at her lodgings at six and do the thing in style.'

'I don't need—' Alastair started, but Bert was on a roll.

'You ask a lady to marry you, you do it properly.'

'I don't want—' Penny-Rose tried, but the stubby finger was pointed at her in turn.

'Give the man a chance. You can always refuse, and that'll be the end of it. You made me listen to him. Now you do the same. If he badgers you after tonight, he'll answer to me.'

'Bert—'

'No argument,' Bert said. He'd wavered, but now his decision was made. It was time to get on with what he was here for—stone-walling. Everything else was a nuisance. 'That's my final word.' He turned back to Alastair. 'Now, you get back to your castle where you belong and you, girl, get back to sorting your stones. There's to be no more talk of marriage before tonight.'

'Bert, I can't go out with this man.'

'You can,' Bert said heavily, and the amusement was suddenly gone from his voice. 'This is the man who's paying us, girl, and he's in trouble. You made me listen to him. Well, I have. You can put the good of the team before everything for the moment and give him a fair hearing. That's all I ask.'

'And that's all I ask,' Alastair said, his calm brown eyes resting on her face in a message of reassurance.

Which was all very well, she thought wildly as she sent him a savage glance. Reassure all you like.

Marriage!

The man was seriously nuts!

'Six o'clock, then,' he said. 'You're staying with the Berics? I'll collect you there.'

'How do you know where I'm staying?'

'I know all about you.'

'Then you know what I'm about to say to your crazy proposition,' she flung at him. 'No and no and no.'

'Just listen.'

'I'll listen. And then I'll say no.'

CHAPTER THREE

THE man who called for Penny-Rose four hours later was the same man—but only just. Madame Beric opened the front door, quivering in excitement. Penny-Rose didn't blame her. She was waiting in the kitchen, trying not to quiver herself, and when Alastair was ushered in, she failed.

She definitely quivered.

Whew! This was Cinderella stuff. And where was her fairy godmother when she was needed? She'd put on her only dress that was halfway decent—a white sundress with tiny shoulder straps that was more useful for a day off than for a dinner date. She'd washed and brushed her curls until they shone, but that was as much as she'd done.

There wasn't anything else to do. She wore no adornment. How could she? She didn't have any adornment. Or any cosmetics. In fact, her entire outfit was worth peanuts!

Alastair, on the other hand, was wearing a formal suit that must have cost a mint. It was deep black, Italian made and fitted perfectly. The black was lightened by the brilliance of his crisp, white shirt and the slash of a crimson silk tie. His normally ruffled black curls had been groomed into submission, there was a faint aroma of very expensive aftershave about him and he looked every inch a man of the world.

Unlike Penny-Rose, who had the look of a woman who'd appreciate diving into a small, dark cupboard.

There wasn't a small, dark cupboard available, and Alastair's dark eyes were twinkling in amusement.

Good grief! She could see why Belle wanted him. In fact, she could see why any woman would want him!

'You look beautiful,' he told her, his wide smile taking in her discomfort and reacting with sympathy.

If she could have known it, he was also reacting with truth.

She did look lovely, Alastair acknowledged as he took in her simple appearance. Money made little difference when it came to pure beauty. Her glossy chestnut curls tumbled about her shoulders. Her face glowed with health and humour, her green eyes were edged with tiny, crinkling laughter lines and her diminutive figure was well suited by the simplicity of her dress. She was five feet four and beautiful, whatever she was wearing.

But Penny-Rose couldn't tell what he was thinking, and the thoughts that were whirling around in her head were very different.

She was about as far from his beautiful Belle as any woman was likely to be, she thought bitterly. She wore little make-up, her nose had the temerity to sport freckles, and as for her hands...

Belle's hands would be flawless—of course. They'd be groomed for wearing fabulous jewellery and doing little else. Penny-Rose's hands had been put to hard physical work from the time she could first remember, and it showed.

Alastair reached out for her hand in greeting and she felt him stiffen as he came into contact with the roughened skin. He looked down involuntarily.

Her hands were worn and calloused. They were Cinderella hands, and no fairy godmother could have altered them in time for a date with a handsome prince.

She saw his face change—twist—in a half-mocking smile.

'It is true,' he said slowly, inspecting her fingers in a way that made her attempt to haul her hands out of reach. But he held on, and kept inspecting. 'What my mother said about you is right.'

She was thoroughly flustered, by his words and the feel

of her hand in his. 'I have no idea what your mother said,' she snapped, hauling free her fingers. 'But if it's that I have no time for nonsense then, yes, it's the truth. So can we get this dinner over and be done with it?'

'You sound like you aren't looking forward to it.'

'I'm not.'

But, in fact, that was a lie. There were few village families prepared to take in lodgers, so Penny-Rose had had to be grateful for what she'd been able to find. Madame Beric was a kindly enough soul but she was a gifted watercolour artist, with little time for anything else. Her cooking was therefore appalling. Penny-Rose was now up to turnip soup version thirty-four, and burned turnip soup version thirty-four at that...

'Where are we going?' she asked, despite herself, and Alastair's face creased again into one of his blindingly attractive smiles.

'Lilie's, of course,' he said softly. 'Where else does a man take a woman when he's asking her to marry him? It's the best, and tonight only the best will do.'

It was a twenty-minute journey—twenty minutes while Penny-Rose sat in stunned silence in the passenger seat of Alastair's car. A Ferrari. Of course. She'd never been near such a car in her life. Alastair's shabby clothes of earlier had been token workman-like apparel, she thought resentfully. No wonder her hands fascinated him. He wouldn't know what it was to work hard with his hands.

Everything about this man screamed money.

And now he wanted more and he was prepared to marry a stranger to get it.

Maybe that was unfair, she acknowledged. Maybe it was true that he was concerned about the villagers.

She glanced across at him as they pulled to a halt in the restaurant car park, and found that he was twisting to survey her with the same intensity she was using on him. Their gazes met. She flushed and turned away.

'You don't approve of me, do you?' he asked cautiously and she bit her lip.

'I'm not here to make a judgement,' she said at last. 'I'm here because my boss told me to be here.'

'And to eat a wonderful dinner?'

There was that. She had the grace to concede the point and her lips gave an involuntary twitch into a smile. 'Um...OK.'

'My mother says you know what it is to be hungry.'

That comment killed her smiling urge. She returned to glaring, shoved the car door open and then stood and waited for him to get out and lock his damned expensive car.

'I said the wrong thing,' he said ruefully, as they turned toward the restaurant.

'My stomach is my business,' she said with dignity.

'I guess it is.'

She said nothing—just concentrated on where they were going. Damn him, he had her right off balance and she didn't know how to deal with it. Somehow she just had to get this over with. Concentrate on dinner...

Luckily, Lilie's was worth concentration.

The restaurant was built into the parapets of another mediaeval castle. Well, why not? This was fairy-tale country, with castles here to spare.

But there were modern touches. A lift swept them to the rooftop, where the restaurant was situated among the battlements. Floor-to-ceiling windows were now installed where archers had once stood to protect their fortress—and Penny-Rose saw the view and gasped in delight. She'd been trying to disregard Alastair's disturbing presence until now, but the view made her almost forget him.

Almost? Well, almost a little bit...

Focus on the view, she told herself. And what a view! It was as if they were perched in an eagle's nest high over the river. Below were river plains, golden with buttercups and inhabited by placidly grazing cattle. At every turn of the river were more ruins, more castles, and more…

More stone!

'What are you thinking?' Alastair asked, watching her with bemused interest.

'I'm thinking…' she said slowly, and paused.

'Yes?'

'That there's a lifetime of work for me in this country,' she managed, and his eyebrows shot to his hairline.

'What on earth…?'

'Stone-walling,' she breathed. 'Look at it out there—all those stones. All those crumbling walls, just waiting for repair.'

He shook his head. 'I don't believe this.'

'What don't you believe?'

That he'd taken a woman out to dinner—and she was talking about stone?

'Um…stone walls are just stone walls,' he managed, and she gazed at him as if he'd just uttered a profanity.

'That's like saying every house is just a house. And they say you're a well-respected architect. Is that what you believe?'

'I… No.' He was flummoxed. This woman was like no woman he'd ever dated.

'Well, there you go, then.' She smirked. 'I rest my case.'

He grinned. They were being led to a discreet table tucked into a niche where all they had for company was the view. 'OK,' he conceded. 'But…'

'But?'

'I never thought I'd be wining and dining a woman who'd look at rock and gasp.'

She gave him a look of gentle mockery. 'Surely not. You must be using the wrong rock. Have you tried diamonds?'

He cast her an amused glance—she certainly was different—but then was distracted by the need to order champagne.

Penny-Rose didn't protest. She could count the times

she'd tasted champagne on one finger. She cast another long look out over the valley, she gazed around her again at the opulent restaurant setting—and she decided there and then that she wasn't about to let scruples get in the way of a very good dinner.

And Alastair saw it. 'You're intending to milk this for everything it's worth,' he said dryly, and she had the grace to blush.

'Um…yes.'

'Because?'

'Because I shouldn't be here. I have no intention of agreeing to any crazy marriage proposal but, as you say, I've been hungry.' She beamed, abandoning herself to enjoyment, and gave a small bounce on the beautifully padded chair. 'Wow. This looks like a very nice place to eat.'

He was fascinated. She'd bounced. She'd definitely bounced.

'What?' she demanded, seeing his expression. 'What did I do wrong?'

'Nothing.'

'I just said it looks a great place to eat.'

He took a deep breath. 'That, Miss O'Shea, is an understatement. Can I interest you in some snails?'

'You can interest me in anything that's not turnip soup,' she said, and received another startled look. 'That's what the Berics live on,' she explained. She shook her head. 'Every night, M'sieur Beric sits down to turnip soup, and every night he finishes it, looks up and tells his wife it was delicious. So she makes it the next night. And if she doesn't, he gets all disappointed.' She grinned. 'So you see why I finally agreed to eat with you?'

'Despite disapproving of me?'

Her smile widened. 'Despite that.'

He paused, but he had to ask. 'Why?'

'Why what?

'Why do you disapprove of me?'

'Because you're a prince and I'm a worker,' she said

frankly. 'Cinderella was a fairy story. It doesn't happen in real life.'

'It might.'

'Oh, yeah?' It was a gentle jeer. 'Even Cinderella's prince didn't propose marriage just for a year!'

Alastair thought that through and disagreed. 'Her guy had his deadlines, too,' he told her, semi-seriously. 'Like midnight. Seeing carriages turn to pumpkins just as the going gets romantic might put a man right off his stride.'

'I'd imagine it might,' she said faintly.

'So Cinderella's beloved had to work fast.' He paused again, and then his smile died. 'As I do.'

'If you want to be Prince.'

'No.' Alastair shook his head.

The champagne arrived. There was a moment's silence while the bubbles were poured, and he waited until she'd taken her first gorgeous sip. He waited for her verdict, and he got it.

'Yum!' she said, and he smiled at her pleasure. *Yum.* It was a word Belle hadn't used in her life!

But he couldn't afford to be distracted by this strange Cinderella his mother had found for him. He had this one meal to persuade her, and he already knew persuasion would take some doing.

'I really don't want to be a prince,' he said, and his eyes met hers over the glass. 'Will you believe that?'

'Um…' She took another cautious sip and made her decision. 'No.'

He had to make her believe. Otherwise nothing would make sense. 'Fame,' he said slowly, 'isn't all it's cracked up to be. This principality is small, but as the eldest—indeed, only—male of the royal family, the spotlight is now on me. There's a population of a tiny country waiting to see what I do.'

He motioned out the window to the tiny holdings scattered along the river. 'There are so many families whose lives depend on my choice—and your choice, too.'

'Don't you dare try to blackmail me,' she snapped, suddenly angry, and his expression softened.

'No. I won't. But according to my mother, our needs mesh.'

She glared some more. 'I don't understand.'

'A year as my wife would set you up for life.'

'I don't need to be set up—'

'You can barely afford to eat now,' he pointed out. 'Michael is still at secondary school and he wants to be an engineer. How are you going to afford three of them at university?'

She placed her champagne glass carefully down on the table. All of a sudden the bubbles tasted like vinegar.

'You really have pried...'

'My mother has on my behalf.' His calm gaze met hers, and his hands reached out across the table and took hers. She didn't pull back. He looked down at those work-worn hands, and his mouth twisted into the mocking smile she was starting to know well.

'You want a résumé of all my mother found out about you?'

'No, I—'

'Because I intend to give it to you.' He shook his head at her indignant protest, released her hands and sat back, assessing. His eyes rested on hers, like she was an enigma he was still trying to figure out.

'Your mother was an invalid,' he started, watching her face. 'She had multiple sclerosis. She should never have had one child, let alone four, but your father was desperate for a son. After three daughters, she finally died giving birth to Michael. That was when you were ten.'

'I don't—'

'I'm saying this no matter how much you interrupt,' he continued. 'So you may as well listen and make sure I have it right. We wouldn't like to make any mistakes here.'

'Of course not,' she said bitterly, and Alastair smiled.

'Very wise. So what did you have? A father who's a

farmer and an expert stone-waller, but who coped with his wife's illness by turning to the bottle.' He held his hand up as Penny-Rose made an involuntary protest and she subsided. Reluctantly. 'And a mother who depended on her eldest daughter for everything.

'And then your mother died.' His voice softened still further. 'Which left you at ten, caring for Heather, six, Elizabeth, four and Michael who was newborn. And a herd of dairy cows and a father who drank himself stupid every night, leaving everything else to you.'

'I don't—'

'Welfare nearly stepped in,' he went on. 'The whole district was concerned. My mother's investigators had no trouble finding people who remembered gossip about your family. I gather you came within an inch of being put into care. But for you.'

'I didn't—'

But he was brooking no interruptions. Like Cinderella's prince, he was working to a deadline. 'You worked your butt off,' he told her. 'You came home from school every night and you milked. You got up at dawn and did the same. The neighbours knew and were horrified but you wouldn't have it any other way, and when Welfare tried to step in they were met by a little girl whose temper matched that of any adult. "Leave us alone," you said. "We'll survive." And somehow you did, until you could leave school at fifteen and work full time on the farm.'

'Yes, but—'

'But it wasn't much easier then, was it, Penny-Rose?' he said gently. 'Because your father drank any profits, and you had your work cut out keeping bread on the table. When your father got drunk one night and smashed his car into a tree, things might have been easier. If the younger children had left school. But you wouldn't let them.'

'Of course not. They're so clever,' she said desperately. 'All of them. Heather wants so much to be a doctor. Like you, Elizabeth wants architecture.' She flashed him a wintry smile. 'And somehow you already know that Michael longs for engineering.'

'You're supporting two at university now and one at school. How are you going to do more?'

'They have part-time jobs. They help.'

'Not enough. It's two more years until Heather finishes and Michael's major expenses haven't started. You're up to your ears in debt already.'

'I don't need to listen to this!'

'No, but you should,' Alastair said ruthlessly. 'You can't do it. You've come to Europe because the pay's better. With a great exchange rate you can send more money home, but there's an end to it. You can't stretch your debts any further.'

'I must,' she said in a small voice, and his hand came back across the table and caught hers.

'You need a life, too.'

'They're great kids.' Her green eyes sparked with anger. 'We've talked it through. As soon as Michael's finished, it's my turn. That's when I can start enjoying myself.'

'Oh, great. In six years? More! How much more turnip soup, Penny-Rose? How long before they're self-supporting and you have your debts paid off?'

'I want them to have the best,' she said stubbornly. 'They shouldn't suffer because my father…'

'Because your father didn't face his responsibilities.' Alastair's voice gentled. 'You face yours, though, don't you? And I do, too. That's what this is all about. Facing responsibilities. That's why I'm asking you to marry me. It could help us both.'

'I don't—'

'No, don't say anything.' He smiled at her, a smile that lit his face and took the heaviness away from her heart. 'First let's eat a very good dinner. And tell me…'

'Tell you what?' She was thoroughly flustered. 'You already know everything.'

'I don't know this.'

'What?'

'Why do they call you Penny-Rose?'

She didn't answer him until she'd demolished the first course. Her snails were magnificent morsels of taste sensation. She'd never tasted anything so delicious in her life. And in a way, it was time out. Her whole attention had to be on conquering the tricky silver tongs and tiny fork—and on not missing a drop of the gorgeous juice.

She finally finished and looked up to find Alastair watching her. The look on his face was strange, as if he couldn't believe she was real.

'Oh, what?' she said crossly. 'Have I made a *faux pas*?'

'On the contrary, you managed beautifully,' he told her, just a hint of a smile lingering in his voice. 'In fact, I don't think I've ever enjoyed watching someone eating snails more.' He left her to make of that what she liked, and then pressed home his question for the third time. 'Before our next distraction comes—'

'Food's not a distraction,' she retorted. 'What a thing to say!'

'OK, I was brought up wrong,' he admitted. 'I could have had snails for breakfast if I'd wanted. But I do want to know—'

'You know everything.'

'Not this.'

'So pay more money to your private investigators.'

'My mother asked them,' he confessed. 'But apart from knowing your full name is Penelope Rose O'Shea…'

'So? That's why I'm called Penny-Rose.'

'No.' He shook his head. 'It'd explain Penny, or Rose, but—'

'I hate Penny.'

Alastair's face was thoughtful, watching hers. 'I see you do. Why don't you call yourself Penelope, then?'

'I'm not much into that either.'

'Would you like to explain?'

'My...' She caught herself. No! This was none of his business. It was no one's business.

But then she looked at him again, and he looked gravely back, and she thought, He *does* want to know. For whatever reason, he's really interested.

In me.

The thought was so novel she could hardly believe it. Talking about herself was something she never did, but suddenly she couldn't resist telling him. Just once.

'My father called me Penelope,' she began. 'He insisted I was called that after a great-aunt, so she'd leave us money. But she never did, and my father hated the name because of it. And I think...' She took a deep breath. 'I think my father hated me.'

'That's a fair indictment of your father.'

She shook her head. 'Maybe I don't blame him. I was his conscience, you see,' she told him. 'From the time my mother died I badgered him. All Dad wanted was to drink himself into oblivion, and I wouldn't let him.'

'How did you stop him?'

She shrugged. 'It was never easy. I'd steal money from his wallet to feed the kids, so when he went to the pub he didn't have enough. A great little thief—that's me. Or I'd wake him up sometimes...' Her voice faltered as she tried to continue. 'When I was ill or when the milking got too much for me, I'd sometimes be able to shame him into helping. And I badgered him into teaching me to build stone fences. He had to work a bit to get money to drink, so he'd take on a stone-walling job, and there I'd be, watching. Because it meant money, I'd help all I could.'

'I'd have thought,' Alastair said thoughtfully, his eyes resting on hers, 'that he'd have been grateful.'

'He wasn't.' There was no question of that. 'He called me Penelope. He'd put on this dreadful voice and he'd say to the kids, ''Penelope says we have to do this. Penelope says there's not enough to eat...''' She broke off. 'He'd tell the kids it was my fault they were hungry—because I'd taken his money! Sometimes it was as if I had another kid to look after, but he was my father. I couldn't stop him hating me. The only way I could get through to him was to threaten to come into the pub and tell his drinking mates how much we'd had to eat that week.'

'You didn't!' Alastair said, awed, and she managed a smile.

'You have no idea what you can do when you're desperate. Only then…after the first time I threatened that, he started calling me Penny instead of Penelope. He said I was constantly grubbing for money so I might as well be named for it. I hated that, too. So, behind his back, the kids started calling me Penny-Rose.'

'I see…'

'And it's sort of stuck,' she told him. 'And maybe it fits me. Penelope Rose is on my passport and job application, but when I got the job with Bert they said I was such a two-bit thing they'd call me Penny-Rose.' She smiled. ''Cos I surely wasn't a two-bob Rose.'

There was silence as he took that on board. The waiter came and cleared their plates, but still Alastair didn't speak.

'I don't think you're a two-bob Rose either,' he said at last, and he couldn't quite keep the emotion out of his voice. He looked at her across the table and he couldn't believe what he was seeing. All this… His mother had told him her background, but until now it had hardly seemed true.

'I don't think you're a two-bob Rose either,' he repeated. 'I refuse to call you Penny. Or Penelope. I think you're a Rose, and a million-pound Rose at that. A Princess Rose. You deserve it, and marriage to me might just make sure that you get it. From this time on…' His voice caught with sudden, unexpected emotion. 'From this time on, you're Rose.'

'Rose…'

'Don't you like it?'

'Yeah, but it doesn't sound like me.' She grinned. 'It sounds too dignified.'

'You can live up to your name.'

'Yeah, right.'

'If you want to…'

The main course arrived then, giving them welcome time out. Penny-Rose—or just Rose—was never going to be distracted from food like this, not for all the princes in the world.

Before her was roast duckling, snow peas and crispy roast potatoes, served with a *jus* that made her mouth water before she even saw it. Penny-Rose-cum-Rose forgot all about dignity and concentrated on what was important.

Which was a novelty in itself to Alastair. He wasn't accustomed to taking a woman out to dinner and having all her attention focussed on the food!

He sat and watched, bemused, waiting for the moment when she'd scraped her plate clean, and then turned back to more mundane questions. Like marriage proposals.

She turned straight back to practicalities.

'I can see you have a problem marrying Belle,' she said at last, popping a final snow pea into her mouth and savouring it with regret that it was the last. 'But why did you choose me as an alternative? I'd imagine there must be lots of nice, virtuous girls in your principality.'

'Um, yes.' He seemed discomfited and she pressed home her point.

'So why did you choose to investigate my background?'

'You were my mother's choice.'

'Oh, right. And you always do what your mother tells you?'

He grinned. 'Always.'

'Why don't I believe you?'

'In this instance I think she's done very well.'

'But why me?' she pressed again.

He hesitated, but decided he might as well be honest. 'Because you're Australian.'

She frowned at that. 'You'll have to explain.'

'At the end of our marriage,' he told her, playing with the cutlery still lying on the table, 'you'll need to walk away. I don't want television and newspapermen in your face for the rest of your life. I'd imagine you don't want that either.'

'No,' she said, startled.

'This marriage will create publicity.' He paused. 'You know I've been engaged to be married before?'

'I did know that,' she said, a trace of sympathy entering her voice. This man stood to inherit the rulership of this tiny country and you couldn't cross the border without hearing the gossip. 'Her name was Lissa and she was killed in a car crash three years ago.'

'With my father.'

'I'd heard that as well.' Her face softened still further. 'I'm sorry.'

He shrugged off her sympathy. He didn't need it. He just needed to make her see why it mattered. 'Then maybe you'll understand why I don't want to get emotionally involved again.'

'Hence Belle.' She nodded wisely, thinking of what the gossip columnists said about Alastair's companion. 'I can see that, too.'

He heard the gentle criticism—the same concern that came from his mother when she asked whether he was sure he was doing the right thing—and it stung. 'Belle will make me a very good wife.'

'I'm sure she will.'

His eyes narrowed, but Penny-Rose's face was cordiality itself.

'Apart from the virtue bit,' she added. 'That's hard. To be hit now for flings you had in your youth. So...' She cocked her head. 'You're not in love with Belle?'

'I'm not in love with anyone.'

'No?' She was like a brightly inquisitive sparrow, he

thought, impossible to take offence at. But she was insistent. She was still waiting.

'No. I'm not in love with anyone,' he repeated stiffly. 'After Lissa, it's impossible.'

'Lissa was some lady?'

'We were second cousins and we grew up together,' he told her, his voice softening. 'We were the best of friends.'

He received a probing look as Penny-Rose thought this through. 'So… You're thirty-two now, and you didn't get engaged until three years ago. They say you'd only just become engaged when she was killed. And you and Lissa were friends for years.' She paused and thought it through some more. 'Then after years of friendship, passion suddenly overtook you so you decided to marry?'

He frowned at that, and fingered his wineglass, sending shards of candlelight glistening through the Burgundy. 'Aged almost thirty, we realised how good friendship could be.'

'So you weren't in love with Lissa either?'

His face darkened. 'I loved Lissa.' And from the way he'd said it, she was sure it was the truth. But maybe he hadn't loved her as a man could love a woman. Or…as she'd always hoped a man could love a woman.

For heaven's sake… What would she know? she thought suddenly. Maybe what she was thinking of was a romantic dream. It was a dream she'd always had at the back of her mind, but still just a dream for all that.

She could hardly probe any further down that road, but there was still something not quite right. She sipped her wine and wrinkled her freckled nose. 'And Belle?' she pressed. 'She's a friend, too?'

'Not like Lissa was, but…' Alastair hesitated, but this was a major commitment he was asking of this woman, and it was important for him to be honest. He knew that. If she agreed, she had to know exactly what she was letting herself in for. 'Belle's an interior decorator—a partner with my Paris architectural firm. She knows what I expect in a woman, she entertains my clients magnificently and she doesn't interfere with my need for privacy.'

'Your need for privacy! That's a wonderful basis for a marriage—I don't think.' Her words were out before she could hide the revulsion in her voice, and he heard it. His brows snapped down in anger.

'Privacy and mutual support is all either Belle or I need.'

'I…I understand.' Penny-Rose did, too, and the thought made a shudder run down her spine. He saw, and his frown deepened even further.

'You're cold?'

'How could I be cold?' It was the most beautiful spring evening. But his concern was warming, she thought. Nice.

'So let me get this right,' she continued. 'You want me to play the fairy-tale princess for a year, then at the end of it to calmly apply for a divorce, hitch up my socks and walk out of here. Leaving you to Belle.'

'I wouldn't have put it quite like that but, yes. That sums it up.'

'And Belle?' Penny-Rose toyed with her wineglass. 'How does she feel about it? If it were me,' she said carefully, 'I wouldn't be happy about seeing my fiancé marry someone else first. In fact,' she added honestly, 'it'd be pistols at dawn if anyone made the attempt.'

He smiled at the image. 'That's hardly sensible. And Belle's sensible. I told you. She understands that the needs of the country have to come first.'

'I see.' Or she saw enough to make her shiver again.

But she needed to concentrate on her own role. Not Belle's future one. 'Is this really going to be OK?' she asked. 'Will the lawyers be happy with a twelve-month marriage?'

'The inheritance doesn't say how long I have to stay married. Legal opinion is that if the marriage doesn't last a year then annulment rather than divorce could be considered and it could risk the inheritance. But if it lasts a year—'

'Then you and Belle can be safe as Prince and Princess and live happily ever after.' She nodded wisely—but there was something else niggling her. Something else that needed asking, and there was no easy way to ask it.

'Um…how do you know I'm unimpeachably virtuous?' she demanded.

He looked across at her, startled, and then he grinned. 'The investigators say you've never had a boyfriend. According to my mother, you haven't had time.'

'Gee, thanks.'

'It does make things easier,' he told her. 'And your maturity helps. If I marry a woman who's not mature then I risk her falling…'

'Falling for you?'

'There's not much chance of that happening,' he said bluntly. 'Not with the way I feel about marriage. But falling for the trappings of the position.'

'What makes you think I won't?'

'You're a pragmatist,' he replied. 'My mother says so, and I'm starting to accept that she's right. You do what you need to do to survive.' He grinned again. 'Besides, you're Australian. If the worst comes to the worst, after twelve months I can kick you out of the country. But I don't think I'll need to do that. You'll be wanting to get back to your sisters and brother. And you'll have your fee.'

Now they were getting down to business. 'My fee,' she said faintly.

The thought suddenly seemed repugnant. But… According to Alastair and his mother, she was a pragmatist. So she'd just better school her features into interest and behave like one. A virtuous pragmatist.

It sounded like something to take for constipation. Or… She grinned. Maybe it sounded more like someone who played very boring music!

Get a grip, she told herself. Was it the champagne that was going to her head? 'What…what exactly were you thinking of as a fee?' she asked unsteadily, and he nodded as if he'd expected the question.

He was certainly prepared—and then some! 'My accountant suggests an allowance of ten thousand English pounds per week, over and above expenses, for the entire time we're married, and a further one million pounds settlement at the time of the divorce.'

She'd raised her wineglass to her lips, she'd taken a sip—but the wine didn't go down. She choked and choked again, and finally Alastair came around to thump her shoulders.

The feel of his hand on the bare skin of her back did nothing at all to help her composure. By the time she'd finished coughing she was bright pink and thoroughly flustered.

'I'm sorry,' she gasped at last. 'I thought you said…a million pounds!'

'I did. Plus the rest.'

'That's ridiculous.' She was almost angry.

'No. I'm rich already. I might not have enough to buy the estate at the values tourists would put on it, but if I inherit, I'll have more money than I know what to do with. My lawyers say that if I'm not generous, I could face a lawsuit later. I don't want that. And my mother says you deserve this windfall, and I'm starting to believe that she's right.'

'And…' She still couldn't take it in. 'Belle agrees to it?'

'Belle's the woman I want with me long term,' he said slowly. 'After losing Lissa, I don't want anyone or anything making emotional demands. Belle's a wonderful partner and she understands—'

'She understands what little you want of her.' Penny-Rose nodded, though the thought of the marriage he was contemplating made her feel dreadful. 'And she understands me?'

'She sees you as a necessary evil.'

'Gee, thanks.'

'Say nothing of it.' He smiled, his dangerous, coaxing smile that had her half-inclined to agree just so she could see it once more. He was still standing, looking down at her, and his very closeness was unnerving.

The whole situation was unnerving.

And there were things she didn't understand. Lots of things.

'I'd imagine, as a prince, yours would be a very public wedding,' she said slowly.

'Yes. It'll need to be.'

'Then how will your people take it?' she went on, thinking it through as she spoke, 'when I disappear after twelve months?'

'My people are pragmatists,' he said. 'Like yourself. There's discontent now because the succession is at risk. Even though my engagement to Belle hasn't been official, the gossip columnists have voiced rumours and disapprove. They know about the inheritance, and they want the principality to continue. Our marriage will dispel that worry.'

But she was no longer listening. She'd been caught by a word. A very major word. Succession... She almost choked again.

'Hey, you don't want me to have a baby, do you?' she demanded, and Alastair smiled. Drat! How could she concentrate when he smiled like that? But she *must* concentrate. 'There's no stipulation about babies in the old prince's will?'

And now he was laughing at her. 'No. I think Belle and I can manage that. Eventually.'

'That fits in the category of what an elegant hostess does?' Penny-Rose enquired politely, and his smile faded.

'There's no need—'

'To be impertinent?' Her equilibrium almost restored, she managed a chuckle as Alastair finally sank down again into his chair. 'I'm sorry but I'm always impertinent. You should know that if you intend marrying me.'

'Then you will marry me?'

She put up a hand. 'I'm thinking about it. Nothing more.'

'That's all I ask.'

'How long do I have to make up my mind?'

'Until coffee,' he told her, and her equilibrium disappeared all over again.

'Help…'

'If you don't agree, I need to find someone else,' he said apologetically. 'And pragmatic single women of unimpeachable virtue…'

'Are a bit thin on the ground?' Penny-Rose was fighting for composure. 'I guess you could always put an advertisement in the international press. WANTED: PRINCESS FOR A YEAR. I imagine you'd be swamped by callers.'

'Maybe I would be.' He smiled faintly. 'But I can't do that.'

'Why not?'

'This marriage,' he said slowly, 'has to appear real.'

'To appease the cousins?'

'And the lawyers. That's right.'

'But…' She thought this through. 'Bert and the team already know it'd be a marriage of convenience.'

He shrugged. 'A marriage of convenience doesn't necessarily mean it's not a real marriage. Royal marriages have been just that for thousands of years. But advertising seems a bit over the top, and I can't publicly stipulate a time frame. I'm running a fine legal line.'

'You certainly are.' She glanced up at him and then away again. He was starting to disconcert her. He was speaking of business. He was planning out his whole life—first with her and then Belle—as if he was planning a commercial venture.

The thought left her feeling almost ill.

What a waste, she thought suddenly. Arranged marriages might be what was expected of royalty, but… With Alastair's wonderful smile, and his caring nature—and his money and his castle…

He was some catch!

He was some prince!

That wasn't the way to think, she told herself hastily. Alastair was planning this as a business proposition, and so must she.

'A million pounds,' she murmured, forcing her thoughts sideways and letting herself dwell on what that could mean. 'A million... Do you have any idea how tempting that sort of money is for a girl like me?'

'I can imagine.' Alastair smiled at her across the table and she had to give herself the same business-only lecture she'd given herself thirty seconds ago. It was either that or go take a cold shower. But he didn't seem to notice. Maybe he had that effect on all women! 'You'd never have to work again,' he was saying.

His words startled her, breaking through her fog of masculine awareness. Of Alastair awareness... 'Not work?' Penny-Rose frowned. 'I wouldn't know how to not work.'

'You could learn,' he said gently, 'during your year as a princess.'

'Oh, right. Just swan around, adjusting my tiara and polishing my throne. I don't think so.'

'You'd be a figurehead...'

'A figurehead who still has to get herself a master stone-waller certificate. I'm not going home without it.'

He stared at her. 'You won't need to stone-wall. A million pounds will set you up for life.'

She looked blankly at him, as if he were speaking some foreign language. 'But I *like* stone-walling.'

'You couldn't possibly stone-wall as my wife.'

'If you stuck me in a castle on a velvet cushion I'd go into a decline,' she said. And then she chuckled. 'Or I'd cause trouble. I just know I would. I'd be sticking my nose into all sorts of things that don't concern me. You need to accept me as a stone-walling bride or not at all.'

Wordless, he sat back and stared some more. Finally he reached across and lifted her fingers again, gazing down at her callouses and scratches left from the day's work. 'You don't want to leave all this?'

'A stone-waller is what I am,' she said simply. She took a deep breath, trying to make him see. 'Alastair, money would be very nice—because of my sisters and my brother—but at the end of the year I've no intention of becoming your pensioner for the rest of my life.'

'There's a lot of women who'd jump at the chance.'

'I'm not a lot of women.'

'I can see that.' He laid her hand down on the table. 'But...if you don't agree to marry me, there's many families here who'll lose their homes.'

'That's the only reason I'm listening.'

'We could make it work.'

Penny-Rose hesitated. 'You'd want a fairy-tale wedding? Lace and chariots and archbishops and the whole catastrophe?'

'Maybe not archbishops. If we're making vows we don't intend to keep, I'd prefer not to do it in a church. The church here is tiny so that can be our excuse. But otherwise, yes, pretty much the whole catastrophe.' And he sounded suddenly as unsure as she felt. They were hurtling into this together and in truth it scared them both.

She stared at him, and she saw his uncertainty—and his need. For some reason, his hesitancy reassured her.

As did his decision not to use a church.

His scruples were the same as hers.

'You'd have to fly my sisters and brother over to watch,' she told him slowly, and for the first time she sounded as if she was starting to think of this marriage as a serious possibility. 'They'd never forgive me if I didn't include them, and if they don't see it for themselves they'll never believe it's real.'

Alastair didn't hesitate. 'I can do that. Of course.'

'And...' She bit her lip, stared at the table for a while and then raised her eyes to meet his. There was something else she had to be sure of, and this was major. 'It really is business only? You wouldn't come near me? As a wife, I mean.' Her face turned pink. 'Um…there'd be separate bedrooms?'

'There are royal precedents for such arrangements.' He grinned, relaxing a little. 'The marriage suite in the castle is two bedrooms with a dressing room in between.'

'How very romantic. And locked doors?'

'Of course,' he said gravely. 'Because you're a lady of unimpeachable virtue.'

'I'm not infringing on Belle's domain.' Her mind was working in overdrive. This was going to be hard, but it had to be said.

'Speaking of Belle… Alastair, she'll have to go.' She hesitated, trying to think of an alternative, but there wasn't one. With Belle included in the arrangement, the marriage idea was preposterous. 'For the full twelve months of our marriage, Belle will need to stay away from the castle. I can't play the part of your wife if you have a mistress in the same house. I'd feel like Belle was watching me, daggers drawn, for the whole year. I'd hate it. She'd hate it. So…' Her troubled eyes managed a twinkle. 'I need to put my wifely foot down.'

Alastair thought that through. It was a reasonable request. Sort of. Belle would resent it, he thought, but on reflection Penny-Rose was right. The whole sham marriage could well founder if she stayed.

Finally he nodded. 'Agreed.'

'And I can keep on stone-walling with Bert?'

That wasn't as easy. 'That'll raise eyebrows. Princesses don't stone-wall.'

'This one does,' she told him. 'Or it's no deal. I'll be your part-time princess and you can be my part-time prince. But from eight to four, it's off with the tiara and on with the overalls. You can lock the gates so there's nobody to see me do it, apart from Bert and the guys. Bert already knows what the deal is. He'll keep his mouth shut and the men think I'm eccentric anyway.'

'You can't keep stone-walling,' he said faintly, looking again at her hands. 'You can't want to.'

'I can and I do.' She leaned forward, trying to make him understand. 'Alastair, will you continue to be an architect as well as a prince?'

That was different. 'Yes, but—'

'But nothing. I've spent years learning how to stone-wall. I'm good at what I do and it took years of negotiating before I got Bert to employ me. He's giving me the chance of being a master waller. I'm not about to give that chance up now.'

'With the money you'll earn, you won't need to be a master waller.'

'Like you won't need to be an architect. But you won't stop.'

'But—'

Penny-Rose shook her head, refusing to be swayed. 'But nothing. There's no negotiating on this one. I can use your money for the kids' education, and I can't tell you how much of a relief that will be, but afterwards I'll put what remains into a nice little pension plan for when my fingers get too feeble to wiggle copestones.'

'It'll be some pension plan.'

'And very nice it'll be, too.' She chuckled, and her green eyes met his and held. 'You are serious about all this?'

There was only one reply to that. Alastair had no choice. 'I am serious.'

'But…you do have reservations?'

And he had to be truthful again. 'I do.'

'Well, so have I,' she told him. 'But if the choice is for Michael not to go to university and for your villagers to lose their homes, I think we could give it a crack, don't you?'

There was a moment's pause. The thing hung in the air between them—a weighty decision, to be made one way or another right now. Because, marriage of convenience or not, they both knew this decision would change their lives for ever.

But he couldn't step back now. Not when so much was at stake.

'I believe we can give it a crack,' he said at last, and finally he allowed himself to relax. He smiled. 'After dessert, of course. Can I interest you in Pierre's excellent raspberry soufflé?'

'You can indeed,' she said cordially. 'And then let's plan how we intend to get married.'

CHAPTER FOUR

IT WAS amazing how quickly, once a decision had been made, that plans were set in concrete. Before she could change her mind, Alastair told Marguerite and Belle, and Penny-Rose was left to tell Bert.

'One wisecrack about romance and you're dead,' she told her boss. 'It's a marriage of convenience for a year, but the world—and the team—has to think it's indefinite. You know why I'm doing it, and it was you who made me listen to the man. So you can just shut up and support me. Or else.'

Bert did. Surprisingly, he met her decision with whole-hearted approval, and proceeded to tell the men—confidentially—that Penny-Rose was taking a step up in the world. He didn't tell them about the time frame, but he did tell them everything else.

The men sat in stunned silence while they took it in.

And then they wholeheartedly approved! In the time they'd worked with her, the team had become extraordinarily fond of their 'Penny-Rose', and in their opinion her stroke of good fortune couldn't have happened to anyone nicer.

But they couldn't understand why she was still sorting rocks as if nothing had happened.

'I'm not royal yet,' she retorted. 'And even when I'm married, I'll still be me.' Still Penny-Rose, she thought. Not Rose yet. 'I'm better off out here.'

Out of the publicity, she meant. Here, in the secluded castle grounds, working alongside her friends, she was shielded from media hype. She could concentrate on what she was good at and block out her increasing nervousness.

She could also block out her siblings' reactions. Which was tricky.

Because she couldn't tell them it was a business arrangement which would last only for a year. They felt so indebted to her already... If they knew she was doing this for them, she'd have a mass educational walk-out, which was the last thing she wanted.

So she told Heather the bare facts and left her sister to fill in the gaps as best she could. Which Heather did, with relish.

'That's just fantastic.' Heather could hardly believe it. 'Oh, Penny-Rose, I always knew you'd marry someone special. A real live prince? Is he fabulous?'

'I guess you could call him fabulous,' she said cautiously, and Heather chuckled.

'He'd have to be if you've decided to marry him. I know what you think of marriage.' She hesitated and Penny-Rose could hear her uncertainty down the line. 'What does he call you? Penelope?'

'Rose.'

'Even though he knows you're called Penelope?'

'Yes.'

'You'll be Princess Rose?'

'I guess so.' She took a deep breath. 'He says...he says he won't call me Penny-Rose because I'm worth much more.' She didn't add that the way he called her Rose made her feel odd—like he was deliberately distancing himself from who she really was.

But Heather loved it. 'Then he is special,' Heather said soundly. 'And...' Penny-Rose could imagine her sister's glee on the other end of the line. 'Is he very rich?'

'Um, yes.'

'Specialler and specialler.'

Penny-Rose grinned. 'Specialler... Is that good grammar?'

'Always the big sister. Leave my grammar alone. When do we get to meet him?'

'The wedding's in six weeks. Alastair will send you plane tickets, if you can come.'

There was a squeal of delight from the other end of the phone. 'Really?'

'Really.'

'Oh…' A long sigh of pure pleasure. 'Try and keep us away. Can we be bridesmaids?'

'I'm not having bridesmaids.'

'Princesses always have bridesmaids.'

'Not this one.'

'But…' There was a slight pause. 'It is going to be a royal wedding—right?'

There was only one answer to that. 'Yes.'

'Fabulous.' Another sigh, then… 'Help, we don't have anything to wear.'

This had already been discussed. 'Alastair's sending you a cheque,' she told her sister. 'So…so you can get something wonderful to wear.' When she revealed how much the cheque would be for, there was a moment's silence.

'Is this guy for real?'

'Yes.'

'Does he have any brothers?'

That brought another grin. 'No.'

'He must be wonderful,' Heather said at last, when she'd caught her breath. 'It'd take a special sort of prince to look at you in your disgusting work clothes and see the gorgeous Penny-Rose underneath.' She sighed once more. 'You'll be able to stop stone-walling.'

'If anyone asked you to marry him,' Rose said carefully, 'would you stop wanting to be a doctor?'

That halted her sister's romanticism in its tracks. 'Um, no.'

'Then leave my career alone.'

'Alastair's happy for you to stay a stone-waller?'

'It's what I am.'

There was a long, thoughtful silence, and then a sigh so

deep it was almost a blessing.

'Oh, Penny-Rose. Oh, love, I'm so happy for you I'm starting to cry.'

There was nothing Penny-Rose could do to prevent her siblings' reactions.

There was also nothing she could do to stop the media frenzy. Even though no formal announcement had been made, their evening at Lilie's had been noticed.

'Stay at the castle from now on,' Alastair told her, and she had no choice. Photographers were camped out at the castle gates. Their night at Lilie's, along with Belle's hasty departure, had been noticed and put together with glee. The media knew how urgently Alastair needed a bride, and Penny-Rose was obviously it.

And she didn't like the sensation at all. The conversion of Penny-Rose to Rose...

'I'm beginning to feel like a poor little rich girl,' she said as she sat down to dinner with Marguerite and Alastair two days later. Reluctantly, she'd moved into the castle guest quarters. At knock-off time she therefore bathed away her grime and presented herself at the dinner table as a normal guest.

A normal guest? Ha! She didn't feel in the least normal. She'd never seen so much glass and silverware in her life, and it took all her courage to stay dignified in front of the servants. Now, as the butler moved away with the dinner plates, she grimaced. 'I can't go anywhere?'

'You couldn't afford to go anywhere before this anyway.' Alastair smiled across the table at her, his gentleness robbing his words of offence. 'And at least we don't serve you turnip soup.'

'I know. I'm not complaining.' Her sense of humour reasserted itself. But she wished he wouldn't smile like that. It put her right off what she was thinking.

What was it? Oh, right. Not complaining...

'Or at least, not very much,' she added, hauling herself back to the matter in hand. 'I just need to remember not to take my wheelbarrow close to the boundary while I'm working. And I dread long-distance lenses.'

'They haven't placed you as one of the stone-walling team,' Alastair told her. 'Heaven forbid that they do. You're sure the team will stay silent? And the Berics?'

'I'd imagine your money will ensure that,' she said dryly. 'Talk about buying silence. So you're right. As long as I stay here I'm fine.'

'But…' Alastair was thinking this through '…there is one problem. You'll need to take a trip to the city.'

'Why?'

'You need clothes.'

She bristled. 'What's wrong with my clothes?'

He hesitated, and then he smiled again, seeking to lessen offence. 'Your dress…' He motioned to her sundress. 'I know I'm not supposed to notice, but it's the third night in a row that you've worn it.'

Her bristle turned into a glower. 'So? I *like* my dress.'

He raised his eyebrows. 'And you have a wardrobe of different evening-wear?'

'I don't need—'

'A stone-waller may not need, but my intended bride does,' he told her. 'Friday is official announcement time, and you should look great.'

'She looks great now.' Marguerite's warmth and approval were the one constant in this arrangement that was making Penny-Rose feel OK with what was happening, and it came to the fore now. 'The media will love her.'

'Rose was photographed leaving Lilie's in that dress,' Alastair said stubbornly. 'She needs another.'

Marguerite was like a defensive mother hen. 'I'm sure she has another.' And then she frowned at her son. 'Why do you call her Rose? Her name is Penny-Rose.'

'Penny-Rose is hardly a name for a princess. Rose is much more dignified.'

Much more *not me*, Penny-Rose thought. Still, this marriage was all about keeping their distance. If that was the way he wanted it…

It seemed he did.

'Do you have anything else to wear?' he asked, deflecting his mother's query nicely.

'Um…' Penny-Rose turned pink. 'Actually I don't.'

'Oh, my dear…' Marguerite sounded horrified.

'Don't let it bother you,' she said hastily. 'I don't understand what women see in choice. It makes dressing a whole lot more complicated.'

'But it also makes it more fun.' Marguerite had swung to her son's point of view in a moment. 'Now, where will you go to shop? You can't go anywhere in this principality. You'll be mobbed before you reach the first boutique. There's nothing for it. Alastair, you'll have to take her to Paris. You need a few days on the rue du Faubourg Saint Honoré…'

'Hey…' The idea startled him. 'I don't have time to go to Paris. It's not me who needs clothes.'

'She can't shop here.'

'No, but—'

'But Paris it must be. Are you saying that you won't take her?' his mother demanded, and fixed him with a look.

'I could have Belle take her…'

There was a collective intake of breath. And then Alastair had the grace to grimace. 'OK. Bad idea. Belle's well known and there are media problems everywhere.' He sighed and appealed again to his mother. 'But you're the obvious one to go.'

'No, dear.' His mother shook her head. 'The press has seen you once together. The more romance we can imbue this with, the better. I'm not saying I hope the photographers find you—you need a couple of days' grace—but if they do eventually track you down, it'd be so romantic to have you photographed strolling down Paris streets, hand in hand.'

'Hey, I don't intend holding anyone's hand,' Penny-Rose retorted, and Marguerite sighed again.

'You two aren't very good at this romance business, are you?'

'We're fine,' Alastair said.

'Right. Good. So hold hands.'

'Mother…'

'You need to get used to it.' His mother looked from Penny-Rose to Alastair and back again. 'In six weeks someone's going to say, "You may kiss the bride." If that means one chaste kiss on the forehead, the lawyers will label this marriage a sham and the castle—and the estate— will be lost. To us and to the villagers.'

'They can't—'

'This marriage has to appear real,' Marguerite said with asperity. 'Alastair, stop treating the girl as if she'll bite. Penny-Rose, stop treating the man as if he's your boss. Get friendly.'

'Yes, ma'am,' Penny-Rose said, and she managed a smile. 'I'll do what I can.'

'Alastair, take the girl to Paris. And start calling her Penny-Rose.'

'Um…'

'Don't "um" me,' his mother snapped. 'Get a handle on this. You never know, you could just enjoy yourselves.'

'Rose could enjoy shopping on her own.'

'Call her Penny-Rose.'

'It's not a princess's name.'

'And she'll only be a princess? Not a friend?'

'We need to keep things formal.'

'Fine,' his mother said, exasperated. 'Just take what's-her-name to Paris.'

His exasperation equalled his mother's.

'What's-her-name can go alone.'

'Excuse me,' Penny-Rose said, grinning slightly at their matching belligerent expressions. They really were very alike. 'But I…I suspect I might need some help. I don't exactly have much experience in shopping.'

They stopped glaring at each other and turned their stunned attention to her.

'No experience in shopping.' Marguerite gasped. 'Oh, my dear…' She sounded as if she'd just heard Penny-Rose had been deprived of something of major importance. Like a leg.

'So where did you find the dress you're wearing?' Alastair demanded in disbelief. All women shopped!

'Actually, I made it myself. I sew all my own clothes.'

That stunned them even more. Alastair stared at her as if she'd announced that she'd come from another planet.

'You're kidding.' Sewing your own clothes… He'd hardly heard of such a thing.

'I'm not kidding.' She met his look head on, defiant. 'I don't just stone-wall. I have other skills, too.' She grinned. 'I can also whistle loud enough to call the kids home from a mile away. Want to hear?' And she put two fingers to her mouth and prepared to whistle.

'No!' Marguerite and Alastair spoke as one, and she chuckled and desisted, but Alastair was still looking at her dress in awe.

'But…' His critical eyes appraised her workmanship and found no fault at all. 'It's lovely.'

She twinkled. 'Thank you.'

He was still having trouble believing her. 'And…your overalls?'

'I made them, too.'

'You really have never shopped for clothes?'

'Sometimes at welfare places,' she said diffidently. 'But not…not at real clothes shops.'

'Oh, Alastair!' Marguerite's eyes were shining. 'What fun. To introduce your bride to shopping!'

'To introduce your future daughter-in-law to shopping,' he retorted, but despite himself his imagination was caught. 'I don't suppose…' His thoughts were heading off at all sorts of wondrous tangents. A woman who'd never shopped…it was almost unbelievable. 'Things like lacy negligees and so on…' he said slowly. 'I can hardly help her there.'

'Of course you can,' his mother said soundly. 'Now…you're to leave tomorrow morning. You're to stay at the Hotel Carlon, which Belle tells me is the most splendid hotel in Paris. You're to spend a fortune and you're to have a very good time. That's an order. Any questions?'

'No, ma'am,' Penny-Rose said faintly. 'Except…' She blinked. 'There's Bert. I need to ask Bert for a couple of days off.'

'Bert and I have an arrangement,' Alastair told her. 'He's a very understanding boss—and employee.'

That didn't please her. 'You mean you'll just bribe him to keep me on the team with no questions asked.'

'I need do no such thing. He's not about to sack you.'

'He mustn't. If I lose my spot on the team…'

'Because you're out buying frilly knickers…'

'If you so much as tell him that…' She was aghast.

'I won't.' Alastair smiled at her.

Drat! His smile was really starting to get to her. For heaven's sake—she'd been living in Alastair's home for only two days. She had over a year of this mock marriage to go, but there was something very strange going on already. Every time the man smiled at her, something in the deeper recesses of her middle did some sort of stupid lurch…

It was just that he was so darned attractive, she thought wildly, and the number of deeply attractive men she'd spent any time with in her life numbered approximately zero.

Or maybe it was just that she hadn't had time to notice, she decided, forcing herself to be practical. Maybe there were plenty of gorgeous guys out there, and after this wedding farce was over—after her twelve-month marriage—maybe she could see for herself…

With her frilly knickers!

The thought made her grin, and Alastair saw it and smiled back.

'What?'

'Sorry?'

'What are you laughing at?'

'The thought of me in frilly knickers underneath my homemade overalls,' she confessed. 'Some things are too ridiculous for words.'

'But you'll come shopping with me?'

'Do I have a choice?'

'No.'

She spread her hands. 'OK. One shopping hit. But it'll have to be just the one. Let's get it all over in one shot. Can we buy a wedding dress while we're at it?'

'I have an idea about that.' Marguerite had been watching the interplay, a small, self-satisfied smile playing on her lips. Who knew what was behind that smile? 'I thought…' She hesitated. 'My dear, if you don't mind, I thought you could wear my wedding dress.' She flickered a questioning look at her son. 'You've always loved the photographs of your father and I being married. The dress I wore belonged to your grandmother before me, and it's lovely. If Penny-Rose agrees, it'd be wonderful for you to have your bride wear it.'

'But won't Belle…?' Penny-Rose started, but was silenced by the sudden frown snapping down on her future mother-in-law's face.

'Belle would die rather than wear an old dress of mine.'

Belle would. The thought of the svelte Belle wearing a traditional, pre-loved wedding gown seemed almost ridiculous.

'I… It seems very personal,' Penny-Rose said, looking sideways at Alastair to see how he was taking it. 'I mean, it *is* a wedding of convenience. It *is* only for a year.'

But, somewhat to her surprise, Alastair liked the idea. 'I bet it'd look gorgeous on you. And it's very economical.'

He smiled. 'That should appeal to your parsimonious streak!'

'If it's your money, I don't mind spending it,' she replied, and got a bark of laughter in response.

'That's very generous.'

'I can be,' she agreed blandly, and just for a moment they were grinning at each other like fools.

Or like…friends?

Or something more.

Which was crazy. But the moment stretched on, for far too long…

It was Alastair who came back to earth first. Penny-Rose's insides were still doing some type of aerobic act she couldn't define. 'You'll wear my mother's dress?' he asked, and if his voice was a trace unsteady it was only Marguerite who noticed. Penny-Rose's thoughts were way too unsteady all on their own.

'Penny-Rose needs to see it first,' Marguerite decreed, smiling complacently at them both. Things were going very well here. Very well indeed! 'She's only wearing it if she loves it. But meanwhile… Eat your supper, turn in for an early night and then head off to Paris in the morning.'

'For knicker shopping,' Alastair agreed, a wicked gleam lurking deep in those dangerous eyes.

'In your dreams, Alastair de Castaliae,' Penny-Rose muttered. 'You buy me frilly knickers? Over my dead body.' She hesitated. 'And maybe it's just as well if we buy me a wedding dress. I'm really not comfortable wearing your mother's.'

'Why not?'

'Because it's real,' she said frankly. Her insides had somehow settled, but with that crazy lurching had come a realisation. Alastair was holding her at arm's length. She needed to do the same. 'Some day you might meet someone even more special than Belle.'

'That's silly.'

'No, it's not.' She turned to Marguerite. 'You must understand. Wearing your wedding dress makes the whole thing personal—and this wedding has to be impersonal or it can't work.'

'I'd like you to wear it,' Marguerite told her, and with a shock Penny-Rose realised what she was saying.

And she knew she was right in her decision.

'I can't,' she told her. 'It's for Alastair's true wife to wear.'

'I don't understand.' Alastair was looking from one to the other. 'You will be my true wife.'

'As I said,' Penny-Rose retorted. 'In your dreams, Alastair de Castaliae. In your dreams.'

The next day was a dream all by itself.

First there was the journey to Paris.

Penny-Rose and her co-workers had taken the train through France when she'd started working in Alastair's tiny border principality, and she'd expected that she and Alastair would take the same train back to Paris. Or they'd drive. Either way, it was a full day's journey.

But they did neither. After an early breakfast, Alastair ushered her into his Ferrari. Ten minutes later they were boarding a private jet, and thirty minutes after that they were at Charles de Gaulle airport.

There was a limousine waiting. Awed into silence, Penny-Rose was ushered into the car like royalty, and she sank back onto leather cushions and thought that was exactly what she was! Royalty.

Sort of.

Or she would be in a matter of weeks, after this fairy-tale wedding had taken place.

And then they reached their hotel. Alastair left her at her suite door and she had to pinch herself to ensure she really was awake.

Her suite was twice as big as the house she'd been raised in. Heck, the bed was almost as big as the house she'd been raised in! There was more gold and silk and brocade than she'd ever seen in her life.

It was great. Great! So why wasn't she bouncing in pleasure?

It was simply too big and too opulent and too damned lonely. Australia and her family seemed suddenly very far away, and she felt herself blinking back a tear.

She wandered around the suite, touching everything, hardly daring to breathe, and when a knock sounded at the door she jumped a foot.

It was Alastair. Of course. She'd been so stunned she'd hardly noticed him leaving to be shown to his own rooms. But all of a sudden she was desperately glad he was back.

This felt over-the-top opulent, and she was way out of her depth.

'This...this is quite some hotel,' she made herself say, and he nodded and watched her face.

'It is. Do you like it?'

She took a deep breath and looked around. And looked around again.

'It lacks something,' she said finally. 'Or some things. It needs half-a-dozen kids, a few cats and dogs, pizza boxes on the floor, a couple of inner tubes and some rubber duckies for the bath, something noisy on television...and maybe then I'd like it. A little bit.'

'You don't like it.'

'Um, no,' she confessed. 'It's like a palace.' She wrinkled her nose. 'You may be used to sleeping in palaces—'

'Hey, I've only just inherited the title.'

'You chose this place.'

'I didn't,' he admitted. 'I've never been in this hotel. But Belle says it's the best and my mother said I should bring you to the best.'

'And you always do what Belle and your mother say. I see.' She chewed her bottom lip. 'My bath,' she said at last, 'is in the shape of a heart. It's a spa with padded seats.

Built for two. The bathroom looks as if it's been designed for Cleopatra.'

'Mmm.'

'You have the same?'

He nodded, unsure where the conversation was leading. 'I have the same.'

'So we have a heart-shaped spa each,' she said. 'That's cosy. Two spas built for two. One in each room.'

'You're telling me it's over the top?' he ventured, his lips twitching, and she tilted her chin and nodded.

'Just a bit. Maybe.'

'We could always share.'

'Oh, right.' She gave him an old-fashioned look. 'And then your requirement that I be a virtuous bride goes right out the window.'

'There is that.'

Alastair's smile faded as he assessed his future wife. Dressed casually in tailored trousers and a linen open-necked shirt, Alastair himself looked supremely at ease in these luxurious surroundings. His future bride, however, looked far from comfortable.

It was her hands, he thought. Always his eyes fell to her hands. Her sundress was lovely, she looked lovely, but her hands were the true Rose. Or Penny-Rose. They made him feel wrong—as if he was pushing her into something she wasn't meant to be.

He was suddenly, irresistibly reminded of a television show he'd once seen, where a much-decorated war veteran had been brought in for 'show and tell'. The man's deeds had been awesome, but the television show had been superficial. It had glamorised and in the process somehow belittled both the man and his actions.

He'd been uncomfortable, watching.

He was uncomfortable now.

'Do you really not like it?'

'It's the gilt and the brocade,' she explained. 'And...'

'And what?'

'The mirrors. Wherever I go I see me.'

'I can think of worse things to look at.'

'Yeah, right, when you have Belle to compare me to. I don't think.' She took a deep breath. 'OK. I'll get over it. But I would prefer something a bit simpler.'

'The Hotel Carlon doesn't do simple.'

'Then I'm stuck with it.' She looked down at her sun-dress and wrinkled her nose. 'But I believe you now when you say I need clothes, especially if I'm to spend any more time in front of these damned mirrors. Fine. Let's get out of here and go shopping.'

'You're seriously not looking forward to this?'

'I'm seriously not looking forward to this.' She grimaced and made a confession. 'I don't exactly know how it's done.'

'What, shopping?'

'Shopping.'

'It's easy,' he told her, suppressing a smile. 'You stand in a shop, you show them your credit card and you watch what happens.' He held out his hand. 'Come and see.'

She stared down at his hand for a long moment. His fingers were tanned and strong and inviting. The gesture to take her hand in his was a casual one, no more.

But what had Marguerite said? *'It'd be so romantic to have you…strolling down Paris streets, hand in hand.'*

Yeah, great.

But the hand was still proffered, and a deal was a deal. What was the man offering? A million pounds. Whew!

It was the stuff of dreams, and if she was to engage in dreams she might as well go the whole distance.

So she smiled up at her intended husband with a confidence she was far from feeling, she put her hand in his and she let herself be led out onto the streets of Paris.

To shop!

It wasn't an introduction into shopping that Alastair gave her. It was a crash course master's degree and then some.

They shopped and shopped and shopped, and when Penny-Rose decided there couldn't be an item of clothing left in Paris that she hadn't tried on, Alastair turned to accessories and shopped some more.

They paused only for meals. He took her to quiet little restaurants where he wasn't likely to be known. They ate wonderful food, but Penny-Rose slipped into a quietness which even Alastair knew was out of character. On their second day he collected her from her room to find she had dark shadows under her eyes, and when questioned she admitted she hadn't slept.

'It's the bed,' she told him. 'It's too big and too cold and too...'

'Too?'

'Lonely.' There. She'd said it. She looked at him, expecting to see laughter, but instead she saw concern.

'Five-star hotels by yourself are a bit echoing,' he agreed. 'My suite's just as barren. But I don't think sharing's an option, do you?'

'No!'

'Then we just get on with it. One more night and then home tomorrow...'

'Home to your castle!'

He thought of the sumptuous guest room in the castle and frowned. 'Do you find that just as lonely?'

'I'm not homesick,' she said, seeing what he was thinking. 'I'm never homesick.'

'No?'

'No,' she lied. 'I'm enjoying myself. These clothes are...fabulous.'

'We have bought some lovely things,' he said gravely. 'And there's more to come.'

Her determined cheerfulness faltered. 'I... Yes.'

'You're not enjoying the shopping either?'

'I feel like a kept woman,' she blurted out. 'It's awful. I don't know that I'm going to be able to stand it for a year.'

'Being a princess?'

'Being a princess.'

He surveyed her face with caution. If he wasn't careful he could blow it, and he knew it.

Most women would jump at the chance she was being offered, he thought, but he knew enough of her now to know that most women didn't include Rose.

'You can back out,' he told her.

'And then what?'

'And then I'd lose my estate and Michael wouldn't go to university.'

'See? We're up against a brick wall—both of us.'

'It's a comfortably padded brick wall,' he said lightly, and she flushed and bit her lip.

'I know. I'm being stupid.'

'It's harder for you than for me,' he acknowledged. 'I'm not being hauled out of my comfort zone.'

Penny-Rose thought that through and found flaws. 'It's not very comfortable, living on turnip soup,' she said, and he smiled. She had courage.

And the only way through this was through it.

'Breakfast?' He proffered his arm.

'Oh, yup, why not? A smorgasbord of two hundred different dishes…'

'Don't tell me you'd prefer a baguette.'

'Well, actually…'

'Actually, yes?'

And there was only one answer to that. The choice in the hotel's lavish restaurant simply overwhelmed her. 'Yes.'

He looked her up and down, and then he sighed. 'Come on,' he said in exasperation. 'Breakfast here is the most magnificent that Paris has to offer, but don't mind that. Let's turn our backs on the Carlon's stupendous breakfast and go find ourselves a baguette.'

'Alastair…'

But he was brooking no argument. 'I can slum it with the best of them,' he told her. His arm linked with hers and held. 'Just watch me.'

CHAPTER FIVE

So INSTEAD of eating the hotel's sumptuous breakfast they found a patisserie and Alastair proceeded to show Penny-Rose that he had absolutely no idea what slumming meant. As a peasant, he failed miserably. Penny-Rose's simple baguette was simply not enough, not faced with the choice of Paris's magnificent pastries.

So while she watched in open-mouthed amazement, he proceeded to buy one of everything he could see. A baguette, croissants and mouth-watering pastries filled with fruit, something chocolate that Penny-Rose, with her limited French, decided was called Death by Explosion, and more...

Then there was coffee in huge take-away mugs, the smell of which made her mouth water.

They emerged finally from their patisserie to find piles of grapes and mandarins on a next-door stall. Ignoring her protests—'You've dragged me away from the Hotel Carlon's breakfast, woman—you can let me buy what I want'—he loaded them with so much breakfast they were having trouble carrying it. And Penny-Rose was caught between laughter and exasperation.

She was given time for neither. 'Now to the Bois de Boulogne,' Alastair decreed. 'It's the closest.'

It was also the loveliest.

The sun was already warm with the promise of a magnificent day to come. The park was filled with mothers and pushchairs, elderly couples sitting soaking up the sun, and small children playing tag or racing with balloons...

In true royal fashion Alastair found a tree and claimed it as their own. He signalled to someone in the distance, and before she knew it there were two deckchairs set up for their comfort.

'Now…' Alastair surveyed his scene with satisfaction. 'Breakfast as Parisians do it.'

'Oh, right. Parisian princes, would that be?'

'You don't like this either?' His face fell ludicrously and it was all Penny-Rose could do not to laugh.

But he was watching her with such an expression of anxiety on his face—and the sun was warm on hers—and it was Paris in the springtime and the coffee smelled tantalising and the pastries were exquisite…

'I'd have to be a mindless idiot not to enjoy this,' she said softly, smiling up at him. 'No, Alastair, I don't like this. I love it!'

After that the shopping was better, though Penny-Rose still found it uncomfortable. She was now wearing some of the clothes she'd purchased the day before. That made her feel less conspicuous in these over-the-top salons, but every time she dressed at the end of each fitting she couldn't help thinking, These aren't my clothes.

These aren't me.

She was buying clothes for a princess, she thought. Not for Penny-Rose O'Shea. Or two-bob Rose. Or whoever she was. She was beginning not to know any more.

Once he'd made the decision to accompany her, Alastair took his duties seriously. He insisted on seeing her as she emerged in each outfit, and his smiles of approval disturbed her still more. She was turning into what he wanted, she thought.

She was becoming no longer herself. She was becoming Alastair's wife-for-a-year, and the prospect was more and more disturbing.

But finally Alastair was satisfied. Almost. At four o'clock he announced her major wardrobe complete, and he escorted her to a tiny shop off the main boulevard.

The shop needed some explaining, and he did it fast.

'Before you get the wrong idea, my mother told me to bring you here,' he told her hastily. At the look on her face, his dark eyes glinted with laughter. 'This,' he said with an evil grin, 'may well be the best part of the whole shopping experience. It's knicker time.'

And as Penny-Rose gazed into the window she could only gasp.

These weren't just knickers. They were flights of fancy. Here were silken wisps of elegance that had nothing at all in common with the sturdy knickers she was wearing— except maybe two holes for legs.

'I can't buy these!'

Alastair's grin faded. 'You can.' He took her hand, imbuing her with the gravity of the occasion. Only his still-lurking glimmer belied his serious tone. 'And you must. The servants will be doing your washing, and they'll expect quality.' His grin returned in full and she stared at him in confusion. The rat—he was enjoying this! 'Remember,' he told her, 'this marriage has to appear real.'

Somehow she found her voice. 'Your wife would wear things like these?'

He nodded, with no hesitation at all. 'Of course she would.' He motioned to a flagrantly indecent set of bra and panties on a flagrantly indecent model, and his laughter became more pronounced. 'My wife would especially wear those.'

'Oh, yeah, I can see Belle in those!'

His smile faded again, but this time the fading was for real. He hadn't been thinking of Belle, she realised as she watched his face. The rat had actually been thinking of her!

This was crazy. The whole situation was absurd!

'So I'm buying these to keep up appearances with the laundress?' she asked carefully.

'That's right.'

'Does the laundress have any colour preference?'

He pointed to the bra and pantie set—bright crimson. 'I bet bright crimson would work a treat.'

'On the laundress.' She glowered.

He assumed an air of injured innocence. 'Who else could I be thinking of?'

'Right.' Her glower intensified. 'Well, if this is just between me and the laundress, you can take yourself off while I make my purchases.'

'Hey…'

'This is between me and the laundress and the shop assistant,' she said firmly. 'Back in your box, mister.'

'That's no way to talk to a prince.'

'A princess can talk any way she wants. And you want a virtuous bride. Virtuous brides wouldn't be seen dead in a shop like this, especially with their prince—and especially before they're married.'

He thought that one through and didn't like it. 'That's not playing fair.'

'Who's playing?'

Their eyes locked.

And suddenly the question was very, very real.

Who was playing? Who could tell?

The scary part was that somewhere in that over-the-top place Penny-Rose finally started to enjoy herself. With Alastair firmly left outside, she let the sales assistant have her head and she tried on set after set of the most gorgeous lingerie she'd ever seen in her life.

And standing in front of the three-way mirror she started to get an inkling of how Cinderella must have felt.

'It's an out-of-body experience,' she told herself, looking at her trim body clothed only in a wisp of lace that could well have been cut—with cloth left over—from a very small handkerchief. She grinned. 'Or an only-just-in-body experience. I guess when this is all done I can donate these to charity.'

Charity would have a fit, she decided, and it was with a chuckle and arms full of packages that she emerged to the street to find her waiting prince.

But her prince wasn't where she'd left him. She searched the street, and found...

A dog. A pup...

The pup was some sort of terrier, knee high, wire-haired and fawn and white. Or he might once have been fawn and white. Now his fur was matted and filthy, and a deep, jagged wound stretched along most of his side. One leg was carried high, his shaggy ears drooped and his eyes were dull with misery.

It was the end of a Paris business day. The boulevard was crowded, with legs going everywhere. Even though Paris was a city of dog lovers, in this crowd one small dog didn't stand a chance of being noticed. Except by Penny-Rose, who was feeling bereft herself and was searching for Alastair.

She saw the dog first. As she emerged from the shop and saw him, the small creature was pushed too close to the road, and she realised how he'd got that wound. He was headed that way again.

'No!' With a cry of dismay she dropped her parcels and darted forward. She was too late to stop the dog being pushed onto the road, but that didn't stop her from diving after him. There was a screech of brakes, and the next moment she was crouched in the gutter, her arms were full of dog and her eyes were reflecting his pain.

'Oh, no...'

'Rose!'

Alastair had been waiting with the patience of a saint— sort of. He'd been across the road, window-shopping and desperately trying not to think of what his intended wife was doing. He hadn't succeeded. For some reason, all he could think of was his bride wearing that lingerie...

So he hadn't noticed the dog through the mass of legs across the street, and the first thing he saw was Rose diving head first into the crazy Parisian traffic.

Hell! What on earth...? His heart hit his mouth. He

lunged across the road, ignoring braking cars. Reaching the gutter where she knelt, he looked down in consternation.

What was wrong? Had she been hit?

'Are you...' His voice was a cracked whisper as he stooped urgently toward her. 'Rose, are you OK?'

'Yes.' She didn't even look up.

His breath came out in a long rush. Dear God...

'What...what on earth are you doing?'

'It's a dog,' she said, as if he were stupid. But he wasn't. After that heart-stopping moment when he thought she'd been hit, his brain was starting to function again. A taxi veered toward them, and before she knew what he was about, she was bodily lifted and carried back toward the shops.

'You'll get yourself killed!' Alastair had been badly shaken and it showed. 'Are you crazy?'

But Penny-Rose wasn't noticing, not even when he carried her across the pavement to the safety of the shop doorway. She had eyes only for the dog she carried. Alastair set her down, and her fingers kept probing, parting matted fur so she could see the damage.

What was wrong with him?

The dog lay limp and unresisting in her arms, past caring. Alastair knelt beside her, and watched woman and dog together. He felt as if all the breath had been knocked out of him.

'Let me see.'

'He's...he's injured.' She opened her arms so Alastair could see the state of her small burden, and it was all Alastair could do not to wince at the sight.

'Hell!'

Penny-Rose wasn't listening. Pedestrians were having to detour around her, but she didn't notice. She sat with her back against the door of the lingerie shop, and her whole attention was on one small dog.

'It's OK,' she comforted him. 'It's OK, little one. You're fine now.'

Only he wasn't fine. He needed a vet.

'Alastair...'

He was way in front. 'Paris is a dog-loving city,' he said, kneeling beside her. He knew without being asked that she'd never abandon this mutt—and in truth he felt the same himself. The dog was gazing at him now, and there was something about those huge brown, pain-filled eyes...
'There are organisations who take in strays, and there are veterinary surgeons everywhere. I'll call a taxi and we'll take him to the closest.'

She breathed a long sigh. She wasn't sure what she'd expected—she knew this man so little—but all she knew now was that he hadn't reacted like her father.

Her father would have taken one look at the dog—and one look at his daughter's concerned face—and fetched his gun.

But Alastair was different! His first thought hadn't been how best to be rid of the problem and how to hurt her in the process, but how best they could help the dog.

He was some man, she thought dazedly.

He was some prince!

But she needed to concentrate on the dog. She turned back to her pup, cradling him close to give him some body warmth. 'He's only a baby.' The pup was still at the gangly half-grown stage, when dogs were most at risk, outgrowing their cuteness and risking abandonment in the process. 'And he's shaking all over.'

'I'd imagine he must be. He looks as if he's been hit by a car.'

'And he's starving. His ribs... Oh, pup...'

'Come on.' Alastair made a decision and glanced round the street with a rueful smile. 'You can't stay here.'

For the first time she seemed to take in her surroundings. They were hardly dignified. She was sitting in the dust with her stockinged legs out in front of her. She'd lost a shoe. The pup was curled into her lap. Her pale lemon suit was filthy, there was blood on her skirt and she must look...

She didn't get any further. A flashbulb went off not four feet from her face.

She looked up blindly and the flash went again.

The cameraman had been in a nearby café and had been attracted by the screech of brakes. This had the makings of a great photo opportunity, he'd thought as he'd watched what had unfolded—a beautiful woman crouched on the pavement among scattered shopping, her arms full of bloodied dog.

So, while the rest of Paris had gone about its business, he'd hauled his camera out of his bag and headed over to take a few snaps.

Penny-Rose looked up, her face uncomprehending. What...?

'Let her be,' Alastair growled, and the man's attention turned to him. His eyes widened in shock.

Alastair de Castaliae!

Alastair wasn't as well known in Paris as he was in his own country but this cameraman was on the fringe of the paparazzi. He knew his celebrities! In one instant his face changed. He saw a fortune dangling before his eyes, and his camera turned onto automatic.

In the next thirty seconds he'd taken maybe a dozen shots—of the couple crouched on the pavement, of the girl trying to protect her dog from the flash of the camera, and Alastair using his body to shield her.

Which left Alastair in a dilemma. Stopping the camera was impossible. Short of doing the man harm, he had to be allowed to take what he wanted.

He had a choice. He could treat the cameraman as the enemy—which would get them nowhere—or he could treat him as an accomplice, which might achieve more.

'OK, we're sprung.' Alastair sighed, letting his shielding hand drop. 'Any chance of doing a deal?'

'What sort of deal?' The man was still behind his camera, still clicking, but his mind was in overdrive. There'd be at least three major newspapers who'd bid for these pictures, and that was just in France. In Alastair's principality there'd be more, and then there were the women's magazines…

Alastair could see the way his mind was working. And his thoughts had to move even faster.

'We're making an announcement on Friday,' Alastair told him. 'Back home. Would you like to be around when we do?'

The man's eyes practically started from his head. He was only just getting a toehold in this industry, and this could be the break he'd been looking for.

'Sure.' His camera was lowered as he stared in disbelief. 'Yeah, great.'

'Then give us a day before you publish these pictures,' Alastair said. 'One more day of peace.'

'You're marrying the girl?' The man looked closely at Penny-Rose and tried for the jackpot. 'Will you tell me your name?'

'As I said, we're making an announcement on Friday.' Alastair refused to be drawn further, and Penny-Rose took her cue from him.

What else could it be but an announcement of a marriage? The cameraman knew the conditions of the old prince's will. All the paparazzi did. It was their business to know.

'And you're taking a last fling in Paris before the world catches up with you?' The photographer was a romantic at heart, and he could see the headlines over his pictures. He took an uneasy glance along the street. The last thing he wanted now was someone else with a camera. He wanted a scoop!

And Alastair was as eager to get off the street as the cameraman now was to have them leave. He hauled out a business card and scribbled something on the back. 'Here. Ring this number, ask to speak to Dominic and he'll organise you a free return flight.'

'You're kidding!'

'I'd never kid about something like this.'

The man stared down at the card and his face twisted. And he decided on a bit of honesty himself. 'You know, this could be just what I need...'

'I know. But *we* need another day by ourselves.'

The man hesitated. 'I won't be scooped?'

'Not if you keep your mouth shut for twenty-four hours.'

'I can do that.' The photographer grinned, making up his mind. 'One more day with your lady, your dog and your...' His grin broadened. 'Your lingerie.'

With a gasp, Penny-Rose realised what had happened. She'd thrown aside her bags as she'd dived for the dog. She was now sitting among a pile of...

Oh, good grief!

'Can you edit those out?' Alastair demanded, glancing around at the wisps of silk. He fished in his wallet. 'I'll make it worthwhile.'

'Nothing would make editing this out worthwhile,' the man said bluntly. Then, as Alastair signalled for a taxi, he threw in a last question. 'The dog—I assume it's a stray?'

'I imagine he is,' Penny-Rose said shortly.

'Are you keeping it?'

A taxi drew to a halt. Alastair helped Penny-Rose to her feet and thankfully she tumbled into the car, still clutching her pup.

'Just tell me,' the photographer said, this time more urgently. *'Are you keeping the dog?'*

Alastair was gathering knickers and bras and shopping bags together. They needed to get out of there, fast!

'Are you keeping it?' the photographer demanded a third time, and Alastair turned to Rose.

Her face was white and strained. She'd had enough, he knew. These days in unfamiliar territory had taken their toll.

She was so far from home, he thought as he watched her hug the pup. She'd come close to being killed, she was badly shocked, and now... Suddenly he realised he'd never seen anyone look so alone.

She wasn't alone. She was with him. He needed her—and if he wasn't careful he'd lose himself a wife!

Were they keeping the dog? She was holding on as if she needed the pathetic little creature more than the pup needed her.

'Yes,' Alastair said strongly, and with the same flash of insight that had seen her homesickness, he knew this was the only sensible thing to do. 'Of course we're keeping the dog. Why not?'

The cab driver took them to the nearest veterinarian.

'Not to the animal shelter?' Penny-Rose asked, and Alastair shook his head. For some reason he was unsure what to say—they were both in unfamiliar territory.

So they stayed silent while the vet clucked over the little dog, cleaned and stitched the gash on his side, examined his leg and told them the pup was starving but the leg itself was just badly bruised.

'Take him home and give him a light meal—not too much as his stomach won't be accustomed to big feeds. Look after him well, Madame.'

The vet smiled, speaking in halting English. Normally this man didn't deign to use English—it was his opinion that foreigners should speak French in France—but there was something about Penny-Rose that made a man want to help all he could. Her halting thanks in French had made him smile. 'Though I have no need to tell you to take care of him,' he said gently. 'I believe you are doing so already.'

Unlike the photographer, he didn't ask if she intended keeping him. That was assumed.

But she'd been thinking, and there were problems.

'I don't think I *can* take him,' she faltered as they emerged again to the streets of Paris. She looked up and found Alastair's eyes gravely watchful. 'At the end of the year I need to go home. The quarantine between here and Australia takes months.'

'What's a few months between friends?' Alastair smiled. OK, if he was getting committed, he might as well get really committed. To a dog, mind, he told himself hastily. Just to a dog! 'If there are problems, I'll look after him when you go.' He looked down at the disreputable mutt, the pup looked mournfully back and Alastair's grin broadened. OK. Commitment here didn't seem too hard. 'My castle could do with an aristocratic hound as watch dog.'

'Alastair...' Penny-Rose caught her breath at the enormity of his offer. She felt like she'd been handed the crown jewels. 'You're kidding?'

'Would I kid about something that means so much?'

She stared up at him, and something caught in her throat. Penny-Rose had never been handed a gift like this in her life. Gifts weren't something that came in her direction—ever.

With a struggle she kept her voice light, though she felt tears of gratitude welling and it was all she could do to fight them back. 'An...an aristocratic hound,' she managed. 'I don't think so.'

'He'll do.'

She thought about this. 'As I'll do for a wife. Make-believe until the real thing comes along.'

'That's right.' He was looking at her strangely, and her insides were kicking—hard.

Someone had to be practical.

Penny-Rose had to be practical! It was the only way if she wasn't going to sink into the man's chest and sob.

'Well, let's go, then.' She set her chin with resolution. 'Take us home. Your temporary wife and your aristocratic hound. You're getting yourself quite a collection, Alastair de Castaliae.'

'I believe I am,' Alastair murmured.

And he didn't look like a man fighting against the odds one bit.

* * *

To her surprise their cab didn't take them back to Hotel Carlon.

'I've arranged something different,' Alastair told her as they drove in the opposite direction. 'While you were trying on knickers, I made a few phone calls and had our bags moved.' He grinned. 'Maybe it's just as well. Something tells me Scruffy will be more comfortable there.'

'Scruffy…' She was confused, but recovering. 'Who are you calling Scruffy?'

'Not you.' Alastair's eyes teased her. 'Though come to think of it…' At the look in her eyes he held up his hands in mock defence. 'No. The pup. Of course I mean the pup. Scruffy.'

'His name,' she said with injured dignity, 'is *not* Scruffy.'

'Well, what else would you call him?'

Scruffy! Humph. 'His name is Leo.' With her equilibrium almost restored, with it came decisiveness. She raised her eyebrows with aristocratic hauteur, a princess in the making. 'It means king.'

'A king.' He sounded stunned. 'Like in Leo the lion?' He looked down at the bandaged, bedraggled mutt in her arms, his lips twitched and he nodded. 'Oh, right. I see it.'

'You will.' She smiled. 'Just wait until he recovers.'

'So I have a Leo and a Rose,' he told her, but he was half talking to himself. 'What next?'

What next indeed?

What next was introducing her to their hotel, which was pure pleasure. Penny-Rose walked through unassuming street doors and was stunned into silence, but this time it wasn't grandeur that was taking her breath away. It was loveliness.

The hotel's two floors were sedate and low. Built in pink-washed stone, the buildings circled a cobbled courtyard. French windows opened out to the garden, and her first impression was the fluttering of soft drapes in the evening air.

And that air was gorgeous! The courtyard was a mass of flowers. Wisteria clung to hundred-year-old vines, there were early roses, delicate pink tulips, soft blue forget-me-nots... And more.

The hotel itself looked almost inconspicuous in the garden setting. Chairs and tables were scattered under the trees, comfortable and inviting. There was a well-used bird-bath, a sculpture of a woman drooping over a fishpond; there was the gurgle of running water behind...

This was just fabulous, Penny-Rose decided, and when Alastair showed her to her room—no porters here—it was even better. Her bedroom was simplicity itself, its major adornment being the window-framed courtyard. There was crisp white linen, fluffy white towels, a bath with no fancy gadgets at all, mounds and mounds of pillows and...

A dog basket!

She looked an astonished question at Alastair. How had he managed this?

'I told Madame what our problem was,' he told her. 'She moves fast. Someone will be here any minute with minced steak for Leo.'

'Oh, Alastair...' She found herself suddenly close to tears again. Drat the man. She didn't give way to emotion—she *never* gave way to emotion—and here he was unsettling her as no one else could.

As usual, when things got too much for her she resorted to practical matters. Or tried to. 'Thank you,' she said simply. 'But...' She glanced at her watch. It was well past eight and even her own stomach was rumbling. 'How...how can *we* eat?'

'We're in the middle of the best eating district in Paris. We can eat any time we want.'

She bit her lip. He'd done so much already, and this was hard. 'I mean... I can't leave Leo.'

'Now, how did I know you'd say that?' He smiled down

at her, that heart-stopping smile that made her insides do somersaults. 'No problem. While you feed Leo I'll make a foray out into the big, bad world and bring us back food. We can eat in the courtyard.'

'Two picnics in one day!'

He nodded. 'I can handle it. Can you?'

'Yes. Oh, yes.'

She couldn't think of anything more perfect.

CHAPTER SIX

SO WHILE Leo, fed and cuddled and exhausted, slept as he'd never slept in his life before, his new owners ate *pâté de fois gras*, then succulent beef, cooked to perfection in a rich Burgundy sauce, with tiny button mushrooms and crusty bread to soak up the juice. Followed by cheeses...

By the time the last of the main meal was gone, Penny-Rose knew she'd been to heaven and back. This was food at its most exquisite served in take-away containers as if it were everyday food.

And there was more! With the air of a magician conjuring up a rabbit or two, Alastair poured a rich, crimson wine that was full of the sunlight of late harvest, and when he produced bite-sized meringues, luscious strawberries and lashings of clotted cream, she could hardly believe her eyes. She'd never eaten like this.

She hadn't known such food existed!

'I can't believe you found all this,' she told him and he looked smug. In truth, he was enjoying himself hugely. He was accustomed to women who treated great food as an everyday event. Rose's delight made him smile.

It also made his chest expand a notch or two. 'I'm a hunter-gatherer from way back,' he said as his smug look intensified. 'There's not a lot me and my trusty club can't do.' He pointed to the remnants of the beef. 'That's Brontosaurus Rex. Or ex-Rex. Whatever.' He pushed his chest out another notch. 'But there's no need to congratulate me. A man does what he must in order to survive.'

'Yeah, right. You survive on this kind of food?'

'I can survive on less,' he told her. 'If I need to. One

Rex drumstick instead of two.' His smile faded. 'As I imagine you have in the past.'

Unaware of the way his gaze had just changed, she popped a strawberry into her mouth and sighed in bliss. 'Oh, yes. You know, I may well go home at the end of our twelve-month marriage the size of a house.'

'That's fine by me.' More of Rose? He could handle that.

Her smile disappeared as she thought about it. 'I guess…me getting fat would give you your excuse to divorce me.'

'I doubt anyone would think that was a reasonable excuse,' he said, and suddenly thought, Hell, what excuse was he going to use? Mutual incompatibility?

The more he was getting to know her, the more that reason wouldn't wash.

'It'll have to be homesickness on my part,' she said, watching his face and guessing where his thoughts were headed. 'Or I'll suddenly find out about Belle.'

'And you didn't know about Belle beforehand?'

'I was stupid,' she said cheerfully. 'Thick as a brick. I can be when I want to be. Or even…' her smile deepened '…when I don't want to be.' She decided to confess all. 'You know, the day before we came here, I started adding a fourth layer to my wall without putting in throughstones.'

'Throughstones?' He was lost.

'Stones stretching across the wall to tie the sides,' she said patiently. 'Ask Bert how stupid that is.'

'I…um…I see. An unforgivable sin.'

'You'll think so if your wall falls down in two hundred years,' she retorted, and he smiled.

'I'll be watching for it.'

'And you'll deduct the cost of repair from my wages? That'd be right.'

'Or from your great-great-grandchildren's wages,' he told her. 'Remind me to put something in my will to that effect. My great-great-grandchildren can gather stupidity compensation when it's due.'

'It won't be necessary,' she said with dignity. 'I was only three stones along before I realised. The throughstones are now in place.'

'You relieve my mind enormously.'

'That's the plan.' Her green eyes twinkled and a faintly remembered phrase came wafting thought her consciousness. 'After all, as long as domestic service survives, the convenience of the employer comes first.'

He grinned at that. 'Very good. I like it. And it's not convenient to me if my wall falls down.'

'That's the ticket.' She chuckled. 'Your wife and your dog will have fallen down in their duty, and that would never do.'

It took Alastair a while to answer that. He sat and watched her as she tackled a last strawberry. The day had taken its toll. She looked ruffled and tired, but she'd showered and changed into her own faded jeans and cotton blouse. She looked fresh and clean and lovely—but she was as far from the circle of women he usually moved in as she could be. Her toes were bare, her hair was gently stirring in the warm night air and she wasn't wearing a scrap of make-up.

Domestic servant?

She was Cinderella to a tee, he thought ruefully. But all at once he knew that if the fairy godmother were to arrive with her magic wand, he wouldn't have her wave it.

'I suppose not,' he said at last, and he sounded suddenly bewildered.

But Penny-Rose's own confusion was settling. The last rays of evening sun were lingering over the courtyard, with their echoes of warmth from a perfect spring day. Her little dog lay fast asleep in her room. Soon she'd go up to him, and sleep in her wonderful bed, and wake tomorrow morning to sunshine and...

And to Alastair.

The direction her thoughts were headed suddenly jarred home with a vengeance, and her eyes flew wide with shock.

'What's wrong?' Alastair saw the look.

'I...'

'Rose?'

'Sorry.' She shook her head. 'It's nothing.'

'But something's bothering you.'

'No. It was just something...' She fought for an explanation—any explanation—because the real one surely wouldn't do. 'It was something I forgot to tell Bert, but it'll be OK.'

'You're not still worrying about your wall?' He was gently teasing, but the concern in his voice deepened her sense of shock.

Because she knew now what was happening. There was no question about it. It had never happened in her life before—it was something she'd read about but had never believed was real—but there was now no doubting its reality.

It was happening to her right now.

Help!

'We can go home tomorrow—back to your precious stone-walling,' Alastair was saying, and she had to concentrate fiercely to hear him. 'The only task we have left is to order your wedding dress.'

She thought that through. They'd left her wedding dress to the end of their stay because they knew their chances of making such a purchase without publicity were remote. But now it didn't matter. Tomorrow was Thursday. They'd make their purchase and then they'd fly home to announce their plans.

But Penny-Rose's plans had suddenly changed.

A wedding for a year...

She looked at Alastair and the familiar lurch happened all over again. She knew it now for what it was. It was inescapable, and it had changed things for ever.

This was serious commitment, she thought desperately. This man was *some* prince and he was offering her marriage. It might only be for a year, but she'd still agreed to marry him. What would she say?

'With this ring I thee wed. With my body I thee worship...'

The words of the wedding vow came to her as clearly as a song on the late night air.

'To love and to cherish... From this day forward...'

They'd be making the vows in jest—to last for a year.

But why?

Alastair wasn't in love with Belle. Penny-Rose's thoughts were flying every which way and it was a wonder she wasn't saying things out loud. Confusion was certainly washing over her face. He wasn't in love with anyone, she thought. After the shock of Lissa's death, Alastair had been deeply wary of commitment. He wanted a wife of convenience, and that was all.

So...she was to be his wife of convenience for a year and after that she'd be followed by another convenient bride.

Belle.

It was all wrong, she thought wildly. This man should be loved to distraction. He deserved to be loved to distraction.

As Leo was going to be. As much as she was capable of loving.

Or...as she loved already.

This had never happened to her before, but she knew she was right. Somehow her heart had been handed over, like it or not. Whether or not it was sensible, she was head over heels in love with Alastair de Castaliae, and she didn't know what to do with it.

But she knew now that when she made her wedding vows, she'd be incapable of lying.

'From this day forward...' There'd be a part of her that was desperate for those words to mean exactly what they said. And they meant for ever.

If that was what she wanted...

The old Penny-Rose was surfacing. The Penny-Rose who was prepared to fight and steal and do anything she must to protect her sisters and brother. The Penny-Rose who knew the only way to get what she wanted was to fight with everything she possessed and then more.

Well, maybe she didn't have enough armoury to win this battle, but she knew where she'd start.

'I don't think I will buy a wedding dress,' she told him, fighting to keep her voice casual and watching his face as she did.

He frowned, thrown off balance. 'Why not?' He hesitated, and the forlorn look she'd been wearing came back to him. 'You're not thinking of pulling out, are you?' His voice was anxious. Hell, if she pulled out now... 'You'll still marry me?'

'Now, what have you done in the last couple of hours to make me change my mind?' she teased. 'You've been a model fiancé.'

The lurching in the pit of his stomach settled. A bit. 'Gee, thanks.'

'Think nothing of it.' And then her smile died. 'I've... It's just I've been thinking about your mother's offer.' She bit her lip, hardly daring to go on, but her commitment had already been made, and she had no control over it now. She was suddenly playing for keeps and, whether Alastair knew it or not, his precious independence was in deadly trouble.

But she couldn't tell him that. She had to keep her voice practical and sensible. As all her plans must be.

'I'm tired of spending your money, and I'm tired of shopping,' she declared. 'I've decided I'll wear your grandmother's wedding dress after all.'

'But...' He frowned. 'I thought you objected to the idea. That it's for my true wife to wear.'

'Belle doesn't want to wear it, and you said that's what I'll be,' she told him. 'Your legal wife. For a year.'

And however long I can manage, she told herself silently. From this day forward... For ever if I can manage it.

* * *

Penny-Rose lay in bed that night and thought, 'What have I done?'

Beside her, Leo slept the sleep of the dead. Filled with food for maybe the first time in his life, his wounds eased with painkillers and his body snuggled into soft cushions, he lay beside his new mistress and thought he was in doggy heaven.

Her fingers trailed down to touch the pup's wet nose, and she thought she was pretty much in the same place.

But not doggy heaven. Penny-Rose heaven.

'He's given me so much,' she told the sleeping Leo, her conscience giving her a swift kick in the ribs. 'He's handed me a dream for a year. And he's handed me you. It's dreadful of me to go for more.'

But that was just what she was doing. Because somewhere during the last few days, something strange had happened. Her heart had been twisted and turned till she hardly knew herself.

'I've fallen in love,' she whispered. 'So help me, Leo, I've fallen for the man. Now what?'

Fight?

'Just try,' she said to the darkened room. 'Just…take this marriage as it comes but say my vows as if I mean them. And then cross every finger and every toe that I can work a little magic. See if I can change his formal Princess Rose into a Penny-Rose he can love.

'And you'll wear his mother's wedding dress?'

She was questioning her own motives. Leo wuffled in his sleep and Penny-Rose grimaced and buried her nose in the soft pillows.

'It's very wrong.

'But if you don't try…

'If you don't try then Belle will end up with her prince,' she told herself. 'Or with *my* prince. And he doesn't want her any more than he wants me. It's such a waste!

'So what makes you think you can win his heart?

'Nothing at all.' She was two voices. The voice of reason

and the voice of hope. 'Nothing at all,' she repeated into the stillness. 'Oh, but, Leo, I can only try!

'You'll have to do more than try, girl.'

'I'll do whatever it takes,' she said, with a resolution she was far from sure of. 'That and a bit more. Heaven help me, I can't do anything else.'

She flicked on her light with sudden determination and crossed to where the day's parcels had been stacked. In a minute she'd discarded her much-patched pyjamas and was standing in front of the mirror.

She was now wearing one of today's purchases—a soft white nightgown of the sheerest silk. It was cut low across her breasts, it was embroidered white on white with tiny rosebuds and she'd never seen anything so exquisite in her life.

'I can't wear this,' she told her reflection. 'I bought this for the laundress.'

Her curls were tumbled to her shoulders, her face was tinged with a faint embarrassed pink and the reflection that looked at her was...

'I'm not wasting this on the laundress,' she addressed the sleeping Leo. She gave her reflection a rueful grimace. 'It makes me look almost lovely.

'Lovelier than Belle?'

She glowered. 'It doesn't matter how lovely Belle is. She doesn't love him.'

And she herself did!

Alastair was sleeping just the other side of the wall. This was a suite, meant for a family. A door connected the rooms. All she had to do was turn the key on her side, and Alastair turn the key on his...

If I was a bit more brazen I'd knock, she thought suddenly, and then she gasped and took a step back as she realised where her thoughts were taking her. 'Penny-Rose O'Shea... You hussy!' she said aloud.

'If that's what it takes,' her reflection answered her.

'Nope.' She slid the nightgown off and reached for her pyjamas. 'I'm not into seduction.

'So what are you into?

'I'm into loving the man to bits,' she responded to herself. 'It's all I have, and if that's not enough…'

The nightie lay on the floor and mocked her.

'We'll see,' she said, and grinned. 'All's fair in love and war. This is a combination of both!'

And in the next room, Alastair lay and stared at the ceiling with a lot more uncertainty. There were things going on in his life that he no longer understood.

It had all seemed so straightforward, he thought grimly. After Lissa's death he'd made the decision to stay uninvolved, and he'd succeeded. His life was what he wanted.

He had a profession he was proud of. He had more than enough money. And he had Belle, available when he needed her, with the thought of a couple of children down the track.

Children…

They'd be quiet little things, he thought, conjuring them from the darkness. Maybe they'd have pigtails and hula hoops. Whatever, they'd be kids for his mother to pamper…

Marguerite deserved grandchildren.

He checked out his vision of his children—but something strange was happening. Instead of faceless prettiness, as there always had been, he now had Penny-Rose's face before him.

Rose, he told himself. It's Rose… Not Penny-Rose. It was stupid, but it was important somehow. He had to keep this formal.

So she was Rose. But why did his kids suddenly have Rose's twinkle, and Rose's cheekiness, and…?

For heaven's sake, no! If they had personality like Penny-Rose—no, *Rose*—then how could he not love them? he thought, and loving anything…

It didn't work. He'd watched his mother break her heart when his father had died, and his own gut had been wrenched enough when Lissa had been killed. Lissa had been such a good friend that the hurt had been dreadful.

So... It was a lesson he'd learned the hard way, but he'd learned it well. You don't give your heart!

He wasn't giving his heart now. This was a marriage of convenience.

What had Rose said? 'The convenience of the employer comes first.'

That was what he was, he thought grimly. An employer. He was paying her to be his wife for a year, and emotional ties didn't come into it.

How could they? She didn't need him long term. That was why he'd chosen her. She was Australian, and she'd be off home as soon as she had her money.

Leaving him with Belle.

Which was the way he wanted it, he told himself hastily. The way it had to be.

The sensible way.

As was Rose's decision to wear his mother's wedding dress. It was economical. Wedding dresses—especially ones suitable for a royal wedding—cost a fortune. She was saving him money with her decision.

Putting the convenience of the employer first!

So why didn't she feel like one of his employees?

'I'm not very good at this Cinderella thing,' he said out loud. 'I'm not comfortable with it. It's the fact that she has nothing and deserves so much that's making this all so damned gut-wrenching.

'That's why you gave her the dog.

'That's right. She has nothing. A dog can't hurt.

'And you're comfortable with her wearing your mother's wedding dress?

'It's sensible.

'Hell!'

He turned over and pummelled his pillows, trying not to

envisage Rose in his mother's wedding dress. And then trying not to envisage Rose sleeping just through the wall. Could he hear her? There was a soft murmuring through the door. She was awake. She was probably lonely. All he had to do, he thought, was take his key and—

No!

That was the way of madness. He had to stop Rose from turning into Penny-Rose every time he thought of her.

But she was so close...

How could he block her out? Out of his thoughts? Out of his life?

He'd ring Belle, he decided. She'd talk sense into him. He'd phone her and talk through the Palmerstone job. They'd been working on it together, so she wouldn't think it was strange...

It was one in the morning!

He put the phone down with a reluctant grin. This was *not* a good plan. Belle would think such a phone call was weird. He'd never hear the end of it.

But he had to speak to someone or he'd go nuts.

'What I need,' he told the darkness, 'is another Leo. I wonder whether Rose will let me share...'

His key lay in his hand, and he held it so hard that it hurt.

CHAPTER SEVEN

'JUST leave everything to me.'

Back at the castle, groomed to an inch of her life, Penny-Rose was waiting to become Alastair's official fiancée. They'd called a press conference, the gallery was packed and it was all Penny-Rose could do not to bolt for Australia.

She might have recovered her equilibrium since Paris, she thought desperately. She might have made a few resolutions, but she wasn't a limelight kind of girl.

'This is Belle's forte,' she muttered. 'Can't a substitute wife do as well?'

'You *are* a substitute wife,' Alastair reminded her, and she grimaced.

Oh, great. As if she needed reminding of *that*.

'You don't need to be nervous. Leave the talking to me.'

'I can't do much else with my grasp of French,' she said bitterly. Then she took two deep breaths and got a grip. Cowardice was not what was needed. Resolution was what was needed. From this moment on.

'I do know a phrase that might be useful,' she said thoughtfully. 'How about, *Vous ne me ferez jamais parler*?' She clutched her throat with melodramatic flourish. '*Jamais, jamais, jamais…*'

'*You'll never make me talk*,' Alastair translated faintly. He grinned as the tension eased a bit. '*Never, never, never.* Very useful. Where on earth did you learn that?'

She arched her eyebrows in superior fashion. 'Where else but from my "Use-full Frase For Toorist" book? It's the same place I learned *I am bleeding to death*, *That man has a gun* and *Can you tell me how to reach the border*?' She managed a smirk. 'See? I'm ready for anything.'

Alastair choked on laughter and the tension dissipated even further. But... This was serious. 'As I said, maybe it's best if I do the talking. Most of the press have a solid grasp of English, but—'

'But you don't want me to mess things up by threatening border runs.' Penny-Rose nodded her understanding. 'OK. I know my place. We Cinderella types are designed to sit and simper and look beautiful, and hope like hell the pumpkins stay at bay.'

'Rose...'

She put up her hands. 'I know. I know. I'm being paid heaps, and I'll be good. I promise.' Then she peeped through a crack in the door, trying to see what was waiting for them. 'I wonder if our cameraman from Paris is here? That'll be one friendly face.'

'Yeah, he knows us intimately, right down to the colour of your knickers.' Alastair grimaced.

'He doesn't know the real me wears cotton-tails.'

'Cotton-tails?' Alastair said faintly. 'What are—'

'You don't want to know.' She chuckled. 'If you want to keep your delusion that real women wear black lace thongs, it's fine by me. Oh, he is here. I can see him.'

'He'll be here.' Marguerite was fluttering round the edges, adjusting Alastair's tie and putting one last dab of powder on Rose's nose. 'He'd be mad not to be. A new princess... It's what the press have been waiting for for years.'

'Then let's not keep them waiting.' Alastair's mind was still on the cotton-tail conversation and he was finding it hard to concentrate. But he had to get a grip. Somehow... He swung the door wide. 'But, Rose, for heaven's sake, *leave the talking to me*!'

Only, of course, she couldn't. Because, after the first brief announcement, the press didn't want to hear from Alastair alone. They knew this man. Who they didn't know was the lady he was with, and they were fascinated.

'Tell us about yourself,' one asked in English, and Penny-Rose hesitated, obedient to instruction.

'May I leave that to my—'

'No,' she was told very definitely, and before Alastair could get a word in they'd pushed her further. 'Tell us what you think of our country.'

Well, she'd been obedient for all of a minute. It hadn't worked. So what else was a girl to do but tell the truth?

'It's the most beautiful country I've ever been in,' she said frankly. And then, despite her nervousness, her eyes twinkled. 'Apart from mine.'

'You love Australia?'

'Of course I do!'

'Then what's the attraction here?'

She rolled her eyes at that, and turned toward her intended. She looked Alastair up and down, taking in his immaculate suit and gorgeous tie and the way his eyes creased into laughter lines and...and all of him. Her laughter lines creased into readiness.

'Need you ask?' She chuckled, and the room laughed with her.

They loved her. There were flashbulbs going everywhere and the questioning intensified.

'People are saying this is a marriage of convenience,' she was told. 'What do you say to that?'

Alastair opened his mouth to answer, but his bride-to-be was in her stride and unstoppable.

'They're right, of course.' Her twinkle stayed firmly in place. The only way to meet an accusation of an arranged marriage was partial honesty. 'I imagine you know the terms of my future husband's inheritance? If he doesn't marry then the estate will be dispersed and that'll cause hardship. So...'

Her eyes strayed around the members of the press and it was as if she was speaking to each person in turn. In moments, she'd made a big impersonal gathering seem like a cosy afternoon-tea chat. 'It's convenient for Alastair to be married to me, and it's convenient for me to be married to Alastair.' She smiled, and her hand reached out to lightly touch his. 'Very convenient. And apart from that, we think we'll like it very, very much.'

'You're in love with him!' one of the female reporters said, on a note of discovery, and Penny-Rose refused to be disconcerted.

'Of course. Aren't you?' she asked innocently. 'I thought everybody was.'

There was general laughter and then the questioning turned back to Alastair. 'So what makes this lady special?'

Alastair took a deep breath. But suddenly his rehearsed answer went out the window because the touch of her hand on his had thoroughly unnerved him, and so had the way she'd handled this terrifying occasion. Then there was the fascination of the cotton-tail question...

All at once there was only one answer to make.

'If you can't see that, you must be blind,' he said, and there was a note of sincerity in his voice which gave Penny-Rose pause. Her laughter died.

If it were this easy...

'Where's your engagement ring?' someone asked, and she put up her hand to display a family heirloom. That rightly took the press's attention, giving them both much-needed breathing space. Things were moving way, way too fast!

And it was some rock, Penny-Rose thought, gazing down at her ring. Alastair had only produced it this morning and she wasn't accustomed to its weight on her finger. Its weight wasn't insignificant.

Pity it wasn't granite...

What had Alastair had once said? *I never thought I'd be wining and dining a woman who'd look at rock and gasp...*

She looked up and found his eyes on hers—and she knew he realised exactly what she was thinking. Laughter sprang between them. And something else...

'Where's your dog?' a voice called, breaking the moment. Which was just as well, because neither of them knew where the moment had been leading. Into unknown territory... She broke from Alastair's gaze to see the cameraman from Paris beaming at her from across the room. 'Where's the pup you found?'

'You mean...' Her voice wasn't quite steady. She adjusted it and tried again. 'You mean Leo?'

'Leo!' the man said, and his grin broadened. 'I might have known you'd call him something daft like that.'

The rest of the press gallery were fascinated.

'He was a stray,' the cameraman explained to the room in general. Maybe he was giving away a scoop, but it was he and only he who had the pictures from Paris. Generating interest would do no harm at all. 'The lady rescued him.'

That had everyone enthralled—as did the looks that were being exchanged between Alastair and Penny-Rose. A love story and a rescued dog... Well, well. This, then, was the human-interest story they'd craved.

Readers didn't want to hear about a marriage of convenience. Readers wanted romance—and, amazingly, it seemed as if it was romance they were being given.

'Can we see your dog?'

Penny-Rose raised her eyebrows at Alastair and he gave an imperceptible nod. Anything to get the spotlight off them, his eyes told her.

She knew exactly how he felt. 'No flashlights, then,' she said sternly, and escaped Leo-wards.

'Is it true Miss O'Shea is a stone-waller?' she heard as she left the room.

'Of course it is,' Alastair replied. 'It's an unusual occupation, but you have to agree that Miss O'Shea is an unusual woman.'

'You've never met anyone like her?'

'Why do you think I'm marrying her?' was the last thing she heard as she fled.

*　　*　　*

With Leo in her arms, she managed to regain her composure—sort of.

'Isn't he gorgeous?' she demanded of the room full of cynical, case-hardened reporters. Leo was clean—almost—but he was bandaged, he'd lost a heap of hair, one ear was torn and his rib cage protruded for all to see.

But Penny-Rose had decreed he was gorgeous, and there wasn't a person there who would have disagreed.

'Do you like the dog, too?' someone rounded on Alastair, and he managed a grin. The dog... Oh, right. The dog. He'd been looking at the lady.

'I like the dog.'

But he was still looking at the lady.

'This is seeming more and more like a love match,' someone whispered. This was suddenly a very different marriage to the one the press had expected.

Penny-Rose sat by Alastair's side and fielded questions with aplomb—without the least hint of shyness and uncertainty. And she glowed. Nestled on her lap, her disreputable pup wagged his tail and licked her face, then shifted to lick Alastair's face in turn. Alastair pushed the shaggy face away, but it was a very half-hearted push.

'He likes it,' a reporter whispered to a colleague. 'Hell!'

'We have headlines,' another said. 'A royal romance!'

'Followed by a royal marriage,' her colleague agreed. 'All at once, I can't wait!'

There was one more question to ask. A reporter had checked his notes. 'It says here that your name is Penelope,' he said to Penny-Rose. 'But you've been introduced as Rose. Will you be Princess Penelope?'

'No,' Alastair butted in before she could get a word out. 'She'll be Princess Rose.'

Princess Rose...

Penny-Rose looked at him with eyes that were suddenly bright with unshed tears. Princess Rose...

It might be too darned formal—but in that one unguarded moment he'd spoken her name almost as if he loved her!

* * *

'Have you seen the newspapers?'

Belle's voice woke Alastair from sleep. He'd spent the night on interminable paperwork and just before dawn he'd fallen into a troubled sleep where Rose and Leo had mingled with uncertain duty. An hour later the phone had rung.

'How could you humiliate me like this?' Belle's voice was as shrill as he'd ever heard it. 'Our friends know this is a marriage of convenience, but this…' She took a deep breath. 'This is disgusting!'

'What's disgusting?' Alastair's heart sank. Uh-oh.

'Every newspaper has these headlines… ROYAL WEDDING. PRINCE FINDS HIS CINDERELLA…' She seemed to be sorting newspapers as she spoke and he could hear as she tossed them aside. 'They're dreadful.'

'You knew this was going to happen,' Alastair ventured, still not sure what the problem was. 'It was a mutual decision to do this.'

'Yes, but I didn't know this would happen. Alastair, these pictures… You're sitting on the pavement in Paris, she's cuddling a dog and you're *hugging her*. And there are knickers and bras lying everywhere, and some sort of nightgown that only a slut—'

'Hey, hang on…' But he was in trouble. He knew it.

'You look as if you love her!'

And there was the nub of the matter. Alastair closed his eyes, exhaustion washing over him in waves.

'I don't love her,' he told Belle, making his voice as firm as he could. 'She was nearly hit by a car. The dog *was* hit. They were distressed and shaken. I carried both of them off the road and—'

'And you were stupid enough to be photographed.'

Silence.

Alastair thought that through and he didn't like it. He didn't respond, and after a moment of silence Belle decided that maybe she'd gone too far.

'Are you still there?'

'I'm here.' He let the weariness creep into his voice and she heard that, too.

He could hear her rethink. She was playing for a major prize here. It might be wise to draw back.

'Then can I tell my friends it was an accident? That you were playing the hero for a moment—nothing more?'

'I hope you don't tell your friends anything,' he·retorted. 'Belle, you know how much is at stake. The marriage has to seem like it's permanent.'

The silence was from Belle's end now.

'I hate it,' she said at last, and Alastair nodded. So did he. Didn't he?

'But, Belle, if we back out now…'

'We'll lose everything.' She was still focussed on that ultimate prize, he realised, and it was giving her pause. 'I don't want that.'

'So what do you want me to do?'

'Act formally,' she ordered. 'These photos make you look ridiculous. Like a schoolboy with a crush.'

'I'll see what I can do,' he told her, and then he said his goodbyes—as formally as she intended that he act when Rose was around—and he tried for sleep again.

It didn't work.

Formal?

Formal and Rose didn't make sense!

Formal and Belle made sense, but he wasn't marrying Belle.

He was marrying Rose.

The thought suddenly made the thought of sleep impossible.

The next few weeks passed in a blur. There was so much to be done!

Marguerite came down with influenza and retired to bed. 'It must be from too much excitement,' she told her son, and Alastair thought of how much effort his mother had gone to in the past couple of months and felt guilty to the core. He couldn't load her with anything else.

Penny-Rose's knowledge of what was needed for a royal wedding could be written on the palm of one hand. The organisation therefore fell to Alastair, dredging up memories of relatives' weddings in the past.

Finally he located and re-employed the man who'd acted as his uncle's social secretary. He was a godsend, but he wasn't enough.

There were wedding organisers, caterers, state officials—everyone had to put their oar in. Almost the whole principality had to be invited and the production looked bigger than *Ben Hur*!

'Can't we just elope?' Penny-Rose asked as she saw the lists. Every night when she came in from her stone-walling there were more decisions to be made. She did what she could, but the look of exhaustion on Alastair's face was making her feel dreadful.

'It's a State wedding,' Alastair sighed and raked his hand through his hair. 'To be honest, I never imagined it'd get so out of hand. Every politician, every person with any clout, any deserving local…everyone would be offended to their socks if not invited.' He gave a twisted smile. 'It's made use of the chapel unthinkable. There's simply not room. The big marquee has to come all the way from Paris.' He shook his head. 'At least…'

He paused, and she prodded him to continue. 'At least?'

'At least I'll only have to do this once,' he admitted. 'Belle and I will have a simple civil affair.'

'Well, bully for you and Belle.' But she said it under her breath. Alastair was back concentrating on his lists.

She looked across the dining table at him for a long moment. The man looked almost haggard, and the urge to rise from the table and go to him was almost irresistible. To touch him on the shoulders… To massage the tension from his back and to ease the strain…

But she couldn't. She wasn't wanted.

She was simply a name in the marriage ceremony, she thought, and any female would do. His real wife would be Belle.

The thought was almost unbearable.

And dinner was finished.

'Goodnight, Alastair,' she said softly, but he didn't look up from his interminable lists. He was blocking her out.

She pushed back her plate and quietly went back to her living quarters.

Back to Leo.

'He's driving himself into the ground,' she told her little dog. 'As well trying to make everyone happy with the wedding, the estate management's a mess, and he's also trying to keep his architectural projects going. The thing's impossible.'

But he had no choice. The only thing he could give up was his architecture.

'And he can't do that because that's what he is,' she continued. 'An architect.'

Leo wagged his tail in agreement and she gave a rueful smile.

'You understand. He's an architect. Not a prince.'

As Penny-Rose was a stone-waller—not a princess.

'So you and I keep to ourselves, Leo' she murmured. 'We're not wanted. I'm just a name on a marriage certificate.

'For now…'

Penny-Rose might have gone back to Leo, but her presence stayed on with the man she intended to marry, an insistent consciousness that followed him everywhere.

He hadn't said goodnight. He'd been a bore.

But if he'd looked up, he might have said—he would have said, Help me with this. And she'd have stayed and sat beside him and the smell of her would have permeated his consciousness even more and…

And he wouldn't have been able to keep it formal. As he must!

So he'd let her go back to her dog, and he'd gone back to his paperwork, and his exhaustion and sense of confusion deepened by the hour.

He saw her again at breakfast—briefly. They were curt with each other, as formal as Belle would have wanted. Then he saw her from a distance during the day.

It was strange how often his eyes strayed to where the new west wall was gradually taking shape.

Because there'd be his intended bride, filthy and happy, chipping away at stones with Leo scrabbling in the dust beside her. Woman and dog were inseparable and Alastair had to fight an almost irresistible urge to join them.

But… 'Keep it formal,' Belle had demanded, and it was the only sensible thing to do.

Formality increased as the wedding grew closer. It was the only safe barrier. But unknown to Alastair, Penny-Rose was learning more and more about the castle and its workings.

And finally she had to break through Alastair's barriers to use it.

'Henri has bunions,' she informed him as they sat down to dinner a week before the wedding. Marguerite was still keeping to her room—her flu had left her worryingly frail— so Alastair and Penny-Rose dined alone. Formally. But for once Penny-Rose was breaking the ice. 'You should do something about it,' she told him.

Bunions… Alastair frowned. Henri… 'Did you say bunions?'

'I certainly did.' She attacked the last of her salmon with vigour, and as the butler came in to clear the plates, she beamed up at him. 'That was great, Henri. Can you tell Claude that we loved it?'

'Certainly, M'selle. Cook will be delighted.' The elderly man beamed, with a smile that left Alastair in no doubt that Rose was twisting his staff around her little finger. Henri was searching to please her now. 'Claude has made you something called lamingtons for dessert,' he told her. 'He bought a book on Australian cooking, just to make you feel at home.'

Smiling, the butler carried away his plates, and Rose turned back to Alastair as if her point had been made.

'See? He's limping, and it's getting worse.'

'I hadn't noticed,' Alastair confessed, and she smiled her royal forgiveness. If he could be regally formal, then so could she.

'No. That's because you're busy. But I did. The servants talk to me, so I can find out what's wrong.'

He'd noticed that. Often he heard laughter and it'd be Rose and the housekeeper or Rose and a kitchen maid or Rose and the gardener...

And more and more, he felt shut out.

Now, as Henri reappeared bearing a tray of...lamingtons, for heaven's sake, Alastair directed his attention to his butler's feet.

Sure enough, the man was limping.

'Rose says you need time off to have your feet attended to,' he said ruefully. 'Why didn't you tell me? I'm not a slave-driver.'

'I never thought you were,' Henri said with dignity. 'But if it was *your* workload we're talking about, I might agree. You drive yourself too hard, M'sieur.'

'I don't.'

'You do.' Henri paused and then relented. 'But if I may say so, M'sieur, it's a pleasure to work with you. You've been a breath of fresh air in the castle.' He beamed at the pair of them. 'You and M'selle Rose.'

Especially M'selle Rose, his smile said.

'Thank you,' Penny-Rose said faintly, and Henri's beam widened.

'It's my pleasure. So my bunions can stay as they are, thank you very much,' he declared. 'Take time off with your wedding in a week? No, M'sieur. Tomorrow Marie and I intend to attack the marital suite.' His eyes grew misty at the thought. 'It's forty years since your uncle brought his bride home. That marriage didn't last, but…if I may say so, that wedding was an arranged match. Not a match as this is going to be. Oh, no!'

And he limped back to the kitchens, leaving them staring after him in astonishment.

'He thinks it's real,' Alastair said, and Penny-Rose concentrated on her lamington.

'Then I guess we've succeeded.' It took an effort, but she didn't look at him. 'Have a lamington. They're delicious.'

He took a bite of a chocolate-and-coconut-covered square, but his mind wasn't on his lamington.

'What have you been telling them?'

Her eyes widened at that. 'Me? What do you mean?'

'This is a marriage of convenience,' he said heavily. 'I thought it was obvious, but the staff don't believe it.'

'Maybe they don't want to believe it,' she said gently. 'The staff have had a rough time, with the old prince's failing health and then Louis. Maybe they're looking for stability.'

'That doesn't depend on a stable marriage.'

'Of course not.' She lifted another lamington and took a bite, then surveyed it with care. 'I guess Henry the Eighth had quite a stable household.'

'Henry the Eighth?'

'The one with six wives,' she told him.

'Hey!' That was a bit much. 'I only want two.'

'Very moderate, I call it,' she agreed equitably. 'And there's been no suggestion at all of anyone getting their heads chopped off.' She chuckled across the table at him, and it was all he could do not to drop his lamington.

Hell! Things were getting seriously out of hand.

'Rose…'

'These lamingtons are great,' she enthused. 'Maybe we should honeymoon in Australia so we can eat more. I could introduce you to pavlovas and Vegemite sandwiches and pie floaters...'

'Pie floaters?'

'Pies in pea soup,' she explained, and he shuddered.

'If you don't mind, I'll stick to our cuisine. But that reminds me. Our honeymoon...'

'Sorry?'

'The press are expecting us to honeymoon.'

'They can expect all they like. I haven't finished my wall.'

'Oh, for heaven's sake...' His pent-up emotions overflowed and he thumped the table. 'Rose, will you take this seriously?'

'You don't want me to take it seriously.'

'I...'

'It's a mock marriage,' she told him. She rose and gave him a mock curtsey. 'Pardon me, Your Serene Highness, but there's nothing serious about our marriage at all. So I'm not going on a honeymoon anywhere. Sorry, Alastair, but I'm going up to say goodnight to your mother.' Then she flashed her infectious grin at him. 'Stop worrying. Go and design a mansion for someone and stop thinking of weddings. You're getting paranoid.'

And before he could stop her, she'd come around the table and kissed him, very lightly, on the top of his head. It was a teasing kiss—perfunctory and light-hearted.

There was no reason at all for him to put a hand to his forehead.

And for him to leave his hand there for a good three minutes after she'd left the room.

CHAPTER EIGHT

'I HAVE a surprise for you,' Marguerite told her.

It was four days before the wedding. The castle was a hive of activity, and with the invasion of so many strangers, Penny-Rose had grudgingly conceded to stop her walling.

She was feeling like a pampered but caged pet, but at least time with Marguerite was productive. The effects of her influenza were dragging on. Marguerite was wan and listless, she spent most of her day in bed and she had everyone worried.

But she was still scheming.

'I've had the most wonderful plan,' she told Penny-Rose. 'For your honeymoon.'

'We're not having a honeymoon.' Penny-Rose glanced up as Alastair entered the room. 'Tell her, Alastair. We don't want a honeymoon. Just a well mother-in-law.'

'That's all we want.' Alastair crossed the room and gave his mother a kiss. 'Dr Barnard was here earlier. What did he say?'

'Just more rest.' His mother sighed her exasperation. 'You can't expect anything else at my age.'

'That makes you sound as if you're ninety instead of only just seventy,' Penny-Rose retorted. She grinned. 'Madame Beric says all you need is a good tonic. She makes poor M'sieur Beric drink some foul potion full of aniseed and all sorts of horrible herbs and spices that she swears will cure anything from warts to ingrown toenails. Do you want me to get you some?'

'I don't think so,' Marguerite said faintly.

'Are you missing Paris?' Alastair demanded, sitting down on her bed. His mother had a lovely apartment near

112

the Seine. She'd dropped everything to come here when
Louis had died and she hadn't been home since. 'You've
been doing so much—'

'I've hardly done anything,' his mother cut in.

'You have. Without your organisation this household
would be a mess. But you must miss your friends.'

'I'll go back to Paris after I see you safely married,' she
told him, and Penny-Rose gave her a strange look.

'Don't you want to go back to Paris?' she asked, feeling
her way. 'Is that the problem?'

'I do…'

'You don't like it here?'

'I love it here,' Marguerite confessed.

Leo, bored with sitting on the settee with his owner,
jumped down and nosed over to the bed. He leapt onto the
covers and curled into the crook of Marguerite's arm.

'Maybe we could buy you a pup to keep you company,'
Penny-Rose suggested, and Marguerite's face stilled.

'I don't need a dog.'

'Do you have many friends in Paris?'

Alastair frowned. Was this any of Rose's business?

But Marguerite was sighing, preparing to open up to
Penny-Rose as she never talked to him.

'I only moved to Paris after my husband died. But I
have…I have a beautiful apartment. Belle decorated it for
me.'

Oh, great. She could imagine. A big, elegant apartment,
modern and chic and sterile as hell. 'But not company?'

'I don't know many people yet…'

'Then move back here,' Penny-Rose said cheerfully.
'Decide to stay here permanently.' She cast a quick glance
at Alastair and saw she had his approval. 'Leo and I need
company. It'd be great.'

'That'd be lovely dear, but…'

'But?'

Marguerite looked at her son, and then looked away. 'It'd
be worse,' she said softly. 'I'd stay for twelve months and

then you'd leave and Belle would come. And Belle and I don't…don't get along.'

'Belle likes you,' Alastair protested, but Marguerite shook her head.

'Belle's a woman who can't share. Whereas Penny-Rose…' She smiled fondly at her future daughter-in-law. 'Penny-Rose even shares her dog.'

'Certainly, if it means I can get a night's sleep without someone scratching his hindquarters in my face.' Penny-Rose grinned. 'So, yep, I'm extraordinarily generous, and willing to be more so. Stay with us.'

'No.' Marguerite shook her head. 'As soon as the wedding's over, I'll return to Paris.'

'If you're better,' Alastair growled, and she nodded.

'I'll be better. For your wedding I must be.' Her scheming look reappeared. 'But speaking of weddings, I was telling Penny-Rose when you came in. I have a surprise.'

'I don't trust your surprises,' Alastair said cautiously, and his mother flashed him her most innocent of looks.

'That's a dreadful thing to say. As if I'd do anything you mightn't like.'

His look of foreboding deepened. 'What have you done?'

'It's my wedding present to you both. I've booked you a honeymoon.'

'A honeymoon…' Alastair took a deep breath and looked sideways at Rose. 'We're not going on a honeymoon.'

'Of course you are,' his mother said, turning business-like. 'Everyone needs a honeymoon, and you're looking grey with exhaustion. Isn't he, Penny-Rose?'

Penny-Rose could only agree. 'Yes, but—'

'There you are.' Marguerite beamed. 'She agrees. And I'll bet Penny-Rose has never been on a decent holiday in her life. Have you, dear?'

'No, but—'

'You're not refusing to take your wife on a holiday?' Marguerite demanded of her son. 'Especially as it's already booked.' She shifted Leo to retrieve a handful of pamphlets which had been lying on the coverlet. 'These came with this morning's post. Don't they look wonderful?'

Penny-Rose looked at what she was holding up—and was caught.

'Koneata Lau…'

'It's the most beautiful resort in the world,' Marguerite told her. 'It's part of Fiji, but it's a tiny cluster of separate islands, and you book your own island. This is the one I've booked for you.'

She opened a pamphlet to poster size, and a vision of sparkling seas, palm trees, golden beaches and tiny thatched cottages caught Penny-Rose's imagination like nothing else could have.

A beach…

'I've never been to the beach,' Penny-Rose whispered before she could stop herself. 'Not properly. Not to swim. Not to stay.'

'You've never been to the beach?' asked Marguerite in surprise.

'None of us has,' she confessed. 'We lived a hundred miles inland and there was never money or time for holidays.' She took a deep breath and pushed the thought away.

'But no. Marguerite, it looks gorgeous, and thank you, but no. Honeymoons aren't for crazy marriages like ours.'

She flashed an uncertain glance at Alastair. A honeymoon would be pushing him too far and too fast, she thought. She had every intention of trying to make this marriage work, but this was a bit much.

'Besides, there's Leo,' she added, as if that clinched it. 'I couldn't leave him.'

But Marguerite had an answer for that. 'Henri and I will look after Leo as if he's our own,' she said, scratching a floppy and adoring ear. 'The staff are besotted by this dog of yours.' They were, too. In the weeks since his arrival, Leo had crept around the collective castle hearts like a hairy worm.

But that wasn't the issue here. The honeymoon was.

Beaches… Palm trees… A honeymoon with Alastair… It was a fantasy. Nothing more. But it was *some* fantasy.

She had to get away from these brochures!

'My sisters and brother will be here tomorrow,' she told them, and she couldn't stop her voice from sounding a trifle desperate. 'I can hardly get married and leave them to fend for themselves. It wouldn't be fair.'

'You intend to entertain your siblings on your honeymoon?' Marguerite was aghast.

'This is their holiday.' Penny-Rose looked at Alastair, but his face gave nothing away. This was up to her. 'They…they work hard, too, and Alastair's offer of a trip here is unbelievable.' She tilted her chin and ignored Alastair's silence. 'It'll be fun, showing them around.'

'You can hardly take your family sightseeing when you're just married,' Marguerite said, shaking her head. Beside her, Alastair's face didn't reveal one hint of what he was thinking, and it was starting to make Penny-Rose nervous.

But she had to be firm. For both of them. She set her chin in a manner both Alastair and his mother were starting to know. 'Alastair will have work to do, and we don't intend to hang in each other's pockets.' Then she cast one more wistful glance at the posters. One last look! 'So no. Thank you very much, but no.'

She rose and managed a smile at both of them, albeit a shaky one.

'I'll leave you to each other's company. I…have things to do.'

Only, of course, she didn't.

She just needed to get away from the strange expression on Alastair's face.

It was an hour later that Alastair found her.

Strangely unsettled, Penny-Rose had headed up to the battlements. Now she sat on the parapets, hugging her knees and staring out over the countryside below.

Thinking of beaches. And hopeless marriages.

And Alastair!

He found her there. She hadn't heard him climb the stairs, and for a moment he stood in the sunshine and watched her face as she stared out away from him.

She looked bleak, he thought. And why not? She'd spent her life denying herself, and here she was denying herself again.

'I've never been to the beach…'

That one phrase had been enough to give him pause. When she'd left, Alastair had stood with his mother, staring down at the pamphlets.

He had so much…

So would she, he'd told himself. In a year she could afford to go to any beach she wanted.

But…he wouldn't be with her to see.

She'd never been to the beach.

She asked for so little. She wouldn't have entertained the idea of this marriage if it hadn't been for her family and the villagers, he knew, and the thought of her denying herself this was suddenly unbearable.

'Isn't there any way you can organise things and go?' his mother had asked at her most wistful, and he'd looked down at her with suspicion. It had been her wheedling tone.

'Just because you're sick…'

'No, dear. Just because Penny-Rose needs you.' She had hesitated. 'You know, the estate's almost at the stage where it'll run itself. Once you're married, there'll be funds for everything. Your new secretary knows the running of the place. When the wedding's over he can take over with ease.'

'And my architecture?'

'No one's indispensable,' she'd said meekly. 'And you only marry once.'

'Mother…'

'Sorry.' She'd peeped a smile at him. 'But that's what the world needs to think. And they'll think it very odd if you don't honeymoon. It would give Penny-Rose so much pleasure, and I've already booked it...'

Her voice had faded, but her expression had stayed wistful.

It had been more than a man could stand. He'd taken the pamphlets and had gone to find Rose. And now he'd found her...

Leo was sitting by her side, his doleful expression matching hers. The pup looked up at Alastair as he appeared, and the look of reproach he gave him was almost enough to make him laugh. Good grief. You'd have sworn the dog knew!

He crossed to where she was sitting. 'Rose...'

She glanced up, and then looked back out to the river. Fast. 'I'm sorry,' she told him, without looking up at him again. 'I didn't know your mother was planning anything so dire.'

'As dire as a honeymoon?' He sat beside her. Archers had once waited up here for the Vikings to sail up the river to loot and pillage. It was hard to imagine anything so dreadful on a day like today. The sun was warm on their faces and below them the river drifted dreamily on.

'I've never been to the beach...'

'I've just been on the phone to Koneata Lau,' he said.

'Cancelling things?' For the life of her she couldn't keep the desolation out of her voice. 'That's good.'

'No. Confirming them.'

She swung around to face him, disbelief and hope warring within.

Disbelief won.

'We can't.'

'We can.'

Hope flared again, but died just as fast. 'No. It's not possible.'

'If I can, why can't you?' He ruffled Leo's shaggy ears and grinned. 'The only problem that I can see is Leo, and I've fixed that. Henri is having his bunions attended to on the day after the wedding. He'll therefore have two weeks' enforced rest, during which he'll watch daytime television with Leo on his chest. And Madame Henri will dice fillet steak for your pup every night.'

'Alastair…' Rose was half laughing, half exasperated. 'You know I can't. It's a gorgeous offer, but…'

'But what?'

'My sisters and brother…'

'That's what I need to talk to you about,' Alastair took her hands and pulled her to her feet.

Which was maybe a mistake. Her breasts pressed against his chest and, as his hands gripped hers, the texture of her hands and the closeness of her body was doing something really strange.

But he didn't know what.

Just tell her what you need to tell her and then get out of here, he thought desperately. Now.

And somehow he made his voice work.

'You're doing this for your family,' he told her. 'Marrying me. But when you said, "I've never been to the beach", I thought, They won't have either. And they're probably just as deserving as you.'

'But—'

'Shut up and listen, Rose,' he said kindly. 'This is the plan. Your brother and sisters arrive tomorrow. They can have a couple of days looking over the castle. We marry on Thursday. And on Friday the five of us get on a plane and head for Fiji. The press will think your family is going home. Koneata Lau is renowned for its privacy—photographers are shot on sight. The five of us can have a very good time.'

'The five of us…'

'All of us. The very best honeymoons are crowded,' he said, smiling. 'What do you say?'

'Oh, Alastair…' He'd taken her breath away.

All her life she'd wanted to give her family a holiday.

She'd struggled but so had her siblings. Nothing was easy for a family as in debt as they were.

And to take them all to Koneata Lau!

Penny-Rose couldn't resist it. Not when it wasn't just for her. But… All sorts of possibilities were opening up before her.

'Your mother,' she whispered, starry-eyed. 'Alastair, your mother could come, too.'

'Yeah, and my butler could do with a break, and Bert and his team would build great sandcastles.' He grinned. 'No.' Then he relented. 'Actually, I asked my mother, but she refused. She's probably right when she says that a long plane flight would be too much for her.'

'If only she were well…'

'We'll get her well. After our honeymoon we'll pressure her to stay here and give her a real break. But meanwhile, the thing that could give her real pleasure is if we agree to her plan. What do you say, Rose? Can I take you—and all your family—on a honeymoon to die for?'

'Oh, Alastair…'

It was too much. She looked up at him, her eyes shining, and suddenly, before he knew what she was about, she'd stood on tiptoe to kiss him.

It had been intended as a kiss of gratitude—nothing more. But she was emotional, close to tears, and she let her feather-light kiss stay on his lips for just a fraction of a second too long.

Because somehow it became not a feather-light kiss.

In fact, feather-light suddenly didn't come near it.

Beneath the surface, a feeling of warmth and empathy had begun to flow between them, a feeling as powerful as it was real.

They'd started this mad escapade as a business proposition. What had passed between them over the last few weeks had made them friends. And now it was shifting past that, to something deeper.

It had already shifted for Penny-Rose—she knew what she was feeling—but Alastair had no idea. He'd let her lips touch his and he'd expected a soft brush of mouth against mouth. Nothing more. What he received was an electric charge that nearly blew him away.

A surge of wanting engulfed him that was so powerful— so all-engulfing—that his hands moved up instinctively to steady her. As if she could somehow feel it too and be hurt by it…

So it was natural that his hands held her—steadied her and pulled her even closer into him—and the linking of their lips forged an even stronger tie.

Dear heaven…

The taste of her… The feel of her…

He'd never felt like this, he thought dazedly. It was as if her body were merging into his, and there was a sweetness about her that he could hardly believe. She was so innocent and she was lovely and…

She was his for the taking!

She was to be his wife!

For a whole minute he gave himself up to the exquisite sensation of savouring her touch. Of believing that something could come of this. Something magical—that he could let himself love.

That in four days' time he could marry this woman and take her to him and have her for ever. That he could let this sensation run where it would, letting it take its own sweet course and be damned with the consequences.

The kiss grew deeper. Neither could break the moment— break the contact. It was too precious. Too infinitely valuable.

It was as unexpected as it was magical.

'M'sieur…'

The voice came from below, echoing up toward the open door of the battlements. Henri must have seen Alastair come up and was calling for him. 'M'sieur, are you there?'

With his feet, it would have been agonising for the old butler to climb the spiral staircase, but they heard the heavy tread as he started.

It was enough.

Penny-Rose broke away. For one long moment Alastair still held her, his hands on her arms and his gaze locked on hers. Their eyes reflected mutual confusion, mutual need.

But...

'I'm coming, Henri,' Alastair called, halting the man before he could do himself any damage. 'What is it?'

'Your friend from Paris is on the phone,' Henri announced. He didn't need to say more. The staff hadn't taken to Belle, and Henry used the same words and inflection every time she rang. *Your friend from Paris...*

Belle. It had to be. As usual, her timing was impeccable.

They both knew who it was, and the moment Henri spoke it was as if Belle had planted herself firmly between them. Alastair let his hands fall.

'I'm...I'm sorry,' he managed, and Penny-Rose shook her head. It needed only that. An apology.

'Don't be. I had no business to kiss you.'

'I never meant—'

'Of course you didn't.'

He looked at her uncertainly. 'It was just... I was worried about my mother and—'

'Don't explain things to me, Alastair,' she said gently. Because he couldn't.

Penny-Rose had to let him off the hook. He was confused and angry with himself. She could see that. He'd broken his unwritten rule.

This hadn't been a kiss that could be forgotten. It had been very much more.

Penny-Rose knew how much more.

But Alastair would have to discover it for himself.

* * *

Talk about avoidance! If two people didn't want to see each other, a castle was the perfect home, and over the next twenty-four hours a lot of avoidance took place.

Not deliberately, of course. Never that. But if Penny-Rose happened to be visiting Marguerite and Alastair decided to do the same, he'd hear her voice on the other side of the door and suddenly think of an urgent task down in the offices. Or there was a cow in trouble in the river pasture that he felt sure his farm manager needed a hand with—and it just happened to be dinner-time when it happened.

Or he'd be eating his leftover dinner in the kitchen and hear Henri and Rose walking down the passage toward him—and suddenly he'd had enough to eat. He was no longer hungry.

This was going to be some marriage if he couldn't face the girl!

'Keep it formal,' Belle had said, and he knew he had to do just that. Anything else was the way of madness.

He was *not* going to lose his head like a stupid schoolboy. He was not exposing himself to the pain he'd known when he'd lost Lissa. And what he'd felt for Lissa seemed pale to how he could love—

No! Stupid thought.

Keep it formal. Or keep away entirely.

For twelve months?

He could only try.

It was madness, Penny-Rose thought bleakly to herself as she tried for sleep that night. Loving and marrying without being loved in return?

For the first time she let herself think what would happen if her loving didn't work. What if nothing came of it but cold formality and divorce after twelve months?

'I could go nuts,' she told Leo. 'Seriously, peculiarly nuts.

'Or maybe I am already. Maybe I was nuts to agree to this wedding.

'And now a honeymoon.'

But she wasn't backing out. No way.

And money didn't enter the equation at all.

'He's a dish, but he's awfully formal.' Twenty-four hours into their visit her siblings were ready to pronounce judgement. 'Why doesn't he lighten up a little?'

'He's a prince. He's supposed to be formal,' Penny-Rose retorted, and got howled down for her pains.

'I suppose he wears a crown to bed.' It was Heather, ever the impertinent one. She chuckled, bouncing on her sister's gorgeous bed where they'd retired to gossip. 'What does he wear to bed, by the way? Gold pyjamas?' And then, as Penny-Rose turned an interesting shade of pink, her sister homed in like a bee to honey. 'You mean you don't know?' Her jaw dropped in amazement. 'You're engaged to be married and you don't know what he wears to bed?'

'Maybe he doesn't wear anything to bed,' Elizabeth butted in, and Penny-Rose sighed. Honestly, her sisters were incorrigible.

'Do you two mind? Mike's here.'

'Michael's sixteen years old and sixteen-year-olds know more than you do,' Heather retorted. 'I'll bet!'

It was Mike's turn to blush, but still he grinned.

'Does he lighten up?' he persisted. Accompanying Penny-Rose, Alastair had met them off the plane. He'd been welcoming and pleasant but distant, and as soon as they'd reached the castle he'd excused himself, saying Rose needed time with her family. They'd hardly seen him since.

'He's busy,' Penny-Rose said. 'He has a wedding to organise the day after tomorrow, and it's getting to him.'

But the question stayed the same. 'Does he lighten up?'

'He does.'

'If you say so.' Heather was fidgeting with her fingers. Finally she found the courage to say what needed to be said. 'Love, you're not just doing this for the money, are you? For...for us?'

If ever there was a time to admit that this was a marriage of convenience, this was it. But Penny-Rose gazed around at the anxious faces of her family and found she couldn't do it. They were obligated to her enough, she thought. It wasn't fair to make the debt deeper.

'Stoopid, why would I—?'

'You would.' Heather sounded seriously perturbed. 'I know you would. It's been getting harder and harder for us all to stay at uni, and the burden's been heaviest on you. But I can leave. I can defer for a couple of years.'

'You'd never go back.'

'I would.'

'The odds are against it.' Penny-Rose spread her hands. 'I love stone-walling and that's what I'm doing. We're all doing what we want. So...you're going to be a doctor, Liz will be an architect and Mike will be the world's greatest engineer.'

'But...' Heather was still threading her fingers. 'Not if it means you're making an unhappy marriage.' Her chin lifted and her eyes met her sister's. Really, they were very alike. 'Do you love him?' she asked directly.

And there was only one answer to that.

'Yes, I do,' Penny-Rose said, in a voice that left no room for doubt.

And how could she doubt? Marriage to Alastair? It was what she wanted, even more than stone-walling.

But what was she being offered?

Not a proper marriage. A marriage of convenience.

'Of course I love him,' she said, even more strongly. 'And how can I want any more than that?'

How indeed?

CHAPTER NINE

AND then there was the wedding.

It was a wedding that Cinderella's fairy godmother would have approved of, Penny-Rose thought dazedly. Because the magic wands were certainly out in force today.

She'd seen the plans for the ceremony taking shape but until now everything had seemed a chaotic muddle. But on her wedding morning she woke and looked out of her window, to find the mass of canvas and poles and ropes had suddenly transformed themselves into the most beautiful marquee imaginable.

The thing was huge—almost as big as the ground floor of the castle. It stretched over the river pasture. Part of it was built on a wooden platform over the river, and there were royal pennants flying gaily from each pole. The whole scene looked like something out of a mediaeval pageant.

And the sight made her catch her breath. Up until now this wedding had been all talk. Today it was very, very real.

What on earth was she doing? Doubts crowded in from every side as she showered and left her bedroom. Help!

But who to turn to?

Her siblings were nowhere to be found—they only had three days in this magic place and they were making the most of them. Even Leo had deserted her. Confused and aimless, she wandered down to breakfast in a muddle of caterers and guests she didn't know. Then she headed outside.

Here the sense of pageant was even stronger. Carriages were drawn up by the front gates, and horses were being walked up and down in readiness. The servants were in full

126

livery. In her jeans and T-shirt, Penny-Rose felt like some-one who'd wandered onto the wrong stage.

It was someone else's stage. Someone else's life! Not hers.

Where was Leo?

And where was Alastair?

He must be as confused as she was, she thought, but he'd absented himself. Deliberately? Maybe. And maybe he should. It was supposed to be unlucky to see the bride on her wedding day.

The way Alastair was acting, it seemed it was unlucky to see the bride at all!

But he'd organised Koneata Lau. They'd have their hon-eymoon when they'd have to see each other.

'Yeah, it'll be a really romantic honeymoon—just me and Alastair—and Heather and Liz and Mike,' she mur-mured, scooting around the edges of the marquee and trying hard to settle the sick feeling in the pit of her stomach.

Think of the beach! she told herself helplessly. Koneata Lau. It was something to look forward to.

It *should* have been just Alastair and herself, alone on a tropical island.

Which would have been a waste! she acknowledged, be-cause if Alastair had his way they'd probably stay at op-posite ends of the island. It made sense to take the kids with them.

'Be contented with what you have, girl,' she muttered to herself crossly. 'Today you have a truly royal wedding.' She looked around at the marquee with pennants flying, the castle as backdrop, the liveried servants, the carriages and the horses…

'A mediaeval wedding,' she continued.

For a year!

She kicked her toes against a rock, and one corner of her mind registered that it had a very flat base and would make a great foundation stone for the wall she was building.

That was what she felt like doing, she decided. Climbing

back into her overalls and heading back to her stone-walling.

'But I can't,' she told herself. 'Get back to your quarters, woman. Turn yourself into a princess. You have a prince to marry.'

'It's magic,' Heather declared as she bounced into the room an hour later. Penny-Rose's sister looked stunning in a tiny crimson suit—a minuscule leather skirt and matching jacket. Her entrance destroyed the mediaeval air in an instant.

Heather gave her sister a resounding kiss, and whirled to admire herself in the mirror. 'Thank you for not insisting on bridesmaids,' she told her, stroking her leather with sheer joy. 'I spent all my money on this and I'll love it for ever. My friends back home will die of envy.'

Penny-Rose managed a smile. 'It's great. Where…where are the others?' Where's Alastair? she'd meant to say, but she couldn't.

'Elizabeth's flirting with a distant cousin who says he's a count. A count, for heaven's sake! I could end up with a dynasty of royal relations! And Alastair and Mike have taken Leo for a walk by the river.'

Penny-Rose took a deep breath. She might have known. Her little brother was almost overwhelmed by all of this. While her sisters thought it was exciting, Mike had been growing quieter and quieter, and to take him for a walk had been pure kindness.

Her Alastair, she thought, was the very nicest prince a girl could ever marry!

She forced her voice to stay casual, but emotion was threatening to overwhelm her. 'They'll…they'll be back on time?'

'Of course. There's hours to go.' Heather plonked herself down on the bed, and bounced. 'This is the most gorgeous bed!' She bounced again, and then focussed on her sister's face. 'Oh, stop worrying. Alastair doesn't have to get his hair done. Like you do.' Then she grinned. 'That's what I'm here for. The team are ready. Can I tell them to come up?

'The team?'

'Wait till you see what Marguerite has in store for you.' Heather giggled. 'You'll die of shock.'

Penny-Rose didn't quite die of shock but she came close. Marguerite had decreed what was necessary and into her room came hairdresser, manicurist, beautician, florist...

A fairy godmother would have been much simpler, Penny-Rose thought, dazed. As it was, she was twisted this way and that, pampered and petted, and turned into something she'd never dreamed was possible.

And an hour later, Marguerite, looking stunning herself in a blue silk suit which must have cost a fortune, carried in *the* dress.

She had tried it on just once. It had been taken away to be altered, and now it appeared again in all its shimmering glory.

The rest of the entourage stood respectfully back, the gown was slipped over her shoulders and there was a collective gasp from the entire room.

The gown was deceptively simple. It was of made of smooth ivory silk, with a scooped neckline, tiny filigree sleeves and a bodice that showed every lovely curve. Beneath the bodice, the gown clung revealingly to her hips. Then, with a rope of rich ivory braid to delineate the skirt, it flared out into fold upon fold, sweeping to the floor at the front and drifting into a lovely rich train behind.

The skirt was so heavy! Alastair's grandmother hadn't skimped when she'd had this dress made, and the hidden folds made the gown flare and swirl like magic.

Marguerite darted forward and threaded a tiny delicate diamond tiara on Penny-Rose's head. Then the florist fixed a trace of lily of the valley into her mass of tumbling curls and the hairdresser tweaked the curls this way and that, wanting just one curl to lie on the soft curve of her breast.

And that was that. Finished.

The effect was ethereal.

'And I thought my leathers were fabulous,' Heather breathed, and it broke the ice. There was a general chuckle, the beautician made one final adjustment and Marguerite stepped forward and took Penny-Rose's hand.

'Are you ready to meet your husband, my love?'

Penny-Rose met Marguerite's eyes. They were calm and steady, and they knew exactly what they were asking. And she drew in her breath. Marguerite knew!

'I...'

'I think you're ready,' Marguerite said softly. 'Oh, my dear, this is just what I always dreamed of.'

'Marguerite—'

'Now, not another word,' her soon-to-be-mother-in-law told her, and patted her hand. 'You'll spoil your make-up.'

'Or I might crack it,' she whispered, and managed a smile. But it was nonsense. The beautician had had enough sense to leave her skin flawlessly natural.

'You'll knock your husband's socks off,' Heather declared, and Penny-Rose's smile faltered. She turned and took one last, long look in the mirror. The woman who looked back at her was a fairy princess.

She'd been handed every weapon she could possibly need, she thought.

The rest of it was up to her.

Or how strong Alastair's defences could be.

She'd knock his socks off?

'That's my intention,' she murmured. 'OK, Alastair de Castaliae. Prince Alastair. Here I come. Ready or not.'

They'd decided on no formal bridal party.

'If you don't want bridesmaids, I won't have groomsmen,' Alastair had said. 'It's just as well. There's no one close enough to be an obvious best man. Whoever I ask, someone else is bound to be offended.'

And it was ridiculous, given Penny-Rose's fierce independence, that someone give her away.

So they'd decided that she'd walk up the aisle by herself, she'd have no attendants, and Alastair would carry his own ring.

Her sisters fussed around her as she arrived, but with her train arranged beautifully to sweep down the aisle behind her, they took themselves to the front row to watch her make her way to her bridegroom in solitary splendour.

And all at once, solitary splendour felt very, very lonely.

There must be a thousand people present, she thought dazedly, starting that long solemn walk as a lone trumpeter sounded.

And then she saw Alastair.

He was dressed in a soft grey morning suit—of course— and he looked magnificent. The only touch of colour was a crimson rosebud in his lapel.

A rose... The flower of love... Marguerite had chosen the flowers, and Penny-Rose carried twelve matching buds in her bouquet.

The sight, for some reason, made her feel like weeping. Red roses for her wedding day... It seemed almost a mockery.

But Alastair was watching her, and his eyes were calm and reassuring. A tiny smile creased the corner of his mouth.

Dear God, he was so...so...

So Alastair. There was no other way of describing him, because that was who he was, and she loved him so much that she felt she was close to breaking.

How could she do this? she thought wildly. She was marrying the man under false pretences. Alastair didn't want a wife who loved him to bits. He didn't even really want a wife...

Panic was suddenly close to overwhelming her.

And then she saw Michael. Her baby brother.

Alastair's promise that he'd have no attendants had gone out the window. Michael had Alastair's ring in his hand, he was wearing a morning suit to match Alastair's and the look on his face was as if he'd been handed the world.

The sixteen-year-old had flown halfway around the globe to be at his sister's wedding, but until this moment he'd been thoroughly confused by everything that was going on. Sixteen-year-olds were insecure at the best of times. Unlike Heather and Liz, he'd hated this.

But now he'd been handed a part to play, and what a part! Best man! And in his free hand—the one that wasn't holding the ring…

For heaven's sake, Mike was holding a leash. He was holding Leo!

The pup had been brushed to an inch of his life, and he'd never looked so splendid. The scars on his side were almost healed, but they were completely covered by a magnificent crimson doggy coat. He wore a studded collar, his lead was crimson suede and he beamed at the approaching bride and wagged his tail as if this entire ceremony was being put on for his benefit.

Her brother. And her dog…

Alastair had done this—for her!

She couldn't help it. Panic subsided, and despite the aura of solemnity—despite the state officials and the hundreds of people she'd never seen in her life, despite the grandeur and the fuss—she chuckled.

This would be OK.

She loved this man so much… He'd known how alone this ceremony would make her feel, so he'd done the two things that could ease her fears.

He was *some* prince!

And surely the only thing to do with a prince like this was to marry him?

* * *

And Alastair watched his bride come toward him with a feeling in his chest that was almost as close to panic as hers.

What was he doing? *Marrying?*

This wasn't real, he told himself. It was a pretence. It was a mock wedding, made for the best of purposes—to protect his tenants and to provide for their future.

In twelve months he'd let this woman go and he'd marry a sensible woman—a woman who suited his lifestyle.

Belle.

But the thought of Belle was suddenly very far away. What was real was Penny-Rose.

No! She was Rose, he told himself. For some reason it was a distinction it was important to keep. Penny-Rose was for those who loved her. Rose… Rose was to be his formal wife.

So it was Rose who was walking toward him, her eyes wide and her face determined. Despite her determination, her steps were faltering.

She was fearful, he thought. Damn, it hadn't been fair to drag her into this. Into the goldfish bowl of royalty.

But she was so beautiful she took his breath away! She was wearing his mother's dress, a dress that would have been equally beautiful a hundred years ago. She looked timeless and serene and incredibly lovely. In fact, she looked just as a princess should.

His princess.

For a year.

The time frame was suddenly gut-wrenching. But then…he saw the exact moment she registered that Mike and Leo were by his side. He saw the serenity and solemnity vanish, along with the fear. Laughter flashed into her lovely eyes, her lips twitched with pleasure and as she reached him he heard a low, lovely chuckle.

'Oh, Alastair…'

Her laughing face was raised to his and he gazed down at her for a long, long moment.

Then he calmly took her hand and smiled back.

This was suddenly very, very OK.

His princess.

Her prince.

And while the world watched, they turned together to be made one.

The wedding celebrations went on through the day and far into the night. And what a night! Because the weather was perfect, the sides of the marquee were raised so the dance floor was partly over the river and partly over the pasture. The moon was brilliant. The night was brilliant! No one wanted to go home.

And everyone wished to dance with the bride. She was passed from one partner to another and her feet barely had time to touch the ground. Alastair was free to do as he willed.

Which was just what he wanted, he told himself, trying not to follow his new wife with his eyes. She was dancing with one of his business partners now, clasped around the waist in a manner that made him want to—

'Alastair?'

He paused as he realised who was calling. Belle…

Belle's presence had been necessary here, if only to allay gossip, and there was no reason now that they shouldn't speak.

Strange that it felt almost like a betrayal…

But Belle didn't notice. She looked very pleased with herself. 'I've been talking to Marguerite,' she announced. 'She tells me you're taking Rose's family on your honeymoon. That's a great idea.'

'It'll take the pressure off,' he agreed, still watching his wife twirling across the floor. Then he thought about what he'd said. Why should there be any pressure?

Belle was raising one elegant eyebrow. 'Pressure? Surely you're not worried that she'll ravish you?' She wasn't worried at all. Rose was such an insignificant little thing, her tone implied, and Alastair was forced to smile.

'Of course not. I mean…having other people to share the conversation. It'll help.'

He received a blinding smile of sympathy. 'She'll bore you within a day,' Belle agreed. 'Poor darling.'

It wasn't fear of boredom that was worrying him, he decided, but if that's what Belle thought, maybe it was just as well.

'I can cope. This marriage is only for twelve months,' he reiterated, and it was as if he was reassuring himself.

'Of course it is.' Belle kissed him lightly—a gesture that was as natural as any guest congratulating a bridegroom— and then she stepped back. Their path was set and she, for one, was sure of the rightness of what they were doing. 'Secure your fortune and then we're settled for life. Off and do your duty, my darling. Just don't let the creature fall in love with you.'

The creature…

Belle hadn't meant it as it had sounded, Alastair decided as he succeeded in claiming and dancing with his lovely new wife, but the description rankled.

It rankled for the rest of the evening.

She was *not* a creature. She was his wife.

Just for a year.

His hold grew imperceptibly tighter, and his patience with other men wishing to claim her grew thin. A year wasn't very long…

'Belle's looking lovely,' she told him as the music slowed and he held her close.

'She is.' He swirled her around and smiled down into her dancing eyes. 'And so's the man you were just dancing with.'

That had her startled. 'What—lovely?'

'You might say that. He wouldn't mind. Maurice is gay.'

'Oh…' She choked on laughter. 'Are you sure?'

'No, but if he insists on wearing a pink bow-tie and matching braces he has to expect a suspicion or two.'

She choked again. 'What an ungentlemanly thing to say. You sound almost jealous, Alastair de Castaliae.'

'How could I be jealous?'

'How indeed? When you have Belle right where you want her.'

Right. She was right. He did have Belle. Sort of.

But meanwhile, he had his wife right where he wanted her.

In his arms.

They danced until dawn. Then, as they bade farewell to the last stray guest, Alastair glanced at his weary bride and felt an almost overwhelming urge to pick her up and carry her back to his castle. Further. Back to the ready and waiting bridal chamber.

Which was all very well, but he wanted a change to their plans. He wanted the door between them to be unlocked!

In days of old he could have done it, he thought savagely. If the prince were the real lord of the manor, he could have claimed this woman for twelve months—properly taken her—then discarded her and taken another.

But he couldn't think of another. He could only think of the woman by his side. He absorbed the weariness on her lovely face, the way her soft body yielded to his touch, the fragrance of her. The way she looked...

He'd never seen a woman as lovely as his wife looked tonight.

His wife?

He was going nuts, he thought. He should stop thinking like this. He must! She was just...Rose. There was no 'his wife' about it. Not really.

This was a business arrangement and nothing else.

'Tired?' he managed, and she chuckled.

'How can you doubt it? Oh, but, Alastair, it's been the most wonderful day. A day to remember for ever. And my gorgeous gown hasn't turned to rags yet.' She managed another chuckle. 'The pumpkins have stayed at bay, and I have twelve months to go before my midnight.'

She did. Twelve months. Twelve whole months. The thought was suddenly immensely cheering. She'd be with him until then, working as he worked...

The thought of her work reminded him of something important.

'I have a wedding gift for you,' he told her.

'A wedding gift...' She gazed up at him in surprise. 'There's no need. You've given me enough.'

'Not quite enough.' He smiled down at her. 'I realise I don't know you very well, so I asked Bert what you most wanted, and I've got you just that.'

'You asked Bert... Then I can't imagine,' she said faintly.

'Shut your eyes.' The dawn was just starting to break. The bride and groom had decided not to make a formal departure, which left them now at the entrance to the marquee, on the river bank and alone.

'I'll lead you,' he said softly, and he took her hand in his. 'Trust me?'

With all my heart, she thought, but she didn't say it. She merely nodded, and let herself be led.

Her wedding gift was on the other side of the castle. They made their way in the soft dawn light across the pastures of buttercups and poppies, to where the new wall was being built.

The team had finished the most urgent repairs, but there were miles of fencing yet to go. A whole year's worth of stone-walling, Penny-Rose thought happily.

And then she saw Alastair's gift.

It was a vast mound, about six feet high and eight feet square. It was wrapped in some sort of white parchment, and a vast gold bow about three feet high adorned the whole thing.

What on earth...?

'It's soap and a hand-towel,' Penny-Rose said faintly and Alastair grinned.

'Some soap! Nope. Bad guess. Try again.'

'A toaster, then?' She giggled. 'Or a casserole?' Her thoughts slipped sideways. 'We've been given so much… We'll have to keep careful notes and send everything back.'

At the end of the year…

It was a bad thought. It sobered them both. But the parcel was still in front of them, enticing in its mystery.

'Aren't you going to open it?' Alastair demanded.

'I don't think I dare.' She was eyeing it as if it might bite. 'It looks like it could be a rhinoceros.'

He grinned. 'Damn, you guessed.'

She smiled, but her smile was troubled. 'Alastair, you needn't have done this. It makes it seem…'

'Makes it seem what?'

'It makes it seem almost a proper wedding,' she whispered, and her words felt good to Alastair.

He might only have her for a year, but a year was better than nothing.

For heaven's sake, what was he thinking?

The current had caught him unawares, and he was being swept along without realising it. Which was ridiculous, he thought savagely, hauling himself back to some sort of common sense. Hadn't he made himself a vow when Lissa died? Had Lissa's death taught him nothing?

This was a marriage of convenience. Nothing more.

As was this gift to his wife. It wasn't a proper gift. It was only…

'Open it,' he said, and she cast him an uncertain glance. Something had changed.

'Open it,' he growled, and she took a deep breath. OK. Keep it formal. Concentrate on the parcel.

And what a parcel! She had to tug the vast ribbon until it floated free, and after that she had to pull aside the parchment. And inside were…

'*Copestones?*' She stood back in incredulity. 'You've given me *copestones*?'

'Bert said one of the reasons he employed you was that you were a copestone perfectionist,' Alastair said, trying not to sound *too* pleased with himself. These stones had taken a lot of organising. 'He also told me the main reason your hands are a mess is because you chip the damn things until they're perfect.'

'But otherwise they don't look good.' Penny-Rose was lifting a single stone and staring at it in disbelief. Copestones were the stones used to top and weight her wall. Chosen and chipped well, they made the wall look great—the icing on the cake! But it could take her almost half an hour to chip a stone to this shape, and on this job Bert had refused to give her the time.

'There's too much to do. We can't afford your standards here,' he'd told her. 'This is farmwork. We have a job to do and we need to be economical.'

She'd agreed, but she made them perfect anyway, working into her lunch-hours and evenings to get them right so her stones would still look magnificent in hundreds of years.

But they took so much effort, and here they were, already cut.

'How...?' She couldn't believe what she was seeing. 'How...?'

'I employed men off site,' Alastair explained. 'Bert showed them what you've been doing and said we wanted more of the same. They delivered them this morning.' As she replaced her stone, he lifted her hands and fingered her rough skin. 'So, for the next year you can go on stone-walling all you like, but the hardest bit's done.'

'Oh, Alastair...'

'It was Bert's idea.'

'It was no such thing.' She knew that much at least. Alastair must have thought of this all by himself. She thought back to the day a couple of weeks ago when he'd discovered her swearing over a gashed hand and a cope-stone that wouldn't cut as she'd wanted it. 'Bert wouldn't have thought of this as a gift.' She managed a wavering smile. 'Not in a million years. As a matter of fact, I think one of our toasters is his.'

'It would be.'

Silence. She carefully disengaged his hand. For some reason it was suddenly important that she do so.

A thousand copestones...

She couldn't have thought of a better wedding gift if she'd tried.

Damn, there was a tear trickling down her nose—and then another one. She wiped them fiercely away with the back of her hand, and gave a very unromantic sniff.

Which suddenly made Alastair feel very romantic indeed.

This was unreal. Standing in the dawn light, beside a mound of stones, with a woman in bridal attire... A woman who sniffed and tried to look fierce when he knew she wanted to burst into tears. And the reason for those tears? Because here was a woman who thought a pile of cope-stones was the greatest present...

He put a hand out to touch her, but she backed away as if she were scared of being scorched. 'No!'

'No, what?' His eyes were on hers. 'Don't you like my gift?'

'I...I do.' But Penny-Rose knew what she'd stepped back from. She knew what was close to happening. And she didn't want this man to kiss her.

Not yet. It wasn't right.

She didn't want to seduce him, she thought frantically. Nor did she want him to make love to her because she was convenient.

She wanted him to fall in love with her. As she loved him. So intensely that she ached...

'I...I have a gift for you, too,' she murmured softly, and it brought him up short. A gift...

'You don't have any money,' he said before he could stop himself, and she glared.

'Yeah, well, there are some things that can be gained without money. Like Leo.'

'Like our aristocratic dog,' he agreed. 'A gift without price.' And then his brow creased and he grinned in mock dismay. 'Oh, hell. Don't tell me. Another dog?'

'It's nothing of the kind,' she said with dignity. 'Though if I find one with just the right pedigree…'

'To match Leo's.'

'That's right.' She was relaxing again now. The moment of tension had passed. 'So…do you want to see my gift?'

'Of course I do.' He was fascinated.

'It doesn't come in a velvet box either,' she told him. 'And it's not gift-wrapped. It's no toaster.'

'Rose, there's no need to give me anything.'

'You brought the kids over for the wedding,' she said simply. 'You've given me the earth. So of course there's a need for a gift. It took me a while to figure out what, but I finally did.'

'What—?'

'Come and see.'

Once again they walked around the castle, but this time south, where pastures gave way to woodland. Here there was a small rise, looking back over the castle to the cliffs and river plains beyond. It was a place of absolute beauty. Penny-Rose had found it one day when she'd sought a quiet place to eat her lunch, and she'd been back again and again ever since.

And finally she'd asked Marguerite about it.

'My husband loved the castle,' Marguerite had said. 'In a way, he felt it was his ancestral home. And Lissa's family couldn't bear for her to be buried alone. There's a crypt for the royal family underneath the chapel, but we thought…it'd be lovely if they were buried here.'

So there were two simple gravestones, nestled among the woodland. And surrounded by flowers…

'Alastair planted them,' Marguerite had told her. 'All the flowers we both love. Wildflowers and roses and daffodils and tulips and honeysuckle and wisteria… So it'll be a mass of flowers all year round.'

The only jarring note, to Penny-Rose's mind, was the fence. They'd erected a simple wire fence around the graves to keep the cattle out, and it looked discordant in such a lovely place.

So she'd fixed it.

Alastair hadn't been here for weeks. He'd had so much on his plate he hadn't had time.

But now… He saw what she'd done before he reached the graves. His steps slowed. He walked up to the fence and he stopped and took it in.

It was the most beautiful fence he'd seen in his life. Made of simple sandstone, every stone was perfect. The fence formed a tiny fold about ten feet square, a croft where the graves were protected against the weather and against the cattle.

And the fence was built with such care and craftsmanship that the graves would be protected for a thousand years.

It was high—four feet or so—so the sturdiest sheep couldn't climb over, but there were throughstones forming a stile so one could enter.

And she'd formed smoots—narrow slits in the stone—regularly spaced, all the way along. 'To let light in, and so the woodland creatures can enjoy your garden,' she explained, watching his face with some anxiety. 'The first morning I walked up here I saw a litter of tiny rabbits munching on your buttercups. And I thought…if this was my grave that's what I'd want.'

Silence.

'I can pull it down if you don't like it,' she whispered, still anxious. 'But it was the one thing I could do for you.

I know you loved your dad and you loved Lissa. And somehow this seemed right.'

It did, too.

It seemed perfect.

Alastair climbed the stile without a word. Reaching the
top, he held out his hand. After the briefest of hesitations,
Penny-Rose placed her hand in his and climbed the stile
with him. Her wedding dress was lifted carefully over, and
then they were together in the fold.

Around them, wildflowers blossomed around masses of
tulips. Wisteria had been carefully restrung against the
stones. As it was late spring it was losing its flowers so a
carpet of soft blue petals lay everywhere, and the wild roses
were just starting to bloom.

The smell of the morning was with them. The dew on
the grass left a pungent fragrance where they walked, and
the two simple graves lay gently side by side. Like two
friends.

As they had been, Marguerite had told her. Lissa had
been almost a daughter to Alastair's parents. These were
Alastair's people, and it was right that they be buried together.

'Thank...thank you,' he said in a voice that wasn't too
steady, and this time it was he who badly wanted to sniff.
Penny-Rose heard it and managed a grin. She was still feeling distinctly sniffy herself.

Keep it practical... 'Not carrying a handkerchief?' she
managed.

'They gave me a buttonhole instead.' He smiled, and
plucked the crimson rose from his lapel. 'As a handkerchief
it makes a very poor substitute, but here it is. What's mine
is yours.'

It was a simple statement—a jest—but it hung between
them like the promise of the morning to come.

Only...the morning was already here.

'We...we'd best get back to the castle,' Penny-Rose said

uncertainly. 'We have a plane to catch this afternoon and we haven't had any sleep.'

'That's right.' But he couldn't keep his eyes from her. 'We have a honeymoon to begin.'

'A holiday,' she corrected him. 'You need to be really married to go on a honeymoon.'

'And we're not really married?'

She hitched her dress high. This scene was threatening to run away with her, and she wasn't ready. Alastair wasn't ready.

Seduction wasn't her scene. She was playing for keeps, so she had to be practical. Somehow.

'No, Alastair, we're not,' she told him. She looked down at Lissa's grave, and a tiny smile curved her lips. 'I hope we're becoming like you and Lissa...good friends. But that's not a basis for a marriage.'

'Lissa and I thought so.'

'Well, I'm not Lissa.' She stepped up onto the stile and stayed on the fence-top for a moment, looking down. She looked immeasurably lovely, dressed in her bridal finery, with the dawn light behind her and the carpet of wildflowers at her feet. 'I'm me. I'm Penny-Rose. The girl who married for money. I'm your bride for a year, but just for a year, Alastair de Castaliae. So let's not forget it.'

The door between Alastair and his new bride was firmly locked.

'Goodnight,' she'd said sweetly as they'd arrived back at the castle. She'd stood on tiptoe to kiss him but it had been a fleeting kiss of farewell—nothing more. 'We only have eight hours till we catch our plane. I'm off to get some beauty sleep and I suggest you do the same.'

But how could he, when every nerve in his body screamed that his bride was just on the other side of the door?

Belle.

Think of Belle, he told himself desperately. He'd promised to marry her. That was the sort of marriage he wanted. Not…not what he could have with Rose.

And what sort of marriage was the one he envisaged with Rose? If he allowed it to become…proper.

It was the sort of marriage his mother had had, he acknowledged, because if he allowed himself to give—as Rose gave—there'd be no holding back.

And if anything happened…

As it did. As life had taught him it always did. He'd committed himself to Lissa and it had ended in tragedy.

If something like that happened again, he'd go crazy, he told himself fiercely.

But maybe he was going crazy already!

CHAPTER TEN

TAKING the kids on their honeymoon didn't make it less romantic, Alastair decided a few days later. It made it more so. After initial polite protests, the kids had agreed to accompany them. They intended to have a great time but they also intended their sister to have a honeymoon to remember for ever.

Which included romantic seclusion.

'We want to spend time with you,' both Penny-Rose and Alastair protested, but their words fell on deaf ears.

'Well, we don't want to spend time with you,' Heather declared. 'So this morning we've booked the catamarans. One each. We're having lessons and the instructor can only take three, so you guys will just have to find something else to do. Hmm. I wonder what?' She threw them a cheeky grin and disappeared.

Which left them alone. Again.

'I...I'll take a walk,' Penny-Rose said, and Alastair gazed at her in exasperation. In three days she hadn't relaxed once, and the island wasn't big enough to stay away from each other for ever.

'Can I come with you?'

She appeared to give it serious thought. As if she didn't really want to. 'I... If you like.'

'I do like.'

Of course he liked. Who wouldn't? OK, it might be unwise, but in a simple sarong, with her hair hanging free and her nose sporting a touch of sunburn, she looked almost breathtakingly lovely. What man could resist walking beside a woman like this?

Especially when that woman was his wife.

In name only!

He had to keep reminding himself of that. Ever since they'd arrived they'd been treated as being very much in love, and formality was harder and harder to maintain.

The sleeping arrangements were the hardest. There were three guest cottages on the island—gorgeous thatched bures. If Alastair and Penny-Rose had done what they'd first planned and had the island to themselves, they could have had a cottage each. But Liz and Heather had taken one and Michael another. Which left only the honeymoon suite.

The suite was gorgeous. Built right on the edge of the waves, whenever they liked they could push back the folding walls so that sea air and moonlight drifted right into the room with them. Simple but beautifully built, it was almost erotic in its design, with one enormous bed taking up over half the room.

So... The sensible plan had been to place a row of cushions down the middle of the bed.

It worked—sort of. But the trace of shadows under Rose's eyes told Alastair that she was feeling the strain almost as much as he was.

She was so near and yet so far.

She was his wife!

She was his paid companion for a year, he reminded himself harshly as they walked slowly along the sand. Nothing more. He couldn't let her any closer than this. Otherwise when it ended he'd go nuts.

Did it have to end?

Yes, he told himself fiercely. It must. Even if he was stupid enough to lose his heart, there was Belle to consider.

And it was just plain stupid to let himself lose his heart. Hadn't life taught him anything?

'Penny for them?' Penny-Rose asked, and he lifted his head with surprise. They were in the shallows, barefooted and kicking their way through the foam. Alastair was wearing his bathing trunks and nothing else. Which was just as well. Any minute now he could end up swimming.

If things became too hot…

'I beg your pardon?' He had trouble forcing his thoughts from where they'd been straying.

'Penny for your thoughts?' she repeated. 'You look away with the fairies.'

He managed a smile. 'Was I? Sorry. I was thinking of Belle.'

Penny-Rose's smile faded. Belle. Of course. She was between them all the time. 'You must miss her.'

'I… Yes.'

'This'll be hard on you both,' Penny-Rose admitted. 'Knowing how beautiful this is…' She brightened a little. 'Still, the fact that my sisters and brother are here must make it easier for her.'

'I…' Hell, concentrate! Make yourself talk sensibly, he told himself. 'It does. Belle approves of the idea.'

'I'm glad.'

But Belle had called Rose 'the creature'.

Alastair looked across at the creature in question. The soft breeze was blowing her hair into a tumble of riotous curls. The sun was warm on her face and she was lifting her nose to smell the sea.

'Isn't it gorgeous?' she breathed, and he was forced to smile his agreement.

'Absolutely.' But he wasn't talking about what *she* was talking about.

Maybe he'd better head for the water!

But beside him Penny-Rose had paused. Far out in the bay, just around the headland from where they were, she could see three little catamarans. Her siblings were having a ball. She watched for a while, and then sighed and smiled.

'I want to thank you,' she said seriously. 'Alastair, what you're doing for us…'

'I'm doing it for me.'

'I don't think you are,' she said softly. Before he could

stop her she'd caught his hand and was tracing the strong lines below the wrist. 'I think you're doing this for your tenants and for Belle and for your mother—*and* for me. But maybe not for you. I'm starting to know that you don't really want to be royalty.'

'Being royalty can't hurt.' The feel of her hand was unnerving. One part of him wanted to pull away.

The other part of him wanted to move in closer.

'You dislike the publicity.'

'I... Yes.'

'It'll get worse.'

'For a while.'

'Because of our marriage?'

'I guess.'

'And the divorce at the end—there'll be a heck of a fuss.'

'I can cope.' He shrugged. A year was starting to seem a very long way away.

'I wish I could make it easier for you.'

The only way she could make things easier was to leave right now. He was starting to feel as if he was being torn in two. To have her so near...

'Come in for a swim,' he suggested, and she kicked up some water with her toes.

'I wish I could.'

He'd forgotten. Again.

She couldn't swim. He'd discovered it on the first day. The others had somehow managed to learn but his wife hadn't been so fortunate. In her tough childhood, there'd simply never been time.

And Alastair hadn't found the courage to say what he most wanted to say. That he'd teach her.

Because how could he teach her without touching her? And how could he touch her without—?

He hauled his hand away and grimaced. 'OK. You do your splashing bit and I'll do my lap stuff.'

Which was fine, he thought savagely as he stroked strongly in deep water. This way he could put some of his unused physical energy to good use. So far this holiday he must have swum for twenty miles or more. Every time things got too much for him he swam while Rose enjoyed herself in the shallows.

Did she enjoy herself?

Of course she did, he told himself. She'd never been to the beach. It was a novelty. The shallows were enough!

He was being mean!

But if he wasn't mean…that way led to disaster. Teaching her to swim… Letting her close…

Alastair paused but as he did so a movement caught his eye. Entranced, he trod water and watched.

Out past the breakers, where the waves were forming into massive, rolling swells, a pod of dolphins had come in to surf. They were darting into the sapphire crests, row upon row of them—there had to be thirty—using the force of the waves to surf gloriously toward shore.

Alastair was just far enough out to see. They were past the sand-bar which created the lagoon effect where Alastair swam and Rose paddled. Between sand-bar and the beach, the water sloped gently, meaning he had to be a hundred yards from the beach before he could swim.

And that meant Rose could hardly see the dolphins from where she was.

She'd love them. Alastair watched the sea creatures for a moment longer, and then he glanced back at Rose. She was lying full length in the shallows, letting the foam trickle through her toes. She was wearing a crimson bikini, and nothing more.

She looked blissfully happy, and very, very lovely.

But the dolphins were a sight to be seen maybe once in a lifetime, Alastair thought desperately. She should see them.

She couldn't see them from where she was. Not properly.

And there was a channel fifteen or twenty feet wide of deep water between shore and the sand-bar. That was where he'd been swimming.

Maybe she'd trust him to tow her through the deep water to where the sand-bar created a ledge, he thought. If she let him do that, then they could both see.

To have him carry her through deep water when she couldn't swim she'd have to trust him absolutely.

And suddenly there was no reason why not. And every reason why.

'Rose,' he shouted, and started over to where she lay. 'Come and see. It's magic.'

And it *was* magic. As was her trust. She lay limply in his hold, totally reliant on his strength as he carried her out to sea. And he knew how reliant she must be. The channel of deep water was maybe only fifteen feet wide, but for a non-swimmer to trust that much was no mean feat.

'Kick your legs,' he said, and felt her do just that.

Her courage was immutable. She was some lady!

But touching her, towing her strongly alongside him in the deep water with his arm holding her close...

This was an indescribable sensation!

Finally he felt the sand-bar rise underneath him, and he guided her feet so she could stand.

But then, somehow, he didn't—couldn't—quite let her go. After all, he had to guide her so she was looking toward the dolphins. And they were still near deep water, so if she fell he'd have to support her.

And she felt so good by his side. So right!

But she seemed almost unaware of the man by her side. She was totally focussed on the dolphins.

And why not? For someone who'd never been to the beach, the creatures were entrancing. They surfed and tumbled and dived, swimming for the sheer exuberance of being alive. Time after time, they darted into the waves, streaming through the sapphire waters, their bodies like glinting silver arrows, and the joy they felt was almost a tangible thing.

'They're just…they're just magic,' Rose whispered, and Alastair could only agree. It *was* magic.

The whole morning was magic. This place. The island. The dolphins, the sun on his face…

This woman!

And then, as suddenly as they'd appeared, the dolphins departed, backing out of the waves and leaping and cresting along the shoreline, around the headland and off to thrill the three younger ones on their catamarans.

'Do you think they're paid by the island management?' Penny-Rose whispered, her voice still awed, and Alastair managed a smile. It was a wonder he could manage anything. His body was doing very, very strange things.

His head was also doing strange things!

But he had to force his voice to sound normal. 'With the price we're paying, they've probably been trained in Miami,' he told her, and then he laughed at the expression on her face. 'Nope. They were the real thing, lady. Totally wild and totally free, giving us the performance of their lives just for their pleasure. And ours.'

She closed her eyes, and he felt her take it all in. The sheer loveliness of it. The wonder.

And then she opened her eyes again and he saw that the real world had intruded. She shifted away from him—imperceptibly, but it was a shift for all that.

'Take me back to shore,' she said simply. 'Thank you for bringing me out, but it's time my feet hit the ground.'

'You should be able to swim,' he growled, and she nodded.

'Yes.' She couldn't quite keep the note of wistfulness from her voice. 'But I can't. So I need a tow. And then you can get back to your swimming.'

And all at once Alastair couldn't bear it. She asked for nothing, he thought savagely. She gave and gave and gave. If he hadn't had a damned good reason—like saving the tenants' livelihoods—for this marriage, she'd never have made it.

She wouldn't marry for profit. She wouldn't do anything for profit, he thought. Not for herself.

'Would you like to learn to swim?' he asked, and it was as if someone else were doing the asking. He hadn't meant to. Had he?

'Would I like…?'

'I can teach you.' He smiled. 'I taught Lissa.'

The name came up naturally, with no strain at all. Lissa… He'd hardly talked about Lissa since her death. He'd tried not to think of her. But now the memories came flooding back, of Alastair as a ten-year-old, holding his six-year-old cousin under the tummy and yelling, 'Kick, kick…'

And Lissa kicking so hard he'd been bruised for weeks!

He grinned suddenly, and it was as if a weight had been lifted that he hadn't known was there. The grieving had shifted imperceptibly, and the memories that remained were full of sunlight and laughter and love.

But not passion…

The passion he was learning about hadn't come into the equation, he thought as Penny-Rose watched his face. He and Lissa had been such good friends that they hadn't wanted more—or simply hadn't known that more existed. And she'd been killed before they'd found out.

And now…

Now he knew more existed. Because what he was feeling for the woman by his side was very, very different.

Hell!

But Penny-Rose was lifting her eyes to his, and the expression on her face said she understood.

She couldn't understand. How could she? It was his imagination.

'If you could teach Lissa, then you can teach me,' she said softly. 'Oh, Alastair, I'd love it.'

Thus began one of the funniest, most precious days of Alastair's life. All the rest of the morning they worked at it. Her trust was absolute, and her faith paid dividends.

'You'll do dead-man's float first,' he told her, and made her lie face down in the water. 'Lie as flat as a board and don't let yourself put your head up until I touch your shoulders.'

And she didn't. He put his hand under the flatness of her stomach and held her—supporting her totally—and the feeling it gave him was spine-tingling. She lay still and trusting, until he touched her shoulder. Then she gasped and spluttered and knelt up on the sand to laugh in sheer delight.

They did it again and again, until she was almost floating by herself. 'It feels wonderful. It feels weird.'

'It'll feel weirder. This time I'm going to lower my hand and you'll feel the water supporting you instead of me. You'll float.'

And she did! She floated as if she'd done it since childhood, and he gazed down at her beautiful body—and almost forgot to touch her shoulder! When he did, she spluttered a whole lot more as she struggled to her feet. He expected indignation but what he received instead was blazing joy.

'I floated. I floated! All by myself, I floated!'

'If I don't touch your shoulder you can decide to put your head up yourself,' he managed, laughing with her joy but trying desperately to ignore the strange feelings coursing through his body.

Penny-Rose didn't understand. 'Why would I? You'll touch me when it's time to surface. I trust you.'

He knew it. The thought was incredible. 'But…if I'm eaten by a shark…'

She grinned, delirious with sun and surf and happiness. 'Then I'll drown of a broken heart, dead-man's-floating to my doom. What a princess! people would say. Romeo and Juliet would have nothing on a scenario like that.'

He chuckled. 'Hey, there's no need to go to extremes. Dying of devotion…'

All of a sudden the lightness faded. They were standing in the shallows, looking at each other, and her words hung between them.

'I'll drown of a broken heart…'

And his.

'Dying of devotion…'

The words had been said in jest, but suddenly things weren't light at all. Things were moving fast here, changing every minute. The magnetism between them was a tangible power. It was gaining strength every second, and to resist the pull…

How was he to sleep next to her tonight? he asked himself desperately. On the other side of the mound of pillows…

Concentrate on practicalities.

'Speaking of lunch,' he said, and her look of uncertainty faded. She was starving, and passion could maybe take a back seat. It was a shame, but where he led, she'd follow. Don't push the pace…

'Now you're talking. I wonder if flake's on the menu?'

'You mean we get to eat shark before it eats us? How very wise.' He managed a grin and glanced at his watch. 'It'll be on the table right now. Race you up to the dining room, Rose O'Shea.'

'It's Penny-Rose de Castaliae to you, sir,' she said meekly, and while he took that on board she gained so much of a head start that she beat him to lunch, hands down.

And by nightfall she could swim. Not very far, but she could manage half a dozen strokes before she had to surface, and she was so proud of herself she was threatening to burst.

'I can swim, I can swim,' she crowed at dinner, and her sisters and brother looked on with wonder.

'You sound like a ten-year-old.'

'I feel like a ten-year-old.'

'Except,' Heather said slowly, watching her sister with delight, 'that when you were ten you sounded thirty.' She turned to Alastair and her eyes shone with pleasure. 'We can't tell you how much it means to us—that our Penny-Rose met you.'

Alastair smiled, but inside he didn't smile at all. Their pleasure in this marriage made him feel like a traitor. Why? He'd paid for this, he thought grimly. He'd paid money for a bride. So why was he feeling like a rat?

Because they were assuming he was doing this because he loved her, he thought, and he did no such thing. In twelve months he'd walk away.

Back to Belle.

Belle would never come to dinner with sand on her nose, bare toes and a make-up-free face that glowed with happiness, he thought suddenly, watching Rose's lovely, laughing face.

It was just as well. Belle would be a sensible, practical wife.

'Have some lobster,' Penny-Rose said, and handed him a claw. She seemed totally oblivious of his confusion. 'This guy's defending his territory even in death. I can't get the meat out.'

That made him grin. She was in lobster up to her elbows, and her enjoyment was obvious to all. He thought back to the night she'd eaten her first snail, and he knew without asking that this was her first lobster.

'Allow me.' He cracked the shell with practised ease. The long, smooth sliver of meat slid free, and then, because he couldn't resist it, he leaned forward and popped it between her lips. She gazed up at him as the meat disappeared and...

And it was suddenly an incredibly sexy moment, and behind them he heard Heather snigger.

'Um...excuse me, are we in the way?'

'No,' said Penny-Rose, and blushed to the roots of her hair. 'I... Thank you.'

'That's quite all right.' Alastair tried for an unflustered voice but it didn't quite come off. 'Cracking lobsters is one of my splinter skills. Along with swimming lessons.'

And he badly wanted to do it again. Pop a little more lobster between those lips... In fact, he wanted to desperately. But Rose was pushing her plate away decisively.

'Swimming's worse than stone-walling,' she said, and her voice sounded even more flustered than he was feeling. 'I'm going to bed.'

'But there's meringue for dessert.' Mike couldn't believe that she could leave, and Penny-Rose turned her attention gratefully to her younger brother.

'I'm sure you won't have any trouble eating my share. Or Alastair will help.' And then she caught the way Alastair was looking at her. 'G-goodnight.'

And she fled.

Which left Alastair sitting with her sisters and brother. Who were all looking at him with an air of bright expectancy.

And he couldn't disappoint them. Could he?

'I guess I'll turn in, too,' he said, and they beamed their approval. After all, this was how honeymoons were supposed to proceed.

Help!

But he left anyway. How could he not?

Because Rose was waiting.

This bedroom arrangement was impossible.

When he got back to their cottage, Rose was already in the bathroom. She was running a bath, so there was nothing for Alastair to do but to lie on the bed and listen to her wallowing in the vast white tub.

He could imagine her so vividly she might as well have left the door open. He knew how it would be...

The bathroom was a tiny walled patio with three sheltered walls and the fourth side open to the sea. The bathtub was sunk into the decking. It had two soft headrests, and it was designed so lovers could lie side by side. They could soak in the warm water and watch the moon over the sea.

Only…one side would be empty, Alastair thought. *His* side. The other side would have Rose.

Rose…

He let his imagination wander. Lovely, naked Rose, slippery with soap suds, lying back, letting the salt and sand wash away from her gorgeous body. Penny-Rose lying alone in a bath built for two…

Rose! Not Penny-Rose.

Stop thinking like this! You'll go stark, staring crazy— if you're not already, he said desperately to himself, and took himself out for a walk.

Where could he go? If he walked around the cottage and down to their secluded cove, he'd be able to look up and see…

No. Damn, he was turning into a peeping Tom!

He strode deliberately back up to the management lodge where the kids were setting up a game of cards. From the darkness he could see them out on the verandah, laughing as they played some silly game of snap.

He couldn't go there. What would he say?

'Can I play, too? Your sister's taking a bath and it's driving me nuts!'

They'd think he *was* nuts. They were such nice kids. And they thought he was in love with their sister.

Which was nonsense. He wasn't in love with anyone.

But he was definitely in lust with her.

That was it. He'd found the answer. Only lust. He just wanted her body. He was as aroused as he'd ever been in his life, and the fact that she was a virgin bride…

She was *his* virgin bride.

She wasn't *his* anything. And she had to stay a virgin, he told himself desperately. Hell, wasn't that why he'd married her? Because he didn't want commitment? So it had to stay that way. The last thing he wanted was to make it hard for her to walk away.

But was he sure about what he wanted?

He knew what he didn't want. He didn't want commitment.

In fact, he didn't want marriage. He'd agreed to marry Belle because his mother had wanted grandchildren, he'd quite liked the idea of kids, he'd needed a hostess and the whole thing had been sensible. That was a decent basis for a marriage. Sense.

Not lust.

So he should walk right back to his cottage, settle down on the far side of the pile of cushions and go straight to sleep.

But...he just might take a cold shower first.

A cold shower didn't help.

Alastair returned to the cottage to find Rose glowing from the warmth of the bath. She was wearing one of those damned lingerie-type nightdresses she'd bought in Paris and she was curled into her half of the bed with the sheet drawn up to her waist.

The sheet wasn't drawn up far enough. The nightgown was cut low over her lovely curving breasts, her curls were sprayed out over the pillow—and it was as much as he could do not to groan.

So he stood under the cold shower for a very long time. When he emerged she was lying in the half-dark. Only his bedside light was on. She was still awake, smiling up at him in the dim light as he walked around to his side of the bed.

And heaven only knew how heavy his feet felt. It was so darned hard to make himself walk around her.

This was crazy!

'Feeling better?' she whispered, and he managed a nod. 'Yes. Thanks.' But he'd lied.

'It's been the most gorgeous day,' she said sleepily as

he slid down under the sheet—still on his side. 'Thank you, Alastair.'

'Think nothing of it.' That sounded curt. He forced himself to smile, and then flicked off the light so he wouldn't need to hide his expression. But he could still see the curves of her in the moonlight. She was too damned close! 'I enjoyed myself, too.'

'You'd never seen yourself as a swimming master extraordinaire?'

'There's a whole lot of things I'd never seen myself as,' he said bitterly. 'A prince. A swimming master—'

'A husband?'

'The kids think it's real,' he burst out, and there was surely the nub of the matter. If no one thought it was real, he wouldn't have to pretend. It was the pretence that was driving him crazy—wasn't it?

'They do,' she said softly. 'Do you mind?'

'I… No. Only if you do,' he managed. 'It'll make it harder at the end of the year.'

'Alastair, let's worry about the end of the year at the end of the year. For now…this is the honeymoon of my dreams. The holiday of my dreams. I've learned to swim five strokes. I'm here with my sisters and brother—and with you. I couldn't be any happier if I tried.'

He could be. He could be a whole lot happier. All he had to do was shift these damned cushions!

He had to stay formal. Somehow. 'I'm glad you're having a good time.'

'I'm having a wonderful time.' And then, before he knew what she was about, she slipped her hand under the pillows and found his hand. Her fingers were warm and sure as she pulled his hand toward her, and then she raised his hand to her lips and gently kissed his fingertips.

It was a gesture of thanks. Nothing more. Wasn't it?

'This is magic,' she said softly. 'A magic day. A magic prince.'

'It'll end.' He somehow managed to haul his hand away,

and it nearly tore him apart to do it. His voice came out as a sort of strangled croak. 'After all, Cinderella had her midnight to contend with. Your midnight is just taking a while longer to come.'

'I won't forget.' Her voice was suddenly serious, but she was still whispering into the dark. The sensation was unutterably intimate. 'Alastair, why are you so afraid of commitment?'

'I'm not.'

'You are.' He heard her smile in her voice. 'You're just a great big chicken.'

He drew in his breath. How to answer that one?

With the truth. 'I'd rather be a chicken than a squashed hen.'

'There's a brave prince.' She chuckled. 'Is that your royal creed? "He who fights and runs away lives to fight another day."'

'It has a whole lot going for it.' It was surreal. Lying in the dark, talking to her as if nothing was between them.

Only these damned cushions!

'Seriously, though…'

'Seriously what?'

'Why don't you let yourself love…Belle?'

Because I've never been the least bit tempted to love Belle, he thought, but he didn't say it. Whereas you…

But he had to give her a reasonable answer. An answer he thought was the truth. 'I've told you before. I don't do love.'

'Because you might get hurt?' Her voice was carefully neutral.

'Because I *will* get hurt. Eventually. Or you…or Belle would. Nothing lasts for ever.'

'So…' She'd forgotten to whisper. Her voice was curious now. Nothing more. 'So when you're designing buildings, you're planning on them lasting a thousand years?' she asked.

'Like your fences?' He smiled into the dark. 'Nope. You're the master builder in that direction.'

'So how long would a building of yours last—on average, say?'

He didn't understand what she was getting at. 'I'd like to think a hundred years.' He shrugged. 'But probably only forty. Maybe less.'

'But you still think it's worthwhile building them.'

Damn. He'd walked straight into her trap. And the cushions weren't high enough!

'Buildings are different,' he managed.

'I imagine they are,' she said softly. 'Different to relationships. But in some ways they're the same. If they only last for forty years they can still be incredibly wonderful while they last.' She frowned then, and he heard the frown in the dark. He was starting to know her so well...

'You lost Lissa,' she said gently. 'You said she was your best friend. Today you told me about teaching her to swim when you were kids. If you had your time again, would you choose not to have that time with her? Because she might die?'

'That's none of your business.' She was cutting too close to the bone here.

'I'm just interested.'

'Well, stop being interested. Go to sleep.'

Ha! That was a good one. How could they possibly sleep?

'I don't think you're being fair on Belle—that's all.' She was still probing, right where it hurt most. 'I think marriage is all about loving someone to bits.'

'Like your father's and mother's marriage?'

'That's not fair.'

'Isn't it?'

'At least they took a chance,' she said, and now she sounded angry. 'At least they tried. They didn't lock themselves up in some antiseptic world in case the big bad love-bug bit them so hard it hurt. So, yes, they loved and, yes, it did hurt. My mother made a bad marriage but she had four kids and she had a life. And she loved my dad to bits, even if he was a loser. She loved him and even when she knew she was dying, I suspect she never regretted a thing.'

'Apart from leaving you all.'

'We had her,' Penny-Rose said strongly. 'We had her for enough time to love her and be proud to be her kids. Even Michael has the stories we tell about her, and the knowledge that he was loved. You think we'd abandon that love or not embrace it in the first place because we knew she'd die? If you do, then you don't know what way your head is screwed on, Alastair de Castaliae.'

'Oh, for heaven's sake…'

'There's no "for heaven's sake" about it. You loved Lissa. You should try loving Belle.'

'I can't love Belle.'

There. He'd said it. It hung between them, almost as big a barrier as the cushions.

'Then don't marry her.'

'I'm married to you.'

'No, you're not,' she said reasonably. 'You can't be married to someone when there's two feet of cushions between them. That someone refuses to be married on that basis. This is pretend, Alastair.'

'I… Yes.'

'But you and Belle aren't pretending.'

'We don't need to,' he said, exasperated. 'It's a business arrangement.'

'But…' She reflected on this for a moment. 'You're not paying her.'

'No.'

'And you're intending to have kids?'

'Maybe. Yes! I'll need an heir.'

'Poor little heir,' she said softly. 'I hope Marguerite loves it enough for all of you.'

'I'll love it.'

'No.' Penny-Rose shook her head, and anger vibrated

harshly in her voice. 'How can you? Because that's commitment, too. That's risking your precious independence, and you don't want that.'

'Rose…'

'It's Penny-Rose. And what?' she said crossly.

'Can we go to sleep?'

'How can I go to sleep?' she demanded. 'How can I sleep when I've had such a wonderful, wonderful day, and I've learned to swim and I've seen dolphins and I'm now lying in bed wide awake beside the most gorgeous man I've ever met and…and you expect me to sleep?'

Silence.

Hell, she was feeling the same as he was!

'I…'

'You took a cold shower,' she said carefully. 'I know. The bathroom didn't steam. You think my bath was hot?'

'Rose—'

'This is impossible,' she snapped. 'Cold showers aren't all they're cracked up to be. I'm going nuts, and there's twelve months to go. You'd better take me home to your castle and dig a few moats. Right through the middle of the castle. And fill the moats with alligators—with you on one side and me on the other. Because this year's getting out of hand already.'

Alastair tried reason. 'Rose, if we're sensible—'

And that was enough for her. She sat up, and in the dim light he could see her eyes flashing with temper. 'Why the hell do we need to be sensible?'

'Because…'

'Because why?' A cushion tumbled toward her and she lifted it and hurled it to the other side of the room. 'Stupid cushion.'

'Rose—'

'Don't "Rose" me.' She was so angry she was almost spitting. 'OK. Here's the truth. I didn't want to do this—I didn't want to tell you—but it's too much for me to hide and I can't go around like you—an ostrich with my head in the sand—for twelve months.'

'I don't know what you mean.'

But he did.

'You can't feel this thing between us?'

'No!'

'Liar.'

The word hung in the air between them. A threat…

The truth.

And then she'd had enough. She took a deep breath and she said what she'd promised not to say. Whatever the outcome, it had to be said.

'I love you, Alastair de Castaliae,' she said, and her anger was all around them. She was furious with him. She was also furious with herself for betraying what she hadn't wanted to reveal. But there was suddenly no choice.

He was so close.

And there were these stupid cushions!

Another cushion went flying.

'I love you,' she repeated. 'I know. It's stupid. Stupid, stupid, stupid. But you picked me up and rescued me from a life of poverty, you took me to Paris and fed me snails and cheeses and strawberries, you bought me the sexiest knickers a girl could ever have—and then refused to look at them. And you rescued me from traffic and you gave me the most gorgeous dog…'

That was a good one. The most gorgeous dog…

'Are we talking about Leo here?' he asked cautiously, and she glared and threw away another cushion. She was tempted to whop him with it.

'Shut up.' She glowered. 'Just listen. And then you take my little brother as your best man and you stand there in your gorgeous suit and you smile at me, and you make *those* vows! *And you give me copestones for a wedding present.* Damn, a girl would have to be abnormal to ignore that, and I'm not abnormal. I'm truly, madly, deeply in love with you. So there. I've said it. You can do with it what you like, Your Serene Stupid Highness. Like it or lump it.'

Her breath caught on a sob. 'And you needn't worry that it changes anything. At the end of the year I'll still walk away as I promised. But for what it's worth, you should know what you're letting go. You have a wife. I might not be the wife you planned, but I'm a wife all the same. Not a pretend wife, Alastair. I'm a wife who loves you so much it hurts, and who's given you her heart and who doesn't expect a single thing in return.'

And she flung herself over onto her breast and buried her face in her remaining pillows.

And then she sat up again and swallowed. The situation was impossible and somehow she had to strive for lightness.

'Except another swimming lesson tomorrow,' she managed, while Alastair stared at her in open-mouthed amazement. 'I do expect that. You know, this doesn't mean anything has to change, but I thought you ought to know the facts—and the facts are that I'm yours. If you want me. But if you don't want me then that's OK, too. As long as I get to swim tomorrow.'

And that was the end of that.

She buried her head again, and Alastair sat staring down at her, trying to figure out what the hell to say.

What was there to say?

He could think of exactly nothing.

CHAPTER ELEVEN

ALASTAIR slept on the beach.

Or rather he tossed and turned on the beach. He'd taken a spare blanket and gone down to the sand. Back in the cottage, his wife's body had been rigid. Her breathing had been even and measured but he'd known she hadn't been asleep and there would have been no sleep for either of them if he'd stayed where he was.

So he'd left, and lay in the moonlight and listened to the waves gently lap the shore—and wondered what on earth he had done and where he could go from here.

Back to Rose, his body screamed at him. He had only to make the slightest move...

She...*loved him*?

Nonsense. That was impossible. Fantasy stuff. He'd let himself get too close, he told himself, and she was too alone in the world. She'd built him into something he couldn't be.

He'd never pretended with her. She knew him...

She knew what she wanted to know. Love? It'd fade. Romantic love. Ha!

But...his mother and father had been in love, and their love had endured for over thirty years.

And then it had been shattered in one instant, he remembered bitterly. One drunken driver on a motorway and that love had been splintered into a thousand shards, each one capable of hurting to death...

His mother had shrivelled since his father's death. And so had he.

Lissa had accepted a ride from Paris with Alastair's father, and the two had been wiped out in milliseconds. Love lost…

Love found? Rose was back in their cottage, waiting. Waiting for her husband.

All he had to do was take her, he thought savagely. It would be so easy. To accept her love.

But he was incapable of giving that love in return. Because he knew that giving meant pain. He couldn't… He just couldn't expose himself to that sort of pain again! No matter how desirable she was, he couldn't take that last final step. He couldn't depend on her for his sanity.

And he surely would depend on her if he let himself believe in her loving. It would be so easy to lay his life in her sweet hands.

To love and lose… That was the way of madness!

So he was better here, under the stars. For twelve months, if necessary. For however long it took for this strange marriage to run its course.

Penny-Rose came to find him just before dawn.

He was half awake, half asleep, and his dark form was a mere shadow on the sand. She came flying down to the beach and almost fell over him. As he reached up and steadied her, she fell to her knees.

'Alastair…'

And all of a sudden things had changed. There was no hint of the passion—or the anger—of the night before. There was only fear in her voice, and the fear was raw and real.

'What is it?' He was sitting up, and she was kneeling, still in the lovely negligee of last night, her curls tumbled and wild and her eyes huge in the pre-dawn light.

'Alastair…'

'Just say it.'

'Alastair, it's your mother.'

*   *   *

Marguerite had had a heart attack. The call had come through to the resort, and the manager had come to the cottage to break the news.

'My…my husband's gone for a dawn walk,' Penny-Rose had managed. 'Just tell me what's wrong, and I'll find him.'

So now she told Alastair what the manager had told her.

'Marguerite went back to Paris the day after we were married,' she explained gently. 'But apparently she's had chest pains, and they've been growing worse. Finally she made an appointment to see her local doctor, but by the time she reached him it was a full-stage heart attack. She's in Intensive Care.'

'I'll go.' Alastair was rising, and Penny-Rose was right there with him.

'I'll come with you.'

But Alastair was no longer seeing her. His thoughts were only on his mother. 'I'll find the manager and see how fast I can get back to Paris.'

Getting back to Paris was easier said than done. The supply boat pulled into the island once a week, bringing the guests from the mainland. Otherwise they came by helicopter.

'And the hire chopper's out of action,' the manager said apologetically. By the time Penny-Rose and Alastair reached his office, he'd already made enquiries on their behalf. 'The engine's being reconditioned. I'm afraid it's useless until Thursday.'

'That's two days.' Alastair took a deep breath. 'You mean there's no way I can get off the island until then? I can pay the boat.'

'The boat does the rounds of the islands. It'll take at least a day to get back here. But if I could make a suggestion…'

'Anything.'

'One of the outer islands is owned by a reclusive fisherman.' The manager gave a deprecating smile. 'A rich, reclusive fisherman. He's somewhat of an eccentric. He lives alone and doesn't socialise. But he owns his own hel- icopter.'

Alastair frowned. 'Will he rent it out?'

'Maybe, but it only holds one passenger.' The manager cast an apologetic glance at Penny-Rose. 'And while I might be able to persuade him to make a mercy dash for one, I doubt he'd take kindly to doing more.'

'That's fine. It's only me that's going.'

'But…' Penny-Rose flinched. 'Alastair, I need to go with you.'

'There's no room,' he said briefly. 'And no need either.'

He didn't need her. Of course he didn't. Penny-Rose's face tightened. But it was Marguerite she was worried about. Wasn't it?

Damn it, she was worried about both of them. And if anything happened to Marguerite and she wasn't by Alastair's side…

'I'd still like to come.'

'I'm afraid you can't, ma'am,' the resort manager apol- ogised. 'At least, not straight away.' He lifted the telephone and looked enquiringly at Alastair. 'The plane from Suva to Europe leaves at nine this morning. That means there's very little time. If I make fast arrangements I can have you on it.'

'Do it,' Alastair growled. He turned and found Rose watching him. She looked…

Hell, she looked like she'd been kicked. And like she was expecting to be kicked again.

'The kids are booked back to Australia on Saturday,' he told her, his voice gentling. 'That's when the boat calls. You can't cut it short. You know this is the holiday they've always dreamed of, and so have you.'

He couldn't resist then. He put a hand out to trace the outline of her cheek, and if it had been meant to comfort her, then who could blame him if he took a modicum of comfort himself? 'Have a wonderful time. Come back when they leave.'

'You don't want me.'

'I don't…need you.'

And that was that.

'Belle?'

'Alastair…' It was early evening in Paris.

Alastair telephoned Belle's cellphone while he sat in the departure lounge at Suva, and she answered on the first ring. There was a party of some sort in the background. He could hear laughter and voices and the clink of glasses…

'Alastair, what is it?'

Briefly he outlined what had happened, and she was horrified.

'Oh, Alastair, that's dreadful. You poor darling…'

He didn't want sympathy for himself. That was the last thing he needed. He wanted tangible help.

'Belle, she's alone. You know we have no family in Paris, and my only aunt's in Yorkshire and too frail to travel. It'll take me twenty-four hours to get there. Please… can you go to her?'

'Visit her in hospital, you mean.'

'Yes,' he said gratefully. 'Belle, I know it's a lot to ask, but could you stay with her until I get there? I can't bear to think of her being alone. Of her being in pain…'

'Of course I'll go, darling.' He heard her pause and speak an aside to someone in the background, and then she came on the line again. 'Sorry about that. Damn clients. Just tell me what hospital she's in and as soon as my guests leave I'll go.'

'Not now?'

'Alastair, these are important clients—'

He said something exceedingly rude about the clients.

She didn't appreciate it. 'Alastair! There's no need to be coarse. I'll go as soon as I can.'

And that was all he could do.

Twenty minutes later, the jet lifted off from the international airport, and Alastair was finally away. The plane circled the islands underneath as it veered to face Europe.

And Alastair stared down at the turquoise sea and imagined his wife. Rose. She'd be practising her swimming, he thought, and wondered if she'd have made it past five strokes by the next time he saw her.

She would—and he'd miss seeing her try.

The thought was suddenly almost unbearable. He stared down into the water, willing himself to see, but it was too far away.

But he stayed looking for a very long time.

But Penny-Rose wasn't swimming. As Alastair's helicopter took off for the mainland she sat and watched until the sound had faded to nothing, the seabirds had returned to reclaim the patch of beach where the helicopter had landed and the machine was far out of sight.

Yet still she watched.

Have a wonderful time, he'd said.

How could she do that when Marguerite might be dying? When anything could be happening on the other side of the world.

On *her* side of the world.

And that was the crux of it. This wasn't her home. And neither was Australia. Home was where the heart was.

Home was with Alastair.

Fiji. Los Angeles. London. Paris.

The journey was interminable. Each step seemed to take for ever and sleep was impossible. By the time Alastair reached the hospital he was past the point of rational thinking. So much time had elapsed. What if...?

'What if' didn't bear thinking of. At least Belle was with her, he thought again and again. If the worst came to the worst, his mother wouldn't be completely alone.

But, thankfully, the worst hadn't come to the worst.

'She's had a mild heart attack.' The physician on duty

saw the grey look of strain in his face, and answered his overriding terror straight away. 'She's still very much alive and she should be OK—'

'Should?' He went straight to the nub of the matter. 'Why do you say *should*?'

The physician gave him a smile that didn't quite reassure him. 'The attack itself didn't cause long-term damage, but we've had to operate. One of her arteries has become too thin to allow safe passage of blood. The way it was, it was a miracle she hadn't had an attack earlier. I'm sure she's been suffering angina for some time. She wanted to wait until you arrived but we daren't. In fact, she's in Theatre right now.'

The physician's voice gentled as she tried to ease his strain. 'She's having what's called a coronary artery bypass, and there's every reason to hope she'll come through it with flying colours.'

'But…' Alastair's eyes were searching the doctor's face. 'She mightn't?'

'Your mother is seventy. She's been ill, and it's a major operation. There's always a chance that things won't go well.'

'She could die on the operating table?'

'Yes,' the doctor said frankly. 'There is that chance. But there's every reason to hope that she won't.'

'I wish I could have been here—before she went in.'

'We couldn't wait,' the physician told him. 'I'm sorry.'

Alastair put his hands up and raked his hair, then closed his eyes. 'At least she had Belle.' He opened his eyes again, forcing himself to practicalities. If his mother was in Theatre, there was nothing to do but find Belle. 'Where's she waiting?'

'Belle?'

'My…our friend.' As the doctor looked confused, Alastair explained further. 'Belle will be here somewhere. I rang her…' he glanced at his watch '…twenty-four hours ago.'

'As far as I know, there's been no one with your mother.'

Silence.

'You're kidding.'

'I've spent a lot of time with your mother,' the physician told him. 'I've been on duty in Coronary Care for the last twelve hours.' She gave a rueful smile. 'We've had an epidemic of heart attacks and I've hardly had a break. I would have seen anyone with your mother.'

He couldn't believe it. 'Belle said she'd come.'

'Maybe she's been delayed,' the doctor said gently. She, too, glanced at her watch. Her time with Alastair was over. 'It may well be a couple of hours before your mother's out of Theatre. Can I show you where you can wait, or would you prefer to find yourself a hotel, freshen up and come back when the surgery's finished?'

'I'll wait,' Alastair said grimly. 'Of course I'll wait.'

He waited for four hours. The surgery went on for ever, and Alastair paced the waiting room as if somehow expending energy could help. It didn't.

'There are complications.' The physician popped in to find him before she finally went off duty. 'I'm sorry, but it's taking longer than expected.'

'But—'

'There's still no need to panic,' she reassured him. 'Not yet. It's just been a more extensive repair job than they thought.'

'She'll never make it,' Alastair groaned, and the doctor looked at him and then pushed him gently into a chair.

'Sit,' she ordered. 'I'll ask the staff to bring you sandwiches and coffee.' And then she paused. 'Is there anyone you want us to contact? You mentioned a name before. Belle? Would you like her to be with you?'

'No!'

And suddenly he was very sure of it.

And he was also sure who he really wanted to be by his side.

He wanted his Penny-Rose.

And he wanted her so badly it was as if his heart were as injured as his mother's.

Belle arrived half an hour later, breezing into the waiting room with her arms full of flowers as if she were there to visit a mother with a newborn babe. She looked gorgeous. Chic and immaculate in a tiny black suit that must have cost a mint, not a hair out of place, her face immaculately made up…

Here was every reason he had wanted to marry her, Alastair thought grimly. She was indeed the perfect woman.

So why, as she gave a cry of pleasure, placed her flowers aside and rushed to put her arms around him, did he feel nothing? Nothing at all.

It was as if she were some sort of plastic doll—beautiful, but inside there was nothing.

She didn't notice his reaction. 'Oh, Alastair, what a frightful time you must have had. Poor darling.' She kissed him lightly, then pulled away and made a little moue with her lips. 'Darling, you haven't shaved.'

He hadn't. And he didn't give a damn.

'Has it taken twenty-four hours,' he said carefully, 'for you to decide what to wear when visiting hospital?'

She looked astounded. 'I'm sorry?'

'Where the hell have you been?' His pent-up anxiety exploded in fury. 'I asked you to come. I needed someone to be here with her. What have you been doing?'

'Darling, I knew you couldn't be here until now.'

'I asked you to see my mother. Not me.'

She still looked astonished, as if the idea of spending time with an old lady was preposterous. 'I rang.'

'You rang?'

'Of course I rang.' Belle was defensive and angry in return. She had never been one to take criticism lightly. 'The nurse said she was as well as could be expected and due for surgery. There wasn't any point in coming while she was busy having pre-op examinations and things. I would have just had to sit in the room and wait.'

'Right.' He was past anger now. He was cold and drained and very, very tired. 'What a waste of time. Of course. So when she went to Theatre, she had no one with her at all.'

'She had the staff.'

'It's not the same, Belle.' He drew in an angry breath and he knew what he had to say. 'She had no one with her who loved her. It's important.'

'I don't…'

'You don't love my mother? Of course you don't.' He nodded, his weariness intensifying by the minute. 'I should have thought of that.'

'I'm fond of Marguerite,' she chided him gently. 'Alastair, you're weary. You're not thinking straight.'

'Maybe I am.' He shook his head, trying to clear the fog, but truth was surrounding him, fog or not. He lifted the flowers from the table and handed them back to her. 'Love is…important. I hadn't realised it. Until now. And we don't have it, Belle.'

'What—?'

'We never have had it,' he said grimly. 'And I want it. I want it for my mother, for my children—and for me. And I won't find it with you. So…' He took a deep breath. 'I'm sorry, Belle, but there it is. I organised my life like a business. But it's not like that. Since Lissa died—'

'Alastair, I understand—'

'You don't,' he said bleakly. 'After Lissa died I thought I could do without love. But that was because I didn't know what love was. Not true love. Lissa and I were the best of friends and her death hurt like hell. Maybe if we'd married we would have ended up loving…like it's possible to love. Maybe we wouldn't. All I know is that when I made my vow not to love, I didn't have a clue what I was talking about. I do now.'

She still didn't get it. 'Darling, you're overwrought.'

'I'm overwrought,' he agreed. 'Yes. And maybe I should

have been overwrought a long time ago. Take your flowers, Belle,' he told her. 'I'm sorry if I've messed with the smooth running of your life, but there's no future for us. Take your flowers and go.'

She got it then. Her eyes narrowed in anger. 'Oh, Alastair, for heaven's sake. If that little slut has pulled you in—'

'If you're talking about my wife, I'd advise you to be very, very careful,' he growled. 'My wife is anything but a slut.' He took a deep breath. 'My wife is my love.'

Marguerite came back from Theatre two hours later and they still didn't know if she'd make it. She had tubes and machines hooked up everywhere and the sight of her pale face made Alastair feel sick.

'She arrested on the operating table,' the surgeon explained. 'We've been very lucky to get her back. But the repair work has been done. If she pulls through the next few hours she should be fine.'

So he sat, glued to her bedside, willing her to keep on breathing.

Hour after hour.

Staff came and went. He hardly noticed. All he saw was his mother. All he thought about was his mother.

Or maybe that wasn't quite true. Because at the back of his mind was an aching need for Penny-Rose.

Why was he calling her Penny-Rose in his thoughts?

It was how he'd first seen her, he thought. Diminutive and work-stained and determined. Clad in overalls, ready to take on the world for her siblings, as tough as old boots.

And tender to the core.

She'd said she loved him.

Hell!

He watched his mother, but over and over through that dreadful night he thought of his wife.

* * *

And with the dawn, Marguerite opened her eyes and smiled.

'Alastair.' It was a faint whisper, thready and weak, but she was there, conscious and alive. Her pleasure resonated in her voice. 'What…what are you doing here?'

'I came to be with you.'

'But…' She thought that through. 'You should be with your wife.'

'Penny-Rose…' It was so close to what he'd been thinking that he was thrown off balance. 'You know it's just make-believe. Penny-Rose isn't my wife.'

'Of course she is.' Marguerite squeezed his hand with what little strength she had. 'She loves you just like I loved your father. She loves you even more than I love you. So much…'

And she closed her eyes and slept—and left him wondering.

Finally he was persuaded to take a break. Marguerite was settled, her breathing was deep and even and the doctor said she might well sleep for hours. He was sure now that when she woke she'd remember he'd been here, and the staff were smiling their reassurance and their pleasure. She'd live.

So…a shave and a wash and a sleep were called for. Not necessarily in that order.

'But maybe you'd better see your friend before you go,' the charge nurse said, and he frowned.

'My friend?'

'She's in the main waiting room. She says you won't want to see her—that we're not to disturb you—but she's been waiting for some time now. Maybe seven or eight hours. She looks as worried as you have been. I was just about to send someone down to tell her your mother has every chance of recovering, but if you'd like to tell her yourself…'

It didn't make sense. 'Belle's been waiting?'

'Is that her name? She didn't say. You'll find her down the hall.'

So he went down the hall—and in the waiting room was Penny-Rose.

For a moment he said nothing—just stood staring down at her as if he were seeing an apparition. The waiting room was deserted—no one but the most anxious of relatives would be here at this early hour. So Penny-Rose had sat alone and her eyes had been glued to the door as she'd waited.

When Alastair appeared, she looked up at him without saying a word. Her eyes were huge, questioning and terrified, and he realised with a stabbing certainty that she wasn't concerned about him. Not now.

Unlike Belle, who'd only come to the hospital when she'd been sure of seeing Alastair, all Penny-Rose's thoughts were with Marguerite. That was what she was searching for in his face. Marguerite's fate. And he looked haggard, he knew, and his face must give the worst of impressions.

But for the life of him he couldn't make himself smile.

All he could think of was that she was there. She was his love. The two thoughts crashed down on him with overwhelming force.

How could he have been so stupid as not to have seen it? How could he have thought he couldn't love?

Here she was. Miraculously here. His wonderful, wonderful bride. His wife!

'Penny-Rose…' His voice came out a haggard whisper, and she came straight to the worst conclusion possible.

'Oh, Alastair. Alastair…' It was a whisper of distress and absolute, desolate loss, and she buried her head in her hands and closed her eyes. 'Oh, no.'

He couldn't bear it. It took half a second to cross the room, kneel before her and take those beloved hands in his. To drag her fingers away from her tear-drenched eyes and make her look at him.

'No. Penny-Rose, no! She's alive. She's OK...' As she still looked at him with the remains of horror, he finally made himself smile. 'Sweetheart, I didn't mean to look dreadful. It's just because I haven't shaved and haven't slept. But she's recovering. They've operated and they've repaired the damage. She's woken, she's spoken to me and I've left her to sleep.'

She stared up at him, torn between disbelief and hope. Her eyes were vast pools of exhausted misery. Weariness had put her almost past hope.

But, finally, hope won.

'You mean...she'll live?'

'Yes.'

'You're sure?'

'As sure as I can be. I wouldn't have left her otherwise.'

'Oh, Alastair.'

It was too much. She put her arms around his neck, buried her face in his shoulder and burst into tears.

He didn't let her stay there. Not for long anyway.

For maybe a minute he let her weep, while wonder faded and her touch seeped into his soul. She was real. She was here.

She was his.

And he could wait no longer. He put her back from him, looked at her drowning face and smiled down into her eyes with a smile that held infinite tenderness, infinite wonder—and infinite love.

'My Penny-Rose,' he said softly. 'My love.'

And his mouth found hers, and he kissed her with a passion that threatened to last for ever.

It was a kiss that made a marriage—a marriage that was from this moment forward.

'How did you get here?'

Neither of them knew how long it took before words were possible between them, but when they were, everything that needed to be said somehow already had been.

The kiss had said it all. Penny-Rose was in her husband's arms and it would take the strength of giants to tear her away. 'How on earth did you do it?'

'Magic.' She smiled, and he chuckled.

'I know. More of the fairy godmother stuff. But seriously...'

'Seriously, the resort manager realised how much I wanted to go so he contacted your recluse with the helicopter and used all his charm to persuade him to take me as well. Of course, we didn't make it to Suva in time for your flight, so I caught a flight back to Sydney, then flew to Singapore and on to Paris. I must have landed only about five or six hours after you.'

He stared at her in astonishment. 'You must be exhausted.'

'No more than you.' She was snuggled into him, settled and happy. Happy wasn't a big enough word. Ecstatic!

'But why did you come? You wanted the holiday so much.'

'Do you think I wanted a holiday more than being here...with you?' She was indignant. 'And with Marguerite. If anything had happened to Marguerite and I hadn't been here...'

'For me?'

Penny-Rose looked up at him, her face deadly serious. 'For you,' she agreed. But...Alastair, I love your mother.'

'It's your speciality,' he said softly. 'Giving and giving and giving.'

That puzzled her. 'I don't have anything to give.'

'And I do?' His voice was incredulous—angry even. 'Money, riches, power—sure, I have all of those things. I have so much to give. Just not the thing that counts. Love.'

'But you can't—'

'I couldn't.' He kissed her again, because he couldn't bear not to. Heavens, she still tasted like the sea. It'd be the salt of her tears, he knew, but the smell of her, the feel of her...

She was like the sea and the sky and the heavens all rolled into one.

How had he ever thought he could put her away from him after a year? How had he ever thought he could keep himself from her for a year?

'I can love now,' he said, and all the joy of the morning was in his voice. 'I've learned. I've had the very best of teachers. Oh, Rose…my Penny-Rose…'

Her face clouded, just a little, at the memories the name brought back. 'Penny-Rose?'

'I've been really stupid,' he told her. 'Trying to make you into something that you weren't. But Penny-Rose is how I first saw you. Dressed in those damned overalls, filthy, yet laughing at us, letting us know your values weren't ours. Telling me that a marriage without love was stupid.' He pulled her tightly against him. 'So Rose is a princess. My Princess Rose. But Penny-Rose is the woman I love more than life itself.'

She looked up into his eyes for a long, long moment. And then she sighed with pure happiness.

'Penny-Rose it is,' she said softly. 'I'll go for Penny-Rose any day.'

'You mean you'd rather be the woman I love than a princess?'

'I'd rather be the woman you love than anything in the world.'

'Then so be it,' he said exultantly. 'From this day forth. Because that's exactly what you are.'

And he gathered her against him and kissed her—for a very, very long time.

EPILOGUE

MY WEDDING day. My proper wedding day. A ceremony just for us—with the priest and Alastair and me and Leo. Because we want it to be a proper wedding, there'll be Marguerite and our cameraman to act as witnesses, but there'll be no one else.

A true and legal wedding… It's funny how I'm more nervous now than I was at the big one.

There'll be no velvet coats for Leo today. Or any fancy wedding gowns. We're wearing jeans and bare toes on a beach in the South of France. Where no one knows us. Where we can take each other as we mean to have each other—in the privacy of ourselves.

Just us.

For now and for ever.

'Wilt thou have this woman to be thy wedded wife, to live for ever according to God's law in the Holy estate of matrimony? Wilt thou love her, comfort her, honour and keep her in sickness and in health; and forsaking all others, keep thee only unto her, so long as ye both shall live?'

'I do,' said Alastair.

'And you, Penny-Rose. Wilt thou have this man…?'

'I do,' said Penny-Rose.

'Amen to that,' said Marguerite. Completely recovered, she stood with pride as their witness and she couldn't stop smiling.

'Woof,' said Leo.

'Bless you both,' said their lone cameraman—the man

they'd asked to record this event for their great-grandchildren. 'May you be as happy and successful as you've made me.'

And that was the way it was.

THE SHEIKH'S PROPOSAL

by

Barbara McMahon

Barbara McMahon was born and raised in the south, but settled in California after spending a year flying around the world for an international airline. After settling down to raise a family and work for a computer firm, she began writing when her children started school. Now, feeling fortunate in being able to realise her long-held dream of quitting her 'day job' and writing full-time, she and her husband recently moved to the Sierra Nevada mountains of California, where she finds her desire to write is stronger than ever. With the beauty of the mountains visible from her windows, and the pace of life slower than the hectic San Francisco Bay Area where they previously resided, she finds more time than ever to think up stories and characters and share them with others through writing.

CHAPTER ONE

HER father was going to kill her, she thought, barely suppressing a groan. Sara Kinsale looked around the dusty cell and grimaced. She'd been here two days. Two days when she should have been at the hotel in Staboul. Two days stuck in some backwater jail in the very country in which her father was trying to nail the biggest deal of all time. When he needed everything perfect to convince the powers that be that his company could broker the most favorable deal for the newly-up-for-grabs oil leases.

She jumped up from the narrow cot and began to pace the tiny cell. She'd alternated between contemplating her parents' reaction with impatient pacing all the while trying to come up with a solution to her dilemma that might allow her to keep this from them and the world press.

If her father didn't kill her, her mother would guilt her to death with her soft sighs and her telling looks. She'd ask her father a million times, "Where did we go wrong?"

Sara blew her bangs off her forehead and leaned against the hard cinder block wall. She knew the drill. Her parents hadn't gone wrong, she had. But not intentionally. Things just seemed to go awry when she was involved.

First, she hadn't settled on any one career. Not like

her sister the attorney. Or her brother the nuclear physicist. Or even her mother, the perfect hostess, charity
coordinator and helpmate to an international businessman.

She'd tried to find a niche that she could call her own.
Acting hadn't worked out, to the great relief of her parents. Nor had nursing. She got queasy at the sight of
blood. Being a child-care worker had been lots of fun,
she loved playing with the kids. But her lack of discipline with the children had gotten her fired from both
jobs she'd found.

The latest job might have bordered on acceptable—
photojournalism was a respected profession. If she
proved herself, maybe her family would begin to see her
as a contributing member of society and not a flake who
couldn't settle on anything.

Only now she'd blown that, as well. The editor of the
U.S. tabloid newspaper that had hired her had been
thrilled when she had told him about her upcoming visit
to Kamtansin, one of the newly emerging Arabian countries on the Mediterranean Sea. The plum assignment of
filming the royal enclave and getting photos of some of
the royal family of the small Arabian country had been
hers for the asking.

Interviewing some of the leading members of
Kamtansin society had seemed a piece of cake in Los
Angeles. Especially since several were in deep negotiations with her father over the oil leases. She'd meet
them, bowl them over with her charm and get those photographs.

The reality proved one hundred percent opposite.

She'd been refused the interviews and refused photo opportunities.

The worst, however, was being apprehended trying to film the summer retreat of one of the leading families, despite being warned not to approach them. Now she languished in some horrible jail that didn't even have basic facilities.

Worse, she'd been accused of being a spy!

She'd not been allowed to contact the U.S. embassy. Nor call her father. She had not been permitted to seek an attorney. She had not been able to do anything but fret about the predicament she was in!

Her parents would be frantic. She'd stayed one night in the hotel with them when she first arrived. Then boldly plunged into her trip to get something on film after the string of refusals through normal channels. Even though she couldn't get close to the summer enclave she'd targeted, the telephoto lens would allow her to capture the finest details.

But she'd scarcely shot two views before being captured.

Her parents' worry couldn't compare with her own. The laws of this country were completely unknown to her. Would she be granted a trial, or end up remaining in this hot, dusty cell forever—with no one in her family ever knowing what happened to her?

The door opened. At least she had more privacy than she might have expected. The door to the small cinder block cell was solid wood, with only a small square about midway that permitted food to pass through twice a day, and allowed the jailors to check on her from time to time. Like she was going to escape? The only window in the room was equally small, and set too high in the wall for her to even reach.

The tall man dressed in the traditional Arab robes motioned with his head. He didn't speak English and she didn't understand a word of Arabic.

Sara brushed down her khaki trousers and shook her shirt a little. After two days and two nights with no washing, the sharp creases and crisp look had long since faded. She felt rumpled, dirty and tired. And more than a bit scared.

"I want to call the U.S. embassy," she said. She wasn't sure the man understood English, but she'd go down trying!

He remained silent, pointing down the hall.

She walked toward the door. Once within reach, he clasped her arm in a firm grip then marched her down the long corridor to the wide stairs at the end. Again she wondered what they thought she was going to do—flee from the building and face endless miles of burning desert sand and scorching heat with no vehicle to carry her back to safety? Her hired car was probably still hidden in the hill behind the summer villa. And she had no idea where that was in relation to where she was now.

They climbed two flights. He knocked on a door and upon hearing the reply from within, opened it, pushing Sara in before releasing her.

Sara quickly glanced around. It was an austere office with minimal furniture, no coverings on the windows. A man stood by one of the tall windows, gazing out over the desert landscape. She wasn't sure exactly where this jail was in relation to the capital city, but it wasn't far from the ruling family's retreat—the summer home she had tried to capture on film in order to have something for her newspaper's readers. Something to prove to her boss she was capable of the assignment.

Slowly he turned and looked at her.

Sara felt a warm tendril of awareness curl within when his eyes met hers. He easily stood taller than six feet. His hair was black, gleaming in the sunshine beaming in through the tall window. His eyes were dark, fathomless, with an uncompromising glint in them as he studied her. His cheekbones were high with taut tanned skin covering them. Power seemed to radiate from him, enhanced by the exquisitely tailored suit, the wide shoulders, the decidedly masculine stance. She felt the power through his study of her.

Suddenly aware of her own bedraggled appearance, she wished she could have brushed her hair or washed her face. Done something!

Then the absurdity of the situation hit her. She wanted to get out of this jail, not make some kind of good impression on a stranger. One, moreover, who apparently had some control over her incarceration, else why was she here?

"I wish to call the U.S. embassy," she repeated for at least the hundredth time.

He said something in Arabic and the man behind Sara bowed and left, closing the door.

"Sit," he said in English.

She blinked and looked around, spotting a chair against the wall beside the door. She'd have to pass by the desk to reach it. There was a phone on the desk, a few folders—one opened. Was that on her?

"I'm an American citizen. I wish to call the U.S. embassy. This has been a mistake that can be easily cleared up."

"Sit." It was clearly an order.

Moving quickly, Sara sat gingerly on the edge of the chair. Gorgeous or not, his manners needed work.

He stepped behind the desk and fingered a sheet of paper in the opened file. "You were arrested attempting to photograph a private dwelling—one which had posted signs warning trespassers away. You were trying to photograph members of the ruling family without permission. You carried no passport or other identification." He looked at her. "How did you get into this country and for what purpose?"

Sara swallowed. She needed to keep her father out of this imbroglio if possible. She could just imagine the result of his business negotiations if the world's press caught wind of the situation. Yet she couldn't stay here forever. She couldn't!

"My passport and other identification are in my room." She'd traveled light when heading out on assignment. A blessing, or a curse this time?

"And that would be where?"

Dare she tell him? Would he be discreet, believing she meant no harm? Releasing her to return to the capital city? His dark eyes held her gaze as if by merely looking at her he could determine if she spoke the truth or not.

"At the Presentation Hotel in Staboul."

He tilted his head slightly. "First-class accommodations,'' he said, flicking a glance over her disheveled clothing.

She cleared her throat and tried to smile brightly. "I have a room there, with my family."

"And that family would be?"

Who was this man? His suit was the finest Italian cut. His shirt a pristine white contrasting dramatically with his dark maroon tie. His hair was cut short, and he carried himself with an arrogant air. He looked sophisticated and urbane. And from the way the other man had bowed out of the room, the stranger was apparently someone of rank in this country. How susceptible would he be to keeping quiet about her identity?

"If you'd just let me make a call—"

He shook his head. "First, tell me who you are and why you were photographing the summer residence?"

"I'm Sara K— Sara Kay. I'm a newspaper photographer on assignment. I was just trying to get some photos to show Americans what the sheikh's home looked like. Your ruling family is very secretive—especially since the death of one of the sheikhs six months ago. We're curious, that's all. There's nothing sinister about it."

"Then why not request permission to make the photographs through normal channels?"

"I tried, no go."

"And did you not think there might be a reason for that?" His voice was hard, with an edge that set Sara's back up.

"Like what?"

"Privacy, perhaps?" he said softly.

"In America, once a family is in the public eye, their privacy is gone. The general public wants to know all about them."

"You are not in America."

Sara nodded, eyeing the phone. She couldn't snatch it up and dial her parents. She hadn't a clue how to reach the hotel. And she had a feeling this man would easily stop her if she made any attempt.

"Look, if you just let me make one call, I can get this all cleared up. Or you could let me go. The other guys took my camera. I don't have the film, so no harm done. I promise not to photograph anything ever again if you want. Can I just go?" Preferably with her expensive camera, but at this point, Sara would be grateful just to be allowed to leave.

He closed the folder with finality. Her heart sank. He wasn't going to let her waltz out of here. She'd have to use her family's name, call on the influence of her father. She bit her lip. There had to be another way. Her father would kill her!

"Your actions have put into motion a chain of events that could have serious repercussions," he said slowly.

"From trying to take a few pictures?"

"You are an American. My country is in the midst of delicate negotiations with American business entities over oil reserves recently discovered here in Kamtansin. There are factions in the country who do not wish to work closely with the Americans. The ministers are watching to make sure our country has the best repre- sentation. There are those factions who want the country to move into a new direction. The money the leases would bring in would go a long way to improving the standard of living for all our citizens. Your actions could jeopardize the entire negotiations.''

Sara swallowed. ''You could just let me go,'' she almost whispered. ''I wouldn't tell a soul.''

''Too many people already know you are here and what you did. The charge is espionage. We do not take kindly to people flaunting our laws. You requested permission to film and were denied. How would you describe your actions?''

''I wasn't spying!''

He continued as if she hadn't interrupted. ''The old guard would love nothing more than to prove to the world that we will not tolerate a flaunting of our laws and customs. They wish to make an example of you. It would add weight to our side of the negotiations, as well.''

Oh, great. This was the single biggest screwup she'd ever committed—and could ruin her father's business deal! She could just hear her mother!

''On the other hand, if negotiations are to continue for the oil leases, we dare not risk alienating the Americans by holding one of their citizens to make an example of her. If you truly work for a newspaper, I imagine the press coverage would be rampant.''

She watched him closely. Please decide on the don't-alienate-the-American side, she prayed, realizing the full impact of the situation. She felt a little sick with that realization. She'd only been trying to get pictures for the paper—nothing sinister. She had never envisioned causing an international incident. And she certainly didn't want to jeopardize her father's negotiations.

The door opened behind her. She turned to see the man who had brought her to the room. He spoke rapidly in Arabic. The man behind the desk nodded.

"Go, now," he said in English, turning back to the window deep in thought.

"Wait," Sara said, pulling against the grasp the other man took on her arm. "Please, let me call the hotel, my father can vouch for me. He's Samuel Kinsale. He knows the sheikh!"

Kharun froze at the words. The woman's father was Samuel Kinsale? The man with whom he had been working with for weeks in negotiating oil leases? He spun around and looked at her again.

Her bedraggled appearance didn't suggest the daughter of one of the world's most powerful men, but two days in a local jail could explain that. The prison facilities in his country were not known for their lavish appointments.

Her honey-blond hair needed brushing, but it still looked soft as a woman's hair should. Her expressive gray eyes flashed and sparkled as every emotion showed in her face. Her clothes, if clean and pressed, would have been easily recognized as top quality. He should have noticed that first thing.

But what was that story she gave about being a photographer? Was that a cover? Was she in truth acting as a spy, just like Hamin, Garh and their cohorts claimed?

Trying to find a weakness in their side her father could use to hammer out a better deal?

Or was she just foolishly blundering in where she had no business being?

"And what is the daughter of an American oil magnate doing spying on my family?"

"Your family?"

"I'm Kharun bak Samin. That home you were trying to photograph belongs to my family."

"Oh, sheesh, I'm in deep trouble now!" she said with a groan. At least she was consistent, the older she got, the bigger the mistakes she made.

"You have just made the situation a hundred times worse." He switched to his native tongue and told Jabil to return the woman to her cell. Watching as she protested, he let no expression show on his face. He'd become good at hiding his thoughts during negotiations. Never let the other person know his feelings, had been his motto. It stood him in good stead now.

As soon as they'd left, he turned back to the window. But he didn't see the oasis to the left with the soaring date palms, the green grass that flourished in the midst of the sandy desert, or the drab houses of those who eked out an existence on the edge of the dunes. Nor did he see the endless desert beyond that stretched out to Morocco, wild and free and beckoning.

He saw instead the council chamber he'd left that morning. His uncle's handpicked ministers fighting against the men his father had recommended for the council. New regime against the old. Antiquated ways clashing against the hope of moving his country firmly into the twenty-first century.

And smack in the middle came the daughter of the man he was negotiating for oil leases that would enable the government to make the reforms his father had so longed for.

He had involved himself in the situation before he knew all the facts. Now others knew of his involvement. So the final decision would be his. What to do with Sara Kinsale?

Both sides would be closely watching. His father had served on the council for years, the old faction knew him. Now they watched to see he didn't sell out the country. The newer ministers were still wary about moving forward too quickly, wondering if he had the capability to represent their country in the treaty negotiations. They had trusted his father, and transferred that trust to him. But still, they watched.

Their country was such a dichotomy—rich and modern in the cities, poor and underdeveloped in the desert areas. With the influx of funds the oil leases would provide, much more could be done for the outlying areas—bringing all citizens into the twenty-first century.

Whatever he decided, it must be handled discreetly and with great diplomacy. His years in business had taught him all he needed. Now it was time to implement a strategy to get them out of this sticky situation.

He turned and reached for the phone.

Sara lay on her cot, wishing it had a modicum of comfort. Lumpy and narrow, it was obviously not geared for the Ritz. She'd played her trump card—given her father's position—and it hadn't helped. Maybe the oil leases weren't as important as she thought. Or maybe the sheikh felt he held the trump card with her in jail. Maybe he'd use that to force her father into giving concessions.

She groaned, wishing she'd never started this chain of events!

For the first time since her arrest she considered the possibility of staying in jail for a long time. She shivered, not liking the prospect at all.

She closed her eyes—seeing Kharun bak Samin. The top businessman dealing with her father, nephew of the chosen leader of this beautiful Arabian country. The son of the sheikh who had recently died, and who had played an important role as adviser to the ruler. Things could not possibly be worse. What would her father say?

Restless with her thoughts, she sprang up again and began to pace the small space. If her lapse of good sense resulted in negotiations breaking down, it could mean her father losing the deal—another company getting the oil rights. A major contract going south because of her impetuousness.

What would the sheikh decide?

She tried to blank out the memory of that fluttering of interest in the man—personal interest. Was the desert heat getting to her? He had been part of her assignment—photograph the elusive Kharun bak Samin. Let the women of America get a good look at one of the world's most eligible bachelors—heir to the fortune built by his father and enhanced by his own efforts. Dynamic businessman of this important country on the Mediterranean Sea, and handsome as a movie star.

She'd thought it would be a snap, that she'd be able to sell the story and pictures and make a name for herself with the newspaper. She had wanted the credentials of a job well done to help her move to a more established newspaper. One that delivered news and commentaries, not sensationalism.

Trying to ignore the twinge she felt every time she thought about the tabloid aspect of her job, she focused on the fact it was a step toward more serious photojournalism.

But she couldn't help remembering how she herself cringed when seeing the flashy headlines splashed across the different tabloids at the grocery store checkout stands.

Her impetuosity had once again gotten her in trouble. But this time, her father could also suffer. She'd paid little attention to his plans recently, more concerned with learning how to operate the fancy camera she'd bought for the trip, and trying her hand at reporting news.

The two articles she written that had been accepted had been changed beyond recognition by the time they hit the stands. She tried for the exploitive tone of the paper, but it proved impossible.

She had really wanted to do this story—always hoping for the best—a human interest kind of story, nothing sensational.

Sara couldn't bear the thought of being the one to bring disgrace on her father. All she'd ever wanted was to make him proud of her. Now this. She should have kept her mouth shut! She should never have told the sheikh who she was. Sara Kay was an unknown, no one would rally around to rescue her.

But the daughter of Samuel Kinsale? Her father would spare no expense to find her. And if he didn't like the way she'd been treated, he'd stop the negotiations in a heartbeat.

Pacing back and forth, she wished she could go back in time three days. Wished she could turn back the clock. Would she have done anything differently?

Not get caught, for one thing. But the only way she could have avoided that, if she had the last three days to do over, was to not attempt the photo shoot. She'd gambled her career on that. Gambled and lost.

The afternoon hours dragged. Another day gone and she was no nearer to getting back to her family—or even letting them know she was all right.

Kharun seethed with impatience and frustration. His calls had given him the information he needed—Sara Kinsale was indeed the daughter of the man he was dealing with. The youngest child of a very worried man who was discreetly trying to locate his missing daughter.

Samuel Kinsale, too, was aware of the delicacy of the negotiations. And for the time being, didn't seem interested in upsetting the balance. But that would change if he didn't locate his daughter soon.

What would he do when he found out his daughter was in jail being held on charges of espionage?

Kharun's trusted adviser, Piers, suggested secreting her away, hiding her until after the oil leases were signed. But Kharun didn't see that as a viable option. Keeping her whereabouts hidden from her parents for weeks or months would be needlessly cruel.

Garh Sonharh, leader of the old guard, had been vocal in pushing for full prosecution. Kharun had not spoken to him directly—holding off as long as possible as he mulled the situation over. But he'd heard of Garh's wishes from Piers. Once he spoke directly with his uncle's strongest minister, he would be committed.

Kharun's call to his sister hadn't helped. She'd sympathized, discussed the situation, then offered a bizarre idea for scraping through unscathed. Bizarre nothing—it was plain stupid from start to finish.

Damn! He rose from behind the desk and paced the narrow room, wishing he could get on his horse and ride out into the desert until the entire situation made some kind of sense. The freedom he enjoyed on the back of Satin Magic brought a soothing almost mystic release to tension and turmoil.

But his horse was at his summer villa by the sea, and he was here, fifty miles inland.

Beside, he didn't think Garh would take kindly to being ignored while Kharun went horseback riding.

He smiled cynically. It didn't matter what he did, Garh didn't approve.

Nor did his aunt. If she had her way, his tenure as negotiator would be short. But he had the international business experience to know what to bargain for and to stand for his principles. His uncle trusted him, as had his father.

The bottom line—Kharun had the final recommendation regarding the oil leases. His uncle, the ruler of their country, had utmost faith in him. He had better do something soon before it all blew up in his face.

For the first time, he gave his sister's suggestion serious thought. It was a dumb way to muddle through a crisis, but might be the only way to save face all around. And it would make it very difficult for Garh to carry out his threat for an espionage charge.

He summoned Sara Kinsale.

She entered the room with her head held high. Jabil released her and bowed out, closing the door.

"I want to call the American embassy," she said firmly.

Kharun's lips almost twitched in amusement. She had her own strength, he noted, beginning to notice other things about her. She was taller than the average height of most of the women in his country, and that honey-blond hair shone like a beacon. She'd stand out in a crowd. She carried herself proudly. The curves the khakis displayed were womanly and alluring.

He jerked his gaze back to her blazing eyes. Silvery when she was angry, a light gray when not. If she went for the bizarre suggestion, he wondered if he'd be able to gauge her moods by the color of her eyes alone?

"I have confirmed your identity. Your father is escalating his search for you. Pretty soon it will be impossible to keep the circumstances private. Not that you will mind, will you? Once a public figure, privacy is lost, correct?"

She narrowed her eyes as she gazed at him, obviously not liking her own words thrown back.

"I apologize for infringing on your family's privacy. Next time I'll make sure I have permission for a photo shoot."

"Next time?"

She shrugged, still standing proudly before him.

All her makeup had long since worn off. Her cheeks had a natural color to them, and her lips looked full and sweet.

Kharun frowned and looked away from the tempting lips. He needed to make sure they both understood the proposal—and not get confused with some fantasies about the delectable femininity before him.

"I spoke briefly about the situation and the possible repercussions earlier," he began.

She nodded. "I didn't mean to cause problems."

"There may be a way out of this quagmire with a bit of acting on both our parts. Are you willing to hear my proposal?"

She nodded. Her shoulders relaxed a bit. Was she relieved to let him find a way out of the mess? Thus far she'd come up with nothing.

"I suggest we pretend to the world that we have known each other for some time. That your trip to visit your family is merely a cover to see me. That we became secretly engaged and you were planning on surprising me with photos of my family's home as an engagement present."

She stared at him, not moving. Had she heard what he said?

"Are you totally crazy?" she asked at last, almost exploding the words. "Engaged? As in get married to each other one day? No one in their right mind would believe such a thing! Where did you ever come up with such a ridiculous idea? I can't believe that's the best you can come up with. Aren't you supposed to be some hot-shot businessman? This is your proposal? I can counter it in a heartbeat—just let me go. I won't say a word. Make up something—like you imposed a heavy fine. I can't believe you can't think of a rational reason to release me without repercussions!"

He let her rant and rave for a couple of minutes, fascinated by her passion. Her eyes blazed, her breasts rose and fell as she drew in deep breaths. Her cheeks were flushed with color. Would she look as enticing in bed?

Where had that thought come from? He had no intention of finding out. He was trying to get through this without either side losing.

He held up a hand for silence. She closed her mouth and glared at him. He almost smiled at the picture she presented. However, now was not a time to get side-tracked.

"On the surface, I agree it does seem strange."

Hadn't he ranted and raved at his sister only a couple of hours ago protesting the very idea? "But there is a hint of merit in the idea. Hear me out. If we are allied, if we have a personal reason for your taking pictures of forbidden areas, we can scrape through both the ministers's anger and the embarrassment you'd cause your father if his daughter was publicly prosecuted and condemned. An engagement would only be temporary—until the lease negotiations are finalized. At that point, you can return home and we'll make a joint statement that there were too many differences to overcome.''

She blinked and continued to study him. ''It'd never work,'' she said at last. ''No one would ever believe you'd fall for me.''

That caught him by surprise. ''Why not? You're pretty and adventuresome—traits which would appeal to any man. We could have met in any number of cities we've both visited.''

''Puh-lease. You're the nephew of the ruler of this country. Your own father was an important member of the council before his death. I'm the flaky younger daughter of an oil dealer. If it was my sister, Margaret, I could see it, maybe. She's sophisticated, successful and never puts a step out of place. You don't even want to *suggest* such a proposal with me.''

For a second he wanted to agree with her. But it wasn't for real. Just a mock engagement to appease the ministers and keep scandal from rocking a still precariously run country. And, of course, to ensure the negotiations concerning their newly discovered oil reserves could continue with no awkwardness.

''It would take very little on your part—pretend to be my fiancée, attend a few social events, stay at my place temporarily. You do have some acting skills, surely.''

She shook her head. ''Been there, done that. Didn't take.''

''What?''

''I tried acting. I'm no good at it. That I don't fully

embrace the character, was the kindest criticism I received. The rest pretty much said I was a total flop.''

''Have you had experience at being a fiancée?''

She shook her head. ''Nope, neither pretend nor real. It wouldn't work, you know, but thanks for the thought. Can't you just let me go?''

''It will have to work, I see no other way out of this without complications on one side or the other. The next best suggestion was to secret you away to another facility and play ignorant while your parents worry and search fruitlessly for you. Is that a better choice? Or are you ready for the repercussions that could arise out of being tried for espionage?''

He saw he'd hit home with his first comment. She didn't wish to worry her parents any more than he did. She knew what a trial would do to her father's negotiations. Would she agree to this ludicrous scheme now that he'd played that card? One way or another it was up to him to ensure the negotiations continued with a favorable result. Would she make it easier or harder?

''Just a fiancée, right? Indefinite marriage date. Still in the getting-to-know-each-other stage?'' she clarified.

''Show only,'' he confirmed. Any elation he felt, he kept hidden. Maybe they could brush through, after all. They'd only have to pretend until the deal was finalized in a few weeks, a month at most.

''Okay, then, I guess I'll have to agree. Now can I make a call?''

Before Kharun could respond, the phone rang. He answered it, his eyes never leaving Sara. Could he trust her to fulfill her part? Trust that once she left the jail she wouldn't flee the country and to hell with the consequences?

Or would she hang around hoping to get those pictures that had her risking everything earlier this week?

"Garh, here, Kharun. I've heard some interesting rumors about an American spy you're holding at the jail," the familiar voice said when Kharun picked up the phone.

"You need a better source for rumors, Garh. No spies here. A misunderstanding about a present my fiancée wanted to give me."

The pause was minuscule. "Fiancée? I had no idea you were engaged to be married. Your uncle made no mention of this to me. When did this happen?"

"Some time ago. Out of respect for my father's recent passing and the grief in my family at his death, we elected to wait until a more suitable time to announce our betrothal. However, her zeal to capture the family home as a gift for me has changed our timing. We will let everyone in the family know immediately."

"Interesting, I didn't even know you knew Samuel Kinsale's daughter, much less had enough time for a courtship." Suspicion was evident in his tone.

Kharun remained silent. The less he told the old manipulator, the less he had to remember and deal with later.

But wasn't it interesting that Garh knew who Sara was. How had he found out? Kharun had only found out himself a couple of hours ago when Sara told him.

"And when is the wedding?" Garh asked silkily.

"We haven't set a date yet."

"Ah."

Kharun felt the hair on the back of his neck rise. He didn't trust Garh as far as he could throw him. What was the wily minister thinking?

"Perhaps you should consider setting the date immediately. It is one thing to excuse a flighty fiancée, yet engagements can be so easily broken, correct? It would be something else to forgive a dutiful wife."

Kharun heard the threat in his tone. And knew his sister's idea hadn't been foolproof. Was Garh calling his bluff?

"Perhaps you are correct. I will let you know the date. In the meantime, Sara and I will be returning to the capital this evening if you need to reach me again."

He hung up and stared at the phone. The man suspected a coverup. Of all the ministers, Garh pushed the hardest to hear other proposals for oil sales. Kharun couldn't give him any power to stall the current negotiations.

He looked at Sara harshly. "The plan has changed. We will be married immediately."

CHAPTER TWO

SARA gazed out the limousine window, amazed at how fast things had spun out of control. She longed to look at the man seated beside her, but didn't dare make eye contact, or give him any reason to suspect she was interested in him beyond his being the one responsible for rescuing her from jail.

The desert was cloaked in shadows, deep and mysterious as the sun set in the west. She'd caught a glimpse of an oasis when they'd left the enclave. And the heartbreaking sight of a little child scantily dressed, staring at the costly vehicle as they pulled away.

Somewhere out there was his luxurious family home. The contrast between what she'd glimpsed before being arrested and the tiny child at the side of the road was outrageous. Sara knew the same divisions of wealth existed all over the world, but they just seemed less dramatic.

The meagerness of amenities in the area had been apparent and appalling. Nothing like the bustling modernity of the capital city. How did the city people resolve living with their own abundance when they were surrounded by such destitution?

And who was this stranger next to her and how had she wound up agreeing to his scheme? Was there an alternative to his outrageous proposal? Her mind spun trying to find a solution that would suit them both.

As they sped toward the coast, she reviewed her options. Not many, if her word was to hold. Which it would. Her actions had precipitated the situation. If she could avoid a major scandal with no adverse repercussions to her father and his negotiations, it was important she do so.

Yet the thought of sneaking away in the dark and catching a ride home on the next available plane held a lot of appeal.

Should she just throw herself on her father's good nature and ask for help?

"It will take at least two hours to reach Staboul City," Kharun said from her left.

Sara glanced his way, startled to find his intense gaze focused on her. She felt a shiver of awareness. He seemed to fill the ample space of the limo, though he didn't crowd her to do so.

Upon entering the limousine, he'd closed the glass between them and the driver. They were cocooned in a world of two for the next couple of hours. She could smell his faint aftershave, spicy and masculine. She looked away, aware her heart rate had sped up a notch.

Just then the car hit a pothole, jerked, shuddered and quickly recovered, but not before throwing Sara against his hard chest. She scrambled to regain her seat, even more aware of the differences between them. She was tired, dirty and shaking off the fear of the last few days. He looked as immaculate as he must have done that morning.

He inclined his head slightly. "One of the benefits of the oil leases would mean funds to repair our roads. Perhaps you should fasten your seat belt."

"And help people in villages like the one we just left?" she asked, pulling the belt across her. She didn't want to wind up in his lap again.

"The treaty will allow us to do many things, including extending our education for all children, build new medical facilities, provide new jobs. Bring my country from a nomadic past into the technological future."

Swallowing hard, Sara tried to focus on the words and not the strange sensations that sparkled through her at his tone. She felt as if he'd touched her, when there were at least twelve inches of space between them. The very air seemed to crackle with tension.

She looked away, at the growing darkness. Two hours. It seemed like an interminable time to be cooped up with Sheikh Kharun bak Samin. Though not as long a time as it would be if she went through with his crazy scheme to get married.

"I suggest we use the time until we arrive to get to know each other. If we are to pull this off, I need to know more about you than you tried to take illicit photos in a restricted area and are the daughter of Samuel Kinsale."

"Will we be able to pull this off?" She had her doubts. Though she'd do nothing to harm her father's career, she was afraid her acting skills were far below what was needed to convince people she and this powerful man were in love. She wasn't even comfortable riding in a car with him. What would it be like to pretend devotion? To be touched by those strong hands, be caressed—

She shut down her mind. Taking a deep breath she tried for rational thought. Just because the man beside her was the sexiest male she'd ever met was no reason to lose coherent thought. She'd need all her wits about her if she was to come through unscathed.

"Shall I begin? Hello, I'm Kharun bak Samin." He held his hand out.

Reluctantly Sara placed hers in his, hoping for a quick, formal, means-nothing handshake. Did his comment mean he had a sense of humor? So far she'd seen no evidence of one.

His touch startled her. His hand was warm, firm, holding hers as if she was precious crystal. Tingling sensations danced on her nerve endings, causing her to catch her breath. She felt swept away to another level of existence, as if everything before was a prelude to this wondrous delight.

Snatching her hand free she tried to smile, but her facial muscles refused to cooperate. Her heart raced in her chest. Warmth infused her. She took a deep breath— a mistake since it filled her with his scent. She scrambled for coherence.

"How do you do? I'm Sara Kinsale, youngest child of Samuel and Roberta Kinsale." She could have added "classic misfit," but she had a feeling he suspected that already.

"Now where would we have met, Sara? Not here, this is your first visit to my country. Perhaps another locale to which your father has traveled frequently and I had an occasion to visit?''

''He's traveled all over Europe. I sometimes go with them. How about Paris?''

He appeared lost in thought for a moment, then nodded. ''That'll work. My mother is from France and I visit there often. I've been twice in the last couple of years. I assume you were there sometime during that time span?''

She nodded. ''I haven't lived with my folks since I left for college, but did travel with them a few months ago to Paris.'' She'd been between jobs and at loose ends. Shortly after she'd returned home, she'd landed the photojournalist position.

''So you graduated from college, which one?''

She named one of the famous Ivy League colleges, then frowned slightly. ''Only I didn't graduate. I never could settle on a major.''

''Photography and journalism not being an option?''

''Back when I was eighteen I had visions of following in my father's footsteps. I studied business administration for a while—but found it too heavily focused on math and economics. So then I thought about becoming an interpreter—my French is pretty good. That didn't take, either.''

''So the next course of study was?'' he prompted when she fell silent.

''Next I tried drama. I even had a role in one of the college productions. I didn't succeed beyond my wildest dreams. Actually I was a dismal actress. The reviews didn't even try to be kind. That's why I question how this plan of yours will work. How can I pretend to be your fiancée if my acting skills are nonexistent?''

"As my *wife,* you will be beyond questioning. As long as you can appear dutifully attentive when we are in public, there should be no problem.''

Her heart skipped a beat, resumed with a rapid pace.

"I can't marry you.''

"That was settled before we left the jail.''

"I know you said we had to marry, but think about it—it's crazy.''

He leaned toward her, his eyes hard as flint. "Listen well, Sara Kinsale. Your actions have jeopardized something important for my country. We are not the richest country on earth, with a standard of living above all others. Poverty and disease affect a lot of my people. I want to improve the lot and to do so we need an influx of cash. Your father is brokering an oil lease that will bring in that influx. It's the perfect solution and I will not have it destroyed by the flighty irresponsible actions of one woman. You will marry me, you will appear to be my dutiful wife in public and you will say nothing to anyone until that lease is signed, sealed and delivered. At that time, we can arrange a quiet annulment and you can return to your father's care.''

"Yes, sir!'' She tilted her chin. She was not intimidated by his words, but almost exhilarated. What was wrong with her? She should have been quaking in her shoes. Instead, her blood pounded in her veins, her senses were attuned to every nuance and she felt more alive than at any time in her life.

So he wanted marriage, did he? All right. She'd just show him what being married to her would entail!

"So where did you go to school? What's your favorite color and how come you're not already married?" she asked.

She kept surprising him. It had been a long time since someone had done that. For one moment when he challenged her he'd thought she'd quail under his glare. But that little chin came right up and she stood up for herself. If they'd been standing he had no doubt she would have stood toe-to-toe with him, tilting that stubborn chin and glaring at him with silver eyes.

Jasmine's idea had been ludicrous, but the longer he lived with it, the longer he was around Sara Kinsale, the more it grew on him. At the very least, it wouldn't be a boring marriage—however short.

He almost grinned at the surprise he envisioned on his aunt's face when she met his future bride. His uncle's wife liked to think she ruled the family. While always courteous and polite, Kharun was ruled by no one—especially his aunt who would have been happy living in the early days of the last century.

There would also be the possible added bonus of getting the country more firmly on his side. People always were drawn to the romantic, he thought cynically, wondering how they could put a positive spin on the situation. And counter the rumors Garh would be sure to spread.

"I attended Eton then Harvard, finishing with a graduate degree of business at Wharton in Pennsylvania," he said as he became aware she was waiting for his response.

"Oh." She sat back in her seat, eyeing him with a hint of respect—the first he'd seen in her gaze.

"My favorite color is green." Though silver might be moving up to the top spot. "And why I have not married is none of your business. Neither have you. Do you want to tell me why?"

She opened her mouth and he almost held his breath, wondering what she would come out with. When she snapped it shut and shook her head, he was disappointed.

"Did you know green is the color most likely to be a favorite of geniuses? Are you super smart?"

He questioned that, giving his plan to follow his sister's suggestion.

"Your favorite color?" he asked.

"Blue. Favorite ice cream is vanilla, boring, I know, but I love it. Favorite TV show is 'Star Trek,' any rendition that comes on. Favorite food is chocolate—made any way and every way it can be. I've been supporting myself since I left college. And I don't have any pets, though I always wished we could have a dog."

"Do you ride?"

She nodded. "Finest lessons to be had. Do you?"

"Yes. I have a couple of horses. Maybe we'll find we have something in common after all."

"We don't need anything in common. This is temporary. How long do you think it'll take to sign that deal? If you sign soon, we don't even have to get married."

"I have no way of knowing how long it'll take. If

everything goes smoothly, another few weeks. If we run into complications, it could take longer. We've already been in negotiations for four months.''

"Four months! Good grief, what's the holdup? I mean, don't you read the terms, agree or disagree, hammer them out and sign the darn thing?''

"It's a bit more complex than that. And having an American spy thrown into the mix doesn't help.''

"I'm not a spy,'' she said through gritted teeth.

"I would have thought a spy more adept at blending in, if nothing else.'' He glanced at her hair, still fascinated by it. His fingers itched to test its softness. He wondered if he twirled a curl around a finger if it would cling. "Your hair sets you apart from most of the people in the country. You would have done better to wear a hat or dye your hair.''

"Look, I'll make you a deal. You stop referring to me being a spy and I'll do my best to be an adoring fiancée.''

"Wife,'' he reminded her.

"Fine! Wife for as long as it takes to sign the blasted treaty.''

His cell phone rang. Kharun flipped it open and heard his sister's voice.

"So, what happened?'' Jasmine asked with no ceremony.

"My fiancée and I are on our way to my villa as we speak. There's been a slight change in the plans, however. Garh Sonharh found out about our visitor and began to question our relationship. We will be married immediately.''

Jasmine audibly gasped. "You're kidding. You're not going to actually *marry* the woman! Kharun, that's even more stupid than my original idea. An engagement is one thing—but *marriage?*"

"It is settled. We shall meet the rest of the family in the morning. Tonight would not be auspicious." He glanced at Sara, taking in the rumpled and stained clothing, the tiredness around her eyes, and the glare that met his gaze.

"I'm sorry I suggested the idea. You should listen to Piers, his idea made more sense," Jasmine said.

"We have settled the matter."

"You always were headstrong. Why not stick with the engagement and to hell with Garh? Or let her stay in jail. It's not worth risking your future."

"I can take care of my future. I'll call you in the morning, Jasmine."

"I thought you were taking me to the hotel," Sara said as soon as he'd disconnected.

"Perhaps I shall do that in the morning."

"In the morning? I want to go tonight!"

"Looking like you do? Wouldn't there be a question or two about where you've been and what you've been doing?" he asked silkily.

"I thought you were concerned about my parents worrying about me," she tried.

"My secretary has already phoned them to assure them you are well—and with me. What's more natural than lovers who haven't seen each other in months to wish to be reunited?"

"Lovers?" She almost squeaked the word.

He had not thought beyond the ceremony that would join them in marriage. He had not thought about the reality after their vows. Now he considered how difficult it might prove to be to ignore this woman when she was living in close proximity.

Her turn of mind already intrigued him. Her blond, silky hair drew his gaze time after time, and he found himself deliberately saying things to annoy her just to see the sparkle in her eyes.

She had passion in her. Would that passion carry over to bed? Would she be hot and wild and as captivating as Sheherazade?

For the right man, he had no doubt. Did she even suspect the direction of his thoughts? Was she having similar ones?

"We're not lovers!" she said.

"We could be."

"In your dreams."

"Time will tell."

"Hold on a minute. If you think getting married gives you the right to share my bed, we need to talk about this some more."

"It does give me the right. Whether I exercise that right or not remains to be seen."

"I have some say in this."

"Of course. The same vows give you the right to my bed."

"Oh."

She leaned back in her seat, her eyes wide, staring into space as if she'd just realized the full implication.

Kharun watched her in the dim illumination. She

looked lost and lonely and stunned with the thought. And imminently kissable. His gaze focused on her lips, damp from her tongue, faintly pink and full. What would she taste like? How would she respond if he pulled her into his arms and kissed her? Could he spark all that passion and have it focused on him?

"You stay out of my bed and I'll stay out of yours," she said at long last.

"Shall we continue our briefing?" He didn't agree with her suggestion. Had she noticed? Apparently not, she continued with a litany of likes and dislikes, of vignettes of family life and friends. He settled back to watch her, enjoying the play of emotions across her face. And he continued to fantasize about threading his hands in that silky hair and coaxing curls around his fingers.

It was long after dark when they arrived at his villa. A few miles outside of Staboul City, it hugged the sea. Seventeen acres of privacy, with a beach that he too rarely used. It had been a legacy to him from his father upon his death. He had offered his mother free access for her life and she sometimes resided with him for weeks at a time. Always leaving when the memories became too much and she needed a change of scenery.

For a moment he remembered how happy his parents had been in their marriage. Had his grandparents opposed the match? He'd never heard, but often wondered if they had approved of their son marrying a foreigner. Born in France, his mother had been raised in Morocco. She loved the desert, loved the culture and had adored his father.

His aunt had never fully accepted her sister-in-law.
He had no doubts how she would react to his marriage
to Sara. It was best done quickly. They could excuse the
lack of celebration and ceremony to the untimely death
of his father six months ago. His family was still in
mourning.

"I smell the sea," Sara said.

"My house is on the beach. You can swim in the sea
every day if you wish. Just make sure someone is around
in case you get into trouble." During her recital of likes
and dislikes, she'd revealed how much she loved the
ocean. If nothing else, she should be content living here
until they annulled their marriage.

He had made a quick call to his housekeeper when
they'd been halfway home, requesting she make up a
guest suite for his fiancée. She'd informed him of his
mother's arrival. While he could have used another day
or two before presenting Sara to his family, it wasn't all
bad his mother was already in residence. He'd need all
the allies he could get to pull this off. Jasmine would
help. Now he'd have his mother on his side.

If only his aunt had taken a quick trip somewhere.

But life never ran smoothly. Look at the situation he
was presently in.

"Wow, is that yours?" Sara gazed at the house, lit
up from top to bottom as it awaited the return of its
master.

"It is."

"It looks like a French villa, or something on the
Spanish Riviera, not Arabian."

"My father built it for my mother. She is French. It

is a good thing your French is excellent. She'll love conversing in her native tongue. She learned Arabic, of course, but I know she misses her first language.''

"Maybe this isn't such a good idea. It's one thing to fool your ministers, but your mother?''

"Your parents, too.''

She looked at him. "I thought I could at least explain—''

He shook his head. "Unwise. One wrong word and the entire situation would blow up in our faces. I'd lose whatever steps I've gained and the lease negotiations would be crushed. Only you, me and Jasmine will know the truth.''

"Jasmine is your sister. Why can't I tell someone in my family?''

"No.''

The car slid to a stop before the large double doors. They were opened wide and a woman dressed in a uniform stood quietly to one side.

"Let's see if your acting skills have improved since college days,'' he said as the chauffeur opened the back door.

Sara climbed out, stiff and awkward.

Kharun spoke in Arabic when he asked if Sara's rooms were ready and Aminna responded in the affirmative. His housekeeper was efficient and discreet. And loyal—having been with his parents long before he inherited her services along with the villa.

"Your mother has already retired. I didn't know when you'd be home, so did not inform her of your guest,'' the older woman said.

"Well done, Aminna. Time enough in the morning."

He placed his hand in the small of Sara's back and urged her into the house. "I'll take you to your room," he said in English.

Sara had the impression of space as they hurried down the hallway in the direction he indicated. She'd barely glanced into the entrance, or the rooms beyond, though all were lighted. The ceilings were high. The terrazzo floors were cool beneath her feet and the walls were white, adding to the impression of space. The hall itself was wide, with doors opening off it here and there.

She couldn't take it all in at the pace he directed. Or with the tingling that had begun when his hand touched her back. She could barely walk! Fatigue had to be the cause. She'd not slept well the last two nights. For one foolish moment, she wanted to lean into that hand, rest against the strong shoulders that were so temptingly near.

Realizing how dumb the idea was, she stepped out of reach, but the tingling awareness lingered.

"If you just tell me which room is mine, I'll be fine."

He opened a door, and stepped aside for her to enter.

The bedroom was like a fairy-tale setting. French doors opened onto a veranda. The breeze from the sea billowed the gauzy curtains. The bed was huge, dominating one wall, with netting draped enticingly around it as if waiting to shelter a princess.

A small sitting area was carved out of one side. Beyond the bed a door stood open to a luxuriously appointed bathroom.

"A hot shower sounds wonderful," Sara said as her gaze skimmed across the furnishings, the cool floor beneath. What a dramatic change from the cell she'd inhabited for two nights.

"I'll make sure Aminna has something brought in for you to wear," Kharun said. "Please ring if you need anything." He stepped back into the hall, closing the door behind him.

Sara almost danced across the room. It was heavenly—and a light-year away from the tiny, dusty cell she'd been in that afternoon. She went to the French doors and peered outside. Flowers bloomed near the terrace, a path led away—to the sea?

She turned back. Time enough tomorrow to go exploring. Right now, she wanted that hot shower!

Stripping as she walked, she headed directly for the bathroom. She closed the door behind her and in seconds stood beneath the hot spray, relishing the feel of the water slipping over her body. Slowly she washed her hair, soaped her dusty skin.

As the warm water caressed her skin, her tired, traitorous mind imagined Kharun's hands caressing her body in a similar fashion, following the curves, touching her breasts, learning every inch of her. The heat that built within at the rampant thoughts matched the heat of the water.

A cold shower would be better, she thought, shampooing her hair for the second time. She wanted all trace of her recent experience expunged completely! She'd do better to spend her time thinking how to explain the situation to her father than imagining Kharun's hands roaming.

She wasn't usually given to flights of fancy. This was a platonic situation—forged from necessity, not need or want or desire. And she'd best remember that!

Finally giving in to the tiredness that threatened, she shut off the water. The towels were luxurious—in keeping with everything else she'd seen so far, thick and soft. She wrapped one around her, used another to swathe her hair.

She gazed around the bathroom. Except for her underwear lying on the tiles, she had nothing to wear. And she wouldn't wear them again until clean. Snatching them up, she quickly washed them in the sink and hung them over a towel rod to dry. They'd be ready by morning.

Opening the door, she stepped into the opulent bedroom. Maybe the housekeeper had placed a nightgown on the bed.

Sara stopped short. Kharun sat in one of the chairs in the sitting area, looking completely at home.

She gripped the towel. It was tucked firmly against her, nothing showed—indeed, it covered her almost to her knees. But she knew she had nothing beneath but damp skin, and that made her extremely vulnerable.

She glanced at the trail of dusty clothes and wanted to snatch them up, so he wouldn't notice. But of course he'd had ample time to notice. How long had he been in her room?

He raised an eyebrow, letting his gaze travel from her

wrapped hair, across damp shoulders, down the length of her.

Heat swept through her. Her heart began to pound heavily. She couldn't take her eyes off him.

"What are you doing in here?" she asked, going on the offensive.

He rose and started toward her. His hand held a gossamer nightgown. "I brought you something to sleep in."

She stared at the delicate material, knowing it was as light and sheer as the curtains that billowed in the breeze. She raised her gaze to meet his, surprised by the heat she saw. Her heart raced. Mesmerized by the look in his eyes, she couldn't move. Couldn't utter a word. The fantasy in the shower played out in her mind. She wanted to slam the door shut on the images, but couldn't.

He came so close she could feel the heat from his body, see the fine lines around his eyes, smell the male scent mingling with that from the sea air.

For a moment neither moved. Then slowly—oh, so slowly—he lowered his head, blocking out the room, blocking out everything except him.

When his lips touched hers, Sara gave a small sigh and closed her eyes. His lips were warm and firm, moving gently against hers.

She almost missed it when his arms encircled her, pulling her against his hard body. She was too busy wrapping her own arms around his neck; holding on as his kiss inflamed every cell. His embrace was hot and exciting, as he moved against her with sensuous plea-

sure. Her body felt consumed with growing desire. She
was transported away from the memory of recent events,
away from anything she'd ever experienced. Swept away
with the magic of his touch, of his taste, of his caresses.

When he ended the kiss, she clung. Her lids were so
heavy, she had to force them open, gazing into the deep,
dark eyes of the man who still held her.

"The first kiss is always awkward. Better to have it
in private than before an audience," he said.

Releasing her, he stooped to retrieve the nightgown
that had dropped to the floor. He pressed it into her
hands and then brushed her lips once with his thumb as
if capturing some of the moisture to take with him.

Sara watched, dazed, as he spun around and left. The
slight click when the door shut released her from the
spell.

Dazed, she crossed slowly to the bed, sinking down
on the edge, holding the nightgown against her breasts,
feeling the softness of the material and the damp terry
cloth of the towels.

The first kiss? Oh, Lord, there were going to be more?

CHAPTER THREE

WHEN Sara awoke the next morning, her first thought was of Kharun. Wouldn't that stroke his ego? But not in the way he might like. She'd spent a long time last night trying to figure a way out of this outlandish proposal of his. There had to be a way to scrape through with neither side losing.

Last evening before she slept, Aminna had brought her soup and salad and a soothing pot of tea. Once finished, Sara had slipped into bed, wishing for the oblivion of sleep. It proved elusive as she worried about today.

Her parents were the first obstacle. Or maybe Kharun's mother. Would she meet the ministers who questioned their relationship today? Have to defend herself to them? Show them how much she loved Kharun? A man she'd met less than twenty-four hours ago.

How about his sister, or his trusted adviser, Piers?

She pulled the sheet over her head, wishing she could go back to sleep and not wake up until the leases had been signed. The day loomed ahead, overwhelming and terrifying. They'd never pull this off!

But the scent of the sea beckoned. Long moments later she threw back the covers, rising to pad over to the wide-open French doors. The veranda was covered, sheltered from the morning sun. A narrow width of sunshine still warmed the tiles near the edge. Soon it would be gone. She stepped out, feeling the coolness of the tile gradually warm beneath her bare feet.

The breeze swirled the nightgown around her and she raised her head, letting the air brush through her hair. She wanted to go swimming, splash in the warmth of the Mediterranean, forget for a little while the mess she'd made of things.

But she couldn't. She had first to face the day. She turned and reentered her room. On the chaise longue near the door were her clothes—washed and neatly pressed. Sighing softly, she fetched them and headed for the bathroom. It was time to face reality.

Dressed, hair brushed, and wishing for some makeup, Sara entered the hallway and walked toward the entry-way. She heard the murmur of voices, the clink of silver against china. Following the sound, she reached the dining room. It faced away from the sea. The French doors in this room opened to a garden. Riotous flowers bloomed everywhere—bright yellows, rich reds, and a waterfall of white blossoms, all contrasting with the deep green of leaves and stems.

The scent mingled with that of fresh-baked croissants and heavenly coffee.

Kharun sat at the head of the table, an older woman to his right. She was dressed in a fashionable dress of French design. The pearls around her neck and in her earrings were understated, but undoubtedly worth a fortune. She caught sight of Sara and paused, coffee cup raised halfway to her lips.

Kharun looked up.

''Sara, I thought you'd sleep in longer or we would

have waited.'' He rose and came to the doorway, capturing her hand in his. Raising it to his lips, he pressed a kiss upon her soft skin, his eyes catching hers—narrowed in warning.

"Good morning.'' The tone was intimate, the look one of possession and desire.

All resolve fled. What was it about this man that had her reacting like some teenager when the captain of the football team noticed her?

He switched to French. "May I present my mother, Angelique bak Samin? *Ma mère,* this is Sara Kinsale, my bride-to-be.''

She arose to join them and gave Sara a kiss on each cheek.

"*Enchantée, mademoiselle.* My son was just telling me of your betrothal. I know you kept it a secret because of my husband's recent death, but such happy news deserves its time in the sun. It will lift the gloom that settles on our family. Welcome. You may call me Angelique.''

Next to the two of them, Sara felt frumpy and awkward. She wished she had something to wear beside the khaki safari outfit she had thought so dashing only a few days ago.

"I am happy to meet you,'' she replied in French. At least she'd get some practice out of her expertise in the language.

What else would Kharun wish to practice? she wondered as he solicitously seated her at his left hand and summoned Aminna to bring a new pot of coffee.

"Tell me all about this whirlwind courtship. I was beginning to worry about my son. He has been so consumed with business since his father put him in charge. Now I'm pleased to know he is also taking time to assure his future and that of the family. You have brought joy to my heart.''

Sara smiled awkwardly, feeling guilty as sin, grateful when Aminna arrived with the coffee. She stalled, making a great to-do of preparing the beverage to her liking. Please let something happen to deflect the inquisition, she prayed. She looked at Kharun for help. He got them into this particular situation, he could get them out!

Despite her worry, breakfast proceeded without a hitch. Kharun did indeed get them out of the awkwardness, regaling his mother with the most fantastic tale of how they met. Sara listened spellbound, hoping she could remember every word in case she was asked. It would prove smoother sailing if their stories matched.

By the time breakfast was over, Sara almost believed the fantasy herself—how they met in Paris, fell in love on the Rue de Calais, danced until dawn on the Left Bank, and learned more about each other strolling in the gardens of the Tulleries.

''I had planned to visit for a while,'' Angelique said. ''But I will move immediately to Jasmine's apartment. You two will wish to be alone. Especially if you cannot take a proper honeymoon at this time. Kharun explained that once the oil leases are signed, he'd be able to take time. You are very understanding to allow the delay.''

Sara blinked, her gaze moving to Kharun. What had he been telling his mother before she arrived? She smiled, wondering what she was supposed to say. She hadn't been a good actress when she had lines to memorize. Improvisation was even more difficult!

"We would not cut short your visit, Mother," he said.

"Nonsense, I remember how your father and I were—" Tears welled in her eyes and she blotted them with her linen napkin. She pushed back her chair. "Excuse me. I will instruct one of the maids to begin packing immediately." She left the room almost at a run.

"She should stay," Sara said, looking after her. "It's not like she'd interrupt anything."

"She and my father had a passionate love affair from the moment they met. I suspect she considers our situation similar. It's the only way she would have understood an immediate wedding."

Having experienced one of Kharun's kisses, she had no trouble instantly imagining them in a passionate embrace, ignoring the world around them, caught up in the splendor and excitement of touch and feelings and passion. What would it be like to be loved by this man?

But what he'd just said suddenly hit her. "*Immediate* wedding?"

"The sooner the better. Are you almost finished?"

She gulped the last of her coffee, blotted her lips with her napkin and laid it neatly on the table. Thoughts about Kharun were the last thing she needed. If she was to get through this charade, she needed her wits about her—not be daydreaming.

"I'm ready," she said.

"It's early yet. We have time."

"It's never too early at a hotel—they're open twenty-four hours."

"What do you mean?"

"You said you'd take me to the Presentation Hotel this morning. I'm ready."

"After our wedding." He looked at his watch, then met her stunned gaze. "Which is scheduled for ten. I think Jasmine has found you a suitable dress."

"What?"

He rose and was gone before she could formulate a coherent sentence. She followed him from the room with her gaze, stunned at the announcement. He couldn't have been serious! She couldn't marry him *this* morning. Weddings took tons of planning. Invitations and fittings and…and… She didn't know what else, having never married before. But she didn't think you could schedule a wedding with no more than twelve hours' notice. And without telling the bride first.

She jumped up, intent on finding him and telling him why they couldn't marry today. A few hours away from that awful jail and she'd begun to think of alternative scenarios that would let them off the hook. She had to find Kharun and offer different ideas before this one got out of hand.

As she walked into the entryway searching for her reluctant host, the front door opened and a petite, slender young woman entered, wearing a lovely rose-colored silk suit. Accompanying her was a tall man dressed in a chauffeur's uniform carrying a garment bag over one arm. The woman's dark hair gleamed in the sunshine looking almost blue-black. The two of them stared at each other for a moment.

"You must be Sara," the woman said in flawless English.

"Jasmine, I presume," Sara guessed. The woman looked like a small, feminine version of Kharun.

The sunny smile that broke out was a surprise. Jasmine nodded, studying Sara. "No wonder my brother said yes to that crazy spur-of-the-moment idea."

"It'll never work," Sara said.

"If Kharun says it will, it will. I have brought your wedding dress." She flicked a glance to the man standing beside her. "Which room did Aminna give you?"

"Down there," Sara indicated. "But—"

Jasmine took the garment bag from the chauffeur and dismissed him. She turned to head for Sara's room.

"Quickly, you need to try it on. It wasn't easy to get something in your size on a moment's notice. Kharun called me at seven this morning asking if I would pick up a wedding dress. Doesn't he know most boutiques don't open before ten? Silly question, of course he doesn't. Let's see if this fits."

Sara followed, feeling swept away by a whirlwind.

Twenty minutes later Sara stared at her reflection in the floor-length mirror. Everything was spinning out of control. She hadn't found Kharun, but had been bustled along with Jasmine, coerced into trying on the gown. The creamy-white dress fit as if it had been made for her, lacy and elegant—suitable for cocktails, a trip to the theater, or a morning wedding. The shoes were a size too big, but Jasmine had already stuffed cotton in the toes, and they were low-heeled enough to manage.

Sara's blond curls encircled her head like a soft cloud.

The light touch of makeup Jasmine brought enhanced every feature, deepening the mysterious look of her eyes, bringing a hint of blush to her cheeks—making her look almost like a bride.

What would Kharun think?

At least she looked one hundred times better than when he'd first met her—when he'd made his proposal. Surely he could find no fault with the end result.

Slowly, Sara smiled. She liked how she looked. Maybe, just maybe, people wouldn't wonder what he saw in her. Maybe they could pull this off. For the sake of her father she had to try.

Jasmine met her gaze in the mirror, her expression solemn. "Bring no disgrace on my family. Do no harm to Kharun. Do you understand?"

Sara raised her chin and glared at Jasmine. "I would never do that. Nor bring disgrace to my family—isn't that the entire reason for this charade?"

In those short words, reality returned. She was not a blushing bride going to exchange vows with the man she loved. She was entering into a marriage of convenience—not even her convenience—to rectify a mistake. She would not compound it by forgetting for one second why the marriage was taking place.

Taking a discreet peek at her watch, she realized if the wedding was to begin at ten, she had no time to find Kharun and propose her alternative suggestions. It didn't matter, she knew he would never have accepted her ideas. The time for deciding had long passed.

This could work. Once the leases were signed, they'd

get an annulment and go their separate ways. She could do this. It was only for a few weeks.

Kharun left nothing to chance. He arranged for Samuel Kinsale and his wife to attend the ceremony. To do less might raise suspicions. But he timed their arrival to just minutes before he planned to start. They could visit with their daughter after she was legally his wife.

His mother and sister, of course, would attend. His most trusted adviser, Piers. He did not send an invitation to his aunt and uncle. He wouldn't risk their disrupting the ceremony before it could begin. Being a family in mourning helped. A quiet ceremony would be all that was expected.

Promptly at ten, Samuel Kinsale and his wife Roberta arrived. Angelique greeted them and led the way to the garden nearest the sea. She answered their questions as best she could, but Samuel wasn't satisfied. He and his wife had no indication their youngest even knew Kharun, much less planned to marry him, until that morning when Kharun had phoned. And the explanations had been hasty and brief.

Angelique told him what she knew and urged them to await to question Sara until after the ceremony.

The garden was the perfect setting for a quiet, family wedding. Kharun cynically reviewed everything from his place at the doorway. On the surface the locale presented as romantic a picture as he could devise. As long as no one questioned them closely, or challenged anything, it should go off without a hitch. Kinsale remained a question mark. He hoped the man would listen to Angelique and not question Sara until after the ceremony.

Sara was also an unknown. Would she go through with the bargain? Or would she defect at the last moment—thus giving Garh and his associates a weapon to use in their mind-set against progress?

Jasmine hurried down the hall and smiled uncertainly at her brother.

"She's as ready as I can make her. Good luck, brother. I still think an engagement would have worked."

"Sit with mother, she's a bit overwhelmed."

"I don't blame her. How is the bride's family taking it?"

He glanced out to the garden, frowning slightly. "Better than I expected, actually, though her mother looks shell-shocked. Her father put up a fuss when he first arrived, but seems content with waiting to talk to Sara later. I wonder if he had already heard the rumors? He would appreciate the need for such a step."

"Maybe they're glad to get her off their hands," she murmured as she slipped past on her way to join the others.

He turned and waited until he saw Sara walking down the hall. For a moment Kharun forgot they were entering into a marriage for business necessity. His bride appeared entirely different from anytime he'd seen her—including earlier that morning.

He almost caught his breath. She looked shy, virginal and breathtakingly lovely. There would be few questions asked when his uncle's ministers saw her. They'd immediately conclude the reasons why he was marrying her—for her looks, her mind and her background.

"Are my folks here?" she asked, stepping up to the doorway.

"Everyone is gathered in the garden. Are you ready?"

She hesitated a moment, then nodded.

"Then?" He held out his arm.

She took his elbow, gripping tightly. "Shouldn't my father walk me down the aisle?"

"It is a very informal wedding—only immediate family. I don't think we need stand on protocol."

"Or you don't trust me alone with him before?" she whispered as they stepped into the sunshine. She'd given her word of honor. He might not think much of it given the circumstances, but it meant a lot to her. She smiled at her parents, but continued to hold on to Kharun. She'd set this in motion, she'd see it through. Better her family thought she was rushing into marriage than to learn the truth. When it didn't last, they probably wouldn't be surprised.

Maybe one day, after her father finalized the deal, she'd tell them the whole story.

But not today. Today she was getting married in a lovely garden, with the Mediterranean Sea in the background, to a man who could have been a dream come true—but might prove to be her worst nightmare.

Sara knew the day would forever be etched in her memory as a series of sketches. From the fragrance of the flowers surrounding her while she took vows, to the hot demanding kiss Kharun had given to seal their marriage, to the bewildered look of her mother when she turned to hug her. Both her parents had pulled her aside as soon as the short receiving line ended and questioned her about the totally unexpected wedding.

Sara had her history of impetuousness to stand her in good stead. They were not surprised by anything she did anymore, so accepted the fact she and Kharun had decided to marry after a whirlwind courtship. Her mother had questions galore, but Sara staved her off, promising to visit soon and let her know all the details. Her fingers had been firmly crossed behind her back and she hoped the need for the charade would end before her mother cornered her!

The wedding lunch had been extravagant—as if the staff had had weeks to prepare instead of less than twelve hours. The conversation on the other hand, had proved stilted and awkward as Kharun's family, except for Jasmine, did not speak English, and Samuel and Roberta Kinsale didn't speak Arabic. Her father did have a limited command of French, so there was some conversation between him and Angelique.

It had been a strain—pretending to be a blushing bride, all the time conscious of the man beside her. Of his fingertips brushing against hers, which sent jolts of electricity shooting in every direction. Of the intensity of his gaze—which the others had taken as devotion, but Sara knew was more of an assessment, and warning to keep to their deception.

The trip to the hotel to gather her clothes later that afternoon had been accomplished with no fuss. Kharun never left her side. She knew he didn't trust her, but to anyone else, it looked as if he were a devoted bride-groom who couldn't bear to be parted from his beloved.

The oddest memory was of the confused feelings she'd experienced when Kharun had bid her good-night and left her in the middle of the living room.

By then everyone had left—including Aminna. Only she and Kharun remained in the villa. Aminna would return in two days—it was all Kharun had asked for a honeymoon, alluding to a longer one when the demands of his time were less immediate.

She might as well be alone in the world, Sara thought as she listened for some sound. Once his footsteps faded, she heard nothing except the soft soughing of the sea breeze and the rustle of the curtains as they moved with the wind.

She went to her bedroom and closed the door. Within minutes she was nestled in bed, with a magazine she'd seen earlier in hand. But her thoughts were not on the pages.

She'd never thought about getting married—not for years. And certainly not to prevent an international scandal. But being alone in a big bed was never her fantasy for her wedding night. She was disappointed Kharun had not spent more time with her. Sending away the staff had been brilliant—no one around to see they were not the lovers everyone suspected.

But for a moment, she almost wished he'd taken advantage of his right to share her bed. Shocked at the idea, she clicked off the light, letting the magazine slide to the floor as she scooted down on the bed. Her last thought as she finally drifted to sleep was that she hoped the business talks would conclude soon.

Sara awoke early the next morning, having slept better than she expected. She dressed quickly in a sundress she'd brought and wandered out onto the veranda. The sun was already warming the day. The sea sparkled beneath its rays, looking cool and inviting. She followed the path that led through the gardens to the beach. A quick glance around assured her she was alone. The servants wouldn't return until late tomorrow afternoon. Where was Kharun? Still asleep?

The image of him in a bed flashed into her mind. He'd need a big bed. Would he sprawl across it, taking up all the room, or keep to the edge as if ready to leap up in a second's notice? Did he sleep in anything?

She doubted it.

The thought brought tantalizing new images to mind. Trying to block them out of her mind, she opened the low gate to the sand. Sara kicked off her sandals and walked on the hot surface. Running quickly to the water's edge, she almost danced in relief as the cool sea lapped at her feet. Looking left and then right, she saw she was alone. She tried to imagine such a pristine location being empty in America—impossible. Every time she'd gone to the beach, she'd had to share it with families and couples and teenagers. Today's solitude was blissful.

She began to walk along the water's edge.

When she reached a notice board, written in Arabic, she turned around. Maybe that was the edge of Kharun's property. She'd ask, but in the meantime, she was growing hungry. Longingly, she gazed at the water. She wanted to swim, but knew she needed someone else at hand. Maybe later. Turning, she headed for the villa.

She brushed her feet off when she reached the gate and donned her sandals again. Walking through the gardens, she wondered if it would be okay to pick some of the blossoms to carry to her room. They were so lovely and fragrant, she'd enjoy them where she could see them.

She entered her bedroom, crossing to the hallway. It was the only way she knew to reach the dining room. Maybe she'd spend some time today exploring the villa. If she had to live here for a few weeks, she might as well know the layout.

Just as she reached the entryway, a loud knock sounded on the door. Sara hesitated. Should she see who it was, or wait for Kharun? There was no one else to answer.

The knock sounded again.

Sara opened the door and saw an elderly woman dressed all in black. Her gray hair was pulled tightly back in a bun. Her skin was wrinkled, no makeup softened the aging process. Her eyes snapped when she looked at Sara. Her gaze ran from head to toe and then back.

Beyond her sat a huge old car. The chauffeur stood near the front, watching the scene impassively.

The woman said something.

''I hope you speak English or French, because I don't

speak Arabic,'' Sara said. Then repeated the sentence in French.

The woman responded in that language.

"The wife of a sheikh should at least speak his language,'' she snapped. "Are you going to invite me in?''

"Please,'' Sara said, stepping aside, wondering who in the world the woman was.

"I suppose it's too much to expect my nephew to inform his uncle and me when he weds. Just like him to ignore family in his pursuit of his own ways. I have told Hamsid, but does he listen? No. Just like a man!''

Sara watched the woman—obviously Kharun's aunt. Had he mentioned her to Sara?

"Well, where is he?'' she snapped, glaring at Sara.

"Kharun?'' Sara ventured.

"Of course, who else?'' The woman peered at her as if she were daft.

Sara looked around, hoping inspiration would strike. She knew the circumstances surrounding their marriage were top secret. But everyone would expect a new wife to know where her husband of less than twenty-four hours was.

"Um, I'll go get him,'' she said. "Would you like to wait—''

"I'm not going traipsing all through the place to find him. Where are the servants?''

"They were given a few days off. So we could be alone.''

"Then hurry up.''

Sara turned toward the dining room, almost skipping in her haste. She hoped she could find Kharun, and prayed he hadn't left. What would she do if she had to return and tell the woman he had gone out?

How many rooms did the house have? she wondered five minutes later. She'd tried every door she'd come across. Some of the rooms looked lived in, others like showplaces. But all were empty of human life.

Sara stopped and wanted to scream. The impatient woman was waiting. She had no idea where her husband was, nor what she was going to do next. How dare he put her in this position!

Slowly she retraced her steps, heading for the entryway. If she had any luck, the woman would have tired and left.

The sound of voices alerted her to the fact Kharun had found their guest. Thank goodness!

She drew a deep breath and hurried to join them.

Kharun and his aunt didn't notice Sara slipping into the room, they were too busy arguing. She didn't understand a word, but she understood the anger in their tones, and the hard glares they exchanged.

Suddenly Kharun saw Sara. He stopped talking and smiled.

Sara's heart caught then turned a slow, lazy somersault. It was the first time she'd seen him smile at her. She'd thought him handsome when she'd first seen him, but his smile almost stopped her heart. The man should be labeled as a lethal weapon and a warning issued to all females under the age of ninety-eight!

Caught in his gaze, she walked slowly toward him, her skin tingling with awareness and the potent attraction any woman feels around a stunningly masculine male.

He wasn't wearing a suit, she noticed dimly. His shirt was loose, buttoned only partway up, exposing a wedge of broad tanned chest sprinkled with dark hair. His hair was mussed, as if he'd run his fingers through it while working. Or as if tossed by the sea breeze. Had he walked along the shore today, as well?

His trousers were loose and he was barefooted—his feet planted firmly on the floor as if boldly staking his claim and asserting to the world he was totally, completely male—ready to take on all comers. She swallowed hard, amazed to realize this man was her husband.

"Ah, Sara, I wondered where you were." His voice was sultry, sensuous. His eyes caressed her. His hand reached for hers, drawing her closer, his fingers tightening in warning as he pulled her close enough she felt the heat pouring from his body.

Mesmerized, she could not say a word, but her senses seemed to be on overdrive. Every nuance was clear, dazzling. His fingers holding hers were warm and strong. His eyes tried to convey a message, but she wasn't sure what he wanted.

Until he swept her into his arms and kissed her.

She didn't know this man, wasn't sure she even liked him. His kiss meant nothing—merely show for an audience of one.

But one touch and she felt afloat on a sea of sensation and delight. Bright colors kaleidoscoped behind her lids. Her blood seemed to heat until she wondered if it would evaporate. Her senses swam with delight, with shimmering pleasure.

When his tongue stroked her lips, she parted them.

When it danced in her mouth, she met each foray with a caress of her own. When he deepened the kiss, she pressed against the length of his hard body, shocked with the reaction she was causing. But it wasn't enough. She wanted more.

A harsh exclamation behind her slowly penetrated. Kharun eased back, breathing hard as he gazed down into her eyes, his own shuttered and impossible to read.

He placed his arm on Sara's shoulders and turned her into his body, still holding her as he spoke in French, "What did you expect, Aunt. Sara and I haven't seen each other for months. We are married and don't have time for a honeymoon. We will make our own, here, and with every moment we can spare."

"I do not understand this. Take your honeymoon, there is nothing that cannot wait."

"You forget the oil leases I'm negotiating."

"Bah, you are foolish if you think you will garner the ministers' approval. Your uncle indulges you foolishly. But the treaty has not been signed yet."

"We have discovered a new reserve, a huge one, that will enable us to make deals for years to come. The new influx of cash will enable changes, improvements. Bring us into the twenty-first century."

"Your father—"

"Unfortunately he is dead. Out of deference to our mourning, Sara and I had a quiet ceremony yesterday. Mother and Jasmine represented our family. Sara had her own parents present. When our mourning time is passed, we will have a public reception and you may formally welcome Sara into our family."

The woman glared at Sara. She spoke again in Arabic. Kharun tightened his hold, his eyes blazing with anger. He responded in the language then disengaged himself from Sara and headed for the door.

In a very polite voice, he bid his aunt farewell.

When he shut the door behind her, he spun around and looked at Sara.

"That went well."

"That went well?" she exclaimed. "I didn't understand a word of what she said, but I didn't need to. Her tone of voice spoke volumes!"

"Ah, but she never once suspected this as a coverup. She deplored my choice of brides, warned me to keep a tight rein lest you ruin us all, and railed against me for defying the ministers who have more experience in deciding things than I do. But not once did she act as if she didn't believe the marriage."

CHAPTER FOUR

"IF SHE thought about it for two seconds, she might have," Sara mumbled, annoyed Kharun seemed so pleased with himself.

"Why?" He focused his attention on her.

Sara almost shivered, the memory of that hot kiss sending heat washing through her. He was an intense man, and when he turned that intensity on her, she felt like she was the only person in the world.

"I didn't know where you were, nor how to find you. If you hadn't wandered in on your own, I'd be making up some sort of excuse as to why a bride didn't know where her bridegroom was twenty-four hours after the wedding!"

He nodded. "Good point. Come with me, I will show you around the villa and how to use the intercom system. When Aminna is here, she can always find me. Or one of the maids."

"She'll be back tomorrow. If we don't have any more unexpected guests, I don't need a tour." She couldn't explain her reluctance to spend time with Kharun. They meant nothing to each other, yet he kissed her as if she were his passion. And she responded like a firecracker.

False passion—he turned off the charm instantly when they were alone. Although not quite. Just standing there had her fantasizing about things that could never be. He made no effort to entice her. To him their arrangement was pure expediency to keep scandal from tainting his negotiations. But he didn't have to do anything, but stand there and she was captivated. She looked away, trying to get her wayward emotions under some sort of control.

"Come and see the villa anyway. My mother decorated it over the years. I urged her to take some of the furnishings or paintings for her own apartment when she left after my father's death, but she says the memories become too strong and too sad."

For one foolish moment, Sara wished he'd held out his hand when urging her to come on the tour. She would love to slip her hand into his to feel his strength, to feel anchored. To revel in the shimmering waves of tingling awareness that would shoot up her arm at his touch. To relish his touch, and fantasize a bit more before reality returned.

She frowned as she stepped toward the arched hallway. Where had that last thought come from? She didn't want to be anchored, and she didn't need fantasy in her life.

She was a free spirit, hadn't her parents lamented that fact for years? She still had to make her way in the world and show her parents she could accomplish something worthwhile as her siblings had.

"Do you have my camera, Kharun?" she asked as they walked down the corridor opposite the one that led to her bedroom.

"Planning to complete your assignment?" he asked warily.

She flushed slightly. "No. But it was an expensive piece of equipment."

He paused by an open doorway. It was an office, set up with high-tech communications equipment, two computers, an enormous desk, and rows of bookshelves along one wall. French doors opened to the wrap-around veranda and allowed the cool breeze to waft in.

"It's in here."

On the corner of the desk sat the camera.

She stepped warily inside the office and went to pick it up, checking the exposure indicator. Reset to zero.

"The film was confiscated," he said, leaning against the doorjamb.

"I expected nothing else. Can I have some more?"

"To do what?"

"Exactly what I asked myself earlier," she said, swinging around and leaning against his desk. It was easier to face him with the width of the office between them. "What am I to do all day?"

"What do you do at home?"

"I have a job, so I show up at the office, scout around for new stories. There's shopping to do, friends to meet, laundry, household chores."

He raised an eyebrow. "Do you cook?"

She nodded.

"Since Aminna is not here, maybe you'd like to prepare some food for us."

"I don't suppose sheikhs learn to cook."

"Your assumption is flawed. I was on my own several times—when away at school. I can cook enough to get by when a restaurant isn't convenient."

"And a restaurant isn't convenient today?" Sara asked.

He slowly smiled and shook his head.

Her heart turned over. Her knees grew weak and she thought she'd have to learn to breathe all over again. She had already thought he was a striking specimen of alpha male, dominating any situation he was in, but when he smiled, he was devastating. If he didn't already have a calling, she knew he'd be an instant hit in Hollywood, or on the London stage.

She tried to hide her reactions. "So that gives me something to do today, what about the rest of the time while you're off negotiating oil leases and running a company?"

"We can work on that. It may only be a matter of weeks. Pretend you are on vacation. Enjoy the beach, you love the sea. Maybe go shopping. Come, I'll show you the rest of the villa and then you can prepare lunch for us."

She picked up the camera and looked around the room. "This is command central, I suppose?"

"It is my office at home. As you know I have formal offices in Staboul. But when I'm not there, I still need instant communication and access to my advisers. Unless I am present, please do not enter this room." His voice hardened with the last command.

She tilted her chin and glared at him. "I told you once before, I am not a spy. Anyway, I don't speak Arabic, so any secrets you had would be safe from me. I have no interest in your dumb old office." She swept toward him with as much dignity as she could muster beneath the smoldering anger. What would it take to convince the man she was only a sometimes inept novice reporter for a second-rate U.S. tabloid and not a sexy, conniving spy?

Not that the sexy spy role didn't have advantages, she thought as he stepped aside to allow her into the hall. Weren't sexy spies notorious for seducing secrets from lots of men? For a moment Sara wondered if she had the capability to seduce Kharun.

The tour took more than an hour. She was impressed with the comfort level of the villa despite the antiques and costly items that predominated. The paintings on the walls were originals. Her favorite room was the one where Matisse paintings dominated an entire wall. She knew she'd come back on her own just to soak up the ambience.

There were formal rooms, a quiet little sunroom, guest rooms for both family and visitors. Even an exercise room tucked in a back corner. On the far side of the villa was a pool, surrounded by fragrant flowering shrubs, which provided privacy.

"Why have a pool when the Mediterranean Sea is at your doorstep?" she asked when they entered the pool area.

"Some people prefer artificial to natural." He shrugged. "Here we have both. You are free to use either—provided you don't go swimming alone."

"Who would go with me?"

"If I am available, I will go. Otherwise Aminna or one of the maids or gardeners can watch to make sure you don't get into trouble."

"Afraid I'll swim away?" she asked lightly.

"No, Sara, afraid solely for your well-being. It is not safe to swim alone."

She nodded, suddenly touched he'd extend his concern to her well-being after the trouble she'd caused. He was right, it was unsafe to swim alone.

Kharun ended the tour in the kitchen. Sara stared in amazement. "You must entertain a lot," she murmured, taking in the huge stainless-steel refrigeration unit, the industrial-size gas range, the two huge ovens and three microwave ovens. The counter space would provide enough room to cater a seven-course meal for fifty.

"My parents did a lot of entertaining. I don't do as much. Though now that we are married, I wonder if it will become expected."

"No."

"No?" He looked at her. "Why not?"

"I'm not good at gatherings like that," she said quickly. "Besides, we won't be married that long. No one would expect us to entertain."

"Why are you not good at gatherings?"

"I never know what to say to people. We've been involved with big receptions my whole life. You must know that most business deals are often dealt with at social functions. I never told my father, but I hate going to them. One wrong word and world peace as we know it could end."

Kharun laughed out loud. Sara watched him, fascinated. Her lips twitched, but even his laugher couldn't erase the awkward feelings she got when faced with a roomful of strangers.

"It's not funny," she said.

He came to stand next to her—too close. She wanted to step away. She could feel the heat from his body as it seemed to envelop her, smell the scent from his skin that had her wanting to toss her camera to the floor and draw an enticing finger along the swell of his muscles to test their strength, taste him again.

She swallowed and stood her ground, hoping her pounding heartbeat wasn't evident to the astute man now staring down into her eyes.

"It is not funny, I apologize for laughing. But any faux pas you might make at a reception or dinner would scarcely end world peace. If you are uncomfortable, we will not entertain."

She blinked. That was totally unexpected. "It's your home, if you wish to entertain, I'll do my best. Just understand I'm not so great at it. Now, Margaret, she shines at events like that. She knows just what to say, who're the most important people in the room, what the latest rumors are and how to defuse any awkward situations."

"Margaret, is she your sister?"

Sara nodded. "The attorney," she said flatly.

"Ah, I remember now, the attorney and the physicist and the…photographer."

"Photojournalist, this week." Unless her boss had already fired her. She hadn't reported in for a week. She looked at Kharun, trying to gauge his reaction if she asked to use the phone.

"I probably should let my office know what's happened."

He shrugged. "If they are any kind of newspaper, they

already know. My office released news of our marriage this morning. I have cut off the phones to make sure we are not disturbed by reporters. My advisers will handle the world press.''

''Oh. It must be nice to have a legion of people ready to do your bidding.''

He smiled as if amused by her comment. ''It is. Lunch?''

Glancing around the room again, Sara nodded. She placed her camera on the edge of the counter and started opening cupboard doors, looking for something to start with. ''So I join the legions, here for your bidding.''

''Unless you wish to starve.'' Humor laced his tone.

She ignored him. When she reached the refrigeration unit, she was delighted to see a bowl of freshly cleaned and boiled shrimp. Had Aminna suspected they'd like something like that for lunch? ''I can make a shrimp salad for lunch, will that work?''

''Fine. I'll be back in twenty minutes. Does that give you enough time?''

''Sure.'' The image of the two of them working intimately together in the kitchen vanished. So much for thinking it a way to get to know her husband better.

Temporary husband! Their marriage was a business arrangement, nothing more, she admonished herself as she drew things from the shelves. She didn't want to be here any more than he wanted her here. She wanted to be out proving herself to her family. To show she could find a niche and make a career.

Sara sighed softly. Photojournalism wasn't it, she admitted to herself. She wasn't exactly sure what was, but there was no use kidding herself. She was washed up as a hot-shot reporter—even before she wrote her first big story, too.

Sometimes life wasn't fair.

She loaded a large tray she'd found with the salads, freshly cut French bread, and glasses of a cola she'd found in the refrigerator. Carrying it carefully, she made her way to the terrace beside the sparkling pool. There was shade in the far side and a table conveniently at hand.

Setting the small table, she was pleased with the way lunch had turned out. Now to figure out how to get Kharun out here to eat.

"It looks good."

She jumped at his voice. He'd come up behind her without making a sound.

"Aminna had all the ingredients, it was easy to throw together."

He seated her and sat opposite. She was pleased to note after the first hesitant bite, that he dug in with enthusiasm. She tasted the shrimp salad, pleased at how tasty it was.

Kharun obliquely studied his new bride as they ate. She seemed to pulse with restless energy, looking around her with fresh eyes, smiling in pleasure at the flowers that bloomed near the pool. She seemed to love beauty. He had noticed that as they'd toured the villa. What other interests did this stranger bound to him have?

"I have work to do this afternoon. At five, however, I plan to go riding. Would you care to join me?" he asked out of the blue. He rarely let others accompany him riding—that was his time for himself. Generally in a hectic week if he could carve out a couple of hours for himself, he guarded the time. Why had he invited Sara to join him?

"I'd love to. Where would we ride?"

"Along the beach. Normally I keep Satin in a stable a few miles from the city. I like to ride in the desert at dusk. But I brought him here a couple of weeks ago. It's not quite the same thing, but a good ride."

"How far can we go before we run into people sunbathing or swimming?"

"If we head away from Staboul, we can go for several miles. In the opposite direction—toward the city, only two. Do you have riding clothes?"

"I have jeans, that'll do for today. Who is Satin?"

"My horse. His Arabian name translates to Satin Magic. There are two other horses at the stables, I'll have one saddled for you. Do you prefer a spirited horse or one who is more sedate?"

"Spirited, of course. I want to ride like the wind along the sea."

Her eyes sparkled when she spoke, the gray going silver with delight. So it wasn't only anger that changed the color. Passion also brought out the silvery lights. What else did Sara feel passionately about?

He reined in his thoughts. An occasional kiss in public to maintain their charade was one thing. But this woman was a stranger, one who was here under obscure circumstances. There was no passion to be had between them.

Once the leases for the oil rights were finalized and signed, they would part ways.

He rose, tossing his napkin on the table. "Lunch was delicious. I'll come for you at five." He turned to walk away before he had second thoughts—on anything.

"Kharun?" She spoke before he reached the house.

"Yes?" He turned. She gathered their plates, stacking them on a tray.

"I wish to go swimming this afternoon. I'll use the pool. I'm sure I'll be okay if there's no one around."

He hesitated, but it was not an option. His young cousin had died when they'd been children—drowned in an accident that had burned deep into his consciousness.

"I'll bring my reading to the terrace while you swim," he said.

"Oh." She looked nonplussed. He almost smiled. She fascinated him, this Western woman with the changing eyes. "Give me half an hour."

"Sure, I have to clean up and change and all. That's fine. Thanks." She began humming as she swept the last of the breadcrumbs from the table into her hand, dumping them into one of the used plates.

From jail cell to luxury—Sara seemed to fit into both with a built-in self-sufficiency.

As he headed for his office, he remembered her comment about being uncomfortable at formal gatherings. It was too bad she felt that way. He bet she'd keep people on their toes and intrigue them to boot.

It was forty-five minutes later when Kharun stepped back onto the terrace. He had brought his laptop, and a stack of folders to skim through. Sara was sitting on the side of the pool, dangling her feet in the water.

For the first time, he was glad he'd worn his sun-glasses. He hoped they disguised his reaction to seeing her in that sleek swimsuit. Electric blue, it hugged her body. Her high, firm breasts were clearly displayed, as was her narrow waist and sweet flare of hips. Her legs went on forever when she stood and walked toward the deep end.

"Thanks for coming. I won't swim that long. Then I'll lie in the sun for a while and work on my tan."

He nodded and continued to the table where they'd shared lunch. It remained in the shade and he needed all the cooling he could find. His blood warmed at the sight of her. Desire rose. He had enjoyed kissing her, making the best of a bad situation.

Now he wanted her on another level, one that had nothing to do with their bargain or situation.

He wanted her in every way a man wants a woman.

Kharun set his chair so he could watch her without appearing to. She dove neatly into the water, coming up to begin swimming. Her legs kicked strongly, her arms rose and fell in a steady motion as she cleaved through the water. Turning at the end, she continued to swim. And he continued to watch. She was supple and graceful and strong. Obviously swimming was a sport she en-joyed—and excelled at. It proved a pleasure to watch her.

When at last she rose at the far end and sat on the edge, he looked away. But not before noticing how her breasts rose and fell as she tried to catch her breath.

How her wild curls were weighted down with water and hung like shining waves on either side of her face.

And not before he noticed his desire had increased, not diminished. He flipped open the laptop and clicked it on. He had work to do—and it definitely did not include fantasizing about his wife. His *temporary* wife.

Wife. They were married. Neither were promised to another. And weren't Western women supposed to be much more free with their favors than the women of his culture? Maybe he should explore that avenue a bit further.

He looked at Sara. Would she be willing to have an affair while she was here?

CHAPTER FIVE

SARA was ready at five for the promised ride. She'd donned sturdy shoes, comfortable jeans, and a sleeveless yellow top. The sun had kissed her skin at the pool, and she had a healthy glow about her.

She'd wondered earlier if Kharun would join her in the pool, but he'd diligently worked all afternoon—never looked up once as far as she could tell. She'd done some laps, rested on the side, and then swum some more before lying down on a sunbed at the water's edge.

He'd returned to the house once she'd told him she didn't plan to swim again. In fact, he had departed so fast she might have been insulted under other circumstances. Would it have hurt to stay a few moments and maybe talk?

She refused to let any vague feeling of disappointment color her excitement for the upcoming ride. She loved horses and had often wished she could have owned one. But with her father's constant travels when she was younger, and her own future uncertain lately, she had never felt the time was right.

How lucky for Kharun to have a stable close by. Riding along the beach sounded wildly romantic.

Romantic?

"Fun, I meant fun," she said out loud. "It'll be fun."

A light tap on her door startled her. "Great, now he'll

think I talk to myself,'' she mumbled as she hastened to the door.

"Ready?'' Kharun asked. He was also dressed casually, in light pants and high, glossy riding boots. His loose shirt would shelter him from the sun's rays, yet allow the wind to sweep through keeping him cool in the hot afternoon.

She smiled brightly. "I sure am.'' And glad to have a respite from being cooped up in the house, but she wouldn't tell him that. She was grateful, actually, for the opportunity to keep her embarrassing mistake from her father. She needed to act accordingly.

Obviously not all of the servants had been granted time off, there were several men working in the stables, which proved to be a short walk from the villa. Two Arabian horses were already saddled, standing in the shade near a water trough.

One was larger than the other, as black as midnight, with a long flowing mane and tail. The second horse was a bay with one white stocking dusting the left rear hoof.

"They're beautiful,'' Sara said, enchanted. She walked over to them and patted both on the neck. Fumbling in her pocket, she pulled out two carrots, which she fed to the well-mannered horses.

"A way to make a friend for life,'' Kharun said, watching her.

He stood nearby his feet spread slightly, his hands on his hips. He looked the epitome of wild desert sheikh. Instead of the lush greenery behind him, he should have had miles of golden desert sand, and the crystal blue of a vast and empty sky. Maybe tents to one side, with his trusty desert raiders with him.

Sara almost shivered in reaction. She was here to ride, not to fantasize.

"This must be Satin Magic," she said, patting the gleaming black horse once more. He was sleek and strong—the perfect mount for Kharun.

"And who is this?" she asked as she ran her hand along the neck of the bay.

"Alia. Don't let her docile air fool you. With a rider on her back, she expects to go places and runs like the wind."

"Sounds great."

"Then, if you are ready?"

Kharun held her waist and boosted her to the horse. Sara could have managed by herself, but kept quiet, savoring the tingling sensations where his hands were. He helped her adjust her stirrups, the brush of his arm and hands against her legs heating her blood more than the sun had.

"All set?" he asked, looking up at her.

"Yes." It came out far more breathless than she'd expected. Turning her horse, she waited for him to mount his.

In only moments they were walking the horses out of the stable yard and down a winding path toward the sea.

The Mediterranean sparkled in the late afternoon sunshine, a deep mysterious blue stretching as far as the eye could see. The brassy glare of the midday sun had mellowed as the sun sank lower in the western sky. Colors grew richer. The green of the grass and shrubs gave way to the white of the sand.

Alia seemed impatient, pulling a little on the bit, as if anxious to race along the water's edge. Sara wondered if the horse and she were in communion—that's exactly what she yearned to do, too. Race fast enough to escape her thoughts.

As soon as they reached the sand, the horse pranced.

"She's ready to run," Sara said, glancing at Kharun. He looked as if he'd been born to ride. His control of the powerful horse he rode seemed effortless, yet she knew it was a demonstration of his skill. Horse and rider looked perfect together.

"Then let's oblige her," he said with a sudden wicked grin. Without a visible sign, he gave his horse his head and Satin Magic stretched out into a controlled canter, sand kicking up behind him.

"We can't let them get ahead of us," Sara said as she urged Alia into a gallop, her own competitive instincts rising.

In seconds both horses were running neck and neck along the pristine beach, sand spraying behind the thundering hoofs. The breeze from the Mediterranean enhanced the feeling of speed as they let their horses set the pace. Sara laughed out loud, feeling wild and free. It was exhilarating! She felt as if she could ride forever. As if only the darkness of night could slow them down, and maybe not even then. Alia was a magical horse with a smooth gait and easy disposition. Sara was falling in love with her after only a few minutes. Could they ride every day?

The beach stretched out ahead of them, the blue of the water a blur to the right as the horses seemed to gallop for pure joy. Stretching their legs, bunching and shifting muscles, gaits smooth and synchronous, as if they'd matched strides a million times in the past and would that many more in the future.

Several minutes later Kharun slowed from a gallop to an easy canter. Sara followed suit. It was almost as exciting as a flat-out, go-for-broke run and easier on the horses. She watched where they were going, but had time to enjoy the remoteness of the beach, the cool breeze from the water, the splashes when an errant finger of water crossed their path and they plunged through.

Finally, in the distance, she began to see signs of others on the beach. Kharun motioned for her to slow down. She complied instantly, bringing Alia to a complete stop. Both she and her horse were breathing hard. Her blood pumped through her veins. She felt exhilarated, alive.

"That was fabulous!" she said when Kharun reined in beside her. "That's the public beach ahead, I take it?"

"Yes. We can continue for another half mile or so if you like, but at a much slower pace. I do not wish to take the horses where people are using the beach."

"Just a bit farther, then." She walked her horse and Kharun came along beside her, his knee almost brushing against hers. She could have reached out to touch him with no effort. She glanced his way.

His hair was tousled from their run, but he didn't appear to be having trouble catching his breath. He slid a look in her direction.

"You ride well."

"I told you, best lessons money could buy. I always wanted a horse, but talk about impractical with Dad's job and all."

"If you like, I can arrange for you to ride while you are here. As long as you are accompanied by a groom, of course," Kharun said.

"You're not very trusting. Do you think I'll just ride away and never return?"

He shrugged. "It wouldn't matter if you tried, I would come after you."

His words sent a shiver of awareness down her back. Of course he would. They had an agreement. But even beyond that—if she left, he would be humiliated before everyone. That would prove an even worse situation than the incident she almost caused by being caught taking illegal photographs.

"I wouldn't do that," she said.

"You would do nothing to jeopardize your father's career, right?" His voice held a mocking tone.

Sara flared up. "That's true. But that's not the only reason. I gave you my word, and that means something to me. As long as the situation is as it is, you have nothing to worry about with me, Kharun. I stand by my promises. I said I'd stay until the leases are signed and I will. I said I'd pretend this was a great marriage and I will. I've done nothing to give you cause to think otherwise!"

"It's still early days. Who knows what you might decide to do given the opportunity."

She could tell from his tone he was skeptical. She

chafed at the restrictions but reminded herself she'd brought it all on due to her impetuous actions. Time would show him she could be trusted.

But none of that mattered right now. The ride was not over. She'd enjoy each moment as it came.

So she could remember when she left?

The thought surprised her. Would she want memories about her marriage? It was a sham entered into solely to prevent a scandal.

She began to wonder what a marriage to Kharun would be like if it weren't a sham.

Would he follow his father's example and marry for passionate love? Or would he follow the dictates of his uncle's ministers and his aunt and marry for dynastic reasons?

Her own parents had a solid, loving marriage. But she didn't want to have a marriage like her mother's. Sara wanted to be a person in her own right, have her own interests and goals. Her own career.

Her mother was the perfect businessman's wife, loved to host parties, mingle with strangers, wear the right gown and always knew just what to do at the right time. Always knew the right thing to say.

As Kharun's wife would need to.

Sara sighed. It was hard to follow in such a paragon's steps.

"Why the sigh?" Kharun asked.

"What? Oh, I was thinking about my mother."

"She is a lovely woman. You will look as lovely when you are her age," he said.

She looked at him in startled surprise. "I will?"

He nodded once, abruptly.

"Thank you. That's one of the nicest compliments I've ever had." Made even more special coming from a man who didn't appear to like her, or trust her. "But Mom's a hard act to follow. She always knows what to say, what to wear, how to act."

"Perhaps that's her calling in life. She has made a niche for herself as your father's supporter. Somehow, I don't see you in a similar role."

Sara grinned at him. "Got it in one!"

"So what do you want to do in life, Sara Kinsale?"

Her grin faded. "I don't have a clue. That's what makes it so hard. My sister Margaret always knew she wanted to be an attorney from the day she started high school. Josh was scientific-minded from kindergarten, so they tell me. I know my parents despair of me ever settling down."

She didn't want to mention how pleased her mother had been that she married Kharun. She had to find something she was good at and pursue it. She had hoped the photojournalist job would be it. She had been taking pictures since she was little, and had a flare for it. But she'd blown her first major assignment.

"Did you always know you would one day run your family's business?" she asked.

He shook his head. "When I was growing up, I wanted to drive race cars, fly airplanes and pilot a submarine. But as I grew older, business fascinated me. Especially after my father let me work in various departments of the different family companies between school terms. I was hooked."

She was delighted to learn this tidbit about the serious man beside her. Who would have thought he once had frivolous ideas?

"So did you pursue any of those subjects in school? Maybe not piloting a submarine, but maybe racing?"

"Flying. I have a multi-engine license. But none of the others. By the time I was sent away to school, my father made it clear business acumen was important. So I focused my studies in that direction. My family has several interests that span shipping, manufacturing and exporting. That was the role I was groomed for."

"Did you want it?" she asked. Dynastic family responsibilities were beyond her experience.

"I find it much more challenging and rewarding than trying to garner the consensus of ministers each of whom seem to have their own agenda. My father loved that aspect."

"Do you have to run the companies? Can't you go back to your earlier dreams?"

"One cannot fight one's destiny. Surely you know that by now."

"Ouch." Was it her destiny to roam restlessly searching forever for some career that would hold meaning and interest?

Kharun drew up his horse. "Here is the path back to the stable. Have you had enough riding for today?"

"Yes. It's been great, but such a long time since I've been riding. My legs are a bit stiff already."

He led the way along the path until the stable came into view. Dismounting when the grooms ran out, Kharun tossed the reins to one of the men.

Sara slid off her horse before Kharun could come around to help her and smiled at the groom who took the reins.

"Whoa," she said, as she took a step and felt her legs fold up beneath her. Before she could hit the ground, however, Kharun's arms were around her, beneath her knees, behind her back. In one swoop he picked her up and held her against his chest.

"I can walk," she protested, leaning just a little into his masculine strength. Of course she could walk, but what woman in the world had never fantasized about some dashing, romantic man sweeping her off her feet and into his arms?

"Your legs will feel wobbly for a while. Sit and rest." He set her on a bench near the side of the stable.

Sara blinked. She had visions of Kharun carrying her through the flower-scented garden, through the opened French doors to her bedroom and—

Get a grip, she told herself, feeling the heat of embarrassment sweep up her cheeks.

"You're right, I'll be fine in a minute." She couldn't look at him. What if he suspected where her wild thoughts were running? Theirs was a contrived marriage, lasting only as long as the treaty negotiations. There were no romantic overtones, no enduring emotions between them.

But for a moment, Sara didn't think there had to be. They were married. He had kissed her a couple of times already. She looked up at him, her eyes focused on his mouth. She wanted more from him. And she suspected he wouldn't turn her down. What would happen if she kissed him?

Kharun was sitting at his desk in the study the next morning when Piers knocked on the open door and stuck his head in.

"Got a moment?" he asked. "I took a chance and came by to bring you the latest proposals."

"Piers. I wondered if you'd drop by this morning. Come in." Kharun put down the report he was reading and motioned his long-time friend and most trusted adviser to enter.

"Honeymoon over?" Piers asked, grinning at his friend. He carried his briefcase over to the desk and placed it in a cleared area, then sat in his usual spot.

"Such as it was."

"And?"

"Not that it's any of your business, but it's more difficult being married than I had anticipated."

"An engagement would have been better."

"But probably would not have fooled Garh, Hamin and the others."

Piers laughed. "A hastily planned ceremony doesn't make a marriage."

"It's binding enough."

"True, but an annulment will be easy once the negotiations are finished." He opened his briefcase and pulled out a folder. "The latest from Samuel Kinsale. Do you think he is mellowing because his daughter married you? It seems we may be able to close the deal sooner than anticipated."

Kharun looked up at that. "I can't imagine that tough businessman softening for anyone. How soon?"

Piers shrugged. "Within a few days it looks like. Going to New York for the signing?"

"That's where his corporate offices are. I decided that when we began this I'd go there. Now, I'm not so sure."

"I might join you if you go. How about your wife?"

"Sara will be thrilled to hear the negotiations are progressing so well. She originally came to join her parents while they were here. I suspect she'll wish to continue that vacation when we separate. Has there been any further repercussions due to her actions?"

"All's quiet on the Garh and Hamin front. I think they are beginning to cave on their stance. It wouldn't look good, challenging the new wife of the negotiator, now would it?"

"And when we separate?" Kharun leaned back in his chair and studied his adviser. "What will be the repercussions then?"

"Ah, good question. Perhaps they will surge back stronger than ever in their anti-progress stance. Who can say at this point?"

Kharun rose and walked to the window. He didn't notice the beautiful blossoms in full bloom. Nor the glimpse of the sea beyond. He saw instead Sara's laughing face when she was happy, the sparkle in her silvery eyes when she was angry, and the graceful feminine way she had of walking or swimming or riding.

"Something wrong?" Piers asked, watching Kharun curiously.

"What would be the ramifications of a divorce instead of an annulment?" Kharun asked without turning.

The silence stretched out behind him.

Finally he turned to meet Piers's puzzled gaze.

"I don't understand." He blinked, slapped the side of his forehead with the heel of his hand. "Oh, damn, I do understand. Kharun, you and she didn't—"

"It is a hypothetical question," Kharun said firmly. At least at this point. But the desire he felt around Sara seemed to escalate each time he saw her. And he knew she was aware of the sparks that seemed to fly between them.

Yesterday at the stables, for a moment, he'd thought she'd start something. She'd looked at him intently, then color had risen in her cheeks. She'd been distant ever since. What had she been thinking?

Piers cleared his throat. "Actually, it might be better to divorce, than have an annulment. More believable, if you know what I mean."

"Elaborate."

"Let's face it, Kharun, no one in their right mind is going to think you and she didn't do anything—unless the marriage was a sham. It's one thing to fool your ministers—something else to let them know they've been fooled."

"Ah, so now you think it expedient to get a divorce rather than an annulment?"

"Can I have a few days to think over the situation?" Piers asked warily.

"Take as long as you like. It is hypothetical."

"But for how long, I wonder," his friend asked.

Sara appeared in the doorway, stopping suddenly when she saw Piers.

"Oh, excuse me, I didn't know you had company."

"Come in, Sara. You remember Piers."

"The best man. Of course. How are you?" She smiled warily, but remained at the doorway.

"Was there something you wanted?" Kharun asked politely.

"I wanted to phone my mother. She'll wonder why I haven't contacted her at all. I mean, I did come here to visit them, then disappeared. The next thing she knew, she was attending my wedding."

"She knows you are here and safe," Kharun said.

"So I can't call her?"

"Of course you can." He gestured to the phone.

Piers started to rise, but Kharun shook his head.

He turned to Kharun. "Is it wise, letting her phone?"

"Is it wise to raise suspicions of her parents by not allowing her contact?"

She remained in the doorway, watching the interchange. "I can wait until later, when you've finished your business," she said, turning to leave.

"This gets more complicated by the moment," Piers said.

"Actually, it would probably be all right to let her phone whenever she wishes. Sara gave me her word she'd abide by the terms of our agreement. I trust her to do just that."

Piers did blink at that comment. "You, trust a woman?"

"Within limits."

"That's a first. I thought after Andrea du Polline you'd sworn never to trust a woman again."

"This situation is different. Sara has concerns for her father's reputation, as well."

"As well as her own desire to stay out of one of our jails," Piers muttered sarcastically.

"That can be a strong motivating factor," Kharun agreed. "What did Kinsale concede on?"

Piers opened the folder he'd brought and looked at his friend. "I trust you know what you're doing about your marriage. And about the leases. Tell me what you think about this new counteroffer?" He indicated the paragraph of the report.

Kharun knew Piers was surprised by his comment. Hadn't he said often enough in the past he didn't trust women? They all appeared to be after one thing—his money. From his younger days in Eton, to his college days, and even the beginnings of his career, he'd been sought out by beautiful women who professed an interest in him alone—but had an eye on his inheritance.

Twice he'd come close to asking a woman to marry him, only to discover before he could ask the question that they were more interested in his wealth than their relationship. More interested in being seen in all the right places than in quiet dinners away from the "in" crowd.

How ironic, now he had married—and to a woman who didn't even *profess* to care for him. But by the same token, neither did she seem especially interested in his wealth or indulging in hectic nightlife.

Sara wandered around the patio feeling frustrated and bored. She needed to talk to her mother—though she'd have to reassure her she was deliriously happy being married and probably make vague plans for a dinner together at some point in the not-too-distant future.

Her mother was big on family. She'd adopt Kharun into their extended family immediately. Plopping down on a chaise longue, Sara moodily contemplated Kharun and her mother. How would he take to the informal family gatherings? Was he too steeped in tradition to fit in easily with her parents' casual private life? What did it matter? Theirs was a temporary alliance. They could stall any family overtures until time to separate.

For some reason, the thought didn't make her happy.

"*Bonjour, Sara.*" Kharun's mother stood in the doorway and smiled at her.

Sara scrambled to her feet, surprised to see Angelique. Did Kharun know his mother was here?

"Good morning. I didn't know you were coming. Would you like to sit here, or is it too warm? Perhaps you'd rather go inside."

"Here, of course," Angelique said as she strolled onto the terrace. "The roses are lovely this year. But Matassin is a master gardener and has a special affinity for roses." She sat on the chair beside Sara's and indicated Sara should resume her own seat.

"I understand Kharun is back at work. So tiresome. But there is a lot to do. I do hope it won't be long before he can delegate enough to allow time off. If he ever does. His father loved his work. Runs in the family, I guess. I understand he's planning to go to New York to celebrate when the oil leases are signed. Maybe you and he can squeeze out a few extra days for a honeymoon then. You could show him your home—though I'm sure he's already seen it.''

Sara smiled politely, noncommittally. It was the first she'd heard about a possible trip back to the States. That could simplify things when they separated. She'd have to speak to Kharun about the trip.

''I came on the off chance he was back at work. I know my son, you see.''

''Piers was here first thing this morning to see him.''

''Then perhaps while they attend to business you would like to have lunch with me and Jasmine. Then you and I could stop in a few boutiques afterward, to look for a dress for Friday. Unless you already have a gown you planned to wear.''

''Friday?'' Sara asked.

''The reception at the British embassy. Surely Kharun plans to attend. I'm sure he wouldn't risk slighting everyone by not attending.''

''Friday night?'' Drat, she hated formal receptions. Especially any in which she was sure to be the center of attention. And as the new bride of Kharun bak Samin, she knew she'd be at the top of the list of people to stare at and gossip about.

''I wasn't sure if you brought an appropriate dress, but I'd be happy to introduce you to the delights of several boutiques in Staboul which can provide the most fabulous gowns on short notice.''

Sara wondered if one of them was the place Jasmine had found her wedding gown only an hour before the wedding.

"That would be lovely. I don't have anything suitable for an embassy reception. I'd love to come to lunch." Anything would be preferable to her almost enforced stay at the villa.

Angelique knew nothing of the truth. Jasmine knew, and didn't trust her. It should prove to be an interesting lunch.

Aminna appeared in the doorway, Sara's camera in hand.

"I found this in the kitchen when I returned this morning." Aminna held it out.

"My camera." Sara rose and crossed to the doorway to take it. "I left it there yesterday when I fixed lunch." Automatically, Sara checked the camera indicator.

"There's film in it!"

Aminna nodded gravely. "I saw it was empty and replaced the film. Do you wish to have lunch in the dining room, or on the terrace?"

"I'm taking my new daughter-in-law out to lunch, Aminna. Please inform Kharun."

Aminna nodded gravely and left.

"What a complicated camera. I didn't know you were a photographer. How exciting. What do you like to shoot?" Angelique asked.

Pictures of your summer home without your knowledge, popped into Sara's mind.

"Um, actually I'm still developing my style. I like working to get the right framing, contrast the light and shadows. Things like that."

"What do you photograph? People? Scenes? Closeups of plants?"

"Horses, odd houses, old ruins." She smiled. "Sometimes people. Whatever I find interesting." She'd been taking photographs of her family and friends, of exotic locations and quiet homey places for years. The results had been gratifying. She'd been focused on her aborted plan to get pictures of the Samin's summer place, hoping for unusual angles to make the shots distinctive. Maybe today she could get snapshots of Staboul to take home when she left.

And later, she'd photograph the villa. Surely no one could find fault with her taking photos of her own home, however temporary.

Aminna came quietly onto the terrace, a laden tray of tea and small cakes in her hands. She efficiently set the table, placed the food in the center and returned to the house, never saying a word.

"I would like to photograph her," Sara said musingly. "Her face has such character." She faced Angelique as she poured their tea. "And I'd love to photograph your son riding Satin Magic."

"Do so. If it turns out, I would love to have a copy. He is a fine-looking man, isn't he?" She looked at Sara from beneath her lashes.

The true reason a mother had come—to find out more about her son's new wife. Sara smiled politely, wondering how his mother would feel if she knew Sara's true feelings.

Suddenly, she realized she wasn't even sure of her true feelings. Granted, she felt confined to the house since he'd rescued her from the jail. Understandable, though frustrating. She was counting the days until she would be free.

Yet she was strangely intrigued by the man. Fascinated by the range of sensations that danced through her when in his presence. She liked sparring with him, liked hearing him discuss the matters of change he wanted for his country.

She was completely captivated by his kisses. She warmed at the memory. The last time they'd had someone not privy to their secret come to visit, he'd kissed her. Would he kiss her in his mother's presence?

Her heart rate sped up a notch.

She'd soon find out. Kharun stepped out onto the terrace.

CHAPTER SIX

"MA MÈRE, Aminna told me you were here. I wasn't expecting you." Kharun glanced at Sara as he crossed the terrace to kiss his mother on both cheeks.

"I didn't mean to interrupt you, *chéri.* Aminna told me you were hard at work. I thought Sara might have enticed you away from your duties for a little longer. First you take no honeymoon, now you neglect her. For shame." The twinkle in her eyes belied her words.

"Things needed to be done. Sara understands."

"Always things need to be done. Your new wife is a saint if she allows it. Such virtue deserves a reward. I'm taking Sara to lunch with me and Jasmine. Unless, of course, you have plans yourself."

"Piers is here. We are working."

"Times have changed from when I was young," she said mockingly, with a conspiratorial look at Sara.

"How so?"

"Your father and I made sure our priorities included a long honeymoon."

"It never ended."

Her face saddened. "Not until his death. Cherish the moments you have, *chéri,* they seem so fleeting in retrospect."

She rose and patted him on the cheek. "I will speak with Aminna for a moment, then Sara and I will leave.

We're going shopping after lunch. Bring your camera, Sara, you can start with Jasmine and me.''

He waited until she was out of hearing, then turned to Sara, apparently noticing the camera for the first time.

''Aminna brought me the camera. She found it in the kitchen,'' Sara said, holding it in front of her, almost like a shield. ''You mother suggested the photographs.''

''Take the pictures she wants, then. But I'll have the film developed,'' he said with a warning in his tone. ''And none are to go to your newspaper!''

Sara stiffened. She knew he didn't truly trust her, due to her own actions, but it still rankled. ''I have no intention of sending any to the paper!''

''Jasmine knows the true story about our marriage, but my mother doesn't. Keep it that way,'' he admonished.

''Did you come out here just to tell me that? Of course I can remember that order from one day to the next. No one is to know. If I can't tell my mother, I surely won't be telling yours!''

She hurried into the house to change from the modest white pants she'd donned that morning into something more suitable to lunch with her new in-laws.

When she entered the large foyer several minutes later, Piers and Angelique were talking. Kharun leaned casually against the priceless Louis XV table watching them. He looked at Sara when she joined them. She wondered for a moment if the gleam in his eyes meant more than he still didn't trust her.

''Have a good afternoon,'' he said, deliberately crossing to her. He stood so close she could almost share his breath—if she hadn't been holding hers.

"I wish I were going with you," he said. Only she understood the full truth of the comment. He was wary about letting her out of his sight. Yet his comment undoubtedly sounded totally different to his mother, she was sure. Angelique thought Kharun longed to spend the day with his new bride. If she only knew!

"I'll be back before dinner—nothing will happen." It was the best she could do to offer reassurance.

His lips brushed against hers and he straightened and turned.

It wasn't enough. Sara gripped the straps of her purse tightly. She wanted more!

Yet the brief kiss was more than she could have expected.

Pasting a bright smile on her face she faced Angelique. "Let's do lunch!"

When the women had left, Piers looked at Kharun. "Is that wise?"

"Probably not. But it caused no comment. If I had kept Sara isolated from my mother, she would wonder why, and begin to question me, and speculate to all and sundry. I dare not risk any suspicion."

"I understand, but what's to stop Sara from running off the first moment Angelique turns her back?"

Kharun paused a moment, deep in thought. "Sara said she would stay, I believe her."

"She could be a spy. At best she's a sensationalist hack journalist searching for fodder for that rag she works for."

"But she *is* Samuel Kinsale's daughter. His ethics

have never been questioned. I'm betting she's enough like her father that she won't disappear.''

''I hope you're right,'' Piers said, heading back toward the office.

''Me, too,'' Kharun said softly. He wasn't sure where the feeling of total trust had come from. His experience with women outside his family had done nothing to foster such a trust. But there was something about Sara—

He shook his head and followed his friend back to work. He hoped he wasn't letting his desire for the woman cloud his judgment.

When Angelique's chauffeur dropped Sara back at the villa later that afternoon, Sara held the half dozen bags of purchases balanced in her arms. She rang the bell and wondered if she should have asked for a key.

One of the maids opened the door, smiling shyly when she recognized Sara. She said something in Arabic, which of course Sara didn't understand. Replying in French, she could tell the young woman didn't speak that language. It was frustrating not being able to communicate. But the nods and smiles seemed sufficient.

Sara headed for her room. The afternoon had been unexpectedly fun. Jasmine never let up her cautious air, which thankfully Angelique didn't appear to notice. Sara answered all their questions, dared to ask a couple of her own, and tried to pretend everything was normal for a newly wed woman getting to know her new in-laws.

But always in the background hovered the specter of Kharun and the reality of the true situation.

"Shopping, a woman's delight," Kharun said behind her.

Sara spun around, the packages flying every which way.

"I didn't hear you!" she accused. How did he move so soundlessly?

"My apologies." He leaned over and picked up two of the bags.

Sara reached for the others, and continued on to her room feeling a little snappy, with butterflies dancing in her stomach. What was wrong with her? Too much chocolate mousse for dessert at lunch?

Her skin seemed to tingle at his closeness. She wished she'd checked her hair, made sure her lipstick was fresh. Anticipation hummed through her veins.

He followed her into the bedroom as if he had every right. Which, she thought wryly, he did.

"I bought some things," she said needlessly, dumping her bags on the bed. Kharun placed the two he carried and looked at her, his dark eyes disturbing. She fidgeted beneath his gaze.

"What did you buy?" he asked politely.

"A dress for the reception at the British embassy. Your mother said we would be going."

He nodded his head once.

"When were you planning on telling me?" she asked. "Ten minutes before we were about to leave? Listen to me, Kharun, arranging my life without telling me is not something which I'll put up with." She waved her hands. "The first I knew about our wedding was when Jasmine showed up with the dress. The first I knew about this reception was when your mother told me. What else is going on that I need to know that you haven't told me?''

He shrugged. ''I will have to check my calendar. Would you like to go over it with me?'' he asked politely, amusement dancing in his eyes.

She flushed at the sardonic glint in his eyes.

''Of course not, just let me know ahead of time if there is an event you expect me to attend. And I will let you know, as well.''

He quirked an eyebrow. ''An event you and I would attend that you arranged?''

''My mother will certainly wish to have us over for dinner soon. The few moments we had to talk after our hasty wedding certainly weren't enough to satisfy her curiosity. Nor could we talk while I packed with you hovering around like a vulture.''

''Vulture? Somehow I had hoped for a more romantic turn of phrase. I thought I played the part of doting bridegroom perfectly.''

''I'm sure you'd have received rave reviews if anyone had known. But my mother's big on family. She'll love welcoming you into ours, the sooner the better for her.''

Sara bit her lower lip. ''We'll have to stall her.''

''Why is that?''

''There's no point in her getting used to you when the marriage will be over soon.''

''As you say. Let me see the gown.''

She thought about arguing, but about what? She knew this was solely a marriage of convenience—his convenience. Showing him the clothes effectively changed the subject. Sara was pleased with her selections and wondered what he'd think about them. She pushed aside two of the smaller bags, taking the larger one. Withdrawing the dress, wrapped in layers and layers of tissue paper, she shook it free.

Almost a midnight-blue, shot through with silver threads, it was the loveliest dress she'd ever seen. And it fit like a dream.

She held it up, and looked at him.

His expression gave nothing away.

"Try it on," he invited.

"Now?"

"It's hard to see how it will look on you when merely held up in front." He walked to the sitting area and sat as if he was settled for the rest of the afternoon.

"I guess I could."

Five minutes later Sara emerged from the bathroom dressed in the new gown.

The high jeweled halter neckline gave a false impression of modesty belied by the fitted bodice and the long slinky skirt that sported a slit up one side to mid-thigh. The back was virtually nonexistent until her waist. Sara felt alluring and mysterious wearing it.

She should have found the shoes first, however. Walking barefoot missed the look.

Or maybe not, if the heightened awareness of Kharun's interest was a gauge. He rose and walked to meet her halfway across the room.

"You look exquisite," he said slowly, his gaze running along the length of her body. Heat built as he continued to study her. "Turn around."

Slowly she turned around completely, hearing the hiss as he drew in a sharp breath when he saw her bare back.

"Won't you be cold in that?" he asked, his voice rough.

Sara shook her head. If she didn't bank the fires his look caused, she'd burn up.

"I think I'll be fine," she said, pleased to hear her own voice sounded normal. "Your mother helped pick it out."

"My mother is a Frenchwoman, of course she'd pick out something wildly sexy."

"Wildly sexy? Cool!"

He reached out to draw a warm finger down her bare arm. "The men will be envious of my good fortune. The women will be jealous of your beauty," he said slowly.

Her heart almost flipped over. No one had ever said anything so wonderful to her before.

Mesmerized by the heat in his eyes, Sara stared back at him, licking suddenly dry lips.

Kharun caught the movement and fastened his attention on her mouth.

Before she could say anything, he drew her into his arms and kissed her.

There was no audience, was her last coherent thought before dazzling sensation took over.

His mouth sparked a cascade of shimmering enchantment. Sara stepped closer, as if seeking more. She parted her lips and instantly felt Kharun deepen the kiss. His warm hands on her bare back sent tingling waves of excitement coursing through her. His tongue dancing with hers caused the desire that simmered to explode.

She yearned for more. She couldn't get enough of him. She wanted to taste him everywhere, touch him everywhere. Her hands threaded through his thick hair, relishing the texture and heat. She moved them to trace the muscles of his shoulders, back to his head. When he slowly spun them around, she felt as if the world tilted. She clung, holding on to the one steadfast reality in a fantasy illusion.

Slowly they moved until she felt the world fall away. Only it was the two of them, falling onto the bed, amid the bags, tissue paper and pillows.

He held her tightly, cushioning their soft fall, moving his mouth from hers to her cheek, tracing her jaw, running his tongue lightly against her throat, kissing that frantically beating pulse point.

Sara lay half across him, feeling the rugged strength of his chest beneath her. Savoring the feel of his hands against her skin, touching her, caressing her.

The fresh breeze blowing across the garden from the sea brought with it the scent of flowers and the salt air but no cooling relief for the building heat. She was spellbound by the sensations that clamored for dominance— desire, shivering enchantment, sensuous languor.

When Kharun ran his hand down her side, slipping beneath the bodice of the gown to graze her breast, Sara caught her breath. For an instant sanity reasserted itself.

She pushed back, gazing down at him. Slowly he opened his eyes and gazed back.

Scrambling off the bed, Sara backed away. The breeze suddenly felt cold. The dress offered so little protection.

"What is going on?" she asked. The forceful demand

she had hoped to make fell flat. It came out almost a whisper.

Kharun rose lithely and took a step toward her. Sara backed away, clinging almost desperately to the shred of common sense that told her things were getting out of hand. One part of her wanted to throw herself back into his embrace. Another part questioned her sanity.

"I kissed you, you kissed me back."

"That went far beyond a mere kiss!"

"And that upsets you?"

"Of course it does. What's going on? We agreed to a farce of a marriage to make sure we avoided a scandal. But we agreed it would be strictly platonic."

"I'm afraid I don't remember such an agreement."

She blinked. They had said—what exactly? "I remember in the car—"

He waited, as a panther might wait before leaping on his prey, silently, without moving, but aware of everything. Sara took a nervous step backward.

Her eyes widened as she remembered. They'd been discussing the right to share a bed. She'd said he had to stay out of hers and she'd stay out of his. But now that she recalled the conversation, he had never agreed.

"The dress was a mistake," she said.

"Why? It looks lovely on you."

"It obviously gave the wrong message."

Kharun laughed and shook his head, heading for the door. "Sara, the sight of you in that dress did not inflame passion." He paused at the door and looked back at her. "Just looking at you does that. Whether in jeans or bedraggled khakis. I came to see if you wished to ride again this afternoon?''

She blinked, trying to regain her balance. Had he just said he felt desire for her just by looking at her? Then he asked about riding?

''Ride?''

''Horses?''

The sardonic glint was back. He probably thought her mind had been fried by their kiss.

He wasn't far off the mark.

''Yes, I'd love to go riding. I'll change now and meet you at the stables.''

Kharun waited impatiently in the foyer for Sara to change. He had not trusted himself to stay in her room while she slipped out of that sexy gown and donned jeans.

He hadn't wanted to stop when she'd called a halt. He wanted her. And it had been a long time since he had felt such a strong sense of wanting for a woman.

Brief flings in distant capitals had been the norm over the last few years after his blazing mistake with Andrea du Polline. He'd made a fool of himself over her. She'd made a fool of herself over his money.

And since his father had died, he had not had the time, nor inclination, to seek out female companionship.

But Sara was different. Was that part of the spark that drove him crazy? He was sure she felt something around him. He was too savvy not to recognize the signs. Their kiss had been all he'd hoped. But she'd stopped long before he was ready.

He almost laughed. She thought it was the dress. Did she really not have a clue? Or was she playing a more devious game?

''I'm ready.'' Sara joined him, dressed in jeans, a long-sleeved cotton top and her shoes. He'd have to see about her getting some riding boots. Especially if they went to the desert. Would Sara like riding across the dunes, chasing the stars at night?

They could escape away from everything—until they were alone in the universe. He'd dismount and help her from the saddle, letting her body slide down his, a temptation he knew he couldn't resist. Spreading a blanket on the sands still warm from the day's sun, he'd lay her down and strip her bare—until her soft, feminine skin was bathed in starlight. Then he'd make love to her until dawn.

''Kharun, are we going?''

He looked at her. Yes, one night he'd take her to the desert and make love to her.

''After you.'' He opened the door and waited.

She preceded him and turned toward the walkway that led to the stables. He watched her walk, tall and proud. Her hips swayed gently in the tight jeans.

He felt his own pants tighten against him. But he couldn't look away. He thought about what Piers had said—better a divorce than an annulment—at least the ministers might be fooled by such a decision. An annulment would be a slap in the face.

And after everyone had met her, no one would believe an annulment anyway.

Theirs was a temporary alliance, true. But Kharun

knew something bound them tightly for however long she stayed. He would make Sara his wife in truth as well as on paper.

When they reached the stables, he reached out and took an arm, halting her.

"What?"

"Just so you know, it wasn't the dress."

He leaned over to kiss her again, pleased to note the instant response on her part.

The horses were already saddled. Kharun helped Sara to mount, then swung up onto his own horse. He led the way to the beach, wishing again he was on the desert. The confines of the city and demands of his new position grated. He needed to feel the space and freedom of the desert. Soon, he'd schedule a week and forget Staboul and his uncle's interfering ministers and show Sara the other delights of his country.

Once he reached the beach, he gave Satin Magic his head. He was not surprised to find Sara racing neck and neck beside him in only seconds. Alia was a match for Satin. He urged his horse to greater speed, relishing the sense of freedom, the exhilaration riding Satin always brought.

They thundered down the beach, splashing in the shallows, scattering rainbows of colors behind them, tossing up the sand in a wake they could track. Purely for his own pleasure, Kharun kept up the fast pace, but he also was attuned to Sara. If it became too much, he'd stop.

But she was a woman to rise to challenges. She did her best to coax a faster gait from Alia, never giving up. The sun sparkled on the water, the air was scented with the fragrance of a thousand flowers. Blood pulsed in his veins. It was a great day in which to be alive, made all the more so with Sara's presence.

The thought caught him by surprise.

Seeing the signs of civilization ahead, he slowed Satin. Alia raced past, then slowed and turned. Sara halted, breathing hard, as she waited for Kharun to reach her. Her face was ablaze with happiness.

"That was wonderful!" she said, then burst into laughter. "What a fantasy—racing a sheikh along the sea. Splashing in the water. I'm wet to my knees."

He felt a chill. Was that all the afternoon meant—a fantasy with a title, instead of the real thing with a man who desired her? Was she like the others, after all, caught up in the trappings of wealth and titles?

Even after the hard run, Alia danced in place, anxious to continue.

"What's wrong?" Sara asked, controlling her mount, and holding her still.

"Not a thing. You ride well."

"It's not hard on a sweetie like Alia. She seems ready to continue."

"They have a lot of stamina. I breed them for endurance."

"Do you ever take them out in the desert?"

How had her mind aligned itself with his? Was it fate?

"Sometimes."

"I'd love to try that, if we get a chance. I imagine it's even more wonderful—riding forever in the empty desert. No sign of civilization for miles and miles. There are places like that in the States and I love being there. Maybe I should have been a hermit in another life.''

He edged his horse closer, facing Sara, until their knees almost touched.

She was still breathing fast, her breasts rising and falling rapidly. Her gaze caught his, drifted to his mouth. Did she want another kiss? Was she as caught up in the sensual awareness as he?

Her lids drooped and she looked away, color staining her cheeks.

Kharun felt a wave of satisfaction sweep through. She couldn't hide her own awareness. Now it was only a matter of time before he had her in his bed.

Knowing that gave him the will to be more patient. He would not rush her.

But soon.

Sara started her horse back toward the villa. Kharun turned and eased Satin Magic into step with Alia. The horses tossed their heads, but he and Sara kept them to a walk.

''What else was in the packages you brought home?'' he asked.

''Another dress, and a couple of pairs of shoes. Your mother is a power shopper. She was telling us at lunch how she splurges every now and then and goes to Paris.''

''For her, that is the only place really worth shopping.''

''Yet she loves this country, that much is evident in her conversation.'' Sara cast a sidelong glance. ''And she is very pro you.''

"And you find that surprising? Aren't most mothers for their children?"

"Does she know the real you?"

"Who is the real me?"

"A man who manipulates events to his own purposes."

Kharun suspected where the conversation was headed. Could he defuse it?

"Did you take pictures?"

"I got some great ones. Jasmine was quite annoyed with me by the end of the afternoon. Every time I'd see something new, I'd ask Yasaf, your mother's chauffeur, to stop. Your mother, on the other hand, seemed happy to have me photograph anything that took my fancy— from the lovely inlays lining the outside of a mosque, to the faces of children in the poorer section of town."

"You went to the Sadinn area of town?"

"I think that's what it was called. Angelique gave me a complete tour before we stopped at the first boutique."

Why had his mother done so? She didn't know the full circumstances of his marriage, but even if it had been a true love match, wouldn't she shelter her new daughter-in-law from the rougher sections of town until Sara became more accustomed to their country?

"Your mother offered to have the film developed. I told her you wanted to do so, but she insisted she didn't want to wait to see what I'd done. I'm sure you can intercept them when she brings them over to make sure I'm not photographing top secret places in my role as spy."

CHAPTER SEVEN

KHARUN was going to drive her crazy, Sara just knew it. It wasn't enough he suspected her of being a spy, now he was on some campaign to seduce her. Did he think she would then confess to some nefarious plot?

She paused with mascara wand in hand and peered into the mirror. She had ten more minutes before they were due to depart for the British embassy reception.

She glanced over to the bed and looked at the dress. Would she ever be able to wear it without remembering Kharun's kisses and caresses the afternoon she modeled it for him?

She doubted it. She looked back to the mirror and touched her lashes with the mascara. She was nervous about the evening. She disliked large gatherings, how would she handle being the mysterious new bride of Sheikh Kharun bak Samin? She was sure to be the cynosure of all eyes.

"It's just pretend," she murmured, knowing no one else there would think so.

Her hair brushed, her makeup on—she could put it off no longer. She donned the dress. Immediately she was enveloped in the sensuous feelings she had experienced when she'd modeled it for Kharun. The silky material hugged her body like a second skin. The breeze from the veranda caressed her bare back. Slipping on the high heels, she walked to the full-length mirror. The dress made her eyes look silvery. Nervousness gave color to her cheeks. She rubbed her stomach, trying to quell the butterflies. But she couldn't help wondering how Kharun would react when he saw her again in the sexiest dress she'd ever owned.

No time like the present to find out.

She grabbed a small, jeweled purse and headed out, head held high.

Kharun was waiting for her. His tux was elegantly tailored, fashioned for his wide shoulders, long legs. The ruffled shirt might have looked effeminate on other men, but on him it accentuated his rugged masculinity. He looked as daring as a pirate—or a desert raider.

She walked up to him, holding his gaze with her own. Butterflies danced in her stomach and she had trouble breathing, but she wouldn't let him know. Tilting her chin slightly, she stopped right next to him—much closer than she needed to be. Two could play this sensuous game. She almost touched the arm of his jacket, but settled for looking at him from beneath her lashes and smiling.

"You look lovely," he said. Taking her hand in his, he raised it to his lips. Brushing the back with his lips, he turned it slightly until he could brush the sensitive inner skin of her wrist.

Sara felt a shock of desire flood through her. Almost yanking her hand free, she tried to hold her smile. "Is it time to leave?"

He inclined his head, the amusement in his eyes disturbing her. So much for trying to maintain a sophisticated veneer. She turned to head for the door and heard him catch his breath. The sound gave her a smidgeon of satisfaction—he was still affected by the dress, or lack of its back. Good. She hated to be the only one lost in a fog.

The limousine swiftly transported them to the British embassy. The old building was made of stone, with tall columns holding a wide portico in front. Lights shone from all the many ground-floor windows. As they left the limousine, they could hear the murmur of voices and soft background music wafting out on the warm evening air.

Without time to even think, Sara was whisked up the stairs and into the huge reception hall. The short receiving line was solely comprised of the ambassador and his wife and another high-ranking official from England.

Show time, Sara thought. She slipped her hand onto Kharun's arm. He bent his arm and held her hand close to his body. Head held high, she stepped out and the evening began.

An hour later Sara thought her face would crack from smiling so much. She had met everyone in the room, she was certain, and answered so many questions about how she and Kharun met that she wished she'd printed up cards to hand out.

Kharun stayed by her side, giving her snippets of information about the people she met before he exchanged greetings with them. He seemed to know everyone, she thought, wondering how much longer the evening would last. She longed for the privacy of her room.

To add to the strain, she made every effort to play the part of adoring bride. Why had she ever thought she wanted a career in acting? It was hard to remember to glance up to Kharun with what she hoped was love in her gaze from time to time. Primarily because she was so busy trying to focus on breathing. His touch seemed to short-circuit her normal functions. His hand rested on her bare back at one point and she almost forgot the question he asked her. When he laced his fingers through hers later in the evening, her breath caught again. At the rate she was going, she would be a basket case by the end of the reception.

''Ah, Your Excellency, I have not yet had the opportunity to meet your charming bride.''

Sara turned at the sound of the voice. She took an instant dislike to the man standing beside them. He was not tall, Sara could look him in the eye. His dark gaze narrowed and his voice oozed oily *bonhomie,* which did not cover his insincerity. She wondered if he thought it did.

''Garh Sonharh, my wife Sara. Darling, Garh is one of my uncle's most trusted new ministers.'' Kharun's voice was neutral, void of any intonation that would give Sara a hint of how he felt about the man. And that in itself was a clue.

The name was familiar—she suddenly remembered. It was after talking with this man that Kharun had come up with the outlandish scheme to marry instead of just an engagement.

''How do you do, sir?'' she said sweetly, smiling as vapidly as she could. Maybe the acting lessons would come in handy, after all. ''I'm so delighted to meet you.''

Kharun's hand tightened on hers. She resisted looking at him, knowing she might burst into laughter. Then the seriousness of the matter reasserted itself. This man could be considered an enemy of her husband—and of her father. If he suspected they weren't truly married he could precipitate that international incident she was trying to avoid.

"Did you get those photographs you wanted for your husband?" Garh asked.

"Photographs? Oh, of the summer villa? Unfortunately there was a misunderstanding about that." Sara looked up at Kharun, hoping her expression would be taken as adoring. "We got it cleared up, though, didn't we, darling?"

Suddenly she looked straight at Garh. "But how did you hear about that?"

Garh inclined his head slightly. "Rumors, only, madam."

"There you are, I've been looking all over for you," Jasmine said. She wore a burgundy gown and looked stunning.

"Minister Sonharh," she included him in her greeting, then smiled at Sara. "Come and meet some friends of mine. Yasife is dying to meet an American. I told her all about you and Kharun's wildly romantic courtship."

"Do not end up gossiping with the women all night long," Kharun said, kissing the back of Sara's hand before releasing his hold. He turned to Garh as the two women left.

"Thanks," Sara said softly, once out of earshot.

Jasmine laughed. "Garh's bite is worse than his bark and that's formidable. He is against everything Kharun wants to do—from the oil deal to improving the infrastructure, to enticing tourists to boost our economy. I don't know why Kharun doesn't prevail upon our uncle to get rid of him," Jasmine said with a frown.

"Have you asked him?"

"He says it's easier to keep an eye on him at the ministerial level than to constantly wonder what the man might be doing behind his back. Come, here's Yasife."

"So, how did your first reception in Kamtansin go?" Kharun asked as they settled in the limousine after bidding their hosts farewell two hours later.

"Better than I expected," Sara admitted. She kicked off her shoes and wiggled her toes. Frowning, she then wrinkled up her face.

"Is something wrong?"

"I thought I'd try to relax my facial muscles. I hope you don't expect a smile out of me for two days. It'll be that long before my cheeks stop aching."

He laughed softly. The sound was like mulled wine on a cold winter's day. It seeped through Sara, warm and intoxicating.

"I hope you don't expect me to remember the names of the four million people I met tonight," she said brightly to cover her reactions.

"It was only a few dozen, and no, for the most part, you'll remember them after seeing them again and again at various functions. There are a few who are personal friends, do remember them, please."

"Who?" She rested her head against the cushions and closed her eyes, listening to Kharun talk. She could listen to his voice from now until forever.

She felt a brush against her cheek. Slowly she opened her eyes. Kharun was leaning over her.

"We're home."

Sara blinked, awareness gradually returning. Awareness of Kharun growing.

"Did I fall asleep?"

"Just as I was telling you about some friends. I'll have to make sure I don't bore you next time."

"Oh, no, not that!" She sat up, pressing against his shoulder. "I'm sorry. I was just so tired from the strain of the reception—and meeting Garh Sonharh. Jasmine told me about him. He's the real reason we got married, isn't he? He doesn't suspect anything, does he? Jasmine said he was a real thorn in your side."

"I can handle Garh. Come, you can be in bed in only a couple of minutes."

She followed him into the villa and turned to head for her room when he stopped her.

"Your acting was more than adequate for our deception. Thank you for tonight." He leaned closer and kissed her.

Still half-asleep, still remembering the intoxicating effect of his voice in the darkness of the car, Sara stepped into his embrace and his kiss.

The lassitude from her brief nap vanished. Blood began to pound through her veins as his mouth caressed hers, as his lips moved persuasively to coax hers into a response. When she parted her lips, his tongue teased her. She returned the favor, relishing the wild freedom she felt when in Kharun's arms.

His hands were warm on her bare back, sending tendrils of pure pleasure through her. She encircled his neck with her arms and tried to get even closer. She could feel the hard length of him against her and savored the differences between them.

She felt as if she were floating.

He ended the kiss, resting his forehead on hers and gazing deep into her eyes when she reluctantly opened them. The fiery passion he kept under strict control was visible in his eyes. The desire he couldn't completely hide sent a shiver of anticipation and reckless abandonment through her. What would it be like to make love with Kharun?

"You had better go to bed now, if you wish to sleep alone," his voice said roughly.

Sara hesitated a split second. One part of her didn't want to go to bed alone, but the other part knew it would be a mistake not to. This was a temporary, short-term, marriage-in-name-only, not the prelude to a lifelong commitment.

She nodded, pulled her arms from around his neck and turned, walking swiftly to her room.

"Damn!" he said softly as the door closed behind her. Angrily, he ran the fingers of one hand through his hair, and back to his neck, easing some of the tension. Since when had he become a blasted Boy Scout? He wasn't known for his altruism. He was ruthless in his pursuit of a business deal, or in dealing with mistakes at work.

If he'd kept his mouth on hers, they would be in bed together at this very moment. Instead, he was left in the hallway, staring at a blank door as if he hoped for X-ray vision to see through to Sara's room.

She was probably sliding out of that dress now. It clung to her like a second skin, showing off every de-

lectable curve and valley. He wanted to be the one to
slip it from her shoulders, to watch it puddle at her feet
on the floor, then raise his gaze to see her wearing nothing at all.

Turning before he did something rash, Kharun strode
to his own bedroom. What had possessed him to put her
in the room the farthest from his own? What if she
needed something in the night?

Like what? his consciousness jeered. Someone to tuck
her into bed? Someone to soothe away any nightmares?

Someone to kiss her to sleep?

The truth was he wasn't used to denying himself anything. All evening he'd watched for a sign from Sara
that she wasn't immune to the sparks that seemed to fill
the room whenever the two of them were together.

Just a hint, and he would not have sent her to bed
alone.

But either she was a terrific actress, or she didn't have
a clue. Or maybe she didn't feel the attraction he felt,
didn't find anything intriguing about him, like he did
with her. Perhaps she was counting the days until the oil
deal was finalized and she could return to her parents.

For a moment, the thought of Sara returning to
America, never returning to Kamtansin, was more than
he cared to deal with. He'd better make the most of her
stay. Once she was gone, he'd likely never see her again.

The next morning Kharun ate alone. He wondered if
Sara was avoiding him, or just tired from last night and
sleeping in. He almost went to check, but for the arrival
of his mother.

"Good morning, Kharun," she said, smiling as he

rose to greet her. "I hope I'm not visiting too early, but I'm excited about a project I think you will love." Angelique looked around. "Where is Sara?"

"We went to the embassy reception last night, she's sleeping in this morning."

"No, I'm not. I just got a late start," Sara said from the doorway.

Kharun looked at her and schooled his features to hide his reaction. She looked lovely today—her blond hair like a nimbus around her face. Despite her claim to not smile for a week, she was smiling at his mother. For a moment he was jealous of that smile. Sara never smiled at him that way.

Foolishness! He greeted her formally and held a chair for his mother. Sara went to the far side of the table and sat down before he could reach her.

Aminna entered, carrying a tray of croissants, muffins, and various breads. She placed it in the center of the table, pausing to greet Kharun's mother.

Kharun waited until everyone had begun to eat before asking his mother why she'd come to visit so early.

"I thought it would be the best time to reach you both—before you began work for the day and Sara took off."

"Took off?" He looked at Sara.

She shrugged. "I'm not going anywhere."

"You will once you see what I've brought," Angelique said. She smiled at her son. "You will love this."

She rose and left the room, returning two minutes later with a handful of photographs.

With a dramatic gesture, she spread them on the table beside Kharun.

He glanced at the pictures and then at his mother. "And they are?"

"The photographs Sara took."

Sara rose and looked over Kharun's shoulder at the pictures.

"They're the ones I took the other day when Angelique drove me around Staboul." She smiled when she saw the little children crowding around a tourist. "That one came out well, it looks just like I imagined it."

Kharun studied each one in turn. There weren't many. He looked at his mother. She was brimming with excitement.

"Nice pictures," he said.

"Kharun—they're perfect for use as a tourist draw. What person seeing these wouldn't want to come to visit our country?"

"Tourist draw?" Sara repeated.

"It's one of Kharun's and Jasmine's special projects. They've been assigned unofficially to initiate a tourist bureau. We want more visitors to our country—to boost the economy, to share our lovely beaches with those who like to vacation at the sea, to show our historic buildings and offer another attraction for the world traveler. Kharun, don't you see? These are perfect. Sara could take more, and work on a brochure we could then send to the world! And think of the interest because Sara took them."

"I don't know what you mean," Kharun said slowly, but he suspected.

"Thanks to the clandestine manner of your marriage, you are making headlines in all the world's press. People read newspapers! There is a fascination with wealthy men, and an aura around those who don't normally seek publicity. Capitalize on it, as you always say!"

Sara looked at him in horror. "We're in the newspapers?"

He glanced over and almost smiled at her horrified expression. "We're news, why not. Isn't that what you said initially—once in the public eye privacy vanishes?"

He wanted to brush away the lines her frown caused, caress her cheek, excuse themselves from his mother and take her into another part of the house to kiss and caress and see if he could spark an answering desire in this golden girl.

Instead, he forced himself to look away and give serious consideration to the suggestion his mother made.

He picked up the pictures and studied each one in detail. Two he tossed aside, they were good but nothing special. But the rest he held captured his attention. Would they work toward promoting his country? The added money tourists would bring would help finance the improvements he and his father had tirelessly worked for. As would the oil deal he was trying to conclude.

"Would you be interested in taking more photographs, with that end in view?" he asked Sara.

She blinked and nodded, looking amazed. Once again he wanted to whisk her away where the two of them could be alone and undisturbed.

Sara took the photographs from Kharun, careful not to touch his fingers, he noticed. He watched as she studied each one in turn. Slowly her smile came out.

"I did pretty well, didn't I?" She looked up and he caught the slight catch in her breath. Satisfaction swept through. She wasn't as immune to the attraction between them as she'd been pretending. It wasn't one-sided! Wasn't that interesting?

"So you'll do more?" Angelique asked impatiently.

"I would be delighted, if you think any picture I take would be worth something," Sara said, stepping away as if she'd get burned if she stayed so close to him.

"Tourism has not been made a formal part of the government as of yet," he said slowly once they'd all resumed their seats and began eating again. "Jasmine and I have asked our uncle to make it a priority, but he moves slowly."

"He's a turtle when it comes to change," his mother said. "Oh, the arguments your father and he had!" She smiled mistily, remembering.

"A fresh perspective would be good, as well. If you'd let us know what appeals to you about visiting our country, we can capitalize on that."

Angelique laughed softly. "This will be wonderful. And give Sara something to do while you are working. This is supposed to be your honeymoon. But if you insist on working during the day, Sara needs something to occupy herself. And what better time than now, when everything is fresh and new to her. Once she's lived here for a few decades, it'll be as if she's always been here. At least that's how I feel."

Kharun looked at Sara, his eyes focusing on the color that sprang into her cheeks, the way she shyly looked at him. Only the two of them knew Sara wouldn't be here for decades. In fact, she may only remain another week or two, until the final papers were signed and the oil agreements firmly in place.

Sara glanced away and tried to take a deep breath. As long as she didn't look at Kharun or touch him, or think about him, she could do this. Surely the oil agreements would be signed soon and their pretense come to an end—hopefully before she made a complete idiot of herself.

But she couldn't stop the warm glow that filled her at his comments. Kharun liked her photographs. Angelique liked them. She stared at the photos again. They were good, even she could see it.

Was this finally something she could build upon? Make a career with photography? Expand on a hobby and make it into something broader than photojournalism? Maybe specialize in scenes for travel brochures?

Taking pictures would be fun, occupy her time and keep her from fantasizing about Kharun.

"I'm happy to take more photos. It's fun."

Aminna appeared in the doorway. She spoke to Kharun.

"It appears your mother is on the phone, wishing to speak with you, Sara," he said. "You may take it in the hallway if you wish, for privacy."

Aminna held out a portable phone to Sara when she reached the door. She smiled her thanks and continued walking, putting the phone to her ear.

"Mother?"

"Hi, sweetie, how are things going? When are you and Kharun coming to dinner with your father and me?

We will be returning home in a few days, surely you can spare enough time for one dinner.''

"You're going home?''

"As soon as the oil agreements are finalized and your father says that'll be soon. So we need to get together soon, or I'll have to fly halfway 'round the world to have dinner!''

"I'll check with Kharun and call you back.''

"Any night next week would work for us. And in the meantime, what about lunch—just you and me. I want to know more about you and Kharun. The wedding came as a complete surprise and we haven't had a chance to talk properly since.''

"Sure, Mom, let me check and call you back. I'd like to have lunch.'' Not. How would she keep the truth from her mother, who knew her so well. She'd just have to stall, or invite Angelique along so there could be no heart-to-heart.

"Oh, one other thing, do you know a Pete Steede?'' her mother asked.

Her editor at the newspaper. "Yes. He's my boss. How did you know his name?''

"He has called at least half a dozen times, insisting he talk with you. Maybe you better return the call to keep him from leaving any more messages. He's a bit pushy.''

Sara almost laughed. Pete was beyond pushy. How like her mother to be so diplomatic.

"I'll call him right away. And once I check with Kharun, I'll let you know about getting together.''

She disconnected, then punched in the familiar number at the newspaper. She tried to calculate the time difference. It would be evening there, but she suspected Pete would still be hanging around.

Sure enough, he picked up on the second ring.

"Where the hell is your story?" he blurted when he heard her voice.

"I don't have a story," Sara replied, beginning to explain how she'd been caught without getting the photographs or interviews.

"Don't give me that, babe, you are the story. Did you know going over you'd end up married to the guy? Was that part of the plan? Give the details. We're getting killed in the ratings. Every other damn paper out there is scooping us left and right—and one of our reporters is actually part of the scene. Give."

"There's nothing to say, Pete. And I'm quitting. I can't work for you anymore."

"Hey, babe, you owe me. I gave you a job without any experience. Gave you a chance to scoop the world with some photo snaps of one of the world's most eligible bachelors. I could have sent someone else. Give with some details! What's it like living in the lap of luxury? Does anyone speak English? Are you in a harem?"

"For heaven's sake, Pete, you make it sound like I've gone back to the Dark Ages. Most of Kamtansin is as modern as Algiers. There are some lovely old mosques and buildings, small tiny streets with a lot of traffic, and the people are friendly. I haven't had a chance to do much shopping, but I bet there are some real bargains to be found. I am not in a harem. Kharun has a beautiful villa right on the Mediterranean Sea."

"So if you're not a prisoner, why not contact me?

We've been waiting for a week for some news. That country's hot—with the proposed new oil leases and the potential for more.''

''It's also pretty, but deprived in many ways. That's why the oil leases are so crucial. The new income will enable them to progress more rapidly. Not that everyone is in agreement over that. But it doesn't matter, family rules over here.''

''Your guy's rich, the country's poor, what else?''

''Stop, Pete. I'm not giving a report. I called to tell you to stop calling my mother.''

''Give me your number then. I don't like one of my reporters being out of touch.''

''Didn't you hear me, I quit! You can't call here.'' Sara looked up—Kharun stood in the doorway watching her.

''I've got to go, goodbye.'' She disconnected and looked at him wondering how to explain.

''Your mother is welcome to call anytime she wishes,'' he said mildly.

Flustered she tried to smile. Not for anything did she want him to know she was speaking with her editor. He'd be convinced she still planned to do a story!

CHAPTER EIGHT

"UM, MY mother wants to know when we are available to have dinner with them," Sara said, hoping her flustered feeling didn't show. "I knew it wouldn't be long before she invited us."

Kharun tilted his head slightly, his eyes studying her. "Whenever you would like."

"In a couple of days, then?"

"Fine. You took longer than I expected with your call. My mother needs to leave soon for an appointment and she wishes to discuss your taking more pictures with a view to working to devise a campaign for promoting our country."

"Do you think I can take that quality of pictures? Wouldn't a professional be better?"

"What do you think?"

She almost held her breath. Had she finally found something she was good at? "I'd give it my best shot. But I'm really a novice at this. Photography has always been a hobby."

"The quality of the pictures is assured by the camera you have. It's the composition and artistic eye that captures the essence of what you see. Your unique perspective will insure the attraction of the pictures."

"You're good for a woman's ego," she said, warming with a heartfelt glow at his praise.

"By speaking the truth?"

"By bolstering my courage to try."

"That is within you, Sara. Come, arrange things with my mother. I have work to do. Shall we ride this afternoon at five?"

"I'd like that."

The day passed swiftly. Sara went with Angelique when she left for Staboul, catching a ride to the Samin Industries headquarters.

Meeting up again with Jasmine was an eye-opener for Sara. The tall building in the heart of the business section housed several businesses owned and run by the Samin family, from shipping lines to oil exploration to import-export. The latter was headed by Jasmine herself.

"Mother said you could help with the idea we have of trying to bolster the tourist trade," Jasmine said after welcoming Sara to her office.

Glancing around the lavishly appointed office, Sara was envious. She had had a tiny cubbyhole of space at the newspaper. Nothing like the splendid view Jasmine had, nor the solid furnishings or artwork on the walls. The carpet beneath her feet was thicker than in her apartment at home!

"I'm glad to do what I can, but I don't know much about luring tourists."

Jasmine laughed. "Neither do we! But it's something my father supported. Kharun and I have badgered our uncle tirelessly until he finally told us to do what we wanted. Carte blanche is great, except that we don't have any idea how to proceed. I have one person working on it, though it technically shouldn't be done by a private firm. Still, we can get it rolling. You'll be perfect for telling us what would appeal to an American tourist—you're so new here.''

''That's what your mother said. I must say, before my father became interested in dealing for the oil leases, I hadn't heard anything about your country.''

Jasmine made a face. ''So true for everyone, I suspect. So that's a good place to start. Come, I'll introduce you to Tamil, who has started this project. Between the two of you, maybe we can really get going.''

Jasmine's enthusiasm was catching. Sara felt excited for the first time since she started work at the newspaper with such high hopes. But as she followed Jasmine to a lower floor, she began to question what she was doing. Her stay in Kamtansin wouldn't be lengthy. Once her marriage to Kharun ended, she had no reason to remain. Jasmine should have thought of that, as well—she was the only other person privy to the reason for their hasty marriage.

Before she could voice her concerns, however, Jasmine stepped into an office and introduced Sara to Tamil.

Sara was relieved to discover he spoke English, though rather slowly and formally. Still, it would facilitate working together.

By the end of the afternoon, Sara's head was swimming with ideas and plans. They had discussed various strategies and ambitions, jotted pages of notes, and arranged to meet in another couple of days to take a tour of what Tamil considered the most appealing aspects of the city to get Sara's opinions.

She was delivered back to the villa by Angelique's driver. She rang the doorbell and the same maid who had let her in before opened the door. She smiled and again said something to Sara.

"Probably telling me to get a key," Sara murmured as she headed for her room. Glancing at her watch, she saw it was almost five. If she wanted to be on time for her ride with Kharun, she had better hurry.

She was bubbling with all she wanted to tell him. As she donned her jeans, she almost laughed. They would be just like regular married couples—telling each other about their day.

Except, Kharun didn't tell her about his day—did he still suspect she was a spy? How absurd. Maybe if she tried—

Tried what? She sat on the edge of her bed. What did she want? To get to know Kharun better? Theirs was a temporary arrangement—to avoid scandal and make sure the oil treaties weren't jeopardized. They'd already discussed an annulment once the leases were signed.

She glanced around her room and then out at the garden, taking a deep breath. The fragrance of the flowers was light, mingling with that of the warm sea air. Her restlessness wasn't as strong when she was here. The setting was idyllic. And despite the suspicions Kharun seemed to hold, she enjoyed being with him.

Liked his kisses.

Whoa, don't go there! She jumped up and finished

changing, hurrying to the stables as if trying to flee her own thoughts.

The horses were already saddled. Kharun was talking with one of the grooms. He turned and watched as she came up to him.

"Ready?"

"As ever."

They followed the trail to the beach, Sara in the lead. Alia was prancing impatiently, anxious for the run she expected.

"Beat you!" Sara called, tearing down the beach. She could hear Kharun following, the pounding hoofs of Satin Magic drawing closer every moment. Laughing in exhilaration, Sara urged Alia faster. The wind blew through her hair, the sea sparkled like diamonds in the sun.

This is what she should capture to lure tourists. The sheer joy would entice even the most jaded traveler. How could she convey this feeling to the world?

Satin Magic was gaining. He was a strong horse, with a longer stride. Sara knew she couldn't keep her lead, but she and Alia would give it their best. Soon they were neck and neck, then Kharun pulled ahead.

Sara began to ease Alia down into a slower gait until they were trotting. Kharun slowed, turned and came back to where they were.

"You win!" Sara called.

He was grinning as he fell into step with her. "Next time, I'll win quicker with an equal start. I take it by your absence all day that you and Jasmine agreed to work together?"

"Tamil and I will be working on the project. We have so many ideas. He's traveled a bit, and so have I, so we each have ideas on what we look for and what's appealing. We need to explore hotels and restaurants and see who is ready for an influx of customers. See what tours we might devise. Decide where to target our campaign initially. There's so much to do!"

Sara was full of her day and wanted to share the excitement. She told Kharun every idea, from their plans to visit the various sights in the city of Staboul, to interviewing hotel managers, to testing restaurants. She was unaware of how her eyes sparkled in excitement, or how the color flooded her cheeks from her ride.

"Of course, what would make it perfect would be a desert trip. It's so different from what most of the world knows, I'm sure it would be a draw unto itself."

He looked at her. "You like the desert?"

"I don't know, except for my foray to try to photograph your retreat, I've never been." She patted Alia's neck. "The thought of riding a horse along the dunes has a lot of appeal. The oasis where the jail was rose so unexpectedly from the barren land. I imagine it could be romantic given the proper preparation. And you have to admit it would be quite different from what most people are used to—always supposing there's enough water and shade to support a tour group."

"Sometimes I go beyond the oasis. Satin Magic and I spend days on the desert. It is cleansing. Rejuvenating, yet relaxing."

She nodded. "I would love to see it sometime," she said wistfully. "But this is nice, along the sea. Look, there are pleasure boats out today. I haven't noticed them before—just the big ships out on the horizon.''

He glanced at the two boats apparently at anchor a few hundred yards from the shore. ''Another feature you can include. For those who sail the Med, we can offer docking facilities. We already have a couple of large marinas in Staboul. Others could be built.''

''How about docks large enough for pleasure cruises?''

''Ah, you think big. We could convert one or two of our deep water docks from freight, I suppose.''

''I can't wait to talk to Tamil about that! So I told you about my day, how was yours?'' she asked daringly. They turned the horses for home. She liked the ride back each afternoon, it was slower, took longer and allowed them to talk. Gave her time with Kharun—just the two of them. For a while she could forget he didn't trust her. For a while it was just Kharun and Sara.

She watched as he sat on his horse. His dark hair gleamed in the sunshine, his shoulders broad and strong. Savoring the image, she burned it into her memory. She never wanted to forget a single minute with him.

''I didn't realize your family was involved in so many businesses. Jasmine runs the import-export firm. Do you oversee them all?''

''You didn't know?'' he asked. Suspiciously, she thought.

She shook her head. ''I was very impressed,'' she said. ''I thought you just helped out your uncle with the oil leases and other projects he needed done.''

''My father started two of the firms. Jasmine and I

started the import-export. She assumed full control when our father died. By then I was heavily involved in the shipping lines, and now oversee the other company, as well. It's a family concern. Some cousins are involved. And my mother takes an interest, though not an active role.''

''No wonder you work all the time,'' she murmured.

''When a person enjoys what he does, it's not a hardship.''

''What do you do for fun?'' Sara asked as they neared the path leading back to the stables. Was their ride coming to an end so soon? She wanted to cling to the moments, stretch them out.

''I enjoy riding.''

''How about swimming? You've never gone once since I've been here. Living right by the sea, having that lovely pool, I'd think you'd take advantage of the water.''

''Ah, but I do. I usually swim first thing in the mornings, while you're still sleeping.''

''Oh.''

They turned into the path, going single file, Kharun in the lead. Sara watched him as they rode quietly, wondering if it would look suspiciously obvious if she arose early the next morning and happened to wish to go swimming.

''Do you ever swim at night?'' she called.

He looked over his shoulder, his dark eyes enigmatic. ''Sometimes. Want to go tonight?''

Her heart skipped a beat. She nodded.

''After dinner, we can take a walk. If the warmth

holds, we'll swim in the sea,'' he said. His voice was rife with sensual promise, his eyes captivating.

Sara felt the heat rise in her cheeks, but smiled slowly, hoping the sheer joy she felt didn't show. ''I'd like that.''

Sara wondered if their walk would take place when they reached the house and found Piers waiting for Kharun.

''It's late,'' Kharun said when greeting his friend and adviser. ''Couldn't whatever you're here for have waited until morning?''

Piers shrugged, looked at Sara. ''You never minded before.''

''Things change,'' Kharun answered shortly. He lifted Sara's hand and kissed it blatantly. ''Change for dinner. I'll see to Piers.''

Sara was aware of the men watching her as she headed for her wing of the house. She paused just around the bend and stopped.

''You play a dangerous game, my friend,'' she heard Piers say in English. His voice grew fainter as they moved away from her. ''You still don't know for sure she wasn't sent as a spy. Does she have access to your office?''

She knew he didn't trust her. How did Kharun really feel? His voice was too indistinct from the distance. Maybe he'd even switched to Arabic. With a sigh, she continued to her room.

Kharun closed the door to his office. ''Do you have reasons for thinking she is here to spy? A woman who speaks no Arabic and has yet to ask one question about our position on the oil leases?''

"It's just odd she showed up at this particular time, that's all.''

Kharun shrugged. "What is so important you have to come this late?''

"I believe the Americans have agreed to your last counteroffer. We should go over it all in great detail, but I believe we are almost ready for you to send the version to your uncle for his approval. Then we can sign.''

Kharun nodded, his expression schooled to show no emotion. *It was too soon.* He shook his head. They'd been working on this deal for weeks now. The new leases would mean a great deal to his country.

But it would also mean the need to be married to Sara would end. And he wasn't ready for that. Not yet.

"I thought you would be elated,'' Piers murmured, drawing out the thick folder from his briefcase.

"I'm pleased,'' Kharun said. "But let's make sure before we begin to celebrate. No use anticipating.''

But it was clear when he read the counteroffer acceptance that the contracts were almost ready to be drawn and signed.

"It doesn't look like anything Sara could have told her father has changed our position on this,'' Kharun said.

"Doesn't mean they didn't try, that's all I'm saying. So, is it an annulment, or divorce?''

Kharun looked at his friend, his eyes cold and hard. "You'll be one of the first to know—when the time is right.''

''Sorry, I didn't mean to overstep my bounds,'' Piers said hastily.

Kharun was still considering the question, and the possible answer when he changed for dinner. He had Aminna set the table on the patio overlooking the garden. After dinner, he and Sara would take that walk along the beach, and maybe go swimming.

The more he grew to know her, the more she fascinated him. Was it her quicksilver mind, flitting from one topic to another that entertained? Or the way she had of looking at him sometimes like he was the most important person in the world, that he found so beguiling? Or that air of innocence she portrayed so well?

Maybe Piers had been correct, she'd come to seduce him into revealing secrets. Yet she'd made no overt attempts at seduction. He wanted to believe she had been caught up in circumstances. Nothing so far had shown him differently.

Sara dressed with care for dinner. The sundress she donned was her favorite, loose and flowing, yet clinging as she walked, displaying her figure to full advantage. She felt she needed all the advantage she could get. Time was growing short.

She'd resented being forced into this marriage of convenience. But it had turned out to be much more pleasant than she'd expected. Granted she would change some things if she could, but for the most part she was satisfied with avoiding the scandal, which would have reflected so poorly on her father.

She had not counted on developing such an interest in her husband, however. Would he want to continue to see her after they parted?

A pang struck her. What if he didn't?

"All the more reason to make memories while I can," she said, staring at herself in the mirror. She dabbed on a hint of perfume, and recapped the bottle. Taking a deep breath, she turned and headed for dinner.

A most romantic setting, she thought, stepping into the patio after Aminna told her where to find Kharun when she found the dining room empty.

Discreet lighting gave soft illumination. The breeze had died down. The air was redolent with the fragrance of roses. And the soft murmur of the sea made a soft, melodic background.

The small table had been set with gleaming silverware, sparkling crystal. Candles shimmered, their flames dancing, reflected in Kharun's dark eyes.

"You look lovely," he said softly, reaching out his hand.

Sara slipped hers into his, feeling the shock of awareness that always took her by surprise when he touched her. Her heart pounded, and her skin grew tight with sensitivity and longing.

"Let's eat, then we'll take that walk," he said, seating her.

Dinner flew by. Sara was aware of every second, wondering what the future held. Not endless days ahead, but later tonight. Would their walk draw them even closer? Would he kiss her again?

She could scarcely eat, despite the wonderful aromas and tastes of the meal Aminna had prepared.

Kharun spoke of cities he'd visited when he lived in America, and she told him about growing up with a father who traveled the world. They shared their favorite places in Paris, and their love for riding, arguing the various merits of different breeds of horses.

By the time they finished eating, she was a bundle of nerves. Always in the back of her mind had been the promised walk. Alone with Kharun in the dark, along the sea.

Kharun looked at her gravely. "What's wrong?"

"Nothing."

He didn't look as if the answer satisfied, so she continued. "I'm still excited about the plans Tamil and I made today. I can't wait until tomorrow when we look around the city."

He nodded, his eyes narrowed. "Shall we take that walk?"

She blew out her breath and smiled. "I'd like that."

The moon was full, providing enough light to clearly see the path, bathing the white sand with enough illumination to clearly see their way. Sara stopped when they reached the beach to slip off her sandals.

"I like going barefoot," she said, looping them with one finger.

"Be careful where you step. There are broken shells sometimes," he warned, taking her free hand.

She almost shivered at the sensations that tingled along her arm. Glancing around, she almost didn't recognize the beach as the place she'd visited several mornings.

An air of mystery hovered. The sea was dark, the anchor lights of the pleasure crafts the only break in the blackness. The silvery sheen of the sand added to her pleasure, evoking dreams of romantic settings and faithful lovers.

Kharun began angling toward the water, his presence compelling.

"I think I'd come out every night if I lived here," Sara murmured.

"You do live here."

"Temporarily. How are the lease discussions coming?"

He hesitated a moment. She glanced at him.

"They are progressing. How does your father feel about them?"

"I don't know. I haven't spoken to him since our wedding. I did talk to my mother again and arranged for us to have dinner with them tomorrow night, if that's all right with you. Will that be awkward, you and my father sitting down to dinner when you are on opposite sides of negotiations?"

"We are not enemies, Sara. We both want these leases, we're just hammering out the details."

"Mom doesn't like business discussions at the table," she warned.

"A wise woman. I enjoyed meeting her. Are you worried about having dinner with them?"

"A bit. What if they suspect this is all a sham?"

"What would happen?"

She sighed. "They'd be disappointed. I'm a trial to them, I suspect."

"I doubt it. From what I saw, they seemed to delight in your company."

"That's because you saw them at the wedding—when they were predisposed to be happy. Someone else finally took me off their hands."

"Do you think they feel that way? At first they were bewildered. But when they thought you were happy, they were happy."

"So they'll be even more disappointed when the truth comes out. Not that that's your worry."

"We don't have to end the marriage the day we sign the agreements, you know," he said slowly.

"We don't?"

Kharun stopped and turned her so she faced him. He released her hand and placed his on her shoulders. "Piers suggested it might be a slap in the face to the ministers to end it immediately by annulment. We'd be essentially telling them all we'd played a trick."

"Oh." For some reason his rationale depressed her. She'd thought when he first spoke he wanted to keep their arrangement a little longer. Now it was further expediency, nothing more.

"So what do you think?"

"Whatever." She couldn't think with Kharun's hands toying with her hair, his thumbs caressing her jaw. She could only feel the myriad sensations that filled her, that heated her blood and had her longing for things never known.

"I was thinking—"

"What?" She tried breathing normally, every nerve cell at attention and craving more.

"Maybe an annulment isn't such a good idea. A divorce might be more persuasive."

Her heart pounded so hard she wondered if he could see it. Blood pulsed like thunder through her veins. She peered up at him, trying to determine what he was saying—what he really meant.

"A divorce?"

"It is customary when ending a marriage that has been consummated," he said, leaning down to kiss her.

CHAPTER NINE

HE WAS kissing her. He wanted more. More than kisses. Rational thought fled as touch turned her knees wobbly and her thought processes to mush.

He wanted her. Every brush of his lips, stroke of his tongue, caress of his fingertips shouted the message loud and clear.

And she wanted him. Wanted to be closer still, to explore all the cravings that filled her body. Wanted to touch him all over, learn every secret he had to share.

When he pulled back to look at her, she smiled. "I think a divorce is the only way to go," she said huskily.

He swept her up into his arms, her strong desert raider, and turned for the house. She encircled his neck, cherishing every moment. What woman hadn't dreamed of a man sweeping her off her feet since seeing Rhett sweep Scarlet up the steps in *Gone With the Wind*? Was anything more romantic?

Only to have it happen to her.

She scarcely noticed when they reached the garden, except she could see him better with the illumination of the garden lights. He followed the path to her room, entering through the opened French doors.

The soft twinkling from the garden gave all the light they needed. Setting her beside the bed, he took her sandals and dropped them on the floor.

"Are you sure, Sara? There'll be no going back," he said, caressing her cheek.

Her heart exploded with love for this enigmatic man before her. She didn't know him well, but she knew he was honorable and caring. Theirs was an odd arrangement, doomed to end before long. But she loved him as she'd never loved another.

When had that happened?

Could the feelings she had truly be love? Yet what was more natural than a woman wanting to share all she could with the man she loved?

"I'm so very sure, Kharun." So saying, she reached up and pulled his head down for a kiss.

Taking liberties she would never have dared even a day before, she threaded her fingers in his thick hair, relishing her right to touch him.

His hands roamed over her back, pressing her against his hard body, lifting her slightly to bring her even closer. Heat built as his clever fingers found the fastenings for her dress and released them. The cool air on her back should have startled, but she was too caught up in the roiling excitement that grew with each feather stroke of his fingers.

The world spun when he lifted her to place her on the bed. Then it righted itself as he joined her.

Sara awoke when Kharun left her. Dawn was breaking. He was going for his swim, she knew it. For an instant, she considered throwing back the light covering and joining him. But tendrils of passion still filled her, and she wanted to savor the feelings a bit longer. She smiled dreamily and drifted back to sleep hugging the pillow he'd used, breathing in his special scent.

By the time Sara awoke for the day, the sun was high in the sky. Slowly she bathed and dressed. Wondering where Kharun was, she headed for the dining room. Only to be disappointed when it was empty—save for a place set at the table and some food warming on the sideboard. She poured a cup of coffee and selected a couple of croissants. Stepping outside, she went to sit in the shade.

Last night had been beyond her wildest dreams. They'd made love more than once and each time was like it had been invented just to join Kharun and Sara forever.

Wryly she acknowledged he likely didn't feel the same way. The thought threatened to overwhelm her. It was enough she'd had a night with him. Maybe more nights to come. But she'd entered this arrangement with her head fully aware of the consequences. She'd see her commitment through and leave when the time came. She just hoped she was able to leave without clinging, without asking for more than Kharun ever promised to give.

Aminna stepped into the doorway.

"His Excellency said to tell you he had to go to the city today. He will meet you at the hotel for dinner with your parents at seven."

Sara tried to smile, but her hopes and dreams vanished in an instant. Confirmation that last night hadn't meant as much to him as it had to her. Not with such a cryptic message. Not with leaving her alone all day. Leaving without even seeking her out to say goodbye in person.

Without another kiss.

"Thank you. I will be going to the city myself today." At least she still had the appointment with Tamil. How she would have faced the day without that, she didn't know.

"What time? I'll inform the driver."

"I need to be at the company headquarters at ten."

Aminna bowed slightly and left Sara to her rueful thoughts.

By the time seven o'clock rolled around, Sara had been through more emotional turmoil than she cared to repeat anytime soon. She vacillated from being understanding of the demands of Kharun's time and work to being convinced he'd used them as a mere excuse to escape.

She went right up to her parents' suite and knocked on the door a few minutes before seven. Might as well get this over with, and hope for the best.

"Sara!" Her mother swept her into her arms for a brief hug, then held her back, studying her daughter.

"You look radiant."

Sara was startled. Did she? Or was her mother seeing only what she wanted to see?

"Just like a new bride should look. Come in, and tell me all about being married to Kharun. I imagine it would be vastly different from your father."

"One type A personality is similar to another," Sara said, smiling at her mother.

"Ah, but your father wasn't always like that. We married right out of college. We were both so young. But Kharun is already established as a man of the world—

not only in running several international businesses, but negotiating oil treaties on behalf of his country. Vastly different from the early days of our marriage.''

"I guess," Sara said, struck by the difference.

They moved into the sitting room area of the suite and settled on the luxurious sofas.

"Before I forget, though I doubt there's a danger of that, your obnoxious boss keeps calling, demanding to talk to you. He really is getting tiresome."

"Pete? I called him after you told me of his calls. He's still bothering you?"

"Persistent, I have to give him that."

"Can you ignore him? Just hang up the next time he calls, maybe that'll get through to him."

"Actually, I have the front desk screening our calls now. Tiresome, but at least I haven't spoken directly with him today. Ah, here's your father."

"Sara." Samuel Kinsale entered from the adjoining room. He hugged her when she rose, then held her away from him, his hands on her shoulders, studying her.

"Marriage seems to agree with you," he said. Glancing around, he frowned. "Where's Kharun?"

Just then there was a tap at the outer door.

"That's probably him now. He was coming from the office," Sara said, crossing to the door. Her heart skipped a beat in anticipation.

She opened the door, struck anew by Kharun's sexy looks. Her breath caught when he swept her into his arms and kissed her deeply. When he pulled back a moment later, she wanted to grab hold and never let him go.

Startled by the trend of her thoughts, she smiled shakily and stepped back, as if putting distance between them could erase her wanton desires.

"Hi," she said breathlessly.

He smiled that lazy smile then looked beyond her to her parents.

"Good evening."

"Kharun, good to see you."

Samuel and Roberta greeted their guest with obvious warmth. Before long, Roberta had everyone comfortable and at ease.

"No talking shop tonight," she warned the others. "This is a family dinner, not some negotiating session!"

Samuel laughed and nodded. "Very well. Kharun and I get enough negotiating. Tell me, how are you enjoying married life?"

Kharun glanced at Sara then looked at her father. "It is different from what I expected, but it has its compensations."

She pasted an insipid smile on her face and hoped her thoughts weren't reflected. Marriage wasn't what he expected because it was a farce. He deserved to marry a woman he cared about, not to cover up a scandal that might prove an embarrassment to his country.

The comment about compensation didn't go unnoticed. Was that all last night had been to him, a form of compensation for the sacrifice he'd made?

Her head held high, Sara tried to maintain the facade of a radiant bride, happy with life. But she longed for privacy. Even her room at Kharun's villa would be preferable to being with her parents now and trying to keep up appearances with people who knew her so well.

And Kharun didn't help matters. He was sitting far too close. She could feel his thigh against hers, and his shoulder brushed hers when he leaned forward to put his glass on the table. Settling back, he put his arm around her shoulders, his hand lightly tracing circles against the sensitive skin in her upper arm.

She could hardly concentrate on the conversation. Every fiber of her being was attuned to the sensations sweeping through her from his touch. How was anyone supposed to remain coherent when all they could think about was getting alone with the man and seeing if they could take up where they'd left off the night before?

She flicked a quick look at her mother. Roberta was serenely responding to one of Kharun's questions. She didn't seem to notice anything amiss. But Sara felt the entire world had to be able to hear her rapid heartbeat, feel the heat that suffused, know she was focused on Kharun to the exclusion of everything else.

Dinner seemed interminable. She kept her eyes on her plate, lest she give away her emotional turmoil and stare at Kharun for endless moments. Once or twice, when addressed directly, she looked up. Each time Kharun's warm gaze rested on her.

It was all for show. To put on a good front before her parents, to pretend to the world that everything was fine.

Suddenly Sara wished with all her heart it wasn't a charade. That they were married forever and could go home together when the evening ended and close the rest of the world out of their special place.

She stared at the last of the food on her plate. *She'd fallen in love with a man who didn't trust her!* A man who found her a problem to be dealt with and then summarily dismissed once the situation was resolved. Not the best move she'd ever made. Nothing had gone the way she'd expected since she stepped foot onto Kamtansin soil.

She reached for her water and took a long drink, wishing she could catch the next plane home.

She couldn't stay. She'd give herself away any instant, and she couldn't bear the humiliation of his knowing the awkward, flaky daughter of Samuel Kinsale had fallen in love with one of the world's most powerful men.

At least when she made mistakes, they were terrific ones. No little namby-pamby ones for her.

She should have been better prepared. Should have guarded her heart against his appeal and attraction.

What she should have done was refused to go riding with him, ignored his family, fought him at every turn and demanded she be allowed to leave.

Now she didn't ever want to leave, yet the days were counting down and it was only a matter of time before he'd ask her to. Their marriage facade would no longer be needed once the leases were signed. Her ideas for tourism might be utilized, but her presence wouldn't be required.

She could hardly keep from jumping up and screaming at the unfairness of it all. For the first time she'd found someone she truly loved, and it was not meant to be.

"Are you all right?" Kharun asked.

Sara looked up. "Fine."

His eyes narrowed as he studied her. Thankfully, she knew he could not read minds. But his steady regard was making her nervous.

She wasn't fine, she'd made the biggest mess of her life. But she'd bluff her way through. The entire sequence of events was her fault. She would not add to it by letting him suspect her feelings had changed.

The evening seemed interminable, but finally it was time to leave.

Her mother gave her a hug. "I like him so much. I hope you'll always be happy."

Sara smiled, feeling as if a knife was twisting in her heart. What would her mother say in a few weeks, when the marriage was over? Sara didn't even want to think about it.

"You were silent tonight," Kharun said as they settled in the back of the limousine and headed for the villa. "Are you usually so quiet in the presence of your parents?"

"What? Oh, no. We talk a lot, actually."

"So I was the damper on the evening?"

She shook her head, trying to see him in the darkness. The ride reminded her of that first ride from the jail in the desert. She'd never in a million years suspected she'd end up loving the man beside her.

When they reached the villa, Kharun held his hand out for hers to assist her from the car. He didn't release it and Sara tried unsuccessfully to tug free. She didn't need any closer proximity to the man. His attraction was overwhelming. Distance was what she needed.

Lights were on in the house, providing a soft illumination in the living room and halls.

Kharun raised her hand to his lips, brushing a tantalizing kiss to her wrist. "Stay the night with me," he said, his voice low and husky.

It was as if liquid heat poured through her. *He wanted her again tonight!* Dare she follow through?

She loved him, she wanted to be with him in every way. But theirs was only a temporary alliance. Could she spend the night with him and save herself from heartache?

No. But the heartache would come either way. Why not grab the chance to be with him?

"Your place or mine?"

"Tonight, mine."

He leaned over to kiss her. His mouth touched hers with a familiarity that belied the short time they'd known each other. The sensations that filled her were growing familiar with each passing second. She opened her lips to deepen their kiss, thrilled at the responsiveness he displayed.

Slowly, as if dancing to some unheard tune, he turned her and moved with easy abandonment down the long hall, away from her room and the illusion of safety it provided.

Instead, between kisses, she knew they were going to a room she had yet to see. Kharun's private retreat. His own bedroom.

When they reached the door, it stood ajar. Sara loosened her arms, locked around his neck, and peered into the dimness. She could see a bed and the gleam of light on one wall—a mirror reflecting the hallway illumination.

She looked up, into Kharun's dark gaze—alive with desire and impatience, though he kept the latter in check.

"Yes or no?" he said, as if divining uncertainty. He was giving the choice to her.

"Yes." She reached up and kissed him, trying to let him know by touch and actions how much she wanted him. How much she reveled in being with him. If she could offer nothing else, she'd be honest in this. If it had to end, then she'd make sure it ended gloriously. Maybe down through the years, Kharun would think of her once in a while—and think of what might have been.

The next morning Kharun woke early. Sara was snuggled next to him, fast asleep. For a long moment he watched her, fascinated by the hint of color in her cheeks, the sweep of her lashes against her fair skin. Slowly he ran his fingers through her hair, enjoying the shimmering color, and satiny softness. For a moment he thought he could spend the entire day just watching Sara sleep.

Then reality took hold. He had an appointment at nine, and things to see to before that. This was not the time or the place to indulge in fantasies, no matter how tempting.

Once things were resolved, however, he would find the time and place to discover more about this bewitching woman who was his wife before he'd let her go.

Piers was waiting for him when he reached the downtown offices, his face beaming.

"I think you'll be pleased with the lease terms. We've gotten everything we asked for on the last go. I'd say we're ready to sign. You just need to recommend it to your uncle and we can begin further exploration before the month is out."

"Good work."

"Your doing. Not that I want to take anything away from your negotiating skills, but marrying Sara was a stroke of genius. I'm sure some of the concessions we got were a result of her father's feeling generous in light of the marriage."

Kharun frowned. He didn't want favors like that. The relationship between him and Sara was complex. They were both walking a fine line. And after last night, and the night before, the line had blurred.

A quick finish to the business at hand. Was he ready for that? The reason for their marriage would vanish. No matter how much Garh and Hamin wished to discredit the oil deal with his uncle, once the leases were signed, it would prove a moot point.

Kharun's phone rang.

"Yes?" His secretary was on the other end. Hearing the news that Garh Sonharh was in the outer office demanding to see him, he told her to send him in.

"I suspect Garh has heard the news," he said as he hung up.

Piers looked puzzled. "He's here?"

Garh pushed open the door, pausing in the opening for dramatic impact.

"You are a fool, Kharun. It was not enough you wished to jeopardize the future of our country, but to make it possible for the paparazzi to hold us to ridicule is beyond acceptable.'' He strode into the office and tossed several faxed newspapers on the desk.

Kharun looked at the top one. It was from a tabloid newspaper from the United States. A bad photo of Sara stared back at him. The headlines screamed A Hostage To Fortune?

He looked up. ''What is this, Garh?''

''Copies of newspapers on sale in the United States. One of my people saw it, copied it and sent it to me. If your new wife is not a spy, then she certainly is a woman to make the most of her opportunities. In this case, fame and notoriety on a world-wide scale. I cannot help but think your uncle will think twice about signing a lease with a member of the opposition so bent on ridiculing us.''

''I'll deal with it,'' Kharun said evenly. He wanted to smash something—preferably Garh's face. But that would solve nothing. He had to read the newspaper article, assess the damage, then rectify the situation. But not with Garh still in the room.

''I'm taking the papers to your uncle.''

''You must do what you think is right, of course,'' Kharun said disinterestedly. He looked at Piers.

''I'll see you out,'' Piers said, quick to catch on.

Kharun watched as Piers hustled Garh from his office. Once the door was firmly shut behind them, he sat down and drew the damaging fax papers toward him. The second sheet had pictures of them riding on the beach. The caption read ''Aborted escape attempt.'' He almost laughed. The photographer had caught their race—the one where Sara had initially been leading.

The second one was on the beach. He remembered that night, the scent of her that had filled him with such desire. Her laughter, her delight in wading in the warm sea. When she'd almost stepped on a shell, he'd caught her and pulled her back. From a distance, and with the wrong interpretation, he guessed it could look as if she were trying to escape and that he'd stopped her. The pleasure crafts anchored off the beach—a clever cover for the paparazzi.

He set the sheet aside and began to read the inflaming article. Had Sara sent this in? If enough people read it and believed it, it could damage their reputation with the United States.

From the first moment, she'd been trouble. He pushed back his chair and rose. Time to get this settled once and for all.

CHAPTER TEN

SARA was sitting on the patio beside the pool sipping her last cup of coffee for the morning. The air was soft against her skin, a hint of the sea mingled with the faint fragrance of the flowers. She sat beneath an umbrella, which shaded her from the hot rays of the sun. Later she was due to meet Tamil for more discussions. But right now she had nothing to do.

Except dream. And remember.

Remember the most incredible night of her life. She wondered if Kharun had any idea how sexy he was, or how just thinking about him could set her senses spinning. Did the memory of their loving spring to mind when he was at work, or were men better able to compartmentalize their lives?

"Telephone for you," Aminna said in her heavily accented French, standing in the doorway.

Sara smiled and rose, glancing around for the portable phone. She didn't see it.

"Where shall I take it?"

"In the office." She led the way.

Sara slipped into Kharun's office and saw the phone receiver lying on the desk. Aminna nodded and left, shooing out the maid who had obviously been dusting.

"Hello?" She sank into the big chair behind the desk, feeling odd to be in Kharun's office with him not there.

163

"Sara, it's your mother."

"Is something wrong?" She could tell by the tone in her mother's voice something was definitely wrong.

"Your father just got a call from a friend of his in the State Department asking if you were all right."

"Why in the world would he get such a call?"

"Apparently because of a newspaper article that appeared in the U.S. yesterday."

Sara felt her blood grow cold. "A tabloid paper, run by Pete Steede?"

"With headlines implying you are being held hostage while the oil leases are being negotiated."

She muttered an expletive, heard her mother's sharp gasp. She was going to kill Pete! How dare he exploit her life just to sell newspapers! Immediately she thought of Kharun.

"How bad is it?" she asked.

"Your father is getting a copy of the article faxed through. We'll know more then, but it was bad enough for his friend to call to make sure you were all right. You need to verify this with him. Can you call Paul Michaels yourself and tell him it's a mix-up? I've got his phone number right here. Needless to say, your father isn't really happy about this."

"Neither am I!" And she knew for darn sure Kharun would be furious. Especially if it ever got back to this country and the ministers who were so opposed to the oil leases saw the newspaper. Fortunately the tabloid was limited to U.S. distribution.

"His phone number—"

"Wait, I need to find paper and a pencil." She opened

the top drawer of the desk. Neat and tidy, nothing like her own back at work. A workplace she would never see again, unless it was to go and wring Pete's neck.

She picked up a pen. There was no paper.

She closed it and opened the top right drawer.

"Looking for something?" The cold voice at the door stopped her instantly.

She looked up into Kharun's glittering eyes. He was angry. Any idiot could see that.

"I'll call you back," she told her mother, and clicked the phone off.

"Why call back? Why not find what you're looking for while he waits?"

"He? That was my mother."

His patent look of disbelief riled her.

"It was! Call her back yourself if you don't believe me. She wanted to give me a phone number. I was looking for something to write on."

"Try this," he said, tossing the faxed copies of the newspaper article onto the desk.

Sara swallowed hard as she recognized the headline banner. Oh, God, he knew!

Knew and was furious.

She licked her lips nervously. "How did you get a copy?"

He tilted his head slightly. "From Garh Sonharh."

Slowly Sara drew the papers closer. She groaned when she saw the photos and captions. But anger grew as she read the inflammatory article. No wonder Kharun was so furious.

"I didn't write this," she said, standing. "You don't believe I did, do you?"

"Wrote it, collaborated, dictated—it makes no difference. No one but you could have provided all the information—where the villa is, when we would be riding, the hurried wedding, tension between family members. No one but you."

"I didn't do it. Pete did."

"He conjured it up out of thin air?"

She hesitated, but she couldn't let Kharun think she'd betray him. "I talked to him once. But only once. He kept calling—"

"What are you doing in this office?" he interrupted, obviously not interested in her explanation.

"Aminna said I could take the call here. It was my mother. She was giving me a phone number to call and I needed something to write it down on." She drew a deep breath. "I'm not spying on you if that's what you think."

"I'm not sure what I think right now."

"Fine, let me know when you decide." Head held high, she swept from the room, going wide around Kharun as if suspecting he'd try to stop her.

But he said nothing. Made no move.

She didn't know whether to be angry at him or not. She knew she was furious with Pete. She walked back out onto the patio. Her coffee was cold. The pool mocked her with its memories of another time.

She spun around and headed for her room. Snatching up her purse, she left. She'd visit her parents and get to the bottom of this. And she'd call Pete Steede from the privacy of her parents' suite.

Hesitating only a second as she left the villa, she wished Kharun had believed her. Had stood by her. But why should he? She'd messed this up like she did everything.

Yet it was a thousand times worse this time. She loved him. She would never do anything to cause him harm. But would he ever come to see her as anyone but the aggravating woman who threw a wrench into the smooth workings of his negotiations? And how had that blasted article affected his relationship with his uncle's ministers?

She looked at the villa one last time. Would she ever come back?

Highly unlikely.

Kharun's car was parked in front, his chauffeur seated in the driver's seat, reading.

She opened the back door and ignored his start of surprise.

''Presentation Hotel,'' she said, settling in as if she had every right to do so. She prayed he'd comply and not verify her destination with Kharun. The sooner she was away the better.

He nodded, tossed aside the newspaper and started the car.

In moments, she was on her way. It was hard not to look back. Harder still to keep the tears at bay. But it was better this way. Better to leave him, try to clear up the mess Steede had caused and then stay with her parents until the leases were signed, sealed and delivered.

*   *   *

"What the hell do you mean she's gone?" Kharun roared. Aminna stood in the doorway, her face impassive despite his anger.

"Sargon drove her to the Presentation Hotel."

"He didn't check with me first?"

"Why should he? She is your wife. She needed a ride. He has returned and is waiting to take you back to your office when you are ready."

Kharun ran his fingers through his hair and tried to think. His thought processes were short-circuited—thanks to Sara Kinsale bak Samin. Like they had been almost since he met her. Now this.

Conclusive evidence she'd betrayed him? Or just a woman prudently staying out of range until his anger cooled?

Think!

For all he knew, she and her mother had been making lunch plans on the phone.

If she'd been speaking with her mother.

He hated not knowing what to believe.

The phone rang again. He'd been fielding calls ever since Garh had left his office—no doubt to spread the word about the tabloid article. Kharun had already placated his uncle, and Hamin. And his aunt. At least he thought he'd placated his aunt. Time would tell.

In the meantime, he needed to see Sara.

He nodded to Aminna and paced to the window, trying to think. In retrospect, maybe he should have followed Piers's advice way back at the beginning. Shipped her off somewhere and not told a soul.

An idea glimmered. Slowly Kharun began to relax. He'd give Sara until tonight. If she didn't return, then he'd go to get her.

"I don't understand, Sara."

"Mom, just trust me on this, okay?"

"But you didn't bring a suitcase or anything. How can you plan to stay the night? What would Kharun say?"

"He'll be glad to have me out of his hair."

"What? Will you explain? Ever since you got here this morning, you've done little more than make two phone calls and pace around on the carpet so much I think it's wearing thin. You didn't eat enough dinner to keep a bird alive."

"The carpet's fine."

"But you're not."

Sara looked at her mother and almost gave way to tears. But she kept them in. She'd made the mess she was in, and it was up to her to get herself out. She couldn't keep running to Mommy.

"I'm fine."

Roberta shook her head. "I know, you don't want to talk about it. Fine. But I'm here if you need me. And so is your father."

"Thanks." Sara smiled as best she could, and paced to the window. Her father had not been at dinner, finishing up some things, he'd told his wife. At least she'd been spared having to talk to him about the stupid article.

Her conversation with Pete had been less than satisfactory. There was no changing the newspaper once it hit the stands. Now there was only damage control. And a promise to sue him to kingdom come if he didn't print a retraction.

Not that it would do much good. Retractions were never front-page headlines.

Her father entered the suite. "Hello, Sara, I didn't know you were here. But you can hear the news when I tell your mother."

Roberta greeted her husband. "What news?"

"The leases were approved this afternoon. We lost a few concessions thanks to Kharun's tough negotiations, but we now have the exclusive rights for the next ten years. Work will start before the end of the month."

"Darling, that's wonderful! Does that mean we can go home soon?"

"As soon as next week."

Sara felt as if she'd been struck. It was over. There was no reason to continue their marriage. She almost laughed. There'd be no reason for Kharun to seek her out tonight, or wonder where she was. He was probably congratulating himself that he didn't even have to tell her to go, she'd left on her own.

"That's great, Dad," she said brightly. Her face was going to crack if she didn't get away from her parents. She could only fake a smile for so long.

"I'm tired. I think I'll go to bed. Good night."

"What's going on?" Samuel asked as she fled the room.

"I'm not sure," her mother replied just as Sara shut

the door to the room she'd used her first night in Kamtansin.

Leaning against the cool wood, Sara let the tears well into her eyes, wishing the pain in her heart would ease enough to let her find oblivion in sleep.

She'd held heaven in her hands, and lost it.

"Oh, Kharun," she whispered.

He hadn't called, hadn't made any effort to even find her, much less ask her to return home. Now that the leases were approved, there was no reason to see him again.

But she wanted to. Wished she could be with him forever. Explain, make sure he knew she had not betrayed him, that she'd lived up to her commitment.

A knock sounded on the door to the hallway. She pushed away from the door connecting to the sitting room of the suite and crossed the spacious bedroom. Was it the maid to turn down the bed?

She opened the door, shocked to see two uniformed men standing there.

"Sara Kinsale?" one asked.

"Yes."

"Please come with us."

"Who are you? Where do you want me to go?"

"Please come with us."

The second man reached out to take her arm in a firm grasp, pulling her from the room.

"Wait!" She had to tell her parents. She couldn't just disappear. Not again.

The door was pulled shut behind them and they headed down the hall. For a moment, she experienced déjà vu—of a guard holding her arm at the jail in the desert. Was she being returned to jail? Had Kharun reneged on his promise to her because he thought she'd betrayed him with Pete?

"I can't go with you," she said, trying to pull free.

His grip was too solid.

When they bypassed the regular elevators and took the freight elevator, she began to get scared. Her parents didn't know she wasn't in her room. It would be morning before they discovered it. Where would she be?

Before she knew it she was seated between the two men in a fast-moving car. It headed away from the city. Into the desert.

Sara's thoughts swirled. She had to get away, get to a phone.

Call the American embassy? she thought hysterically. Where were they going? And why?

The night was dark once the city lights were left behind. Only the slash of the headlights of the car cut through the impenetrable darkness. Sara gave up demanding to know what was happening. She suspected only the one man knew any English and that sounded very basic.

Despite her worry, she was growing tired. It had been a long day. Emotionally she was exhausted. The monotony of riding through the darkness began to wear her down. Slowly her eyes closed.

Before she could fall asleep, however, the car began to slow.

Snapping open her eyes, she stared around her. Nothing to be seen in the dark. The star-studded sky ended in the far horizon into inky blackness. No lights shone, no buildings were silhouetted against the night sky.

The car stopped and the driver said something in Arabic. The man to her right opened his door and stepped out, motioning for Sara.

She slowly scooted across the seat and stood. The air was warm, a light breeze blowing. But the scent of the sea was missing. This was dry, clear air.

"Why did we stop?"

"We wait," he said.

"For what?"

He shrugged, reached for a cigarette and lit it.

Sara leaned against the car, wondering if she dare try to make a run. She had no idea where she was, or how far from Staboul they were. But the faint glow back from where they came showed her where the city was. On foot it might not take her longer than four or five days' walking.

Her shoes weren't up to it, though the long pants would keep sunburn at bay. She was getting goofy, she thought. She would have no chance to walk back to Staboul—she had no water.

She heard a drumming sound and looked around, trying to figure out what it was, and from where it was coming.

A horse. What was a horse doing out here in the middle of nowhere?

It was coming closer. The man put out his cigarette and said something to the man in the car. The engine started again.

Sara turned to get back into the vehicle, but he stopped her. "No, you wait." He climbed inside and closed the door. The driver turned on his headlights.

Turning to face the direction of the sound, Sara waited, wondering what was next. In only a moment she saw the horse and rider outlined against the stars. The horse looked huge, and the rider was dressed in traditional Arab garb, complete with a folded scarf across his face. Only his eyes were visible in the glow of the headlights.

She reached for the door handle. She didn't want to be left out here at the mercy of some desert raider. Was she to be spirited away, never to be heard from again?

But the car was locked. Once the men saw the rider, the car began to pull away.

Sara felt as if her last hope was disappearing.

The horse took a step forward, another. The rider had said nothing. Sara's heart began to beat rapidly. Glancing on either side, she could see no shelter, no place to hide.

"Come." The man reached out a hand.

Sara took a step back. "I don't think so."

"No adventure?"

She stopped, stared. "Kharun?"

"Come."

She couldn't believe her ears. Was it him? But what would he be doing out in the middle of nowhere? She tried to see if the horse was Satin Magic, but it was too dark.

"Come." The hint of impatience convinced her. She'd recognize that tone anywhere.

She reached up and in seconds sat sideways in front of him. She was barely in place before he drew her close and turned the horse around. Then they were flying across the desert.

She hoped he knew where they were going. Not that it mattered. It was exhilarating, riding along the vast empty space, the wind in her face, the stars like distant diamonds overhead, Kharun's arms tightly around her. She closed her eyes, savoring every moment, committing everything to memory. This was an experience she never wanted to forget.

Sara wasn't certain how long they rode, but when he began to slow, she looked around. No sounds met her ears, except the jingle of the horse's bridle. No building rose.

"Where are we?" she asked.

Kharun pulled the horse to a stop and eased her to the ground, coming to stand beside her a moment later.

"A place where no one else will find us."

She looked at him. "No one?" She almost squeaked it out.

"You said you wanted to see the desert, I've brought you." Swiftly he unsaddled the horse, and tethered him.

He took her arm gently in one hand and led her around a low mound.

"Wait here a minute." He lifted the flap to the large tent and entered. In only seconds, a warm glow emanated.

Sara lifted the flap and followed without waiting for Kharun.

The inside stunned her. Rich Persian carpets covered

the ground. Tapestries hung from the back wall, their vibrant colors reflecting the lamplight. A large bed was erected on one side, draped in gauzy netting. The center brass table gleamed in the light, fruits and nuts heaped in bowls.

"Wow." She lifted her gaze to Kharun. He stood like a bold desert raider in the midst of the splendor. His robes swirled around him as he turned and stared at her, his hands on his hips. The covering from his face was gone, but the rest was pure Arabian fantasy. Her heart skipped into high gear. Her blood raced through her veins faster than ever. She was almost light-headed.

He'd been angry when last she'd seen him.

He didn't look angry now.

Involuntarily her gaze moved to the bed.

"All the comforts of home," she said. She'd meant to be sarcastic. Instead the throaty sound of her voice was sultry, enticing, sexy. Slowly she smiled, hoping he didn't guess how nervous she was.

"Why are we here?" she asked.

"Time alone, just the two of us. The negotiations are concluded."

"I heard. So our marriage is over?"

He tilted his head slightly, then drew the headpiece off and carelessly tossed it to a cushion. His dark hair was mussed. Sara's fingers almost ached with desire to tousle his hair even more, to touch him, feel his heat and strength.

"So, do you mind telling me what we're doing here?" she asked.

"You haven't seen the desert. I wouldn't want you to

go home without experiencing all of my country's delights.''

The primary delight she'd experienced in this country was being with Kharun, but Sara couldn't say that out loud.

''Aren't you worried I'll take photos and send them to the newspaper? Or report some nefarious deeds?''

He laughed, his teeth startling white when compared to his tanned skin. ''You said you didn't write that article.''

''Nor dictate nor collaborate. You seem to be taking this better now than this morning.''

''Perhaps,'' he said, motioning to one of the cushions near the brass table. ''Care to sit?''

She watched him warily for a moment, then nodded, moving to sink on the soft pillow. It felt a bit awkward, but was comfortable. She looked at the food on the table, at the lamp, anywhere but at Kharun.

He sat beside her, crowding her. He could have sat opposite. Did it mean something that he hadn't?

''How did you do all this?'' she asked, sweeping her arm to indicate the tent and the accoutrements.

''I keep the tent for a retreat. It's kept clean and stocked for me. Food is kept for Satin Magic, as well. When I want to use it, I let the caretaker know, and he disappears until I leave.''

''So we really are alone in the middle of the desert?''

''We really are all alone. Does that concern you?'' He leaned closer. Sara could feel the heat from his body envelop her. His breath caressed her cheeks as she looked up into his dark eyes. Her own breath caught.

"No." It came out almost a whisper.

"Good." He closed the distance between them and kissed her.

Reality faded and fantasy took hold. His touch was all she'd ever dreamed of, inflaming her senses, building desire and passion to blend with the love she already felt growing and encompassing her entire being.

She returned his kiss, meeting him halfway, reveling in the sensations that threatened to catapult her into a realm of hedonistic pleasure never known before.

His hand brushed back her hair as he held her face for the kisses that rained down on her. Then he forged a trail of fire and ice as he kissed and nibbled down her neck, to focus on the rapid pulse point at the base of her throat that seemed to fascinate him.

Just maybe she wasn't the only one in this fantasy.

She should be doing something practical about returning to the capital city. About arranging her trip home.

But Sara didn't feel the least bit practical. She craved his touch like she would crave water in the desert. Maybe because he was as important to her life.

"Tonight is ours," he said.

"Yes." She would agree to anything he said, as long as he kept kissing her.

But when he rose and lifted her in his arms, a moment of panic struck. It abated instantly when he pushed through the netting and laid her on the bed.

It was incredibly soft—and large. More room than the two of them needed, she thought hazily as he joined her. When he kissed her again, Sara stopped thinking. She had one last night, and she was going to enjoy every second of being with Kharun.

Dawn was breaking in the east when Kharun woke Sara with a gentle kiss.

"Um?" She burrowed closer. She didn't want to wake up. Didn't want to face the day.

"Come and see the dawn. There's nothing like it as it spreads over the desert, the light faint at first, then growing bolder. The temperature is cool—nothing like the searing heat of midday. And the shadows allow your imagination to fly."

Her imagination was flying right now, and it centered on the two of them in bed, not getting up, going into the cold dawn air.

She didn't want her last night with Kharun to end. She wanted time to stand still.

"Go away," she said grumpily. If he didn't want to stretch it out, so be it. But she could.

"Come on, you'll love it."

"I love you," she mumbled. Then froze, suddenly coming completely awake, though she kept her eyes shut. Tightly shut. Oh, she hadn't really said that out loud, had she?

She held her breath. Please, please, please, she thought, don't let me have said that out loud.

His finger tilted her face up. She kept her eyes shut.

"Sara?"

With a sigh, she slowly opened her eyes. His dark eyes stared down into hers, his expression unreadable.

"Well now that I'm awake, I might as well get up

and see that sunrise. Then we can go back to Staboul and I can make arrangements to head for home,'' she grumbled, starting to get out of bed.

Their legs were tangled, and Kharun clamped a hand on her arm. She couldn't move.

"Maybe we need to talk," he suggested.

"Maybe we need to get on with our lives," she replied. "Let me up, or the sun will beat us."

"We have a few minutes. You know the oil leases were agreed to yesterday. Only the formality of signing remains."

She nodded, longing to escape, longing to leave before she made an even bigger fool of herself. He had to have heard, yet he said nothing. His way of letting her down easy? "Yes. So I can go home today."

"I brought Alia with Satin Magic. I thought we could stay here for a few days. We have food, water, and the desert to ourselves."

She blinked. "Stay here? Are you nuts? There's no reason to stay here. I should be making airline reservations. My parents will be going home soon and I'll go with them. I have a job to get back to—" Not after she'd burned her bridges.

"I thought you were working with Tamil on the tourist project here. That's your job."

She pushed up on one elbow and stared at him. "What's going on?"

"I'd thought you'd stay."

"Why?"

"You love me."

She flopped back on the pillow and closed her eyes again. He had heard!

"And you have a job to do."

"I didn't tell Pete about us. He tweaked some of the stuff I told him and blew it out of proportion."

"Once I cooled down, and Jasmine yelled at me, I suspected that." There was definitely the sound of amusement in his tone.

She opened her eyes and glared at him.

"Are you laughing at me?"

He shook his head, but the laughter lurked in his eyes.

"Kharun, what's going on? Is this marriage over or not?"

"Ah, that's what I wanted to talk about. Don't you think people would find it odd to end it the day after the negotiations were concluded?"

"As compared to when?"

"I don't know, sometime later, so people won't think it was a false marriage."

"Sometime later?" she asked suspiciously.

"Yes."

"How much later?"

"I don't know." He looked at her sharply. "Fifty or sixty years."

She stared at him, her heart beginning to race. Had she heard him correctly? She cleared her throat.

"That's sort of a long time."

"I'm game if you are." He brushed his fingers through her hair, smiling that sexy smile that turned her bones to mush. "I love you, too, Sara. I fought it at first. One day I'll tell you about a woman I thought I loved before. But she doesn't belong with us today. I want you to stay with me forever, but I'll settle for fifty years with an option to renegotiate.''

''And you are so good at negotiating,'' she murmured, moving to meet him halfway with a kiss that sealed their future. ''I love you, Kharun.''

''I was hoping you did.'' His kiss made her blood sing and her heart explode with happiness and love.

Then he ended the kiss. ''Time's up. Come and see the sunrise,'' he said seconds later, throwing back the covers.

It was cold. She frowned and tried to pull the covers back, but he lifted her out of bed and placed her on her feet.

''Hurry.''

''I'd rather stay in bed.''

''We'll come back.'' He tossed her his shirt, the loose one from the night before. Sara slipped it on, tied it closed at the neck and pushed the sleeves up so her hands showed.

''Nothing's been decided. We have to discuss this.''

''We'll have the rest of our lives to discuss anything you wish. But right now, come and see the sunrise. Later this morning—before it gets too hot, we'll go riding.''

He pulled on his pants and waited impatiently by the door. Staring at his chest, she remembered the feel of him last night. Happiness and love blossomed inside, spilling out in her delightful grin. Kharun loved her! Miracles still happened.

''I thought you were furious with me.''

''I was. But love is stronger than anger. And once I

looked at things rationally, and remembered everything you'd ever said to me, I knew you would never have betrayed me."

He'd had faith in her even when the evidence pointed the other way. She'd never had that before. It was amazing how wonderful it felt. For the first time in a long while, Sara didn't feel like a flake.

"Thank you."

"For?"

"Believing in me."

"And loving you?"

She laughed in joy. "That, too. That most of all." She ran across the distance separating them and flung herself into his arms. "I love you so much. I didn't want to leave, but thought it best if I left before you kicked me out."

"Revisionist history? I believe you stormed out, I certainly didn't kick you out."

"Well, I thought you would have, after seeing that damaging report."

"It would never have happened. I knew long ago you were the one I wanted. I told you, one cannot fight destiny. I wasn't sure you felt the same way—especially after our arranged marriage."

"What are you talking about? You thought I was a spy!"

He laughed softly. "Never that. You didn't have the skills to be a spy."

"I resent that!"

"With that honey hair and your flair, you could never fade into the background like a good spy needs to."

"Well, you didn't trust me."

"At first, maybe, but neither did you trust me."

She was quiet for a moment, mulling over what he'd said, afraid to let herself believe what he'd said, that they'd stay married the rest of their lives. Could he truly mean it?

"You forced me into an arranged marriage," she said.

"I hear they can be the best kind. Ours will be the best."

"I love you," she said softly.

"I love you," he replied promptly. He kissed her briefly, then took her hand to lead her outside. "Forget your uncertainty, we will have a wonderful life together. Promise me you'll stay."

She smiled, her joy reflected in her eyes. "I promise!"

Sara stepped forward to greet the dawn, not only of a new day, but of her new life. A life of love and happiness with Kharun, her own desert raider. Her own desert sheikh.

MILLS & BOON®
Live the emotion

0306/01b

Modern
romance™

THE WEDLOCKED WIFE by Maggie Cox

Reece Villiers is handsome, incredibly driven, successful
– and too proud to show his love. Sorrel has left him, and
the only solution can be divorce. Until he realises that
she's pregnant! Suddenly Reece is insisting wedlock is the
only answer if she is to do the right thing for her baby...

AT THE SPANIARD'S CONVENIENCE
by Margaret Mayo

When Spaniard Lucio Masterton discovers he has a child
he knew nothing about, he takes immediate action. And
what better way to start than with Kirstie Rivers, the
child's mother? Kirstie has been terribly hurt by the
billionaire but under the Spanish sun, she finds Lucio hard
to resist...

THE ANTONIDES MARRIAGE DEAL
by Anne McAllister

Greek magnate Elias Antonides has single-handedly turned
his family's fortunes around – so when he discovers his
father has gambled away a vital share he's furious! And
he's stuck with a new business partner – stunning heiress
Tallie Savas...

IN THE SHEIKH'S ARMS by Sue Swift

Cami Elison knew she was playing with fire when she met
Sheikh Rayhan ibn-Malik. He had sworn he would make
her swindling father pay – by stealing Cami's virginity. But
would the Sheikh's lust for revenge turn into love for the
innocent beauty he was determined to possess...?

On sale 7th April 2006

*Available at WHSmith, Tesco, ASDA, Borders, Eason,
Sainsbury's and most bookshops*

www.millsandboon.co.uk

MILLS & BOON®

0306/03b

Live the emotion

_MedicaL
romance™

HER BOSS AND PROTECTOR *by Joanna Neil*

Dr Jade Holbrook's first day in A&E doesn't go
as planned. She discovers her landlord, Callum
Beresford, is also her new boss! Jade knows she
hasn't made a good impression on the handsome
consultant, and is aware that he is watching her
every move…

*A&E DRAMA: Pulses are racing in these
fast-paced dramatic stories*

THE SURGEON'S CONVENIENT FIANCÉE
by Rebecca Lang

Theatre Nurse Deirdre Warwick is determined that
the two children left in her care will have the best
life possible. When Dr Shay Melburne enters her
life suddenly, Deirdre finds herself falling hopelessly
in love with him – and then he offers her a marriage
of convenience…but can he offer her his love?

THE SURGEON'S MARRIAGE RESCUE
by Leah Martyn

Adam Westerman is a successful Sydney surgeon and
has returned to the Outback to find the beautiful
ex-wife he's never managed to forget. Charge
nurse Liv Westerman fears Adam has only come for
custody of their child. She finds herself hoping that
he has come back for both of them…!

On sale 7th April 2006

*Available at WHSmith, Tesco, ASDA, Borders, Eason,
Sainsbury's and most bookshops*

www.millsandboon.co.uk

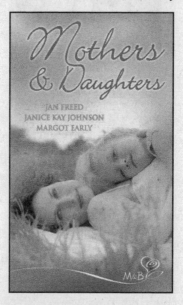